BODIES
FROM THE LIBRARY
5

This anthology brings together 16 forgotten tales that have
either been published only once before—perhaps in a
newspaper or rare magazine—or have never before appeared
in print. Here you will find uncollected cases featuring
H. C. Bailey's Dr Reginald Fortune and A. E. W. Mason's
Inspector Hanaud, as well as early stories by Michael Gilbert
and S. S. Van Dine and a late one by Cyril Hare.

The book also features a previously unpublished mystery by
Edmund Crispin, a little-known short novel by John Bude,
and two radio plays by Dorothy L. Sayers and John Dickson
Carr. Concluding with a murder story by Julian Symons
based on the BBC television game show *What's My Line?*,
this latest volume in the *Bodies from the Library* series spans
50 years of exemplary crime writing with sufficient range to
ensure that all fans of the genre will find something to enjoy.

*For more information about the Golden Age of Detective Fiction
and the conference that inspired this collection, visit:*
bodiesfromthelibrary.com

BODIES FROM THE LIBRARY 5

Forgotten stories of mystery and suspense
by the Queens of Crime
and other Masters of the Golden Age

Selected and introduced by

TONY MEDAWAR

COLLINS
CRIME
CLUB

COLLINS CRIME CLUB
An imprint of HarperCollins*Publishers*
1 London Bridge Street
London SE1 9GF
www.harpercollins.co.uk

HarperCollins*Publishers*
Macken House,
39/40 Mayor Upper Street,
Dublin D01 C9W8, Ireland

This paperback edition 2023
1

First published in Great Britain by Collins Crime Club 2022

Selection, introduction and notes © Tony Medawar 2022
For copyright acknowledgments, see page 407.

*These stories were mostly written in the first half of the twentieth century
and characters sometimes use offensive language or otherwise are described
or behave in ways that reflect the prejudices and insensitivities of the period.*

A catalogue record for this book
is available from the British Library

ISBN 978-0-00-851480-8

Typeset in Minion Pro 11/15 pt by
Palimpsest Book Production Ltd, Falkirk, Stirlingshire

Printed and bound in the UK using 100% renewable electricity
at CPI Group (UK)

MIX
Paper | Supporting
responsible forestry
FSC™ C007454

This book is produced from independently certified FSC™ paper
to ensure responsible forest management.

For more information visit: www.harpercollins.co.uk/green

CONTENTS

INTRODUCTION

'The detective story is written purely to entertain.'
Cyril Hare

Welcome to *Bodies from the Library*, the series that aims to unearth the unknown, to find the forgotten and to locate the lost.

As with the first four volumes, this fifth edition comprises stories from across the genre and includes some that stretch the definition of a detective story. All have one thing in common: none, as far as we are aware, has ever appeared in a dedicated collection of stories by the author concerned.

Here you will find uncollected and hopefully unfamiliar cases featuring H. C. Bailey's Dr Reginald Fortune and A. E. W. Mason's Inspector Hanaud, as well as early stories by Michael Gilbert and S. S. Van Dine, and a late one by Cyril Hare. There is another previously unpublished story by Edmund Crispin and a little-known short novel by John Bude, together with radio plays by Dorothy L. Sayers and John Dickson Carr. And much more besides.

The principal tropes of the detective story were established by the American writer Edgar Allan Poe in 'The Murders in the Rue Morgue', published in *Graham's Magazine* in April 1841. However, the earliest example is probably 'Das Fräulein von Scuderi' (1819), a novella by Ernst Theodor Amadeus Hoffmann, who was born in Königsberg, now the city of Kalingrad in Russia and is best known for his ghastly creation The Sandman.

Today, at a little more than 200 years old, the detective story is in rude health, especially on screen. Television series like Robert Thorogood's *Death in Paradise* and the evergreen *Midsomer Murders* continue to pull in audiences, as do adaptations from the work of Robert Galbraith and Harlan Coben, and new films, such as the forthcoming sequels to Rian Johnson's extravaganza *Knives Out* (2019) and Anthony Horowitz's own adaptation of his extraordinarily clever *Magpie Murders* (2016). Doubtless Sir Kenneth Branagh's new interpretation of *Death on the Nile* (1937) won't be the last cinematic outing for Agatha Christie's Hercule Poirot, and Christie is far from being the only classic author of crime and mystery fiction coming to the screen and streaming services—new incarnations are expected of Margery Allingham's Albert Campion, Georges Simenon's Maigret and Freeman Wills Crofts' Inspector French.

The genre remains enduringly popular too on paper, or e-reader or audiobook, if you prefer. Having defied Christopher Fowler's original intention, the crime-solving team of 'Bryant and May' continue to find mystery and mayhem in London, while 2022 saw the long-awaited return of Miss Marple in a volume of new mysteries by twelve crime writers who have been influenced by Agatha Christie in their own careers. Might this lead to a series of full-length 'Marple' novels, in the vein of Sophie Hannah's Hercule Poirot continuations? The sleuthing team of Dalziel and Pascoe are appearing in new collections of the work of Reginald Hill and we can expect more cases featuring some of the many new and exciting new twenty-first century detectives, among them the group of pensioners that are Richard Osman's *Thursday Murder Club*, Val McDermid's Allie Burns, Ann Cleeves' Matthew Venn, Kate Ellis's Wesley Peterson and Elly Griffiths' Dr Ruth Wainwright, as well as John Tyler in D. L. Marshall's series of thrillers, the sinister protagonist of Jim Noy's *The Red Death Murders* (2022) and many, many, more.

Two hundred years . . . and counting.

Tony Medawar
February 2022

THE PREDESTINED

Q Patrick

It was Jasper's tenth birthday. There had been strawberries and cream for tea on the lawn, and a party of nice-mannered boys and girls had solemnly presented him with gifts and wished him many happy returns.

But Jasper, an ungracious host, had shown more interest in the strawberries and the gifts than in his guests' comfort. In fact, there had been a scuffle with a diminutive female guest, whose pigtails he had so continually tweaked that she had rounded upon him in a sudden burst of impolite ferocity.

Now that the avenger had departed along with the other guests, Jasper seemed the prey to the listlessness of bored repletion. His grandmother was watching him anxiously.

'Is your new collar too tight?' she asked solicitously, as Jasper unloosened his birthday tie and was unbuttoning his first really 'grown-up' shirt. 'Come here, my dear, and let me look.'

Jasper, a handsome, heavy boy, moved sulkily towards her.

'Why, good gracious, your poor neck is all black and blue! Did that horrid little Richards girl scratch you, darling?' Grandmother shook her grey curls as she examined the ugly reddish-blue weal on Jasper's throat. 'It can't be the shirt. I bought it large on purpose to allow for growth. Does it hurt you, my pet?'

Jasper gave a non-committal groan. An orphan child, living

alone with a doting grandmother, he knew that slight indispositions often had their concomitant advantages; such as pleasant pamperings, tempting food and freedom from school. On the other hand . . .

'Or perhaps it's strawberry rash. Your poor father always used to break out after strawberries. It's just struck eight, and if we hurry we'll be in time to catch Dr Barnes. He usually stays late in his surgery Saturday nights.'

Jasper was not so pleased at this. Dr Barnes was apt to pooh-pooh childish malingerings and to prescribe nasty medicines. But this time his neck really *did* hurt him quite badly—a sort of chokey feeling. Perhaps he was going to be ill after all.

A few minutes later Dr Barnes was casting a professional eye over Jasper.

'Where did you say the rash was, Mrs Dogarty? I can't see anything.'

'It wasn't exactly a rash; it was a sort of mark—more like a bruise.' She moved nearer, peering through thick spectacles. 'Well, bless me, it's gone completely. It must have been a trick of light. My eyes are not what they were.'

'But it hurt,' put in Jasper.

'Well it doesn't hurt any more.' Dr Barnes gave him a playful pinch. 'Tummy's a bit fat, but—all's well that ends well.'

He might have added: 'And all's bad that begins badly.'

On the last Saturday of the Summer Term, Dr Hodson, headmaster of St Ewold's School, made a habit of inviting the ten senior boys to a buffet supper at his home. From among these he would choose the prefects for the coming year, to supplant those who were leaving. And, being a wise man, he valued the opinion of his wife and daughters in making his selections.

Like soldiers on parade the boys had lined up outside the headmaster's door, sleek and shiny as soap, shoe-polish and brilliantine could make them. Jasper, third in line of seniority, longed for (and fully expected) the honour of prefecture, with its privileges, comforts, and potentialities of dominance. He had, perhaps, thought too little of its responsibilities.

On the stroke of eight, the senior boy knocked at the headmaster's door. As he did so there was a choking sound, and he turned to see Dogarty staggering out of line, clutching feverishly at his collar and pulling at the neat knot of his tie.

'Fall out, Dogarty,' hissed the senior boy.

The Mesdames Hodson were extremely polite in accepting Jasper's apologies for being late. But their eagle eyes had taken note of the unbuttoned collar, barely hidden by the crooked tie. Nor did his hair have that guardsman 'spit-and-polish' to which these critical ladies were accustomed on such near-formal occasions.

'I don't think so much of your Dogarty,' said Mrs Hodson, after the boys had bowed themselves politely out at ten o'clock.

'Not mine, my dear,' said the headmaster, with his famous whimsical smile, 'but St Ewold's. A good scholar and a good athlete, handsome, but—'

'Handsome is as handsome does,' put in the youngest and most tactless of the girls. 'And Handsome didn't offer me any of that trifle, though he took two helpings himself.'

'His eyes are too close together,' said the eldest daughter, 'and his mouth is too red for a boy's. Besides—if he can't tie his own tie properly, how can he make other boys do it? Jones Minor told me he was a bully; and he's not a bit popular . . .'

Here the headmaster held up his hand with his oft-repeated adjuration against telling tales either in or out of school. Then he added: 'Well, I think Dogarty may go a long way—a very long way.' But he did not say in which direction.

However, it came to pass that, despite his fine athletic record and a brilliant scholarship to Cambridge, Jasper Dogarty never had his name inscribed amongst those who had been prefects at St Ewold's.

*

May-week at Cambridge, with examinations over and dreamy, sunny days—punting along the Cam—moonlit nights with their gay college dances—the announcement of optimistic engagements—with Youth having a final, carefree fling before stepping out from the sheltered groves of Academe into the cold, withering realities of everyday life.

And to Jasper these realities might well prove withering and cold. His grandmother's legacy—aided by his scholarship—had barely seen him through Cambridge. A double first and the glamour surrounding a 'rugger blue' are valuable in their way. But their value so often dies with the shouting and the tumult of graduation, and they are no guarantees of a safe, remunerative job later on. Unless, of course, they have enabled one to find the right connections.

And here Jasper had been lucky, or perhaps clever. Though not generally popular, he had managed to secure the friendship of Douglas Mervyn, who had good-naturedly invited him to share his suite of rooms in Trumpington Street and, more good-naturedly, had invited him to his home during the long vacations. Here Jasper had made good ground with Sir Montague Mervyn, the great industrialist, and also with his only daughter, Eunice. Jasper had managed to convince himself that he would have been genuinely in love with Eunice, even if her father had not been in a position to find a good job for any worthy young man she fancied and, of course, an even better situation for a son-in-law. Jasper felt sure that Eunice, for all her Puritanical upbringing and her ice-clear, grey eyes, was not indifferent to him. For now that the too-red mouth with its petulant lower lip had been brought under control, his perfect physique and regular features were enough to cause a flutter in an even more sternly disciplined heart than Eunice's.

He would have brought matters to a head that last Saturday afternoon in May-week, as they punted down to Byron's Pool between the daisied banks of the Cam. But Eunice—wise girl—

had brought along her Pekinese, Snap, who had a knack of creating some diversion whenever relations threatened to become too intimate.

But he would have his chance with Eunice that night at the Trinity Ball. Jasper had hired 'tails' for the occasion, and their perfect fit had given him much satisfaction when he had tried them on that morning.

Before the dance they were invited to dine with the Dean of Trinity, and Douglas had assembled his party of men and maidens a little before eight. Eunice was there with Snap, who was to be left in the charge of the landlady. In the adjoining bedroom Jasper was putting the finishing touches to his appearance. He was nervous and somewhat afraid. He had learned by now that nervous strain—especially in the evening—was apt to bring on that queer constriction of the throat, followed by a short emotional spasm when he was hardly responsible for his actions.

The college clock struck eight.

'We'll be late, and the dean's a stickler for punctuality,' said Douglas, moving towards the bedroom door.

His sister restrained him, laughingly. 'Let's send little Snappy boy in to hurry him up.' Eunice opened the door just wide enough for the Pekinese to enter.

There was a sound of playful yapping and then a howl of pain. The door was flung wide open and the dog hurtled across the room with Jasper's foot behind it.

'Damn that blasted dog! And damn, triple damn this cursed collar!'

Jasper's eyes were wild and there was an ugly weal on his neck and throat. Oblivious of the ladies, he stood like the mad Hercules pouring his oaths out to heaven and hell.

Then there was a moment of stunned silence, broken only by the whimpering of the dog.

Finally Douglas stammered: 'Look here, old man, this won't—er do, you know—'

But Jasper did not listen. He had gone back into the bedroom. He never saw Eunice Mervyn again.

At thirty-four Jasper Dogarty could hardly be called a success. His latest job of selling on commission for a large perfume company barely paid for the single Bloomsbury room and the commonest necessities of life. It did not cover the rich foods, the pink gins and the double whiskies to which he had become increasingly addicted. But it had one advantage. It brought him into contact with rich—usually older—women who could supply many such little luxuries. But suddenly, it seemed, women had become more sensible, or less sensitive, to Jasper's attractions. Invitations were falling off. His bathroom mirror finally told him the reason. He was getting fat—yes, F-A-T, fat.

He must, he told himself, perpetrate the only dishonesty that he had not as yet tried with the opposite sex. He must get married—and fast.

Quickly, almost feverishly, he reviewed his list of matrimonial prospects.

A few weeks later he was the husband of Sophie Cain, a widow ten years his senior, who enjoyed comfortable ill-health, a more than comfortable income and a magnificent Mayfair flat.

Other appurtenances of wealth included an almost new Rolls-Royce and a nearby doctor who, cheerfully and unashamedly, pandered to her hypochondria.

Such things were, however, mere baubles of a temporal nature. Sophie Cain, now Dogarty, had spiritual wealth, too—a sincere, if rather narrow, religious creed, and the services of a more devout, far narrower female companion—Miss Grace Goodman.

Jasper's bathroom mirror had driven him to matrimony so precipitously that he had had no time to find out that he would be obliged to take on not only the assets but also the liabilities of his beloved. Both her income and her capital were untouchable during her lifetime and, though she consented to make a will largely in his favour, she insisted that Miss Goodman should continue to run the household and hold tight upon the purse-strings.

Jasper, shorter of pocket money than ever, found what solace he could in flaunting the Rolls-Royce before his former 'customers', and in the convivial atmosphere of Dr Belk's flat, which was immediately below his own. The latter, his wife's physician, was a cheerful old rascal, who soon showed that he was more than ready to enter with Jasper into a defensive alliance against Miss Grace Goodman.

'What your wife really needs is cheering up a bit,' said Dr Belk, as he and Jasper sipped their drinks one evening. 'But old goody-goody Goodman is always reminding her of her mortality and scaring the living daylights out of her.'

'My wife isn't seriously ill, then?'

'We—ll, you know how it is with women her age.' The doctor spread out his hands and shrugged. 'I'm not saying she doesn't need medical attention now and then. There is a little cardiac trouble. Flittery, fluttery, you know. A car accident, too hot a bath, a shock, running for a bus might bring on a syncope.'

Dr Belk lifted his glass. 'A little of this—a little fun now and then—theatres, dinner-parties—they would work wonders for Sophie.' He winked.

Of course Jasper realized the meaning of that wink was: 'Get rid of Miss Goodman and there will be the more pickings for you and me.'

But as he thought it over, he was not sure he wanted to get rid of Miss Goodman. The doctor had given him another idea, in which Miss Goodman might be quite useful—quite useful for a plan he had conceived.

*

His chance came about some two weeks later when Mrs Belk sent a polite note, asking Mr and Mrs Dogarty to cocktails and dinner the following Saturday.

'Do you good, dear,' urged Jasper. 'And the doctor wouldn't ask you if he didn't think you up to it. I've promised anyhow, but I'd hate to go and leave you all alone.'

Saturday evening was proverbially Miss Goodman's night off. Every Saturday at seven she marched off on foot—scorning buses and Tubes just as she scorned raincoats and umbrellas—to visit her brother in Maida Vale.

Of course cocktails were out of the question for Sophie. But Jasper could go an hour early and his wife would join later.

Before leaving. Miss Goodman prepared a bath for her mistress (carefully testing it to body temperature) and laid out the least becoming of her evening gowns.

Jasper made a point of leaving the flat a few seconds before she did, and Miss Goodman saw him, as the lift bore her downwards, standing outside the door of the doctor's flat as if waiting for admittance.

But as soon as the lift had passed, Jasper climbed the one flight of stairs to his flat and quietly let himself in. Then, noiselessly, he moved to the bedroom door and waited.

At length the faint sound of splashing told him that his wife was in her bath.

He put on his dressing-gown over his dinner jacket. Then slowly—silently—deliberately—he made for the half-opened bathroom door.

And slowly—silently—deliberately—he entered and did what he had to do. There was no struggle as poor Sophie's head was submerged beneath the water.

He ran some hot water into the bath, remembering the doctor's words that too hot a bath might well cause a syncope. It would be at least an hour and a quarter before he need feign

anxiety as to his wife's non-appearance at the Belks's dinner--
table. After that he had planned to 'discover' the 'accident'
himself. His alibi would be almost spite-proof, and his grief
more than convincing. By the time Miss Goodman returned at
about eleven o'clock, any awkward questions about the temperature of the water or the splashes on the bathroom floor, etc.,
would be unnecessary and out of place. Sophie's body would
(with good luck) have been removed, and her death certificate,
duly signed by the complacent Dr Belk, might well be a *fait
accompli*.

So far so good.

He hung up his dressing-gown in its usual place, and walked
down to the Belks's flat, where he was admitted at less than five
minutes past seven.

He was in splendid form both with his hosts and their guests.
Dr Belk kept plying his glass, whispering: 'Make hay while the
sun's shining, eh, my boy?'

'Talking about the sun's shining,' put in Mrs Belk, 'just look
at that! Why, who'd have thought!' She had pulled aside the
curtain to show a sudden torrential rainstorm. There were
rumblings of thunder and angry tongues of lightning.

The noise was deafening. But the banging at the door and
the screeching of the bell were heard above the thunder.

Instinct told Jasper what it was. Even Grace Goodman's stout
heart had quailed before those drenching floods of rain. She
had returned home—too early.

He was conscious of her standing in the Belks's doorway,
dripping wet, screaming: 'Doctor, come quick. It's Mrs Cain—
she's dead—drowned in her bath!'

Jasper gulped down his own cocktail and another one that
stood nearby. Then, moving like an automaton, he followed the
doctor up to his own flat.

He was a little drunk.

Much later, so it seemed, he heard the doctor's voice, rich and fruity: 'Bear up, old man. I'm afraid she's gone. I always told her that she might have an attack if her bathwater was too hot. Just an accident.'

A few minutes before eight o'clock the police arrived, summoned by Miss Goodman, and again he heard her voice, shrilling protestingly about the heat of the bathwater and the relatively excellent health of Mrs Cain when she had left her.

And then Jasper was aware of a distant church clock striking eight, and a young-looking police officer was questioning him in a polite, BBC voice:

'I know how you feel, Mr Dogarty, but . . .'

But he did not know how Jasper felt. Only Jasper knew the feeling of that dreaded constriction round his throat—that choking sensation that had so often gripped him in moments of crisis. Instinctively his hand went up to loosen his tie and collar.

'That mark on your neck, Mr Dogarty?' said the young officer, less polite now. 'It looks freshly made—as though you'd been—er—struggling with someone.'

And then Jasper, fuddled by cocktails and bewildered by Miss Goodman's accusatory screeching, made the mistake of his life—the mistake which was to cost him his life.

'Struggle? Oh no. She didn't struggle . . .'

It was a slip of the tongue.

The young detective knew, of course, that this little slip of Jasper's could not be used in evidence, since no official warning had been given. But he also knew that, in a murder case, half the battle was won if one knew the identity of the murderer.

It was only a matter of hours before Jasper Dogarty was held without bail, charged with the murder of his wife.

Mr Justice Harriman slumped into his armchair before the fire in his chambers at the Old Bailey. He was tired, and he knew the jury was tired, too, as he had kept them late into the evening.

At a few minutes before eight he was told the jury had agreed upon their verdict.

Back in the Court, his wrinkled old face was an expressionless mask.

'Guilty . . .'

As the clock struck eight, he put his formal question to Jasper. Receiving no reply, he assumed the black cap.

And so, one morning, the governor and his officers proceeded to Jasper's cell, where they pinioned his hands.

On the gallows, Jasper may have heard the first stroke of eight as they shrouded his head.

In the shed below, the rope was loosened from Jasper's neck. The two official doctors, waiting for the last heartbeat, looked indifferently at the ugly, bluish-red marks about his throat— those same marks that had worried the loving eyes of his grandmother at eight o'clock many evenings ago, and, recently, drawn the suspicious eyes of the young police officer who had arrested him.

They were the marks of his predestination.

Q PATRICK

Richard Wilson Webb was born in Burnham-on-Sea in Somerset on 10 June 1901, the youngest of four and the sole son of Frederick Charles Webb and Grace Elizabeth Lucas, who were the joint principals of Oakover Girls' School in Burnham.

Webb went to Clare College, Cambridge, coming down with a second-class degree in English in 1923. In 1926 he emigrated to America to take up a position with a pharmaceutical company in Philadelphia. In the early 1930s, he began writing crime fiction with Martha Mott Kelley (1906–2005), adopting 'Q Patrick' as a pen name by combining his preferred name, 'Rick', with 'Pat', a shortened version of her nickname 'Patsy', topped off with the letter 'Q' to add a note of mystery. When Kelley moved away to England to get married, Webb began a short-lived collaboration with Mary Louise Aswell (1902–1984), who would become a journalist and, later, write one more crime novel, *Far to Go* (1957). Webb's third and final partner would be Hugh Callingham Wheeler, whom Webb had known before he left England.

Wheeler was born in Highgate, London, on 19 March 1912, the younger son of Florence Scammell and Harold Wheeler, an examiner with the Board of Trade. In a 1979 interview, Hugh Wheeler said that he had been writing since he was eight years old, and in 1925 he was sent away by his parents to board at Clayesmore in

Winchester, Hampshire, and then studied English at the University of London, graduating with honours in 1932.

Wheeler emigrated to the United States in 1934 where he met up again with Webb. While their first collaboration, *Death Goes to School* (1936), was poorly received, they wrote dozens of short stories and seven more novels as 'Q Patrick', as well as an as-yet-unpublished novel, *The Secret of the Nine*. They also wrote as 'Patrick Quentin' and 'Jonathan Stagge', enabling them to explore slightly different styles of crime fiction. Sources differ on the number of titles they collaborated on; Wheeler claimed they had co-authored 'about four' as 'Patrick Quentin', while the authority on Webb and Wheeler's work, Curtis Evans, has shown it as seven. What is certain is that the two men wrote together in Massachusetts, first at Hickory Farm in Tyringham—which they rented with Webb's friend, Richard G. Burlingame—then at Red House, Sky Hill Farm in Lee and later at Twin Hills Farm, Monterey, which they bought and, as Evans has established, they would later share with Wheeler's friend, Johnny Grubbs.

In the early 1940s, the friendship between Webb and Wheeler began to fracture. In May 1943, Webb married Frances Winwar, but the marriage collapsed within months. Wheeler joined the US Army Medical Corps while Webb was posted overseas with the Red Cross. After the war, Webb's health began to decline and he all but completely stopped writing in 1952. In 1959, he returned to Europe, where he died in 1966.

Wheeler remained at Twin Hills with Grubbs and continued to write crime fiction as 'Patrick Quentin', eventually receiving a special Edgar from the Mystery Writers of America for *The Ordeal of Mrs Snow* (1961), a collection of stories mostly written before he and Webb had parted ways. However, Wheeler was losing interest in crime fiction. In the late 1950s, he fulfilled a long ambition to write a play, *Big Fish, Little Fish* (1961), a comedy about a failed academic that would be directed on Broadway by Sir John Gielgud. His second play, *Look, We've Come Through* (1961), was also a comedy and concerns a group of young intellectuals struggling to find their place in the world. While the two plays were in rehearsal, Wheeler worked with Peter Viertel on the screenplay for a thriller, *Five Miles to Midnight* (1962), then wrote a stage adaptation of Shirley Jackson's creepily suspenseful novel *We Have Always Lived in the Castle* (1963) and another comedy, *Rich Little Rich Girl* (1964).

The following year, assisting on the book for the American production of *Half a Sixpence* (1965) gave Wheeler his first taste of professional musical theatre and it led to his working on the book for *Softly* (1966), an adaptation of a story about post-war Japan by Santha Rama Rau. In 1968, Wheeler began work on the screenplay for *The Cook*. The film, retitled *Black Flowers for the Bride* (1970) and starring Michael York as a bisexual butler, was directed by Hal Prince. Although Wheeler would write other scripts—including the pilot episode of *The Snoop Sisters* (1973–1974) and, with Jay Presson Allen, *Cabaret* (1972) and *Travels with My Aunt* (1972)—working with Prince would prove a turning point when he invited Wheeler to meet his friend Stephen Sondheim to discuss the possibility of collaboration. Over dinner, Wheeler suggested an adaptation of Ingmar Bergman's film *Smiles on a Summer Night* (1955) and the result, *A Little Night Music* (1973), would go on to win five Antoinette Perry Awards, among them one for Wheeler's libretto. This led to further collaborations with Sondheim, among others, including a new book for *Candide* (1973) and for *Sweeney Todd: The Demon Barber of Fleet Street* (1979), both of which won Tonys and other awards for Wheeler.

Hugh Wheeler continued to work in musical theatre until his death at Berkshire Medical Centre, Pittsfield, Massachusetts, on 26 July 1987. Three years later, the book for *Meet Me in St Louis* (1990) would earn him a fourth Tony nomination.

'The Predestined' was first published in *Britannia and Eve* on 1 August 1953.

VILLA FOR SALE

Ellis Peters

The lady in black, the heavy, elegant, mourning black of southern France, watched the young couple descend from the station bus in the square and hoist their two cases up the steps of the corner hotel.

Over her vermouth she weighed and measured them with cool, illusionless eyes. English, very young, pale, impecunious, and in love. A brand-new wedding ring on the girl's finger, a tenuous black beard on the young man's chin and that drifting look about him that marks the unanchored, those who carry their jobs or their unemployability about with them.

This one, she judged, worked, but at something mulish and unsuccessful of his own. The two meagre cases didn't suggest painting materials. Maybe a writer. Hollow-cheeked, city-bred, hungry for the sun but without the means to stay in it for long.

She thought they would do. When you have nothing to lose, why should you be afraid of being cheated? She ground out her cigarette and was at the bar before them, politely not appearing to listen as they asked for a room.

'Forgive me,' she said, when the bartender had vanished to call his patronne, 'but if you intend to stay any time it could be cheaper to take a house.' She saw the girl's eyes fly to her husband's face solicitously, with the look of a young mother nursing a tuberculous child.

'I'm English, too, by birth,' she said, 'but I've been here half my life. Were you planning to settle here?'

'My husband,' said the girl eagerly, 'ought to be in a warm climate for at least a year. He has a book to finish . . .'

They all have, of course! The improbable masterpieces that no one will ever publish or, even supposing they do, no one will ever buy. Now she knew they would do for her purpose.

'But we couldn't possibly afford . . .'

Of course they couldn't. So much the better.

'You can't afford a hotel for long, that's certain. Even this hotel. But stay overnight and rest, and look around. I live here. My name is Lesoulier, though it used to be Jenkins. I'll look in on you tomorrow, if I may. I know of a place that might suit you here, a bargain. Don't be afraid. Everyone knows me, you'll find. Ask your hotel manager.'

And they did, of course, and they were told what she knew they would be told, that Madame Lesoulier was the recent widow of the wealthiest wine-grower and landowner in the district, and beyond all conception respectable. That made it easy for her to open, over lunch, any delicate question of the Villa des Rosiers.

'There is a house you could buy. No, don't protest yet. It's furnished and, apart from perishables, you could even say it's provisioned for some months. I'm not acting as an agent,' she said drily, seeing the scared glance they exchanged, 'for anyone but myself. This house belonged to my husband. It's the house to which he brought me when we were married.

'Now that he's dead I shall not be living in it; I intend to sell it. It would please me to think that you might be happy in it.'

'It's extraordinarily kind of you,' said the boy carefully, 'but we haven't the money to buy even a suit of clothes.'

'A suit of clothes,' said Madame Lesoulier rather oddly, 'would cost you several hundred francs. At any rate, there's nothing to prevent you from accepting my invitation to view the house.'

So they humoured her and went with her, in her chauffeur-driven car, through the gleams of sea and sun and the garden foaming with flowers. They walked through the Villa des Rosiers at her heels, hand in hand, with wide enchanted eyes, like children in a dream, through all eleven rooms that seemed so many more because of the cunning design. It was neat and manageable—but a palace.

'I am offering you this house,' she said, 'freehold, outright, just as it stands. My price—to you—is fifty francs.'

They stood stunned, even frightened. They would have thought her mad but for the dry curl to her mouth, the cool look in her eyes, and the evidence of money all about her that said she could afford her eccentricities.

'I shall sell it, and for that price,' she assured them. 'I should like it to be to you.'

'This is a joke, of course,' said the young husband from a dry throat. 'It isn't a very kind one.'

'It wouldn't be kind at all if it were a joke. But it isn't. There's no catch in it.'

The fever of desire burned up. They had nothing to lose but 50 francs, and a world to gain. She never told them how many others before them had not been quite desperate enough to overcome their suspicions and grasp at their luck. But she did refer them to her solicitor and left them to satisfy themselves of his stature.

'Madame Lesoulier is empowered to sell,' said Maître Ardouillet austerely. 'It is for her to name her price. That has nothing to do with me. You may be assured the villa will pass into your hands precisely as it stands, with full legal safeguards and no repercussions afterwards.'

'And there's no provision against resale?' Asked the young man tensely. 'In—in case we should have to consider selling it?'

'None whatever. You could resell on completion if you wish.'

'But why?' said the girl, hardly audibly. 'Why is she doing this? She could get hundreds of thousands of francs for it.'

Maître Ardouillet preferred not to reply, nor even to hear the question. But the girl believed she knew the answer already.

'She's rich and kind. She lived all her married life there, and was happy, and now she wants someone else to be happy there, too. It would be barbarous for us to refuse.'

Knowing his wife as he knew her, the young man realised that she meant exactly what she said; that the acceptance was an act of generosity and faith that repaid the gift. That was why, after the incredible bargain was signed and sealed, he never felt mean or indebted in the Villa des Rosiers, but always free and vindicated and glad. He wrote well there, because his heart and mind were liberated by the act of acceptance.

As for Madame Lesoulier, she pulled up her roots and went away to a flat in Paris. She dined with them before she left; and they knew by her smiling tranquillity that she was as content with the transaction as they were. After that they forgot her.

He finished his book and made a good job of it; and after its success as a film they never looked back. All their three children were born in the house, all their friends visited it. Other love affairs began there, and other marriages were made. It was a place saturated with sunlight and happiness.

It was ten years before either of them saw Madame Lesoulier again. Alan was flying back from a conference with his London publisher and stayed overnight in Paris; at a café in Montmartre he found her watching the passing world over the rim of a vermouth, hardly changed at first sight from what she had been when first he encountered her.

On a second glance she seemed to have lost the ten years— and more. Her hair was expertly tinted, her eyes gleamed, and her fair skin bloomed. She was alone and highly content.

'I saw your new book reviewed last month,' she said amiably. 'You've done well in the world.'

He admitted it, still a little amazed. 'We feel we owe it all to you. You started us ahead, and we've never looked back.'

She asked after his wife, and opened her eyes wide to hear of the three children. 'And are you living in Paris now?'

'Oh, no, I'm only here overnight, on my way back from England. I'm off home to the Villa des Rosiers in the morning.'

'You mean,' said Madame Lesoulier blankly, 'that you've hung on all this time? You could have got nearly a quarter of a million francs for it any time you cared.'

Alan stiffened accusingly. 'Then so could you,' he said.

'Of course, if I'd wanted to. But I didn't want to.' She caught his eye and held it; in a moment she relaxed, smiling. 'Don't worry, you never owed me anything. I got my money's worth in return. You did me a favour. You've no idea how most people shy away from a bargain they can't understand.'

For the first time he looked back narrowly and coolly, and saw that the motives they had attributed to her had never been adequate. You may give a house out of pure benevolence, perhaps, if you're rich enough to be able to do that kind of thing. But you don't sell it for fifty francs, not without a reason.

Alan said, 'I'm grown-up now, I'm old enough to be told the facts of life. Why did you do it?'

And she saw that he was, and saw, moreover, that what she told him now could not in any way damage the security and happiness that had never been her gift to them.

'My husband brought me home to the house,' she said with deliberation, 'after our wedding here in Paris. I spent twenty years in hell there. He had vices by the dozen, mistresses by the score. At first I stayed, and stayed faithful because I loved him, and then because I hated him. He'd married me, and I was going to get something out of it if I had to wait years for him to die. When he did die he left me comfortably off. Very comfortably.

'But he got in one dig at the end. I'd suffered from his last mistress for five years. He left me my portion on condition that I sold the villa and handed over the proceeds to "our dear friend Madame Hermine Franck".'

She drank with slow enjoyment, and licked her lips like a cat.

'I was always a dutiful wife,' She purred. 'With my own hands I conveyed to "our dear friend Hermine" the proceeds of that sale. It was worth a quarter of a million francs, believe me. Well worth it!'

ELLIS PETERS

Edith Mary Pargeter was born on 28 September 1913 at 26 Wellington Road in the village of Horsehay, Shropshire—a house now known as *Cadfael Cottage*. Pargeter's father Edmund was a clerk at the local ironworks, and her mother Edith an amateur antiquarian and talented musician who fostered in her children a love of music and a keen interest in local history. Pargeter loved the district where she had been born and although in later years she travelled to Europe, India and eventually America, her home was never more than three miles from her birthplace. She attended Dawley Church of England School where the self-styled 'girl who never stopped writing' contributed poetry and stories to the school magazine, and won first prize in a nationwide essay competition run by the Royal Society for the Prevention of Cruelty to Animals. She also won a scholarship to Coalbrookdale school in 1924 and the following year, when she was only twelve, began her first novel. When she finished it three years later she sent it to William Heinemann, the London publishers. They rejected it for publication but nonetheless asked that she let them see any other novels she might complete.

In 1931 Pargeter left school and after a brief spell working at a labour exchange she became a pharmacist's assistant in the dispensary of Bemrose's, a chemist in the nearby village of Dawley. In the evenings she wrote short stories and worked on a richly detailed novel about ancient Rome. Never shy, she sent the completed typescript to literary agent Gilbert Wright, who placed the novel, *Hortensius—Friend of Nero* (1936), with Lovat Dickson Ltd but sadly did not live to see it published. Pargeter's second novel, *Iron Bound* (1936), was inspired by her father's employment and also appeared from a small publisher, but her third, *The City Lies Four Square* (1939)—an extraordinary ghost story with homoerotic undertones—was published by William Heinemann. Edith Pargeter had achieved her teenage ambition.

Pargeter's first short story to appear in print was 'Mightiest in the Mightiest', published in 1936 in *Everywoman's*. The magazine would feature many more of her stories in the next few years, including a series of rural romances set in the fictional village of Brambleridge. Prompted by her agent, Pargeter tried her hand at writing a romantic novel, albeit pseudonymously to protect her growing reputation as a serious novelist. *Day Star* (1937), inspired by the life of Greta Garbo, appeared under the pen-name of 'Peter Benedict', and Pargeter used the same pseudonym for three newspaper serials: *Rents Are Low in Eden* (1938), a romance centred on a property dispute; a detective story entitled *What Happened at Montalban?* (1939); and *Masters of the Parachute Mail* (1939), a light-hearted thriller that subsequently appeared in hardback as by 'Jolyon Carr', a pseudonym that Pargeter had already used for *Murder in the Dispensary* (1938), a novel that drew on her experience of working at Bemrose's. As 'Jolyon Carr', she also wrote a light-hearted thriller, *Freedom for Two* (1939), and a mystery, *Death Comes by Post* (1940), while a third pseudonym, 'John Redfern', was employed for *The Victim Needs a Nurse* (1940).

At Munich in 1938, out of naïvety or blind hope, Britain's prime minister Neville Chamberlain effectively ceded Czechoslovakia to Germany, an action that left Pargeter desolated. She had been born on Czechoslovakia's national day and had developed a strong interest in the country. As would so often be the case, she felt driven to '*do something*', and so she joined the Women's Royal Naval Service. She received the British Empire Medal for her war work in Liverpool as a teleprinter operator, which she drew upon for *She Goes to War* (1942) and she also completed a trilogy about the war service of a British soldier called Jim Bennison. In 1947, she attended a summer school in Prague where she met various Czechs including Václav Havel, who was the basis for Václav Havelka, the central character of Pargeter's *Black Is the Colour of My True Love's Heart* (1967). Havel would eventually become the country's President in 1989. At the summer school she also met Jiří Edelmann, with whom she would remain close friends for the rest of her life.

In 1948, after the Communist Party seized power, Czechosolvakia fell under the control of the Soviet Union. Despite the difficulties, and 'continually walking a tightrope in order to avoid harming people I wanted only to serve', Pargeter continued to visit Jiří Edelmann and his wife until it became impossible. Nonetheless, determined 'to serve' in some way, she became fluent in Czech and over the next ten years translated at least sixteen notable works, including a volume of stories by Jan Neruda, Josefa Slánská's controversial memoir *Report on My Husband* (1950) and Josef Bor's *Terezin Requiem*, which reduced her to tears as she worked on the translation. Bor's memoir recounts the true story of a production of Verdi's *Requiem*, organized and conducted by a young Czech, Raphael Schachter, whom the Nazis subsequently slaughtered beside the musicians and choir. In 1968, the Czech Society for Foreign Relations awarded Pargeter the Gold Medal and Ribbon for her services to Czechoslovakian literature.

As well as translating Czech books, Pargeter also wrote *The Coast of Bohemia* (1950), a semi-fictional amalgam of travel book and history lesson in which she contrasted the serenity of Prague with the horrors of Terezín and the village of Lidice, which had been razed by the Nazis. And in *Fallen into the Pit* (1951), her first detective story for ten years, the unsympathetic victim was a former Nazi. After *Holiday with Violence* (1952), Pargeter once again seemed to abandon crime fiction until the appearance in 1961 of

'Ellis Peters', named for her older brother, an engineer with whom she lived for many years and nursed until his death in 1985, and Petra, Jiří Edelmann's daughter (whose own daughter would be named Edith). *Fallen into the Pit* had featured a conventional detective, the dull but reliable Inspector George Felse, and between 1961 and 1978 he and members of his family variously appeared in a dozen more novels by 'Ellis Peters'. Two were inspired by a visit to India and one, *Death and the Joyful Woman* (1962), won Pargeter an Edgar from the Mystery Writers of America and, much to her delight, was later the basis of a Czech film, *Smrt a Blazená Paní* (1980).

The 1960s and early 1970s were Pargeter's most productive period. As well as the Felse series, numerous short stories and half a dozen non-series crime novels, she wrote a large number of historical novels, including the *Heaven Tree* trilogy (1960–1963), which she regarded as her best work, and the *Brothers of Gwynned* quartet (1974–1977). Then, inspired by Owen and Blakeway's two-volume *History of Shrewsbury* (1825), which she had been given as a child, and details of monastic life at the 900-year-old Benedictine abbey, she conceived a new novel built around the character of a medieval herbalist called, simply, Cadfael. 'Ellis Peters', crime writer, had finally arrived.

Pargeter's 'one sacred rule' for crime novels was that they must be moral, reflecting her own Anglican sensibilities, and in the worldly Cadfael, named for a Welsh saint, she found the ideal character to fulfil that rule. While she had intended *A Morbid Taste for Bones* (1977) to be a one-off, the enthusiastic response of readers and critics alike ensured that the character would return. And he did, again and again. As she would say in interviews, the twenty Cadfael books and a handful of short stories gave her 'more pleasure than anything else' she wrote in her long career, with her favourite among them being his debut. The books were similarly admired by her peers, with *Monks Hood* (1980) winning the Silver Dagger from the Crime Writers Association. Historical detective stories had existed before her, but their popularity today undoubtedly owes much to Pargeter. In later years she was understandably irritated by the suggestion that the notion of a medieval whodunit was created by Umberto Eco whose global bestseller *The Name of the Rose* (1980) had been published two years after the first of the Cadfael novels.

Pargeter continued to write well into her seventies. In 1993 she was awarded the Cartier Diamond Dagger for her lifetime achievements, and she went on to publish *Brother Cadfael's Penance* in 1994, the same year she was awarded the Order of the British Empire for services to literature in the New Year Honours.

In 1995 the girl who 'never stopped writing' finally stopped. On 14 October, shortly after returning from hospital where she had been suffering from a stroke following a leg amputation, she died in her sleep at her home, a bungalow in Madeley named *Troja* after the suburb where her friends the Edelmanns lived in Prague. By her bedside was Jiří Edelmann, the man to whom she had dedicated *The Fair Young Phoenix* (1948), a semi-fictional love story set in the aftermath of the Second World War.

'Villa for Sale' was published in the *Australian Women's Weekly* on 7 December 1966.

THE GINGER KING

A. E. W. Mason

Monsieur Hanaud was smoking one of Mr Ricardo's special Havanas in the dining-room of Mr Ricardo's fine house in Grosvenor Square. The trial which had fetched him over from Paris had ended that morning. He had eaten a very good lunch with his friend; he had taken the napkin down from his collar; he was at his ease; and as he smoked, alas! he preached.

'Chance, my friend, is the detective's best confederate. A little unimportant word you use and it startles—a strange twist of character is provoked to reveal itself—an odd incident breaks in on the routine of your investigation. And the mind pounces. "Ping," you say, if you play the table-tennis. "Pong," you say, if you play the Mahjong. And there you are! In at the brush.'

'I beg your pardon.'

For the moment Mr Ricardo was baffled.

'I said, "You are in at the brush,"' Hanaud repeated amicably.

Mr Ricardo smiled with indulgence. He too had eaten his share of an admirable saddle of lamb and drunk his half of a bottle of exquisite Haut-Brion.

'You mean, of course, that you are in at the death,' he said.

'No, no,' Hanaud protested, starting forward. 'I do not speak of executions. Detectives are never present at executions and, for me, I find them disgusting. I say, you are in at the brush. It is an idiom from your hunting-field. It means that when all the mess is swept up, you are there, the Man who found the Lady under the thimble.'

Mr Ricardo was in no mood to pursue his large friend through the winding mazes of his metaphors.

'I am beginning to understand you,' he answered with resignation.

'Yes.' Hanaud nodded his head complacently. 'I speak the precision. It is known.'

With a gentle knock, Mr Ricardo's incomparable butler Thomson entered the room.

'A Mr Middleton has called,' he said, offering to Ricardo a visiting-card upon a salver.

Ricardo waved the salver away.

'I do not see visitors immediately after luncheon. It is an unforgivable time to call. Send him away!'

The butler, however, persisted.

'I took the liberty of pointing out that the hour was unseasonable,' he said, 'but Mr Middleton was in hopes that Monsieur Hanaud was staying with you. He seemed very anxious.'

Ricardo took up the card reluctantly. He read aloud.

'Mr John Middleton, Secretary of the Unicorn Fire Insurance Company. I am myself insured with that firm.' He turned towards his guest. 'No doubt he has some reason to excuse him. But it is as you wish.'

Monsieur Hanaud's strange ambition that afternoon was to climb the Monument and after to see the Crown Jewels at the Tower, but his good nature won the day, and since he was to find more than one illustration of the text upon which he had been preaching, he never regretted it.

'I am on view,' he said simply.

'We will see Mr Middleton in the Library,' said Mr Ricardo; and into that spacious dormitory of deep armchairs and noble books Mr Middleton was introduced.

Hanaud was delighted with the look of him. Mr Middleton

was a collector's piece of Victorian England. Middle-aged, with dangling whiskers like lappets at the sides of an otherwise clean-shaved face, very careful and a trifle old-maidish in his speech, he had a tittering laugh and wore the long black frock-coat and the striped trousers which once made the City what is was. He was wreathed in apologies for his intrusion.

'My good friend Superintendent Holloway of Marlborough Street, whose little property is insured with us, thought that I might find you at Mr Ricardo's house. I am very fortunate.'

'I must return to Paris tomorrow,' Hanaud replied. 'For this afternoon I am at your service. You will smoke?'

From his pocket Hanaud tendered a bright blue packet of black stringy cigarettes, and Mr Middleton recoiled as if he suddenly saw a cobra on the carpet ready to strike.

'Oh no, no!' he cried in dismay. 'A small mild cigar when the day's work is done. You will forgive me? I have a little story to tell.'

'Proceed!' said Hanaud graciously.

'It is a Mr Enoch Swallow,' Mr Middleton began. 'I beg you not to be misled by his name. He is a Syrian gentleman by birth and an English gentleman by naturalization. But again I beg you not to be misled. There is nothing of the cunning of the Orient about him. He is a big, plain, simple creature, a peasant, one might say as honest as the day. And it may be so. I make no accusation.'

'He has a business, this honest man?' Hanaud asked.

'He is a furrier.'

'You begin to interest me,' said Hanaud.

'A year ago Enoch Swallow fitted up for his business a house in Berwick Street, towards the Oxford Street end of that long and narrow thoroughfare. The ground floor became his show-rooms, he and his wife with a cook-general to wait on them occupied the first floor, and the two storeys above were elaborately arranged for his valuable stock. Then he came to us for an insurance policy.'

'Aha!' said Monsieur Hanaud.

'We hesitated,' continued Mr Middleton, stroking one of his side whiskers. 'Everything was as it should be—the lease of the house, compliance with the regulations of the County Council, the value of the stock—mink, silver fox, sables—all correct, and yet we hesitated.'

'Why?' asked Hanaud.

'Mind, I make no suggestion.' Mr Middleton was very insistent upon his complete detachment. 'It was held to be an accident. The Société Universelle paid the insurance money. But Mr Enoch Swallow did have a fire in a similar establishment on the Boulevard Haussmann in Paris three years before.'

'Enoch Swallow? The Boulevard Haussmann?' Hanaud dived deep amongst his memories, but came to the surface with empty hands. 'No, I do not remember. There was no case.'

'Oh dear me, no,' Mr Middleton insisted. 'Oh, none at all. Fires happen, else why does one insure? So in the end—it is our business and competition is severe and nothing could have been more straightforward than the conduct of our client—we insured him.'

'For a large sum?'

'For twenty-five thousand pounds.'

Hanaud whistled. He multiplied the amount into francs. It became milliards.

'For a Syrian gentleman, even if he is now an English gentleman, it is a killing.'

'And then last night it all happens again,' cried Mr Middleton, giving his whisker a twist and a slap. 'Would you believe it?'

'I certainly would,' replied Hanaud, 'and without bringing the least pressure upon my credulity.'

Mr Middleton raised a warning hand.

'But, remember please, there is no accusation. No. All is above board. No smell of petrol in the ruins. No little machine with an alarm-clock. Nothing.'

'And yet . . .' said Hanaud with a smile. 'You have your little thoughts.'

The secretary tittered.

'Monsieur Hanaud,' he said coyly, 'I have in my day been something of a dasher. I went once to the Moulin Rouge. I tried once to smoke a stringy black cigarette from a blue packet. But the strings got between my teeth and caused me extreme discomfort. Well, today I have Mr Enoch Swallow between my teeth.'

Mr Ricardo, who all this time had been sitting silent, thought it a happy moment to make a little jest that if the secretary swallowed Mr Swallow, he would suffer even more discomfort. But though Middleton tittered dutifully, Hanaud looked a thousand reproaches and Mr Ricardo subsided.

'I want to hear of last night,' said Hanaud.

It was the cook-general's night out. She had permission, moreover, to stay the night with friends at Balham. She had asked for that permission herself. No hint had been given to her that her absence would be welcome. Her friends had invited her and she had sought for this leave on her own initiative.

'Well, then,' continued Mr Middleton, 'at six o'clock she laid a cold supper for the Swallows in the dining-room and took an omnibus to Balham. The employees had already gone. The showrooms were closed and only Enoch Swallow and his wife were left in the house. At seven those two ate their supper, and after locking the front door behind them went to a cinema-house in Oxford Street where a French film was being shown. *Toto et Fils* was the name of the film.'

They arrived at the cinema-house a few minutes past eight. There was no doubt whatever about that. For in the lobby they met the manager, with whom they were acquainted, and talked with him whilst they waited for the earlier performance to end and its audience to disperse. They had seats in the Grand Circle, and there the manager found them just before eleven o'clock, when he brought them the news that their premises were on fire.

'Yes, the incontestable alibi,' said Hanaud. 'I was waiting for him.'

'They hurried home,' Middleton resumed, but Hanaud would not allow the word.

'Home? Have such people a home? A place full of little valueless treasures which you would ache to lose? The history of your small triumphs, your great griefs, your happy hours? No, no, we keep to facts. They had a store and a shop and a lodging, they come back and it is all in flames. Good! We continue. When was this fire first noticed?'

'About half-past nine, a passer-by saw the smoke curling out from the door. He crossed the street and he saw a flame shoot up and spread behind a window—he thinks on the first floor. But he will not swear that it wasn't on the second. It took him a few minutes to find one of the red pillars where you give the alarm by breaking the glass. The summer has been dry, all those painted pitch-pine shelves in the upper storeys were like tinder. By the time the fire brigade arrived, the house was a bonfire. By the time the Swallows were discovered in the cinema and ran back to Berwick Street, the floors were crashing down. When the cook-general returned at six-thirty this morning, it was a ruin of debris and tottering walls.'

'And the Swallows?' Hanaud asked.

'They had lost everything. They had nothing but the clothes they were wearing. They were taken in for the night at a little hotel in Percy Street.'

'The poor people!' said Hanaud with a voice of commiseration and a face like a mask. 'And how do they explain the fire?'

'They do not,' said Middleton. 'The good wife she weeps, the man is distressed and puzzled. He was most careful, he says, and since the fire did not start until some time after he and his wife had left the house, he thinks some burglar is to blame. Ah yes!' and Mr Middleton pushed himself forward on his chair. 'There is a little something. He suggests—it is not very nice—that the burglar may have been a friend of the cook-general. He has no evidence. No. He used to think her a simple, honest, stupid woman and not a good cook, but now he is not sure. No, it is not a nice suggestion.'

'But we must remember that he was a Syrian gentleman before he became an English one, must we not?' said Hanaud. 'Yes, such suggestions were certainly to be expected. You have seen him?'

'Of course,' cried Mr Middleton, and he edged so much more forward in his chair that it seemed he must topple off. 'And I should esteem it a favour if you, Monsieur Hanaud, and your friend Mr Ricardo'—he gathered the derelict Ricardo gracefully into the council—'would see him too.'

Hanaud raised his hands in protest.

'It would be an irregularity of the most extreme kind. I have no place in this affair. I am the smelly outsider'; and by lighting one of his acrid cigarettes, he substantiated his position.

Mr Middleton waved the epithet and the argument away. He would never think of compromising Monsieur Hanaud. He meant 'see' and not examine, and here his friend Superintendent Holloway had come to his help. The superintendent had also wished to see Mr Enoch Swallow. He had no charge to bring against Enoch. To Superintendent Holloway, as Superintendent, Enoch Swallow was the victim of misfortune, insured of course, but still a victim. None the less the superintendent wanted to have a look at him. He had accordingly asked him to call at Marlborough Street police station at five o'clock.

'You see, the superintendent has a kindly, pleasant reason for his invitation. Mr Swallow will be grateful and the superintendent will see him. Also you, Monsieur Hanaud, from the privacy of the superintendent's office can see him too and perhaps—who knows—a memory may be jogged?'

Mr Middleton stroked a whisker and smiled ingratiatingly. 'After all, twenty-five thousand pounds! It is a sum.'

'It is the whole multiplication table,' Hanaud agreed.

He hesitated for a moment. There was the Monument, there were the Crown Jewels. On the other hand, he liked Mr Middleton's polite, engaging ways, he liked his whiskers and his frock-coat. Also he, too, would like to see the Syrian gentleman. For . . .

'He is either a very honest unlucky man, or he has a formula for fireworks.' Hanaud looked at the clock. It was four.

'We have an hour. I make you a proposal. We will go to Berwick Street and see these ruins, though that beautiful frock-coat will suffer.'

Mr Middleton beamed. 'It would be worth many frock-coats to see Monsieur Hanaud at work,' he exclaimed, and thereupon Mr Ricardo made rather tartly—for undoubtedly he had been neglected—his one effective contribution to this story.

'But the frock-coat won't suffer, Mr Middleton. Ask Hanaud! It will be in at the brush.'

To north and south of the house, Berwick Street had been roped off against the danger of those tottering walls. The salvage company had been at work since the early morning clearing the space within, but there were still beams insecurely poised overhead, and a litter of broken furniture and burnt furrier's stock encumbered the ground. Middleton's pass gave them admittance into the shell of the building. Hanaud looked around with the pleased admiration of a connoisseur for an artist's masterpiece.

'Aha!' he said brightly. 'I fear that Misters the Unicorn pay twenty-five thousand pounds. It is of an admirable completeness, this fire. We say either "What a misfortune!" or "What a formula!"'

He advanced, very wary of the joists and beams balanced above his head, but shirking none of them. 'You will not follow me, please,' he said to Ricardo and Middleton. 'It is not for your safety. But, as my friend Ricardo knows, too many cooks and I'm down the drain.'

He went forward and about, mapping out from the fragments of inner walls the lie of the rooms. Once he stopped and came back to the two visitors.

'There was electric light of course,' he said rather than asked. 'I can see here and there plugs and pipes.'

'There was nothing but electric light and power,' Middleton replied firmly. 'The cooking was done on an electric stove and the wires were all carried in steel tubes. Since the store and the stock were inflammable, we took particular care that these details were carried out.'

Hanaud returned to his pacing. At one place a heavy iron bath had crashed through the first-floor ceiling to the ground, its white paint burnt off and its pipes twisted by the heat. At this bath he stopped again, he raised his head into the air and sniffed, then he bent down towards the ground and sniffed again. He stood up with a look of perplexity upon his face, a man trying to remember and completely baffled.

He moved away from this centre in various directions as though he was walking outwards along the spokes of a wheel, but he always came back to it. Finally, he stooped and began to examine some broken lumps of glass which lay about and in the bath. It seemed to the watchers that he picked one of these pieces up, turned it over in his hands, held it beneath his nose and finally put it away in one of his pockets. He returned to his companions.

'We must be at Marlborough Street at five,' he said. 'Let us go!'

Mr Ricardo at the rope-barrier signalled to a taxi driver. They climbed into it, and sat in a row, both Middleton and Ricardo watching Hanaud expectantly, Hanaud sitting between them very upright with no more expression upon his face than has the image of an Egyptian king. At last he spoke.

'I tell you something.'

A sigh of relief broke from Mr Middleton. Mr Ricardo smiled and looked proud. His friend was certainly the Man who found the Lady under the thimble.

'Yes, I tell you. The Syrian gentleman has become an English gentleman. He owns a bath.'

Mr Middleton groaned. Ricardo shrugged his shoulders. It was a deplorable fact that Hanaud never knew when not to be funny.

'But you smelt something,' said Mr Middleton reproachfully.

'You definitely sniffed,' said Ricardo.

'Twice,' Mr Middleton insisted.

'Three times,' replied Hanaud.

'Ah!' cried Ricardo. 'I know. It was petrol.'

'Yes,' exclaimed Mr Middleton excitedly. 'Petrol stored secretly in the bath.'

Hanaud shook his head.

'Not 'arf,' he said. 'No, but perhaps I sniff,' and he laid a hand upon an arm of each of his companions, 'a formula. But here we are, are we not? I see a policeman at a door.'

They had indeed reached Marlborough Street police station. A constable raised the flap of a counter and they passed into a large room. An inner door opened and Superintendent Holloway appeared on the threshold, a large man with his hair speckled with grey, and a genial, intelligent face.

'Monsieur Hanaud!' he said, coming forward with an outstretched hand. 'This is a pleasant moment for me.'

'And the same to you,' said Hanaud in his best English.

'You had better perhaps come into my room,' the super-intendent continued. 'Mr Swallow has not yet arrived.'

He led his visitors into a comfortable office and, shutting the door, invited them all to be seated. A large—everything about Marlborough Street police station seemed to Hanaud to be large—a large beautiful ginger cat with amber-coloured lambent eyes lay with his paws doubled up under his chest on a fourth chair, and surveyed the party with a godlike indifference.

'You will understand, Monsieur Hanaud,' said the superintendent, 'that I have nothing against Mr Swallow at all. But I thought that I would like to see him, and I had an excellent excuse for asking him to call. I like to see people.'

'I too,' Hanaud answered politely. 'I am of the sociables.'

'You will have the advantage over me, of seeing without being seen,' said the superintendent, and he broke off with an exclamation.

The ginger cat had risen from the chair and jumped down on to the floor. There it stretched out one hind leg and then the other, deliberately, as though it had the whole day for that and nothing else. Next it stepped daintily across the floor to Hanaud, licked like a dog the hand which he dropped to stroke it, and then sprang on to his knee and settled down. Settled down, however, is not the word. It kept its head in the air and looked about in a curious excitement whilst its brown eyes shone like jewels.

'Well, upon my word,' said the superintendent. 'That's the first time that cat has recognized the existence of anyone in the station. But there it is. All cats are snobs.'

It was a pretty compliment, and doubtless Monsieur Hanaud would have found a fitting reply had not the constable in the outer office raised his voice.

'If you'll come through and take a seat, sir, I'll tell the superintendent,' he was heard to say, and Holloway rose to his feet.

'I'll leave the door ajar,' he said in a low voice, and he went into the outer office.

Through the slit left open, Hanaud and Ricardo saw Enoch Swallow rise from his chair. He was a tall, broad man, almost as tall and broad as the superintendent himself, with black short hair and a flat, open, peasant face.

'You wished to see me?' he asked. He had a harsh metallic voice, but the question itself was ordinary and civil. The man was neither frightened, nor arrogant, nor indeed curious.

'Yes,' replied the superintendent. 'I must apologize for asking you to call at a time which must be very inconvenient to you. But we have something of yours.'

'Something of mine?' asked Mr Swallow, perhaps a little more slowly than was quite natural.

'Yes,' said the superintendent briskly, 'and I thought that you would probably like it returned to you at once.'

'Of course. I thank you very much. I thought we had lost everything. What is it?' asked Mr Swallow.

'A cat,' the superintendent answered, and Mr Swallow stood with his mouth open and the colour ebbing from his cheeks. The change in him was astonishing. A moment before he had been at his ease, confident, a trifle curious; now he was a man struck out of his wits; he watched the superintendent with dazed eyes, he swallowed, and his face was the colour of dirty parchment.

'Yes, a big ginger cat,' Holloway continued easily, 'with the disdain of an Emperor. But the poor beast wasn't disdainful last night, I can tell you. As soon as the door was broken in—you had a pretty good door, Mr Swallow, and a pretty strong lock—no burglars for you, Mr Swallow, eh?' and the superintendent laughed genially—'well, as soon as it was broken in, the cat scampered out and ran up one of my officer's legs under his cape and clung there, whimpering and shaking and terrified out of its senses. And I don't wonder. It had a near shave of a cruel death.'

'And you have it here, Superintendent?'

'Yes. I brought it here, gave it some milk, and it has owned my room ever since.'

Enoch Swallow sat down again in his chair, and rather suddenly, for his knees were shaking. He gave one rather furtive look round the room and the ceiling. Then he said:

'I am grateful.'

But he became aware with the mere speaking of the words that his exhibition of emotion required an ampler apology. 'I explain to you,' he said spreading out his hands. 'For me cats are not so important. But my poor wife—she loves them. All last night, all today, she has made great trouble for me over the loss of our cat. In her mind she saw it burnt, its fur first sparks then flames. Horrible!' and Enoch Swallow shut his eyes. 'Now that it is found unhurt, she will be happy. My store, my stock all gone, pouf! Of no consequence. But the Ginger King back again, all is well,' and with a broad smile, Enoch Swallow called the whole station to join him a humorous appreciation of the eccentricities of women.

'Right!' the superintendent exclaimed. 'I'll fetch the Ginger King for you'; and at once all Enoch Swallow's muscles tightened and up went his hands in the air.

'Wait, please!' he cried. 'There is a shop in Regent Street where they sell everything. I will run there and buy a basket with a lid for the Ginger King. Then you shall strap him in and I will take him to my wife, and tonight there will be no unpleasantness. One little moment!'

Mr Enoch Swallow backed out of the entrance and was gone. Superintendent Holloway returned to his office with all the geniality gone from his face. He was frowning heavily.

'Did you ever see that man before, Monsieur Hanaud?' he asked.

'Never,' said Hanaud decisively.

The superintendent shook his head.

'Funny! That's what I call him. Yes, funny.'

Mr Ricardo laughed in a superior way. There was no problem for him.

'"Some that are mad if they behold a cat,"' he quoted. 'Really, really our William knew everything.'

Monsieur Hanaud caught him up quickly.

'Yes, this Enoch Swallow, he hates a cat. He has the cat complex. He grows green at the thought that he must carry a cat in a basket, yes. Yet he has a cat in the house, he submits to a cat which he cannot endure without being sick, because his wife loves it! Do you think it likely? Again I say, "not 'arf."'

A rattle and creak of wickerwork against the raised flap of the counter in the outer office announced Enoch Swallow's return.

The superintendent picked up the Ginger King and walked with it into the outer office. Mr Ricardo, glancing through the open doorway, saw Mr Swallow's dark face turn actually green. The sergeant at the desk, indeed, thought that he was going to faint, and started forward. Enoch Swallow caught hold upon himself. He held out the basket to the superintendent.

'If you will put him into it and strap the lid down, it will be all right. I make myself ridiculous,' he said, with a feeble attempt at a smile. 'A big strong fellow whose stomach turns over at the sight of a cat. But it is so.'

The Ginger King resented the indignity of being imprisoned in a basket; it struggled and spat and bit as if it were the most communistic of cats, but the superintendent and the sergeant between them got it strapped down at last.

'I'll tell you what I'll do, sir,' said Holloway. 'I'll send the little brute by one of my men round to your hotel—Percy Street, wasn't it?—and then you won't be bothered with it at all.'

But Enoch wouldn't hear of putting the station to so much trouble.

'Oh no, no! You are kindness itself, Superintendent. But once he is in the basket, I shall not mind him. I shall take him home at once and my wife will keep him away from me. It is all right. See, I carry him.'

Enoch Swallow certainly did carry him, but very gingerly, and with the basket held well away from his side.

'It would be no trouble to send him along,' the superintendent urged, but again the Syrian refused, and with the same vehemence which he had shown before. The police had its work to do. It would humiliate him to interfere with it for so small a reason.

'I have after all not very far to go,' and with still more effusive protestations of his gratitude, he backed out of the police station.

The superintendent returned to his office.

'He wouldn't let me send it home for him,' he said. He was a very mystified man. 'Funny! That's what I call it. Yes, funny.' He looked up and broke off suddenly. 'Hallo! Where's Monsieur Hanaud gone to?'

Both Middleton and Ricardo had been watching through the crack in the door the scene in the outer office. Neither of them had seen or heard Hanaud go. There was a second door which opened on the passage to the street, and by that second door Hanaud had slipped away.

'I am sorry,' said the superintendent, a little stiffly. 'I should have liked to say goodbye to him.'

The superintendent was hurt, and Mr Ricardo hastened to reassure him.

'It wasn't discourtesy,' he said staunchly. 'Hanaud has manners. There is some reason.'

Middleton and Ricardo returned to the latter's house in Grosvenor Square, and there, a little more than an hour afterwards, Hanaud rejoined them. To their amazement he was carrying Enoch Swallow's basket, and from the basket he took out a contented, purring, gracious Ginger King.

'A little milk, perhaps?' Hanaud suggested. And having lapped up the milk, the Ginger King mounted a chair, turned in his paws under his chest and once more surveyed the world with indifferent eyes.

Hanaud explained his sudden departure.

'I could not understand why this man who could not abide a cat refused to let the superintendent send it home for him. No, however much he shivered and puked, he would carry it home himself. I had a little thought in my mind that he didn't mean to carry it home at all. So I slipped out into the street and waited for him and followed him. He had never seen me. It was as easy as the alphabet. He walked in a great hurry down to the Charing Cross Road and past the Trafalgar Square and along the Avenue of Northumberland. At the bottom of the Avenue of Northumberland there is—what? Yes, you have guessed him. The river Thames. "Aha," I say to myself, "my friend Enoch, you are going to drown the Ginger King. But I, Hanaud, will not allow it. For if you are so anxious to drown him, the Ginger King has something to tell us."

'So I close up upon his heels. He crossed the road, he leaned over the parapet, swinging the basket carelessly in his hand as though he was thinking of some important matter and not of the Ginger King at all. He looked on this side and that, and then I slip my hand under the basket from behind, and I say in his ear:

'"Sir, you will drop that basket, if you don't look out."

'Enoch, he gave a great jump and he drop the basket, this time by accident. But my hand is under it. Then I take it by the handle, I make a bow. I hand it to him, I say "Dr Livingstone, I presume?" and lifting my hat, I walk away. But not so far. I see him black in the face with rage. But he dare not try the river again. He thinks for a little. Then he crosses the road and dashes through the Underground Station. I follow as before. But now he has seen me. He knows my dial,' and at Middleton's surprised expression he added, 'my face. It is a little English idiom I use. So I keep further back, but I do not lose him. He runs up that steep street. Half-way up, he turns to the right.'

'John Street,' said Mr Ricardo.

'Half-way up John Street, there is a turning to the left under a building. It is a tunnel and dark. Enoch raced into the tunnel. I follow, and just as I come to the mouth of it, the Ginger King comes flashing out like a strip of yellow lightning. You see. He could not drown him, so in the dark tunnel he turns him loose with a kick no doubt to make him go. The Ginger King is no longer, if he ever was, the pet of the sad Mrs Swallow. He is just a stray cat. Dogs will set on him, no one will find him, all the time he must run and very soon he will die.

'But this time he does not need to run. He sees or smells a friend, Hanaud of the *Sûrété*, that joke, that comic—eh, my friend?' and he dug a fist into Ricardo's ribs which made that fastidious gentleman bend like a sapling in a wind. 'Ah, you do not like the familiarities. But the Ginger King to the contrary. He stops, he mews, he arches his back and rubs his body against Hanaud's leg. So I pick him up and I go on into the tunnel. It winds, and at the point where it bends I find the basket with the lid. It is logical. Enoch has dismissed the Ginger King. Therefore he wants nothing to remind him of the Ginger King. He drops the basket. I insert the Ginger King once more. He has confidence, he does not struggle. I strap down the lid. I come out of the tunnel. I am in the Strand. I look right and left and everywhere. There is no Enoch. I call a taximan.'

'And you are here,' said Ricardo, who thought the story had been more than sufficiently prolonged. But Hanaud shook his head.

'No, I am not here yet. There are matters of importance in between.'

'Very well,' said Ricardo languidly. 'Proceed.'

And Hanaud proceeded.

'I put the basket on the seat and I say to the taximan, "I want"—guess what?—but you will not guess. "I want the top--dog chemist." The taximan wraps himself round and round with clothes and we arrive at the top-dog chemist. There I get just the information which I need and now, my friend Ricardo, here I am with the Ginger King who sits with a Chinese face and will tell us nothing of what he knows.'

But he was unjust. For later on that evening, in his own good time, the Ginger King told them plenty.

They were sitting at dinner at a small mahogany table bright with silver and fine glass: Mr Ricardo between Hanaud and Middleton, and opposite to Ricardo, with his head just showing above the mahogany, the Ginger King. Suddenly one of those little chancy things upon which Hanaud had preached his sermon, happened. The electric light went out.

They sat in the darkness, their voices silenced. Outside the windows the traffic rumbled by, suddenly important. An unreasonable suspense stole into the three men, and they sat very still and aware that each was breathing as lightly as he could. Perhaps for three minutes this odd tension lasted, and then the invaluable Thomson came into the room carrying a lighted lamp. It was an old-fashioned oil affair with a round of baize cloth under the base, a funnel and an opaque globe in the heart of which glowed a red flame.

'A fuse has blown, sir,' he said.

'At a most inconsiderable moment,' Mr Ricardo replied. He had been in the middle of a story and he was not pleased.

'I'll replace it at once, sir.'

'Do so, Thomson.'

Thomson set the glowing lamp in the middle of the table and withdrew. Mr Middleton leaned forward towards Ricardo.

'You had reached the point where you tiptoed down the stairs—'

'No, no,' Ricardo interrupted. 'The chain is broken. The savour of the story gone. It was a poor story, anyway.'

'You mustn't say that,' cried Hanaud. 'The story was of a thrill. The Miss Braddon at her best.'

'Oh well, well, if you really think so,' said Mr Ricardo, tittering modestly; and there were the three faces smiling contentedly in the light of the lamp, when suddenly Hanaud uttered a cry.

'Look! Look!'

It was a cry so sharp that the other two men were captured by it and must look where Hanaud was looking. The Ginger King was staring at the lamp, its amber eyes as red as the flame in the globe, its body trembling. They saw it rise on to its feet and leap on to the edge of the table, where it crouched again, and rose again, its eyes never changing from their direction. Very delicately it padded between the silver ornaments across the shining mahogany. Then it sat back upon its haunches and, raising its forepaws, struck once violently at the globe of the lamp. The blow was so swift, so savage that it shocked the three men who watched. The lamp crashed upon the table with a sound of broken glass and the burning oil was running this way and that and dropping in great gouts of fire on to the carpet.

Middleton and Ricardo sprang up, a chair was overturned.

'We'll have the whole house on fire,' cried Ricardo as he rang the bell in a panic; and Hanaud had just time to snatch up the cat as it dived at the green cloth on the base of the stand, before the flames caught it; and it screamed and fought and clawed like a mad thing. To get away? No, but to get back to the overturned lamp.

Already there was a smell of burning fabrics in the room. Some dried feathery grass in a vase caught a sprinkle of the burning oil and flamed up against the wallpaper. Thomson arrived with all the rugs he could hurriedly gather to smother the fire. Pails of water were brought, but a good many minutes had passed before the conflagration was extinguished, and the four men, with their clothes dishevelled, and their hands and faces begrimed, could look round upon the ruin of the room.

'I should have guessed,' said Hanaud remorsefully. 'The Unicorn Company saves its twenty-five thousand pounds—yes, but Mr Ricardo's fine dining-room will need a good deal of restoration.'

Later on that night, in a smaller room, when the electric light was burning and the three men were washed and refreshed, Hanaud made his apology.

'I asked you, Mr Middleton, inside the burnt walls of the house in Berwick Street, whether it was lit with electric light. And you answered, "with that and with nothing else." But I had seen a broken oil lamp amongst the litter. I suspected that lamp, but the house was empty for an hour and a half before the fire broke out. I couldn't get over that fact. Then I smelt something, something acrid—just a whiff of it. It came from a broken bottle lying by the bath with other broken bottles and a broken glass shelf, such as a man has in his bathroom to hold his little medicines, his toothpaste, his shaving soap. I put the broken bottle in my pocket and a little of that pungent smell clung to my fingers.

'At the police station at once the cat made friends with me. Why? I did not guess. In fact I flattered myself a little. I say, "Hanaud, animals love you." But it was not so. The Ginger King loved my smelly fingers, that was all. Then came the strange behaviour of Enoch Swallow. Cats made him physically sick. Yet this one he must take away before it could betray him. He could not carry it under his coat—no, that was too much. But he could go out and buy a basket—and without any fear. Do you remember, how cunningly he looked around the office, and up at the ceiling, and how satisfied he was to leave the cat with us. Why? I noticed the look, but I could not understand it. It was because all the lights in the room were bulbs hanging from the ceiling. There was not a standing lamp anywhere. Afterwards I get the cat. I drive to the chemist, leaving the cat in its basket in the cab.

'I pull out my broken bottle and I ask the chemist. 'What is it that was in this bottle?'

'He smells and he says at once, "Valerian."'

'I say, "What is valerian?"'

'He answers, "Valerian has a volatile oil which when exposed to the air develops a pungent and unpleasant smell. It is used for hysteria, insomnia and nervous ailments."'

'That does not help me, but I draw a target at a venture. I ask, "Has it anything to do with cats?"'

'The chemist, he looks at me as if I was off my rocker and he says, "It drives them mad, that's all," and at once I say:

'"Give me some!"' and Hanaud fetched out of his pocket a bottle of tincture of valerian.

'I have this—yes. But I am still a little stupid. I do not connect the broken lamp and the valerian and the Ginger King—no, not until I see him step up with his eyes all mad and on fire on to the mahogany table. And then it is too late.

'You see, the good Enoch practiced a little first. He smears the valerian on the base of the lamp and he teaches the cat to knock it over to get at the valerian. Then one night he shuts the cat up in some thin linen bag through which in time it can claw its freedom. He smears the base of the lamp with the valerian, lights it and goes off to the cinema.

'The house is empty—yes. But the cat is there in the bag, and the lamp is lit and every minute the valerian at the bottom of the lamp smells more and more. And more and more the cat is maddened. Tonight there was no valerian on the lamp, but the Ginger King—he knows that that is where valerian is to be found. I shall find out when I get back to Paris whether there was any trace of a burnt cat at the fire on the Boulevard Haussmann.

'But,' and he turned towards Mr Middleton, 'you will keep the Ginger King that he may repeat his performance at the Courts of Law, and you will not pay one brass bean to that honest peasant from Syria.'

A. E. W. MASON

Writer, spy, politician and actor, Alfred Edward Woodley Mason was born in South London in 1865. He attended Dulwich College where he excelled in modern languages. He also took part in the school's theatrical productions, acting in French and German plays as well as Shakespeare, including playing Oliver in *As You Like It* (1883). On leaving Dulwich, Mason went up to Oxford, studying at Trinity, and he joined the Oxford University Dramatic Society. Among many roles, he played Heracles in 1887 in a production of Euripides' *Alcestis*; in the same production the character of Death was played by Arthur Bourchier, who in 1920 would portray the French police officer Gabriel Hanaud in Mason's adaptation of his own novel *At the Villa Rose* (1910).

In 1888, after graduating, Mason joined Sir Frank Benson's repertory company but he was not with them long. He moved to the Compton Comedy Company and then Ben Greet's Company, with both of which he toured the British Isles, fulfilling minor roles in plays like Sheridan's *A School for Scandal* in 1890 and Sydney Grundy's *A Village Priest* in 1891. Mason was not a particularly good actor—at an Old Playgoer's Dinner in 1928, Sir Frank Benson commented drily that, while Mason didn't always know his lines, those he improvised were often better than the original; at the same event Mason acknowledged his own shortcomings, noting his appearance in the first production of George Bernard

Shaw's *Arms and the Man* (1894), at which—on the opening night—Shaw had taken to the stage and panned it as a comedy rather than the tragedy he had written.

While acting, Mason produced his first play, an adaptation in 1894 of the famous French comedy *Frou-Frou* by Ludovic Halévy and Henri Meilhac. He also began writing short stories which appeared in provincial newspapers as well as in journals like *Cassell's Family Magazine*, the *English Illustrated Magazine* and the *Illustrated London News*. Mason completed his first novel, *A Romance of Wastdale* (1895), and then, buoyed by its reception, *The Courtship of Morrice Buckler*, which he would go on to adapt for the stage in 1897, co-authoring the script with the actress Isabel Bateman with whom he had appeared in a production four years earlier.

When his theatrical career came to an end, Mason became a political agent for the Conservative Party and later joined the staff of the Church Defence Society—both undemanding jobs that allowed him to pursue his writing. It was with his ninth novel that his career as a novelist took off. *The Four Feathers* (1902) is a thrilling adventure set during the Mahdist War in North Africa. The book has been filmed six times, most memorably in 1939 under the direction of Zoltan Korda and with a screenplay by R. C. Sheriff, author of the classic anti-war play *Journey's End* (1928).

In 1903, in the wake of the success of *The Four Feathers*, Mason was invited to take up a career in politics. Always up for a challenge, he accepted and, despite living in Queen Anne's Mansions in Westminster, London, he was selected as the Liberal Party's candidate for Coventry, a city in central England. At the General Election in 1906, he won the seat, overturning a massive majority and taking more than half the votes cast. As a politician Mason championed equality and the rights of the individual, arguing against racist exclusionary laws in South Africa and in favour of women's suffrage at home, as well as pushing for free school meals and the provision of land for allotments, arguing that 'the desire for a piece of land was the one sure sign of a healthy mind'.

Although Mason was a tremendous success as a member of Parliament, the pressure of maintaining two careers was enormous. He stepped down at the January 1910 election, at which the Liberal Party's new candidate was another author, Silas K. Hocking, who lost narrowly; other than for the eight years following the December 1910 election—when another man called Mason (but no relation) was elected—the Liberal Party never again won a Coventry constituency. As always, Mason made practical use of his political experience, which he drew on for a play, Colonel Smith (1909), and a novel, The Turnstile (1912); in later years he would criticise the idleness of minor politicians who 'haven't a moment to spare, they do nothing with so much energy and persistence'.

After leaving politics, Mason decided to move into crime fiction and to create a detective who would be a professional, in contrast to the likes of Sherlock Holmes and Father Brown, and credible in his methods rather than a super-normal expert like Dr John Thorndyke. In a profile broadcast on the BBC Empire Service in 1935, Mason explained that while Inspector Gabriel Hanaud was in part a portrait of a detective friend, he had also drawn on the memoirs of several senior French police officers. Like Holmes, Hanaud has his Watson—a retired London banker called Julius Ricardo—but the ebullient Hanaud's investigations focus more on psychological rather than physical clues. Mason had been inspired to write Hanaud's first case, At the Villa Rose (1910), by the chance observation of two French names scratched on the window of an English inn, names connected with the real-life double murder and robbery in 1903 of Eugénie Fougère and her maid Victorine Giriat at Aix-les-Bains in France. The book was an enormous success and has been filmed five times. Hanaud would go on to appear in four more novels (he is mentioned in a fifth but does not appear), the last of which was Mason's final book, The House in Lordship Lane, published in 1946.

In 1914, with the advent of what would come to be called The Great War, Mason and his friend Sir James Barrie travelled to

America on a 'mission of truth' to combat German propaganda. In 1915 he was gazetted a temporary captain in the 21st battalion of the Manchester regiment; and in 1917 he was appointed an honorary major in the Royal Marines and served in the Intelligence department of the Admiralty, working to frustrate the German military in Morocco and Spain and even in Mexico, where Mason helped to destroy an enemy transmitter.

With the war behind him, Mason resumed writing and engaged a secretary, a young woman called Muriel Stephens. In the early 1920s, he published three books, including the second Hanaud novel *The House of the Arrow* (1924), but by the mid-1920s Muriel was ill with 'consumption', or pulmonary tuberculosis. Mason took the unusual step of adopting his secretary and funding her treatment at a sanatorium in the New Forest. Muriel's health did not improve and in 1929, she died in Arosa, Switzerland. She was 27 years old.

Shattered, Mason threw himself into writing and his hobbies— mountain-climbing and sailing his 50-ton ketch *Mannequin*. In 1936 he produced what many regard as his finest novel, *Fire over England* (1936), an Elizabethan romance of espionage that drew in part on his own experiences during the First World War. An enduring classic adventure, the novel was filmed in 1937, featuring Laurence Olivier and Vivien Leigh, with William K. Howard directing and Zoltan Korda's brother Alexander heading production. The same year, Mason renamed *Mannequin* the *Muriel Stephens* and he sailed from Brixham to Gibraltar with the hope of finding inspiration for a novel about the Spanish Civil War. Despite spending three months moored off the coast he did not find it and, on returning to Britain, he decided to resume writing historical fiction.

In 1941, Mason had published a biography of Sir Francis Drake and, at the time of his death from heart trouble and asthma in November 1948, he was working on another biography about the seventeenth-century naval commander Admiral Robert Blake. In his will, Mason left the bulk of his estate—the equivalent of £2.5 million (about $3 million)—to his alma mater, Trinity College, Oxford. As well as large bequests to his secretary and manservant, Mason left a sum 'to be applied for the care or relief of consumption', the disease that nearly twenty years earlier had taken the life of Muriel Stephens.

'The Ginger King' was first published in *The Strand Magazine* in August 1940.

SUGAR-PLUM KILLER

Michael Gilbert

I

'Dangerous criminals?' said Detective-Inspector Chapman doubtfully. 'Yes, I suppose you could call some of 'em dangerous. Like animals.

'There's no rule about it. Take dogs, for instance. Nineteen dogs out of twenty are all right. The twentieth one looks just the same, only he bites. When he's bitten you once you know for next time—if there is a next time.'

'That's right, sir,' said Probationary Detective Walkinshaw. 'Close, isn't it?'

The two men were on their way home. It was past two o'clock in the morning but, being short-handed, the detective staff of Q Division kept no sort of hours.

'Who would you say was the most dangerous man you ever met, Inspector?' said Walkinshaw.

'Peter the Cobbler? Flash Martin? They're both dead now. There was a Pole I had a hand in pulling in at the beginning of the war—Dodrowski, or some such name. Changed it to Dods when he was in prison. Sugar Plum Dods.'

'Sugar Plum?'

'That was how he used to talk to girls he met. Nothing to do with the sweetness of his nature, I should say,' said Chapman shortly. 'He had a gun on him when we took him, only we didn't give him time to use it. I heard stories about him though—things he'd done in the States. Odd-looking cove. Outsize, with a shock of black hair and a white face, dead white, like the belly of a fish.'

'Sounds quite a lad,' said Walkinshaw. 'Do you think it's going to thunder?'

'Might be,' agreed the Inspector. 'It won't be too soon when it does come.'

It was a black night: the air so warm and heavy that it felt almost sticky to the touch.

They walked on in silence for a bit.

'What did he do?' said Walkinshaw suddenly.

'What did who do?'

'Dods.'

'He was a safe-breaker,' said Chapman. 'Specialist in his own line. Here's where I turn down. Good night.'

'Good night, sir,' said Walkinshaw.

He did not make immediately for his own lodging. The attic bedroom where he sweltered through the hot nights held few attractions for him.

He sat down for a moment on the low wall outside the school playground and thought the long thoughts of youth. He thought about Inspector Chapman, who had just left him.

He liked Chapman, a kind man and an easy-going superior. But he didn't admire him, He thought him slow and old--fashioned. One day he, Walkinshaw, was going to outstrip Inspector Chapman. He was going to be a Divisional Detective-Inspector, like Hazlerigg, or even a Superintendent.

Give him a chance. Just one chance, and he'd show them what he was made of.

There was a car in the distance, travelling fast.

The trouble with the system, thought Walkinshaw, swinging his heel hard against the wall, was that all the credit—hello, the car was coming in his direction . . .

Then everything happened at once.

The car came up the hill with the roar of an express train. It was travelling without lights.

Walkinshaw jerked out a torch, stepped into the road and waved.

The car hardly checked. It was almost on top of him. 'He's seen me. He's not going to stop.' As Walkinshaw's mind registered this message, he jumped aside.

The car went past him, brakes squealing, rocketing like a spinning top.

There was a tiny explosion. Sharp splinters spattered into his face.

Then the car turned, left-handed, following the road that Inspector Chapman had taken. The roar of the engine receded.

Walkinshaw found that there was blood on his face and that he was trembling.

He turned his torch on to the pavement and saw that the car, in brushing past the lamp post, must have snapped off its driving mirror. It was the glass which had flown up into his face.

He pulled himself together and started to run. It was a futile gesture. The car was already a hundred yards away and gathering speed.

Suddenly he saw a light flash. Came a shout. Then a crash. Then a thud. The noise of the engine seemed to check for a moment, before gathering speed again.

Walkinshaw ran on. He was feeling sick now, as well.

In the roadway, outside his own front door, he found Inspector Chapman. One glance in the light of his torch was enough. The car had gone over the Inspector.

Walkinshaw dropped on to his knees. Deep silence had followed the passing of the car. Inspector Chapman was whispering something. Walkinshaw bent his head to listen.

Then he realised that what Chapman was saying was his wife's name, over and over.

After a minute this stopped, too.

II

It was stifling hot in the CID office on the first floor of Barley Lane Police Station.

Inspector Hazlerigg was looking through a list of dangerous criminals who specialised in stolen cars. A name caught his eye:

HERMAN DODS. Alias Dodrowski. Polish-American. Deserter. Assault on British Military policeman—1940. Six months. Car stealing—armed robbery . . . Specialist safe-breaker . . . Resisted arrest . . . Thought to carry arms. Dangerous.

The telephone rang.

'Another stolen car,' said Hazlerigg wearily. 'All right. Wait while I write it down. Stolen in Gerrard Street two nights ago. Found on North Hill—yes, I'll see to it.'

Sergeant Pickup came in. He had a report in his hand.

'No. 7 Eton Hill,' he read. 'Housebreaking or burglary. The owner's away on the Continent, but his housekeeper looks in every other day. She's just given us the alarm.'

'What did they take?'

'They took the safe,' said Pickup. 'They couldn't get it out of the wall, so they cut the back off and took the whole thing.'

'We'd better go round right away,' said Hazlerigg. 'Oh, by the way, get Walkinshaw to have a look at this stolen car.'

Walkinshaw found the Station Sergeant in charge. 'There she is, son,' he said. 'Found this morning, at the top of North Hill. Been there since the night before last. The night Inspector Chapman caught it. Nothing to show it's the same car, though.'

Walkinshaw was already head-down inside the car.

'Could you plug in that inspection lamp?' he suggested politely. He was now in the front seat, scraping something off the carpet by the clutch pedal. He marked two more places on the rubber flooring mat, and what he took from each went into a separate envelope and was carefully sealed.

The Sergeant, who had early lost interest, came back an hour later to find Walkinshaw standing thoughtfully beside the running-board. 'Well, young Sherlock,' he said, 'what have you found?'

'Gravel,' said Walkinshaw. 'Paint and sawdust.'

'It hasn't got a driving-mirror,' said the Sergeant. 'Looks at if it's been snapped off.'

'So it does,' said Walkinshaw.

The first rule in any detective force is that everything goes on record.

This rule Walkinshaw was breaking deliberately.

It wouldn't have been easy to explain to an outsider that he had put himself on trial and found himself guilty: that it was he who should have been dead, not Inspector Chapman; that, in that blinding moment two nights before, he had lost his self-respect; and that the only possible way to get it back was to get his hands on the people who had been responsible.

Therefore he kept to himself one vital piece of knowledge which he should have shared.

He had forwarded his samples to a friend at the Police Laboratory for a report, and while he was waiting for the answer he discussed his ideas—or some of them—with Sergeant Pickup.

'Sawdust,' said Walkinshaw, 'means a carpenter. It wasn't ordinary sawdust, though. Not soft and floury. Very fine and dry. Some hardwood, I thought. Mahogany or teak, perhaps.'

'Sounds more like a cabinet-maker,' suggested the Sergeant.

'Yes, that's what I thought. And the paint was high-gloss paint. The flakes were quite hard. It was paint a joiner might use.'

'What's your idea about all this?' said Pickup. 'Are you going round all the cabinet-makers and joiners in the Division? '

'No. The paint and sawdust are just corroboration. It's the gravel that we'll find them by.'

'There's a good deal of gravel in North London.'

'This is a fine top gravel. I asked a builder about it. It's the sort that's used for finishing a high-class drive. The people who left that car there wouldn't want to walk far. Too risky. A quarter of a mile at the outside. There can't be many newly laid drive-ways within a quarter of a mile of a district like North Hill.

The following afternoon, just before five o'clock, Sergeant Pickup had cause to recollect this conversation. Hazlerigg called him up and pointed to an envelope he had just opened.

'This seems to be for young Walkinshaw,' he said. 'Do you know about it?'

'Yes, I do, sir. It'll be reports on three samples he sent of the stuff out of that stolen car.'

'I remember.' Hazlerigg glanced down the paper. He didn't make much of the gravel. The paint flakes stopped him. 'Dark green,' he said, 'on a metallic surface. Looks promising. What's this? Sawdust. Hardwood, probably teak, mixed with—*what?*'

He read on quickly.

'Have you seen these?'

'No, sir,' said Pickup.

'Then you didn't know they found alum in the sawdust? When did Walkinshaw go out?'

'About two o'clock.'

Hazlerigg looked at his watch and said quietly: 'We've got to get after him—and damned quick.'

He reached for the telephone.

III

Walkinshaw had started out for North Hill at half past two. It was hotter than ever.

He worked methodically, coming back each time to the place where the car had been abandoned and setting out again in a

different direction. His course on the map would have shown
like the spokes of a great wheel, with the hub resting on the
top of North Hill.

By four-thirty he had covered three segments of the circle.
He was actually on the way back to the centre when his eye
caught a glimpse of fresh yellow. It was a hundred yards ahead
of him, and had he turned a moment sooner he would have
missed it.

When he came up to it, he saw that it was a good class house,
unusually good for the district. It had a long garden and the
trees in it almost hid the front of the house from the road.

The top gravel of the neatly rolled drive was plainly of the
finest quality, and there were indications that a car had been
along it recently

Walkinshaw took a deep breath, walked up the drive, and
rang the bell. The door was opened by a maid.

'I wonder if I might have a word with the gentleman of the
house?' he said. 'I'm from your local police station.' He felt for
his warrant card, but was surprised when the girl said, in the
tone of voice of one who suddenly grasps a difficult situation:
'Oh, you're from the police. Will you wait in here? He's in the
garden.'

Walkinshaw found himself in a room which had the look of
a bachelor's study. It was neat and comfortable, and in some
indefinable way it was an old man's room.

A door led into a further room and as he stood there his
senses were assailed by a faint but characteristic smell. It took
a moment to register. Then he had it. It was varnish.

The house was very quiet. He tiptoed across the room and
turned the handle. The door opened and he found himself
looking at—

'My workroom,' said a polite voice behind him. Walkinshaw
turned and saw a red face under a mop of white hair. It was a
face he was sure he had seen before somewhere.

'Excuse my curiosity,' said Walkinshaw. 'I—that is to say, I see you are a carpenter.'

'A cabinet-maker, really,' said the man with a smile.

'Do you do your own painting?'

'Certainly. Both painting and enamelling.'

'In that case (Walkinshaw swallowed hard) I must ask you to account for your movements on the night of the fourteenth.'

'The fourteenth,' said the man. He seemed a little embarrassed. 'That would be—let me think—well, I was with some friends.'

'Business friends.'

'Yes. I'm retired now. A sort of reunion.'

'Might I ask where this reunion took place?'

'As a matter of fact, I was at Scotland Yard.'

'My God!' said Walkinshaw. He suddenly realised that, standing in front of him, was the recently retired and most celebrated head of the Criminal Investigation Department.

When he had finished apologising, Sir Hector McDonnel said: 'There might be something in that idea of yours, you know. The gravel, I mean. I got mine from the contractor who put up that small block of luxury flats you can see from my back window. The drives and paths are all surfaced with it. They're quite nice flats, but mostly foreigners in 'em.'

'I'll try it at once,' said Walkinshaw gratefully.

Five minutes later Walkinshaw was talking to the commissionaire of the flats. The commissionaire was an ex-serviceman inclined to be helpful as far as he could.

'I don't know of any carpenters in this block,' he said. 'Mostly they're something in the City. From the look of them they wouldn't know a chisel from a screwdriver. And yet—wait a minute—I knew there was something. The big first-floor annexe flat—it stands on its own, really. We built out over the garage. Two foreign gentlemen have got it.'

'What about it?' said Walkinshaw.

'I'm telling you. I was cleaning up the passage carpet the other day, and I picked up a lot of sawdust—right outside their front door.'

IV

'I want two squad cars with full crews to close on the top of North Hill at once,' said Hazlerigg into the telephone. 'I can't tell you exactly where they'll be needed, but when it does come it'll come quickly. I shall be in a wireless car. I'm going out to look for my man now. Tell the squad cars to keep in touch. That's all.'

An exasperating half-hour followed.

They crawled from point to point. A policeman coming off duty had seen Walkinshaw at three o'clock. Another had spoken to him just before four. But after that there was nothing.

He seemed to have walked off the streets and disappeared.

The other cars came on the air from time to time, but Hazlerigg had nothing tangible to offer them.

At five-forty he told his driver to turn back to the police station, where he had left Sergeant Pickup to take incoming calls.

'Nothing, sir. It's getting damned dark, isn't it? Oh—here's somebody. No, it's an outside call.'

'Who is it?' said Hazlerigg. 'I can't—'

'It's Sir Hector McDonnel, sir. He wants to speak to you personally.'

Hazlerigg picked up the receiver. However busy one may be, one does not say 'No' to an ex-head of the C.I.D.

Pickup listened to the telephone cackling and wondered what the old Chief could be talking about.

Then he saw Hazlerigg's face.

'Thank you, sir,' said the Inspector. 'It's very good of you. The flats in Curran Road—yes, I'll go right along.'

The door banged. Footsteps clattered down the stairs. A car started up.

Walkinshaw paused for a moment outside the door of the flat. As the porter had indicated, it was the only flat at the end of the long corridor.

It was now so dark that he looked down with some surprise at his watch. The time was twenty-five to six, but a hard grey cloak of premature dusk lay across the sky, blanketing sound and movement.

In the exaggerated silence he could clearly hear men's voices inside the flat. Some way back in the main block a wireless was playing. A car went by in the street.

He touched the bell. The door was opened by a fat man in overalls. He opened it so quickly that he might almost have been waiting with one hand on the latch.

Walkinshaw introduced himself.

'Why, come in,' said the man. He pointed to an inner door, then walked ahead and half opened it. As Walkinshaw got there he received a violent blow between the shoulders which shot him forward. His head cracked against the edge of the door, which opened under the impact, and he found himself inside the room.

Two men were looking at him.

'Do you always open doors with your head?' said the bigger of the two.

'Hard-headed Harry, the boy detective,' said the smaller man.

Walkinshaw said nothing. He was still seeing sparks.

'Let's hear from you,' said the big man. He had a white face under a heavy shock of black hair. Dead white, like the belly of a fish. His accent was American.

Walkinshaw's head was clearing now. He said: 'You're Herman Dods.'

'Right,' said the man.

'In that case,' said Walkinshaw. 'I shall have to ask you to come with me.' He moved forward.

'Don't try it,' said Dods, 'unless you want to build yourself a new stomach.' His hand moved, flickered lazily inside his coat, came out holding a gun.

Walkinshaw stopped moving.

'That's right,' said Dods. There was another silence.

'What are we going to do with him?' said the man in overalls.

Walkinshaw realised that he had interrupted a move. Shelves and cupboards were empty. Three suitcases stood ready strapped beside the door

'Go and run the bath full of water,' said the big man.

'Hot or cold?'

'Now, that's not kind,' said Dods. 'Just make it warm. Then we'll tie this boy up and dunk him into it while we get going. It'll give him something to think about, keeping his head above water.'

Walkinshaw stood very still. He had realised that his detecting career, so recently and promisingly begun, was already at an end. If he submitted this time he didn't see that he could ever stand on his own feet again. If he didn't . . .

The big man was a full two yards away, watching him. There wasn't a chance in a million of jumping him. Walkinshaw jumped.

Dods's arm came up almost slowly and two reports echoed each other. The one inside the room was loud, but it was swallowed up and drowned by the tearing crash from outside as the storm broke and the sky fell in a blinding cataract of rain.

V

Whether the sudden shock of the storm upset his aim or whether the unexpectedness of Walkinshaw's attack achieved a fraction of a second of surprise will never be known. The result was what counted.

Dods shot high and left.

He didn't miss Walkinshaw, because a miss at that range would have been impossible, but the bullet, instead of hitting him in the stomach or chest, went in under the collarbone and out by the shoulder blade.

It knocked out Walkinshaw's right arm, but it didn't kill him—and it didn't stop him.

He whipped his left arm round Dods's neck and jerked him backwards. He then slid to the floor and Dods, who had no choice, slid with him.

The thin man had also drawn a gun: but he pushed it away again. Walkinshaw was underneath Dods, and with the two of them threshing round on the floor like twin-hooked salmon, there seemed to be very little chance of getting in a useful shot.

Besides, as he soon saw, it wouldn't be necessary.

He picked up a bottle off the table, sidled forward for the kill.

The storm hit Hazlerigg's rescue party as they came skidding into the drive. There was no time to shut windows or lower windscreens. The leading car ploughed up to the entrance with a feather of spray in front of each wheel, and Hazlerigg tumbled out.

Fortunately the porter's army training stood him in good stead.

'Your man's in the flat at the end of the corridor,' he said. 'Up those stairs and at the end of the corridor.'

It wasn't a long sentence; when he started speaking there were eight huge, wet policemen in the entrance hall. By the time he had finished all had gone.

Hazlerigg raced ahead up the stairs. When he came to the door of the flat he paused for a moment to listen, but the drumming of the rain drowned everything. He pivoted on one foot and swung the other foot back and then forward, the sole flat against the door, an inch below the handle.

The door gave and the tide flowed in, across the passageway, and into the front room, like great, grey-blue seals tumbling after a bucket of fish.

The thin man took one look at what was coming and jumped out of the window. It was quite a long drop. The fat man hit one of the policemen once in the face. Roberts, who had played a deal of rugby, took this in very good part. He clasped the fat man round the waist, bore him to the floor and rolled on him.

Dods offered no resistance at all. He seemed relieved when Hazlerigg prised Walkinshaw's forearm away from his windpipe.

Hazlerigg walked to the window. Two of the police car drivers were helping the thin man to his feet. He seemed to have broken an ankle. There was not much more to do.

The postscript was in Hazlerigg's official report to the Assistant Commissioner:

> I commend to your attention the enterprise and persever-
> ance displayed by Probationary Detective Walkinshaw. It
> was only from lack of experience that he did not appreciate
> that hardwood sawdust—particularly when mixed with
> alum crystals—forms the normal fireproof lining of a
> certain type of small safe. Taken in conjunction with the
> dark green paint, this should certainly have suggested that
> the men who stole the car might be—as proved to be the
> case—the persons responsible for the Eton Hill robbery.
> Had he appreciated this point he would not, I feel certain,
> have attempted to tackle them single-handed.

Hazlerigg paused and chewed the end of his pen. Outside the world was fresh and sparkling from its bath. He hated writing reports. What he really wanted to say was that, in the long run, the thing that mattered most in police work was guts, and that he thought the boy had done damned well. He could think of no official phraseology to convey it.

MICHAEL GILBERT

Michael Gilbert was born on 17 July 1912 in Billinghay, Lincolnshire, the son of Anne Cuthbert, a journalist, and Bernard Gilbert, a McGonagallesque poet and author of an unfinished history of rural life in England. Gilbert was educated at St Peter's School in Seaford, Sussex, and at Blundell's School, which he left in 1931. For a short period, he taught at Salisbury Cathedral School and outside work secured an external law degree from London University.

In 1938, Gilbert joined Ellis, Bickersteth, Aglionby & Hazel as an articled clerk. At the same time, and doubtless inspired by his parents, he began writing a novel inspired in part by his time as a teacher. However, career and novel were to be interrupted by the outbreak of the Second World War, during which Gilbert served with the Honourable Artillery Company in North Africa. He was captured in 1943 and held as a prisoner of war in Northern Italy, but when the camp guards fled after Italy's surrender, Gilbert and two other POWs were able to escape.

On his return to England, he completed the final chapters of *Close Quarters* (1947), but only, he would claim in later years, after he had managed to work out which of the many suspects was guilty! In the same year, he married Roberta Marsden, with whom he would have seven children, and he resumed his career as a solicitor, joining Trower, Still & Keeling. He became a partner in

1952 and remained with the firm until his retirement in 1983, having specialized in copyright and company law.

Over the next 50 years, while maintaining a successful career as a solicitor, Gilbert wrote more than 80 novels. In the words of Francis Iles, he was a 'determined experimentalist' and his work includes historical mysteries, detective stories and realistic police procedurals, as well as thrillers dealing with terrorism, apartheid or espionage, such as *Be Shot for Sixpence* (1956) and the tales of *Mr Calder and Mr Behrens* (1982). Gilbert also wrote around 150 short stories as well as stage plays and scripts for radio and television. Like many authors, he drew on his own experiences. His time in the Italian POW camp provided the background for *Death in Captivity* (1952), while the novel that some regard as his masterpiece, *Smallbone Deceased* (1949), is set largely in a solicitors' office.

In interviews, Gilbert regularly recounted how he would write during the 50 minutes it took to travel to London by train from Sole Street station in Kent. Seated always in a less crowded first-class carriage, he aimed to write a minimum of two sides of foolscap on the way in, while keeping the journey home for research. What he also made clear in interviews, but is less often remembered, is that he always planned at home *what* he was going to write about. Typically he made a synopsis of the next two chapters in a legal notebook, which he would then flesh out during the morning commute. Ideas for plots and characters generally came from his work as a solicitor or while walking on the North Downs, but the mayhem of *The Night of the Twelfth* was inspired by the antics of a cherubic choir boy. Gilbert also reviewed books for the *Times Literary Supplement* and the *Sunday Telegraph*, wrote several true crime studies and edited three widely praised anthologies: the *Oxford Book of Legal Anecdotes* (1986); *Prep School* (1991), an anthology of reminiscences of school life; and *Crime in Good Company* (1959) for the Crime Writers' Association.

As well as being a founder member of the CWA, Gilbert was a member of the Detection Club and in 1988 he was named a Grand

Master by the Mystery Writers of America. Perhaps his greatest honour, however, was being made a Commander of the Order of the British Empire by Her Majesty Queen Elizabeth II. He died on 8 February 2006 at his home, the Old Rectory in the village of Luddesdown near Gravesend in Kent.

'Sugar-Plum Killer' was first published as a five-part serial in the *Daily Herald* between 18 and 22 December 1950. The authority on Gilbert's work, John Cooper, has noted that some years later Gilbert reworked the story to include Patrick Petrella; as 'Kendrew's Private War' it was first published in *Argosy* in April 1959 and collected in *Even Murderers Take Holidays and Other Mysteries* (2007).

VACANCY WITH CORPSE

Anthony Boucher

I

Felicity Cain's hair had started out to be red. It had stayed red until halfway through her high school days. This was why she had come to be known as 'Liz'. You can't call a freckle-faced carrot-top Felicity. That suggests lace and dimity and demureness, and there was nothing demure about Liz, not even after her hair turned the brownish blond you've seen in her publicity pictures.

The freckles had vanished when the red hair changed colour, but her eyes still had a greenish glint, and her spirit was still flamboyantly flame-crowned. Yet, here in the quiet, civilized atmosphere of the fashionable cocktail lounge, atop San Francisco's most impressive skyscraper, with the clink of ice and glass to soothe the ear, she was more strikingly lovely than Ben Latimer ever remembered. It was a beauty that fascinated him, left him oddly breathless.

Out of the broad plate glass windows there was a noble view of the bay, bright with the afternoon sun. But he had no eyes for the view—not when Felicity was around. She had her arm in a sling, the result of an aeroplane accident—she was America's most noted aviatrix—but the injury made no difference to Latimer. She still looked good to him.

He grinned as he set down his glass. 'You're like the bay, Liz,' he said. 'Wonderful.'

She smiled back. 'You really mean I'm an institution, like the Barbary Coast, the cable cars—and the Cains! See any guide book.'

Ben Latimer winced. 'No. You're wrong.' He waved his arm. 'See that view. At first glance it's perfect beauty. But look again and you notice a carrier and a couple of destroyers. There's toughness under that beauty.'

'La, sir!' Liz said. 'And likewise fie. Is that any way to speak of the woman you love? Don't you know I'm all sweet femininity? At least as long as this damned arm keeps me grounded.'

Ben laughed. 'It's funny, Liz. When I think about you, it's always with red hair. Even when I look at you I can't get over being surprised.'

'And when I think of you I still see you back on campus in a Letterman's sweater. I just can't get used to the idea that you're now a policeman.'

'Detective-Lieutenant, Liz, please,' he corrected her. 'Can you imagine the society pages of the papers writing up the marriage of a Cain to a mere policeman?'

'I know.' Her green eyes sparkled with glee. 'At our wedding, do we line up your squad, or whatever you call them, and march out of the church under an arch of crossed rubber hoses.'

Ben shook his head. 'No rubber hoses in war time,' he said solemnly. 'In fact, we haven't had a single voluntary confession since the rubber shortage started.'

Liz fished in her glass, and said, 'I like onions better than olives any time.'

'What's the matter?'

'Why? What should be?'

'Whenever you begin making irrelevant remarks like an Odets character, I know you're shying away from something that bothers you. What is it?'

Liz hesitated. 'I don't know how to converse with a policeman.'

'That's never bothered you before.'

'I've never done it before. I mean I've always just talked to

Ben—my Ben!' A smile softened her face, a smile such as you never saw in any of the press photos. 'Now I want to consult with Detective-Lieutenant Latimer.'

Ben Latimer frowned. 'What on earth kind of official business can you have on your mind? Remember I'm on Homicide.'

Liz vigorously nodded her brownish blond head. 'Uh-huh.'

It wasn't a gag. Her face was serious. She kept it averted as she carefully drew geometric patterns with the cocktail's tooth-pick.

'All right,' Ben said. 'I'll try to look official even though I'm in plainclothes. What's the trouble? Anybody I know? No, that doesn't sound official. What, madam, is your complaint?'

'It isn't mine. It's Graffer's.'

'Your grandfather? You mean there's something sinister about his illness?'

'Of course not!' Liz smiled. 'Graffer's illness, God bless him, is just age and heart and things. You don't think Dr Frayne could be fooled, do you? This is something else. It's—it's funny. Ben, if you hated a man and he was going to— to die, wouldn't you just say to yourself, "Goody, goody," and that'd be that?'

'No,' Ben said reflectively. 'That's not the way some minds work. You might say, "Damn it, he can't die all by himself and do me out of the pleasure of killing him." Is that what you mean?'

'Uh-huh. Graffer's been getting notes. Crazy notes. *The Black Angel cannot claim you who belong to us.* Strange things like that.'

Ben frowned. 'It happens to every judge, I guess, if he's been on the bench as long as your grandfather was. Half the time they're from neurotic cranks. Are they signed, these notes?'

'With a rubber stamp of a pointing hand. You know, what printers call a fist. I don't know what it means.'

'The Fist.' Ben nodded. 'It's an imitation Black Hand racket which sprang up in the Italian colony here. And your grandfather did send Almoneri and de Santis to the gallows.'

'But it's so silly,' Liz insisted. 'That was twenty years ago. And now, when maybe he's dying, why should they suddenly write him threatening notes? Perhaps I shouldn't take them seriously. It must be some screwy kind of a gag. But Graffer wanted me to tell you about it.'

Ben shook his head. 'I don't know if it's silly, at that. You remember Vitelli wasn't hanged? He got paroled a few weeks ago. He managed to disappear somehow and he hasn't been reporting either to parole or alien authorities. Does your grandfather want a police guard?'

'Uh-huh. Only quiet-like. You know Mother. You know what a policeman in the house would do to her. Especially at a time like this with my cousin, Sherry, coming and the servants changing all the time. Also, Graffer didn't tell anybody but me. Not even Graffer's secretary, Roger Garvey, knows. So could you arrange it somehow?'

'I'll fix things.' Ben spoke in reassuring tones. 'If it's to be secret, I can't do more than put a couple of men to watch the entrances to the house.' He groped in his pocket. 'Here—give your grandfather this whistle. It may set his mind at ease.'

'Thanks, Ben. It seems so funny, talking to you official-like. You never did mention your work around me. Not even when you were on that suitcase murder and all the papers were full of it. Then, again, maybe I'd better not know too much. Just keep you for my Ben and not think of you that way.'

A bespectacled, studious-looking young man at the next table rose. started out of the room, but detoured to halt beside them.

'Felicity!' The man was Roger Garvey, Graffer's secretary. He grinned. 'Headed home? Oh, hello, Latimer.'

'Hi, Garvey,' Ben grunted.

Liz smiled at the difference between the two men. They were equally tall, equally well-built, but made from different moulds. Ben's suit looked rather sloppy beside the sleek perfection of Roger Garvey's well-tailored grey. Then, again, the detective's broken nose—which had healed remarkably well from a wound inflicted by a three-time murderer—served to emphasize the pleasing profile of her grandfather's handsome secretary. Even Ben's easy casualness seemed rather crude when contrasted with Roger's graceful suavity.

'Roger's right, Ben,' she said. 'I should be headed home. Mother's got so much to do.'

'I'll squire you on the cable car, Felicity,' Roger Garvey suggested. 'Ridiculous nuisance, this having to leave one's car at home. And I've no doubt the street-car will be full of filthy workmen in oil-stained overalls. Oh, well! The Japanese war'll be over soon. Until then, I suppose we have to put up with these things.'

Ben's face turned brick red. He opened his mouth to make an angry retort, but Liz gave him a warning glance so he only said, 'Take good care of her, Garvey.'

'That's something I like to do, Latimer. I'll never forgive you for getting the inside track. I suppose we'll be seeing you at the great family dinner tonight?'

'Sorry. I'm on duty.'

The secretary looked wise. 'Oh, you remember that Sherry's to be there?'

Ben didn't answer for a minute. There was no sound but the clinking of glasses and the babble of voices.

'Yes, I remember,' Ben said at last. 'Tell her I'll try and get around tomorrow.'

'I'm sure that even in her present state she'll be anxious to see you, Latimer. Don't you think so, Felicity?'

Liz said, 'Come on. You can't tempt Ben when he's on duty. The only way we could inveigle him to the house tonight would be to stage a murder for him.'

After they had left, Detective-Lieutenant Ben Latimer sat alone at the table for some minutes. He frowned, and his finger outlined a pointing fist on the damp surface Then his frown deepened and he murmured, 'Sherry!'

He was unreasonably annoyed when the waiter brought him a glass of light brown wine.

II

Mrs Vicky Cain's hair was red, too, and people used to think that Liz had inherited hers from her mother. If so, it would have been a striking example of the transmission of acquired characteristics, and worthy of note in learned journals.

Usually Mrs Cain's face was as skilfully made up as her hennaed hair, and she never looked old enough to have a famous aviatrix for a daughter. But now, as she greeted Liz, her face was hot and dripping, and her charmingly decorative apron had failed to protect her best tea-gown from unidentifiable stains.

As for the house, it was old-fashioned but wonderfully kept up. There were deep-piled rugs, waxed hardwood floors, panelled walls and tapestries, Chippendale cabinets, urns and Oriental vases, and overstuffed furniture, all blending into the colour scheme with excellent taste. At one side of the great front hall was the massive staircase, with its heavy newel-post and bronze figures, leading up to the second floor.

'Mother!' Liz gasped. 'What *have* you been doing?'

Mrs Cain sighed. 'It isn't what I've been doing, it's what other people have been doing. It's all because Mary wanted to bend wires.'

'To bend wires?'

Roger Garvey apparently foresaw trouble. He said, 'Good evening, Mrs Cain,' and vanished upstairs unobtrusively, to his secretarial duties.

'Yes, she took a course at night school, and now she's gone into your Uncle Brian's factory.' Mrs Cain sighed deeply. 'What's the good of my hiring good cooks if your Uncle Brian keeps stealing them away?'

Liz smiled and nodded. 'Oh. The way you spoke it sounded as if she'd gone into an institution to cut out paper dolls. Well, aeroplanes are important to the progress of our country. Remember that.'

'But why did your Uncle Brian need Mary to build aero-planes?' Mrs Vicky Cain persisted. 'She's better off in the kitchen.'

Liz patted her arm. 'Don't worry, Mother. The agency will find us another cook. They always do.'

'But that isn't the worst of it,' went on Mrs Cain, smoothing her stained apron. 'Today your grandfather decided to move into the west bedroom because he says he wants to be facing the sea when he dies. Which isn't very cheerful, you'll admit. As if we didn't have trouble enough being without servants. How the nurse, Miss Kramer, and I ever got him moved there, I'm sure I don't know!'

'When did the cook leave?' Liz asked.

'This morning. I had to go out and do the marketing myself and the butcher was short of meat, and there are so many guests coming, I guess we'll have to eat out of cans. When there was enough food, they wouldn't let us buy it because that was hoarding, and now there isn't any left. And if there was, we couldn't get it anyway. So I don't know where we are. Do you? It's completely beyond me.'

Liz laughed. 'I certainly can't answer that one. Now I'm going upstairs, darling, and change into slacks, and be useful. Mother, haven't you anything but gold lamé to wear in the kitchen?'

Mrs Cain gave a hasty glance downward and a look of surprise spread over her face.

'Certainly, Liz. But I forgot. You know, I'm used to wearing something nice in the afternoon.'

Liz shook her head reproachfully and began to climb the broad staircase. This had been San Francisco's showplace once, she reflected—the Cain Mansion. Now all its grand old neigh-bouring houses, on top of the hill, had been converted into three- or four-flat dwellings, housing families whom the Cains did not know. The one time 'mansion' had become just a funny old building. Her mother's ideas were like that, too—all very well for a life of privilege, but hopeless in these changed times.

Nothing that might happen in the way of new ideas, new modes of living, could ever have demolished her mother's concept of the world and her place in it.

Liz paused in front of the room to which her grandfather had been moved. She was about to knock when Roger Garvey came out.

'Miss Kramer says he's asleep,' the secretary told her.

'All right,' Liz said. 'He needs all the sleep he can get, poor man.' She smiled at Roger. 'Miss Kramer knows her business. I believe she's the most efficient nurse Graffer has had.'

The natty secretary lingered. 'Had you anything important you wanted to say to your grandfather? I might be able to help you.'

Liz shook her head. 'No. I just wanted to find out how he was.'

Garvey betrayed curiosity. 'I thought perhaps you had some message for him?'

'No, nothing. I've got to go change now, Roger.'

But he stood blocking her way in the hall. 'Felicity, won't you listen?' he pleaded. Behind his gold-rimmed glasses his eyes had begun to glow.

'I'm sorry, Roger. Let's not go all over that again.'

'Tell me, Felicity. What do you suppose your detective--lieutenant thinks of your cousin Sherry now?'

'I'm damned if I know,' Liz said truthfully, and pushed her way past him to her room.

Sleek Roger! It was like him to remind her. If she could only forget that she'd caught Ben Latimer on the rebound from Sherry, forget it as completely as she was sure that Ben himself had forgotten it by now. But with Sherry coming here today to see her dying grandfather, Liz's mind was upset, anyway. And Roger's question hadn't helped her.

She changed as rapidly as one can with a bad arm. The doorbell rang as she started downstairs, and she finished the flight at top speed. She was careful to use the banister, however, as she was taking no chances on being grounded for a longer time. Notwithstanding her worry about Sherry and Ben, she still retained all her childhood friendship for her pretty cousin. It would be good to see Sherry again, in spite of the fact that Ben had once cared for her so much.

But it was Uncle Brian Cain who was at the front door. And it was Mrs Cain who let him in. When Liz arrived he was removing his gloves in the front hall, with a puzzled expression upon his face.

'Liz,' he called to his niece as soon as he saw her, 'come here and translate. I am trying to persuade your mother that I never stole anybody's cook in my life.'

At that moment, the doorbell rang again. Liz smiled at her young and distinguished looking uncle and dashed past him to the door. But it was only Dr Frayne, their family physician, complete with the bag and the beard that always reminded Liz of a doctor from some period motion picture.

'Hi, Frayne!' Uncle Brian called out. 'How's the last bearded medico outside of a museum?'

Dr Frayne grunted. 'Sir, I retired happily ten years ago, and settled down to cultivating my roses and my beard,' he said. 'Just because this war called me back into practice, I don't intend to relinquish everything. How's your father?'

Uncle Brian shrugged. 'I haven't seen him yet.'

'Miss Kramer says Graffer's asleep,' Liz added.

'I'll run up and have a look at him,' the doctor said. 'Has the prodigal Sherry returned yet, Vicky?'

Mrs Cain shook her head.

'Curious to see her, after this great transformation.' Dr Frayne winked at Liz. 'Think I'll invite myself to dinner. Thanks.'

Mrs Cain stared after him as he mounted the stairs, leaving his black bag on the table near the newel-post.

'Don't say it, Mother,' Liz cautioned her. 'Don't say anything. One more won't make it any worse. Oh, Uncle Brian, did you see the *News* this evening?'

Uncle Brian Cain was lighting a cigar. 'No. Why?'

'Your new plane got plenty of space on the front page as a result of that last flight to China,' Liz said. 'Isn't that what's known as knocking them into the aisles?'

Cain chuckled. 'Now, Liz, you know I'm not interested in the publicity. The main thing is we're doing a job—a good job, if I do say it myself. Until the cutbacks come, we'll manage to keep up production and turn out the latest quirks in aircraft.'

The doorbell rang again. Liz flung the door open, and threw both arms around her cousin Sherry's neck, without any thought of the bad arm.

It wasn't the twinge of pain that made her draw back. It was the feel of the heavy white wool and the scent of starchy cleanness. But the young woman she had embraced wasn't Sherry. It was a stranger—a nun in a hood, stiff linen and robes, with a rosary at her waist. Sherry was the girl standing beside her.

Liz gasped, drew back, and remained very still while her mother and her uncle uttered loud greetings. It is a strange thing to look at your closest girlhood friend and see her in the convent garb of a novice.

'Sister Ursula, I want you to meet my cousin, Felicity Cain,' Sherry was saying. Her voice was still low and rich and warm. 'This is Sister Ursula who came up with me.'

'Oh, there are two of you!' Mrs Cain exclaimed in surprise. 'I should have known nuns always travel in pairs, but I just can't get used to thinking of you as a nun, Sherry. I fixed up the north room for you. Luckily we have another spare bedroom, so we can manage to take care of you both splendidly.'

The doorbell rang again. Mrs Cain gave a start and turned. 'Now who can that be?'

The latest ringer of the front doorbell was a small, middle-aged man in dingy overalls. He was waiting on the porch, carrying a battered suitcase. He had a grimy, good-natured face and sharp restless little eyes. 'Is this the Cain place?' he asked.

'Yes,' Liz answered.

'Some hills you got here in San Francisco, lady.' He set down his suitcase with a sigh of relief. 'I'm Homer Hatch, from the shipyards. Would you mind showing me to my room?'

III

It was Liz's uncle, Brian Cain, who broke the amazed silence.

'I'm afraid I don't understand, my friend,' he said. 'Does this look like a rooming house?'

'The City Housing Bureau sent me,' the man explained. 'This address is listed there as being open for tenants.'

'The Housing Bureau?'

'Look,' the man said. 'If anything's gone haywire, it ain't me. I've got credentials.' He pulled a sheaf of papers and cards out of his pocket and began thumbing through them. 'See—here's my union card—Homer Hatch. I've been a top-hand welder for years. I work at Marinship. Take a gander at my gate pass and my button. All right, so far?'

'All right.' Uncle Brian nodded. 'So you're Homer Hatch, a shipyard worker. But who sent you to this address?'

'I'm coming to that. Now have a squint at this letter from the Housing Bureau. It says: "Report to home of Mrs Michael Cain."' He held up the letter for them to read. 'You can see for yourselves.'

Liz glanced at her mother. Her married name was Mrs Michael Cain. Liz saw memory dawning in her mother's eyes and with it a trace of guilt.

'Mother!' Liz cried.

Suddenly Mrs Cain was all the gracious hostess. 'I remember!' she cried. 'You're the man I'm taking in for Mrs Vansittart! Do come right on in!'

It was Homer Hatch's turn to look puzzled.

'Lady, I don't know no Mrs Vansittart,' he said. 'But I want a room and a clean bed so bad that I ain't arguing. Not even if

Mrs Vansittart's in it.' He saw the nuns and hastily added, 'Meaning no offence, y'understand, Sisters.'

'Now, let me see!' Mrs Cain began to calculate aloud. 'You're going to remain over until tomorrow, Brian, because this is a family gathering. You can use the small room downstairs near the kitchen just for tonight, and I'll put Mr Hatch in Graffer's old room. There! That's settled.'

'How about grandfather?' Mr Hatch asked. 'Maybe I ought to tell you—I snore some.'

'Oh, so does Graffer. But I meant the room he just left, which is vacant. Now, Brian, will you show Mr Hatch upstairs while Liz and I look after Sherry and Sister Veronica?'

'Ursula,' the nun said quietly. Her face was calm, beautiful, serene.

Hatch reached down and picked up his suitcase. 'Let's go. Lead the way, Mister.' He walked into the house.

'My name is Cain,' said Uncle Brian, closing the door after him. 'Come on, Hatch. We'll see how you like the room.'

'If it's got four walls and a bed, I'll like it,' said Hatch.

Liz watched the two men ascend the big staircase and disappear at the top.

'Now, Mother,' she said.

With Mrs Cain leading, and Liz, Sister Ursula and Sherry following, the four women started upstairs. The two nuns quietly but firmly had insisted on carrying their own bags. All the way up to the second floor, Mrs Cain kept chattering away steadily.

'It was Mrs Vansittart's idea,' Mrs Cain explained. 'At the Tuesday Morning club she told me all about the housing shortage and I foolishly expressed sympathy for the poor ship-yard workers. Then she told me everybody with spare rooms should register with the Housing Bureau and I let her call up and put in my name. That was a month ago. I never dreamed your grandfather would be so ill, and I thought you, Liz, would be off somewhere, ferrying aeroplanes.'

They had reached the second floor now and were moving along the hall. Mrs Cain was trotting ahead, brisk and chipper. From behind, Liz could hear the soft sound of Sherry's laughter. Sherry's laugh had always been low and musical, but now Liz thought she had never heard anything sound so soft and contented.

'You haven't changed a bit, Aunt Vicky,' Sherry called out. 'You don't know how nice it is to hear you all muddled, after the sensible women I have recently met.' Liz glanced back over her shoulder and saw Sherry exchanging a smile with Sister Ursula.

'Sherry, here's a real muddle for you,' said Liz. 'First we'll show you to your rooms. Then, believe it or not, Mother and I are going to get dinner, and not out of cans either. Can you put up with what two amateurs can dredge out of the pantry, Sherry?' Liz had dropped back beside them.

'If a cook is all you need, may I offer to help?' suggested Sister Ursula.

'Can you cook?' Liz faltered, glancing at the long draped sleeves of the nun's habit. It was very strange. She had never thought of a nun standing before a stove.

Sister Ursula laughed. 'Oh, these roll back easily. Housework is our speciality, you know. We are the Sisters of Martha of Bethany. And Martha, you remember, was the one who did all the housework.'

'Then Sherry is going to do housework?' Liz stared at her cousin in surprise. 'I didn't understand. I thought she would turn to other things.'

'Spending a life of cloistered contemplation behind an iron grille?' Sister Ursula was smiling broadly. 'I'm afraid we're not that kind of nuns. Not good enough, perhaps. I doubt if Sherry here could ever measure up to such a life. I'm sure I couldn't.'

'But I thought nuns were devoted to prayer, and acts of charity and mercy.'

'There are nuns and nuns,' Sister Ursula said. 'Brother Gregory used to say, 'There are three things known only to God in his infinite wisdom. One is how much a Dominican knows. Another is what a Jesuit is thinking about. And the third is how many Orders of Sisterhoods there are.' Ours—well, we're the etceteras who do the work. And now about dinner. How many do you expect?'

Later, as Liz set the table—making an awkward job of it with her one arm—she was more puzzled than ever. The other nun—was her name Ursula? She was a surprising person. She was so quiet you didn't know she was there, at first—just a funny habit with a round face looking out. Until she spoke. Then, in a few sentences, she had become a clear and definite person—efficient, administrative, capable, wise, and even humorous. If that was what the Sisters of Martha of Bethany did to you, maybe Sherry's choice made sense after all.

Liz was remembering. It had been ten or twelve years ago—the time she and Sherry had stayed overnight at Mina Drake's house. They had sat up until all hours, sleepless and babbling, plotting their futures and leaving brown smudges of chocolate on Mrs Drake's sheets.

Mina was going to be an actress like Jean Harlow, who had just burst on an astonished public in *Hell's Angels*.

'And when he comes to see her on account of his friend, he starts to fall for her himself,' Mina had said. 'She wore a white evening dress and she looked *simply gorgeous!*'

Liz had liked *Hell's Angels*. In fact, she thought it was the most wonderful picture she had ever seen, but not because of Miss Harlow.

'I know,' she had answered. 'That's the one where the Zeppelin comes out of the clouds over London and he crashes his ship into it. But, Mina, who wants to be like that kind of a woman? What's the fun of letting the man do all the flying?' Her own idol had been Amelia Earhart.

Sherry had been very quiet until they finally asked her, 'And how about you?'

'Oh,' Sherry said simply. 'I'm going to be a nun.'

They'd hooted at that, Mina and Liz. It was so silly. Why, Sherry hadn't even been disappointed in love yet.

Sherry hadn't mentioned her choice of vocation again for years. She'd led a normal life on campus, spent a couple of years employed as a secretary. Then she had disappeared.

Liz had heard it first from Ben. That was when Ben Latimer was Sherry's young man, and Liz had thought men were all very well as mechanics or co-pilots, but otherwise unnecessary.

There'd been a long post-mortem after she'd heard Hinchcliff read his paper on his new direction finder, and she got home late. She had heard voices in the west room and had wandered in. Even before Sherry hastily excused herself and went upstairs, Liz realized she'd interrupted a scene. Liz hadn't known whether to go or remain, so she'd stood there, looking at Latimer.

Ben had taken a long time lighting his pipe.

'I want you to be the first to know, Liz,' he said at last. 'I've been jilted.'

Liz gasped. 'Why, Ben! We've all always believed it was completely settled.'

Ben got up from the chair slowly, standing very tall and straight. He was still in uniform then.

'I've bumped into a powerful rival,' he said. 'A rival too strong to buck. The Church. Sherry's determined to become a nun. There's nothing I can do about it.'

Afterwards, when Liz had gone upstairs to bed, Sherry had told her about it.

'I didn't want to do it blind, Liz,' Sherry had said. 'I wanted to see enough of the world first so I'd be sure. And now I know. There's no mistake about it.'

Now here it was, settled. All the hopes of that chocolate--smeared confab had been carried out. Wilhelmina—now Lorna—Drake was in Hollywood, and one of the most celebrated stars in the country, for reasons which had not been especially apparent twelve years ago. Liz was a grade A aviator—she hated the word 'aviatrix'—and would be flying again as soon as this damned arm healed. And Sherry was a nun—or at least, well on the road to being one.

How about that? How close to being a nun was a novice? How irrevocable was it if you changed your mind? Liz wasn't sure. But she felt absurdly glad that Ben Latimer wouldn't be present for dinner tonight, Liz even hoped something might come up to keep him busy for the next few days.

IV

Dr Frayne tasted the contents of the casserole and his white teeth glistened as he beamed with pleasure above his beard.

'Magnificent!' he proclaimed. 'And you concocted this out of canned remnants, Vicky?'

Mrs Cain shook her head. 'She did it. Sister Helena.'

'Ursula,' the nun said quietly.

Dr Frayne turned his smile down the table and eyed her with an approving gaze.

'As an atheist of long and solid standing, I have always admired monks, if only because they know how to make wine and liqueurs,' Dr Frayne announced. 'But I had no notion that nuns had their fleshly virtues, too. If this is a sample, Sister, you must publish a Convent Cook Book.'

'As a matter of fact, I didn't learn this in a convent,' the nun confessed. 'Oh, we cook, of course—and Sister Immaculata could shame many a *cordon bleu*—but this recipe I learned from the wife of a lieutenant on the Homicide Squad. She is the best cook I have ever known.'

Liz felt a little shudder run up and down her spine. A lieutenant on the Homicide Squad? She hadn't mentioned Ben Latimer since Sherry had arrived. Now she let her eyes meet those of her cousin, and wondered if her own were as unreadable as

Sherry's. She caught sight of a dangerous smile on Roger Garvey's handsome features and saw his full lips part as if to speak.

Hastily she plunged in. 'How on earth do you happen to know such strange people, Sister?'

She didn't hear what Garvey said, though she knew it was some question directed at Sherry and Ben. His speech and hers had overlapped and cancelled each other. There was another awkward silence.

Then Liz's mother took a taste and stared at the untouched plate before Uncle Brian.

'Brian, Dr Frayne's right,' Mrs Cain said. 'It really is wonderful. I'm almost tempted to enter a convent myself. How can you sit there, not touching a morsel of it? You look pale.' Her face grew anxious. 'Are you ill?'

'I'm all right, Vicky.' Brian Cain forced a smile. 'Something must have upset me at lunch. I feel a little squeamish.'

'Overwork,' Dr Frayne diagnosed. 'You won't be much use to the war effort if you wear yourself out, Brian.'

Mrs Cain spoke to everyone. 'There's plenty of seconds for everybody.' Her face brightened. 'Ah—I know!'

'What, Mother?' Liz always feared the worst from her mother's sudden inspirations.

'That poor Mr Thatch! He must be terribly hungry after welding things all day. I'm sure he'd be glad to eat up whatever is left over.'

She bustled out of the room. Sister Ursula smiled approval, but Roger Garvey lifted his carefully brushed eyebrows.

'At least I hope she's able to persuade Hatch to wash his hands,' Roger said. 'Changing his clothes would be too much to hope for.'

Nobody had a chance to answer him. From the second floor they heard Mrs Cain's shrill, terrified scream.

It was an unearthly sound that came quavering through the old house. It caused them to hold their knives and forks suspended and sit for a brief space in stunned surprise.

Dr Frayne recovered first. His professional duties had trained him to rise to emergencies. He jumped out of his chair and darted out of the room. Sister Ursula was not far behind him. Liz and Sherry momentarily got tangled up in the doorway, then went racing for the stairs, with Brian Cain close on their heels. Only Roger Garvey did not move. He shrugged wearily and went on eating.

When Liz reached the bend, Sister Ursula was already well up the steps. But Dr Frayne had halted at the small table at the bottom of the flight and was looking about him in a perplexed manner.

'Where is it?' he was muttering. 'I'm sure I left it here.'

Then he looked under the table, saw his bag, snatched it up, and started to climb the steps, two at time. Liz followed.

There had been only one scream. Now silence reigned on the upper floor. Automatically Liz headed for Graffer's room.

'The poor old man is dead and Mother must have found him,' she was thinking. 'Too bad! But perhaps it's for the best. He's been in pain so long.'

Just as she remembered about Fists and those threatening notes, she saw Graffer's door open and Miss Kramer, starched and efficient, with her cap on, come out into the hall. As the nurse headed towards the east bedroom, Liz glanced into Graffer's room. The old man was sleeping peacefully, with his veined aged hands resting upon the folded sheet.

Liz turned and hastened towards the east bedroom, too. Down the hall she could see Sister Ursula about to enter that room. Liz ran forward past Miss Kramer and stopped in the doorway. Her mother was lying on the floor in a faint, but when Liz's glance went to the bed, she forgot about everything else.

The little shipyard worker, who had been so perkily alive an hour before, was lying upon the bed with his head on the pillow, face upward. He was dead. But it was something more than mere death that halted Liz in the doorway of the room—something that jarred her nerves as they had never been jarred before. It was the expression upon the face of the corpse. The features were screwed up into a grin which was indescribably appalling.

Grins are supposed to depict mirth but this grimace was anything but humorous. It expressed pain—nothing else. Homer Hatch had died in agony and that last contortion of his features remained frozen there.

The effect was heightened by the stringy, greasy hair that hung down over his high forehead and the gleam of his yellow, bared teeth.

It was Dr Frayne's dry voice, behind Liz, as he spoke to the nurse, which broke the spell of her horror.

'Miss Kramer, you stay here and assist me,' said the doctor, as he pushed Liz to one side, and moved forward into the room. He glanced at Sister Ursula who had stopped at the foot of the bed. 'Everybody else must clear out. Brian, carry Vicky to her room. Liz, you go with him, undress her and put her to bed. No—of course you can't do that with your lame arm. Sister, will you help?'

The nun nodded and Liz, recovering from her shock, turned. They were all there now, Uncle Brian, Sherry, Miss Kramer— everybody except Roger Garvey.

Brian Cain picked up Mrs Cain and went out, followed by Liz, Sherry and Sister Ursula. Miss Kramer remained with Dr Frayne who stood at the door and closed it after them. They followed Brian as he carried his sister-in-law down the hallway.

Sherry had lingered in the doorway. Her face was as white as her wimple.

'Is—is Hatch dead?' she asked Liz.

'Yes.'

'I never saw death like that before,' Sherry said in shaky tones. 'I know I'll have to. We do so much nursing work. But it's awful, just the same.'

Her voice dropped. For the first time since her mother's scream Liz had the chance to ask herself how, what, why? Why had Hatch died almost on the instant he entered their home?

She had plenty of time to think, too, for when they arrived at Vicky's room and Uncle Brian had laid her down on a couch, Sister Ursula took charge and shooed them all out, just as Dr Frayne had done.

Brian Cain went downstairs again, perhaps to finish his interrupted dinner. Liz and Sherry remained in the hallway, too excited to care about food. The two girls didn't say much to each other. They just stood there, thinking about what had happened.

After about fifteen minutes had passed, the doorway of the east bedroom opened and Miss Kramer came out. She motioned to them and they hurried forward.

'I'm going to see how Mrs Cain is getting along,' said the nurse. 'Dr Frayne told me to. You better go in and see if you can help him. He may need someone.'

Then with a nod at Liz, she went up the hall to Mrs Cain's room.

Liz could feel Sherry steeling herself, tightening her nerves against the death-chamber. She took the novice's hand in her good one and squeezed it reassuringly.

'Come on,' she whispered.

The body had been clothed at Liz's first glimpse of it. Now the clothing lay on the floor, and when Dr Frayne caught sight of the two girls, he hastily pulled a sheet over the corpse.

'Have to report this to the coroner's office right away,' he told them. 'Although I couldn't very well give a certificate, I was curious to see for myself.'

'Why did he die?' Liz asked. She tried to forget about that grin. The doctor frowned and tugged at his beard. 'Damned if I know why, but I'm getting an idea of how. Thought at first it was tetanus. Typical enough spasm. But if that was it, we'd have noticed he was sick when he came.'

'He looked fine then,' Liz said. 'Just a little tired.'

'Sure. That's why I checked over the body. Tetanus could have resulted from an industrial accident, but with modern precautions, it's unlikely. Also, there's no abrasion or wound on the body.'

'Then what killed him?'

Dr Frayne pulled down the sheet. The distorted grin seemed to have no effect upon his hardened nerves.

'Look at those eyebrows,' the physician said. 'Look at the mouth. Indisputable signs. Has to be either tetanus or strychnine. Since it wasn't tetanus, it must have been strychnine.'

Liz shuddered. She heard a small groan from Sherry. 'You mean he killed himself?'

'That's what the poor devil wanted the room for. Suicide in privacy. That's why he needed a room so badly. He did it quick, too.'

'But if it's suicide, shouldn't there be a glass or something?' Liz asked.

'Why?' Dr Frayne retorted. 'Pills in your pocket—gulp 'em down.' He was still oblivious of the womens' reaction to the casual vividness of his picture and the twisted features of the dead man.

There was a sound from the doorway and Liz glanced around to see Sister Ursula standing there. How long she had been in the doorway Liz didn't know.

'May I come in?' the nun asked. 'Mrs Cain is in bed. She seems to have passed into a normal sleep. And this poor man, God rest his soul! I wonder where he got the strychnine.'

Dr Frayne raised his eyebrows. He could not conceal his astonishment. 'You go in for diagnosis, too, Sister? Or did you hear what I said?'

'No, I didn't hear.' The nun gestured at the contorted dead face. 'It is easy to surmise the cause of death must have been strychnine.'

The doctor grunted. 'Also, it might have been tetanus. Trust an amateur to jump to the sensational.'

'Remember, Doctor, I saw him only an hour ago. He was well then.' She moved quietly to the bed. 'He'd been drinking, hadn't he?'

Dr Frayne nodded. 'Common prelude. Nerve yourself up to it.'

'But when he came here, I stood close to him and smelled no liquor. Have you sent for the police?'

'Police?' Sherry gasped.

'They check up on suicides,' Dr Frayne said. 'Liz, will you please put in the call?'

V

Liz left the room. As she walked out she heard the nun's quiet voice.

'Dr Frayne, why are you so sure it was suicide?'

Liz dialled OPERATOR and said, 'I want a policeman.' She gave the address and hung up. When she turned, Roger Garvey was standing behind her.

He glanced at her unsteady hand and wordlessly offered her a cigarette. After he had lighted it, he puffed on his own.

'I know to my sorrow, my dear Felicity, that you yearn for a specific policeman,' he drawled. 'But what drives you to this step? What has been happening?'

'You don't know?'

'When a woman screams, and a doctor, a nurse and a nun are all available, it strikes me that I'd be more of a hindrance than a help. I decided to finish dinner. But what happened?'

'That little defence worker, Mr Hatch, just killed himself in the room Mother let him have.'

Garvey blew out a smoke ring. 'And you still find death moving? Even in this year of death? But why the police?'

'Dr Frayne says suicides must be reported.'

'Of course. I should have remembered. But why just "a policeman"? Why not give the family business to a family friend?'

'Please, Roger. Don't heckle me. I've got to get back.'

Roger Garvey halted her by placing his hand on her shoulder. 'Felicity, you still misunderstand me. I don't mean to heckle.

I only want you to see yourself clearly. Don't you know why you didn't call Ben?'

Liz's eyebrows went up.

'Why should I? It isn't his sort of job. He wouldn't want to be bothered.'

'Of course, you can rationalize it.' Roger sounded impatient. 'But can't you see why you subconsciously shrank from calling Ben? Because you don't want him to come here, not while Sherry is in the house. It's because you still aren't sure of him.'

'Let me go, Roger.'

'Felicity.' His voice was low and urgent. 'You could be sure of me. You should know that.'

'Let me go!'

She jerked away and ran upstairs. She could almost feel Garvey's eyes following her, although he had let her go.

At the head of the stairs she met Miss Kramer.

'Oh, Miss Cain,' the nurse said, 'would you please go in to your grandfather? He's awake now and he's demanding to see you and Miss—Sister—his other granddaughter,' she concluded, uncertain of the correct designation for a novice.

'Right away.' Liz again went into the room where Hatch had died. 'I put in that call, Doctor,' she told Frayne. 'A prowl car should be here any minute.'

'Thank you, Liz.' The doctor turned to the nun. 'And please, Sister Ursula! Leave it up to them when they arrive. After all, it's their business.'

'I hope they know their business,' the nun said.

Liz turned away and hurried up the hall to see her grandfather.

Graffer had always been old, as Liz remembered him. He had always had that white hair, that heavily lined face. But there had been strength and vigour under the semblance of age; now he was just an old man, weak and helpless and very much alone.

He sat propped up with pillows and a bedrest. He smiled as Liz came in. The smile lit up his grey, wrinkled face.

'Did you see your young man today?' he asked. His voice was gentle, but probing.

She understood what he meant. 'He said he'd see to it, Graffer. He promised to have men posted around the house. You can rely on him. He'll take care of it.'

'Good. I feel like an old fool, calling for help from the police.' His withered face took on a cunning expression. 'But Vitelli always meant what he said. Can't take chances with you and your mother here in the house. What's been happening?' he demanded with considerable abruptness.

Liz tried to stall off his question. 'I haven't heard the news yet this evening,' she said. 'What makes you ask that?'

'People tramping up and down halls, in and out of rooms. What's been going on? Or has that fool of a doctor decided it's not good for my heart to let me know? Come on. Tell me.'

Liz tried to smile. 'You're imagining things, Graffer. Of course, it takes a lot of shuffling around, getting people settled in guest rooms, when we're having a family reunion.'

He gave Liz a sceptical stare, then shrugged his shoulders.

She was glad that Sherry came in just then. Graffer took one look at this other granddaughter and shut his eyes in a wry grimace.

'Mary Sheridan Cain!' he barked. 'What are you doing in that masquerade costume?'

Sherry stiffened. 'It's my uniform,' she said.

Graffer snorted. 'Hmf! I warned your father what would come of your mother's religion. But I never expected to see a granddaughter of mine dressed that way.'

'If we're going to start this again, I think I'd better go,' Sherry answered quietly.

Graffer opened his eyes and laughed. 'You're a good girl, Sherry,' he said. 'You know what you want and you've got the courage to stick to it. You're kind enough to come to see your old grandfather because the idiot doctors say he's dying. But you're strong enough to hold on to what you believe, and no pampering of an old man who might cut you out of his will. You're all right, Sherry. And I like your uniform.'

Sherry stood still for an instant of amazement. Then she moved swiftly and gracefully to the side of the bed, leaned over, and kissed the old man.

'I'm glad,' she said simply. 'I've prayed that we could love and understand each other again.'

They were silent for a moment. Liz smiled and felt good—the kind of feeling that leaves your eyes not quite dry.

'Intolerance is a bane of good times,' Graffer said slowly. 'I've been pig-headed in my day. I've been proud of it, and declaimed that tolerance is the limp virtue of the feeble-minded. But I was a fool. Emotions run high. Hatred runs high. What might have been mere irritable prejudice ten years ago now can turn to vicious hate. We've got to watch ourselves. We've got to understand—and to love.'

He paused and then barked out a loud laugh. 'How the boys down at the Hall of Justice would enjoy this! Old Tim Cain turns soft! But Sherry understands.'

'Yes, Graffer.'

There were noises in the hall—the clumping of heavy feet.

'Sherry, now that we're friends again, maybe you'll tell me what the hell goes on out there?'

'What do you mean, Graffer?'

'Why are the bulls here?'

'Bulls?'

'Or do you forget such words in the convent? The harness bulls, the cops. After ten years in the district attorney's office and twenty on the bench, do you think I don't know a policeman's footsteps when I hear them?'

He was leaning forward from his pillows, his old blue eyes aglint.

'I'll go see, Graffer,' Liz said. 'You stay here, Sherry.'

Miss Kramer was in the hall. 'I thought he wanted to see you alone,' the nurse said to Liz. 'That's why I didn't interrupt you.'

Liz nodded. 'Thanks. But please go in now and see if you can calm him down. He knows something's going on and he wants to hear all about it.'

The nurse went into Graffer's room, while Liz followed the sound of loud bass voices to the room that had been Homer Hatch's.

Dr Frayne was there, and Sister Ursula, and two men in uniform. They paid no attention to Liz. The short and wiry policeman was talking to the doctor.

'And nobody around this place ever seen this Joe before today?' he asked.

'No one,' Dr Frayne said. 'It was pure chance that the Housing Bureau should have sent him here.'

The officer turned to the nun. 'And you still insist this ain't no suicide?'

'I do,' said Sister Ursula firmly.

'Look, Sister. Accordin' to you, inside an hour after he gets a room here, he makes a total stranger mad enough to kill him. The mysterious stranger has strychnine somewheres, and this dope obligingly ups and drinks it. Now I ask you does that make sense?'

'Patience is one of the seven cardinal virtues,' Sister Ursula answered with a sigh. 'In this instance, I fear time will show I am correct.'

'Huh?'

'I was simply reminding myself. Let me tell you again, officer, when I saw the man this afternoon there was no liquor on his breath. When I saw him dead there was a pronounced smell of whisky. Dr Frayne will corroborate me.'

'So what? He took one to give himself some Dutch courage.'

'And what did he drink it out of? There is no glass here.'

'Look, Sister. Not everybody's so polite they got to drink out of a glass.'

'Then where is the flask or bottle or whatever he had?'

'Maybe he got really good and mellow and heaved it out the window.'

'Better search for it before you dismiss this as suicide. If you don't find it, admit that someone must have been drinking with him, and that someone carried away the flask or glasses. No one in this house confesses to having visited Hatch.'

The policeman was heavily patient. 'Sister, you been reading stuff they hadn't ought to let get into convents. This poor sap comes here to bump himself off in peace and quiet. So let him. Leave him alone. Chuck, you go phone the coroner's office and let 'em cart him to the morgue.'

The doorbell rang just as Sister Ursula started to speak. Liz thought hastily of where the others were, and concluded answering doorbells was her job. She turned towards the hall.

'I should warn you that, with the family's permission, I intend to report this death to the proper authorities,' she heard Sister Ursula say as she left the room.

VI

Descending the stairs, Liz reached the front door and opened it. The man there promptly kissed her.

'Good evening, darling,' said Detective-Lieutenant Ben Latimer.

'Oh, Ben! My! I *am* glad to see you!'

Ben looked at her upturned face, smiled, and kissed her again. Then he released her reluctantly.

'Fun's fun, but what's been going on here?' he asked.

'I don't know. It's all so confused. But maybe you can help me. Mother went and told the Housing Bureau that we could rent a room to a defence worker. Then she forgot all about it and today, in the midst of everything, he showed up, and now he's dead and—my, it's even got me talking like Mother.'

'Dead? Uh—naturally?'

'We don't know. Sister Ursula was talking about notifying Homicide, but now you're here, there's no necessity for that.' She stopped short.

'What's the matter?'

'You're here.'

'Yes?'

'But why? It's marvellous and just when we need you; but how could you know?'

'Ben grinned. 'Fine chance for an act, isn't it? I could spin you a nice convincing story about a detective's intuition. But no mirrors are needed, darling. It's all perfectly straightforward. My men, who were watching the house, saw the patrol car drive up and thought I ought to be told about it.'

'Your men, of course! I almost forgot them. Did they see any strangers around?' Liz had a crawling premonition of what their presence might disclose. 'But come on upstairs. Now that you're here I feel as if everything's going to turn out all right.'

The two men in uniform were leaving Hatch's room. The short policeman recognized Latimer and stopped.

'Nothing for you, sir,' he said. 'Suicide, even if that good Sister in there does insist—'

Ben interrupted him. 'Come on back inside with me while I take a look.'

Liz tried to keep her eyes from the bed as she made introductions. 'Sister Ursula, this is Lieutenant Latimer. Dr Frayne, you know Ben?'

The doctor nodded. 'Of course. Glad you came, my boy. We need the professional mind.'

'Sister Ursula?' Ben repeated musingly. 'Sister, do you know Terence Marshall, on the Los Angeles force?'

'Very well. In fact, I'm his daughter's godmother.'

Ben turned to the men in uniform. 'I think you might pay some attention to what she says. I met Marshall while I was down south on the Rothmann matter. He told me that the two toughest cases in his entire career had been broken by his friend, Sister Ursula.'

The short policeman's eyes boggled.

'Sister Ursula—Jeez!' he said. 'So it's *her*! Yeah, I know.'

'Please, Lieutenant,' said Sister Ursula. 'I've simply taken an interest in Lieutenant Marshall's cases because my father, God rest his soul, was a chief of police back in Iowa. There was a time when I almost became a policewoman myself and naturally I was interested. It also made it impossible for me to remain silent when I knew there was something very wrong.'

'Of course,' Ben said. 'Now will somebody give me a clear idea of just what happened?'

He listened to Dr Frayne's terse, clear account, occasionally nodding or frowning. At the end he said:

'To sum up—pending the findings of an autopsy, we can assume that this man died of strychnine poisoning. Natural or accidental death is therefore out. Suicide and murder remain, but are equally unlikely. Until we investigate his past, we can't speak of motives, but renting a room through the Housing Bureau for the purpose of having a place to gulp down strychnine doesn't seem plausible. Yet as to murder—he's a stranger to everybody here, and his coming was purest chance, unless some enemy had trailed him to this house.

'But he's dead. So murder or suicide it must be. And the one piece of evidence pointing either way is the fact that he had a drink of whisky from a vanished container.'

'That's what I told you, Lieutenant,' the shorter man in uniform persisted. 'There ain't a thing to show it was murder.'

'But there isn't a thing to let you write it off so easily as suicide, either,' Ben answered. 'Further investigation is indicated. I want a look. Would you like to leave Sister, or Liz?'

Liz couldn't move. She stood rooted—fascinated—while Ben Latimer walked over to the bed. He pulled down the sheet, and her throat went dry as she saw Hatch's sardonic smile again, those stringy locks of hair, those yellow teeth. Ben stooped over the bed, then abruptly straightened up, with something in his hand.

'I don't think there's much doubt of murder, now,' he said slowly. 'This is a case for the Homicide Department, all right. Doctor, you examined the body?'

'Yes. When I thought it might be tetanus—looking for a wound—focus of infection.'

'And did you notice this?' Ben held up what he had found so all could see it. It was a small rumpled oblong sheet of white paper.

'There was a scrap of paper like that on the bed, yes,' Frayne said. 'The body was partly rolled over on it. Didn't notice what it was. Thought it was a farewell note.'

Ben turned the paper so Liz and Sister Ursula could observe it. It bore nothing but the outline of a clenched list, with the index finger extended.

Liz looked up at Ben Latimer. For years he had been a friend, and for almost a year he had been the man she loved and was going to marry. Now he was a detective, working on a case. His lips, his eyes, the set of his jaw—everything about him was new and unfamiliar to her.

This strange Lieutenant Latimer turned to the short policeman. 'You'll relieve him until I can get more men out here. You,' he added to the other officer, 'round up all the people in this house and take them to the drawing-room, downstairs.'

'But Ben,' Liz protested. 'You can't go sending a man around into all these rooms. Graffer's sick, and the shock might be fatal. And I don't know if Mother's come to yet. She found the body.'

'Very well. I'll give you that job, Liz. Round everybody up.'

'Miss Kramer will have to stay with her patient, Judge Cain,' Dr Frayne broke in authoritatively. 'I will not permit him to be left alone.'

'All right.' Ben gave his assent impatiently. 'Officer, I'll leave you here with the body until the boys come. Dr Frayne, Sister—

you will please go down to the drawing-room and wait for me.'

He left the room. Liz followed him. She felt helpless, caught up in something vast and stern and machine-like. An hour earlier domestic life had been chaotic, but at least it had been familiar. Now a stranger had died, and everything was changed. The police were in charge and they were giving orders, and she had her job to do. Round them up, he had said, as though her people were so many cattle.

But it would keep her occupied. It would be something which might efface the haunting memory of Hatch's bared teeth and grotesque smile.

Liz received two surprises during the roundup. The first came when she found Uncle Brian visiting in Roger Garvey's room. This was totally unexpected and a complete reversal of Uncle Brian's ideas of social propriety. He had never bothered to conceal his dislike and distrust of Graffer's secretary. The antagonism between the two men was evident even now, when Liz opened the door to their call and delivered her message.

They had been talking—Liz could see that. Brian Cain had been chewing on a cigar and glowering, while Roger Garvey was looking pale and distraught. It was the first time Liz had ever seen the secretary when he didn't seem sure of himself.

'In the drawing-room?' Uncle Brian said, rising to his feet. 'Sure. I'll come with you, right now.'

'I'll be along in a minute or so,' said Roger.

It was Uncle Brian who closed the door. As he walked down the hallway with Liz, he muttered aloud:

'I can't see how Father tolerates that young upstart. His ideas are all twisted.'

'I don't think he talks much about them to Graffer.'

'The nerve of him—asking me for a job! Why is he so anxious to get out of this house all of a sudden? I don't understand it.'

The second surprise Liz was to remember came when she stopped to tell Miss Kramer to remain with Graffer until relieved. Sherry was also in the room, so Liz took her down the hall to sit for a while with Mrs Cain.

'You'll watch after Mother, won't you, Sherry?' Liz said. 'Later, when she wakes up, you can bring her downstairs to the drawing-room, if you feel she's up to it. Ben Latimer wants to question her.'

Sherry nodded. Then she said slowly, 'So Ben is here.'

Liz said, 'Yes.'

'You said "Ben Latimer wants" as though it were—oh, just anybody.'

'That's the way he is now. He's different, all of a sudden.'

'But he's there. Ah!'

Sherry turned away, crossed the room to the window, and stood looking out with her back to Liz.

VII

Slowly Liz walked downstairs to the drawing-room. There she found Dr Frayne, Sister Ursula, Roger Garvey and Uncle Brian gathered in a group, waiting for Ben Latimer. They did not talk much. They were silent and nervous. And all the time the golden hands of the marble clock, on the huge old-fashioned mantle, kept ticking noisily along, just as if nothing at all were happening.

'But why here?' Liz thought, and was amazed to discover she had spoken aloud.

Dr Frayne jumped. 'What do you mean, Liz?'

'I mean, whoever killed Hatch. Why should he follow Hatch here?'

'Nobody killed Hatch.' It was Uncle Brian who spoke. He was still sceptical.

'But if someone did, why did he choose this house? It's strange, with Graffer so sick and Sherry arriving on a visit.'

Sister Ursula said, 'There was a reason.' It was hard to tell whether it was a theoretical remark or deduction.

Ben came in then. Or rather Detective-Lieutenant Latimer came in.

'I've talked to Sergeant Verdi,' he said. 'There isn't much else I can do until the squad gets here, except talk to you. Perhaps I may be able to turn up something that will give the squad a lead. That room used to be Judge Cain's, didn't it?'

'Until this morning,' Liz said.

'So that anything we find there, from prints to the traditional gold cufflinks, might reasonably belong there. They are either his or those of visitors who called on your grandfather?'

'Lieutenant!' said Brian Cain, suddenly.

'Yes, Mr Cain?'

Uncle Brian had a sudden light in his eyes. 'If that poor devil Hatch was in my father's room, perhaps somebody made a mistake—a perfectly natural one, under the circumstances. The Judge changed his room only today.'

Liz uttered a gasp. 'I see what you mean.' She looked at Ben Latimer. 'It was the Fist, Ben. Remember those threatening notes? It fits. They thought Hatch was Graffer.'

'Ingenious,' Ben said dryly. 'And it might make good sense if Hatch had been, say, shot through the window. But a murderer who could get close enough to Homer Hatch to poison him and still be unable to distinguish him from your grandfather must be a curious individual. I'd like to meet him.'

'How did the poison get into the room?' Uncle Brian asked.

His question aroused a doubt in Liz's mind also. It was odd about the poison. How *had* it gotten into the room? The more she thought of it, the more puzzled she became.

'That's right,' she said. 'It is mysterious. How was the poison put into Hatch's room? Was it by some strange method? You read about poison wallpaper, pillows and things like that. Could it have been something similar?'

Dr Frayne emitted a snort of disgust.

'No.' Ben shook his head at Liz. 'Strychnine gas doesn't explain it either. Hatch was poisoned in the normal manner. Somebody gave him poisoned whisky. Which means, in all likelihood, that he knew and trusted his murderer and would accept a drink from him. You still maintain that none of you knew him?'

The silence was sufficient answer.

'And no one recognized him after Mr Cain showed him to his room?'

Again there was silence. Liz happened to be watching Roger Garvey. She wondered what that quick puzzled contraction of his features meant, and whether Ben also had noticed it.

Dr Frayne said, 'Then you're sure that it's murder?'

'Not sure, no. But sure that it deserves investigation. If my man can't find a whisky bottle within throwing range of that window, I'll be morally certain he didn't kill himself. Then again there's the Fist. That we should find that symbol of death and revenge beside a suicide is asking too much of coincidence.'

'Are you suggesting there were two victims in the same house?' Liz exclaimed in shocked tones. 'I mean two persons condemned to death by the Fist?'

Uncle Brian started. 'What on earth are you driving at, Liz? Two? Has someone else here had trouble with the Fists?' He seemed to understand abruptly. 'Oh!'

Ben nodded. 'Today your father sent word to me by Liz that he'd been threatened. He asked me to put a guard on the house. And that brings me to the most important point in this case.'

He paused. At that moment the door slid back and Sherry appeared, helping Mrs Cain into the room.

They stood near the doorway for an instant. There was a lamp on a low table beside Sherry, throwing its light upwards at an oblique angle, giving that oval face a quality at once both ethereal and human. Yes, Sherry was beautiful.

Ben turned and faced her. For a terrible moment Liz held her breath. They'd met again now, under strange and frightening circumstances. What would Ben do? What would he say?

Lieutenant Latimer spoke curtly. 'Good. Now we're all here. Sit down, please.'

Uncle Brian hardly waited for his sister-in-law to settle herself. 'Well, Lieutenant? What is this important point you mentioned?'

'I complied with your father's request for protection,' Ben said slowly. 'I sent two good men out here. They're experts, both of them, and this house is simple to watch from a spotter's viewpoint. The two of them have had it constantly covered.'

'Yes?'

'They got here shortly before Hatch arrived. Verdi saw him go up the steps and was preparing to intervene when Mrs Cain apparently welcomed him. They've been on guard ever since. No one has entered or left this house.'

The clock ticked very loudly while the group assimilated that explanation. It was Dr Frayne who summed it up.

'That shows that the murderer got here before Hatch and was here waiting for him?'

'Yes,' Ben said.

'And he's still here?'

'He's still here,' Ben replied.

Uncle Brian was on his feet. 'Then we've got to search this house from top to bottom. We've got him trapped. If he tries to sneak out, your men will get him. He hasn't got a chance.'

'We'll postpone the searching party till my squad gets here,' Ben said.

His voice, however, told how slight was his hope of their finding anything.

'I'll take the women first,' Ben continued. 'After that they can go to bed and get some rest. Mrs Cain, will you come to the library with me? Sergeant Verdi can remain with the rest of you.'

He paused in the doorway and added, 'Maybe you'd better come with us, Liz.'

Liz smiled to herself. She understood the suggestion; anyone interviewing her mother would need an interpreter.

But there was nothing to interpret. Out of all the blithe chaos of her mother's remarks, out of all the dissertations on domestic problems and all the questions from Mrs Vansittart on the Housing Situation, there emerged not a single fact beyond what was already known. Mrs Vansittart had been responsible for Hatch's arrival. Apparently it was purest chance that he, rather than any other stranger, should have been sent by the Housing Bureau.

'So you see, Ben, it was all just fate,' Mrs Cain concluded. 'Why don't you go home, take a hot bath and get a good night's sleep? Because you can't arrest fate, can you?'

Ben nodded to himself as Mrs Cain left. 'The damnedest thing is that in a way she's right. Call it fate, call it circumstance, call it the pure cussedness of things, but too many times a detective discovers a criminal is almost guiltless of his own crime. Since you can't arrest the true causes, you nab some poor dope because there has to be an arrest. Now tell me what you know, Liz.'

Liz found that she was hardly more helpful than her mother. A stranger had come to the house and died there. That was all she knew.

When she had finished her futile contribution, she studied the face of the detective-lieutenant.

'Ben,' she said.

'Yes?'

'Will you tell me what you think about this?'

Ben hesitated. 'If it wasn't for that Fist, I might ignore even Sister Ursula's point about the bottle,' he admitted. 'The whole situation is unique—such an unlikely set-up for murder. But I can't disregard the Fist. And I can't get what we know to make sense either. Poisoning Hatch by mistake for your grandfather is impossible, but the Fist angle positively connects Hatch's death with these threats. I've got to plough through this until I turn up the explanation.'

There was a knock at the door, and Sergeant Verdi came in. He was tall for an Italian, and his body was built along generous lines. Now, obviously, he found it awkward to maintain a professional attitude in front of Liz whom he had met a dozen times before as the Loot's girl friend.

'The squad's here,' he said. 'You want to talk to 'em before they start in?'

Ben rose. 'I guess that's all we're apt to get out of you, Liz. Go catch yourself some sleep while the search goes on.'

'What about Graffer?' she said. 'Hadn't I better look in his room myself? If the squad goes bursting in there, he might get excited.'

'Right. I'll send a man with you to stay outside within easy earshot. And here. You might need this.' He handed her his service automatic.

VIII

The men from Homicide were waiting in the front hall. Ben gave them their instructions briefly. They were to search every inch of hiding place in the house. But before they could set off, Sister Ursula entered the hall from the drawing-room.

'Lieutenant!' she called out sharply.

Sergeant Verdi had followed her in. His sheepish face and his clumsily gesticulating hands seemed to say, 'I know I should've stopped her, but you can't lay hands on a nun, can you?'

Ben grinned at him. 'All right, Sergeant,' he said. 'What is it, Sister?'

'Are you sending your search party into old Mr Cain's room?'

'No. Miss Cain thought of that; she's taking that room herself.'

The nun sighed with relief. 'Thank God! And thank you, Felicity.'

'Hooker, you go with Miss Cain, and do whatever she says,' Ben said. 'And since you're here, Sister, I'll take you next.'

The lanky, gangling Hooker talked cheerfully as he and Liz went upstairs.

'Want some gum, Miss? Always helps me concentrate when

I'm working and I ain't supposed to smoke. Used to buy gum by the carton, I did, until we got into this here shortage. Got this pack from a soldier. Give him a lift across the bridge and he says to me, "Guess a pack of gum is the least we can do to help the morale on the home front!"'

Liz hardly heard him. The automatic she was still holding seemed to weigh tons. It felt awkward and strange in her left hand. Because of her interest in aviation, she understood engines, and her hands had developed a knack with machines. but firearms were something else again. If she had to use this weapon, she wondered what she would do.

Also, her mind fretted over Sister Ursula's sudden appearance in the hall. Of course, it was important that Graffer shouldn't be disturbed or shocked. But the nun had seemed to lay more importance on it than simply that. There had been worried tension on her usually smooth face. The nun had thought of something. It was not obvious. It was some new and perilous reason why the police must not penetrate the bedchamber.

She reached Graffer's room. Here there was peace. Outside the door Hooker took his post, a living symbol of the new strangeness that had invaded the house. Across the hall was the room where Homer Hatch still lay grinning. But here there was only an old man calmly asleep and a nurse seated under a shaded reading lamp. Miss Kramer looked up and said, 'Sh!' to Liz.

Yet this peaceful room was somehow the focus of all that new strangeness. For the threat of the Fists had been directed at this room, and the sign of the Fists had tied into Hatch's death. With her body Liz shielded the automatic from Miss Kramer's eyes, but she held a firm and ready grip on it.

Searching the room was simple. There were only a couple of places to look—the closet and the window recess. Both were empty. The nurse watched Liz curiously, but her sleeping patient kept her from asking questions.

The bed was a low one. There could be no hiding place underneath. This room was safe.

Liz returned to the hall, thanked Hooker, and went downstairs again. Catch some sleep, Ben had said. But who could sleep while murder stalked near at hand?

Liz saw Sister Ursula come out of the library, and hurried towards her. She had questions to ask.

'Sister, why were you so worried about having the squad search Graffer's room?'

'How are you fixed here for cocoa?' the nun replied.

'Why? I think we have some.'

'One never knows, nowadays, if anyone has anything. Would you like to join me in the kitchen for a hot cup? We can talk better there,' she added.

'Thanks. I think I'd better give this gun back to Ben first. See you in a minute.' She knocked on the library door and went in.

She made a left-handed mock salute and said, 'Special Agent Cain reporting, sir. No one in Graffer's bedroom. And here is the sidearm issued to me.'

Ben took it and held it tentatively in his hands. 'You wouldn't like to keep it?'

'Why?'

'You're the most sensible and capable person I know here.'

Liz could not conceal her astonishment. 'But why should I need it?'

'If the squad flushes this murderer, there could be trouble,' Ben said. 'He mightn't like being arrested. And if they don't flush him, you might feel better if you have it.'

He hadn't said what he really meant. He didn't need to. 'If they don't flush him, then you're living with a murderer,' was his implication.

Liz shook her head. 'Thanks. I'll make out.'

'As you please.' He looked down at three almost blank sheets of paper before him. 'I'll take Sherry next, and doubtless will continue to learn precisely nothing. Will you please send her in?'

Out in the kitchen with Sister Ursula, the cocoa was hot and rich and soothing.

'You're wise, Sister,' Liz said. 'You know what people need.'

'I'm afraid I know very little,' said Sister Ursula. 'But I must confess, to avoid the appearance of false modesty, that my guesses have a very high average of success.'

'Sister,' Liz began, then stopped in embarrassment.

'Yes?'

'What is a novice?'

The nun looked surprised. 'I thought you were going to ask me about the murder.'

'Later. But what is a novice?'

'Why, I suppose you might say a novice is an apprentice nun, an undergraduate of the Order.'

'Just—just in training for it? Not really one yet?' Liz felt her face flush. Also, to her mortification, she had stumbled over the words.

'Not really, no.' Sister Ursula's eyes had begun to twinkle. She was shrewd, clever. How much had she guessed? How much did she know? How well did she understand?

'And if she changes her mind?' Liz went on.

'Then she does as her changed mind indicates.'

'But I thought novices had to go through with it.'

Sister Ursula smiled. 'I'm not surprised. You've heard stories of the unwilling novices and bitter frustrated lives, to say nothing of the juicier tales of immurings. But girls who become nuns against their will are forced into it by their parents or by circumstances, certainly not by the Order. It wouldn't make sense. The Army exempts conscientious objectors and neurotics and others, not so much out of kindness, but simply because they'd make very bad soldiers. We feel the same way. A woman who became a nun against her will would be useless to the Order.'

'Then Sherry can still change her mind!' Liz took a deep breath and sipped more cocoa. 'Now, please tell me about Graffer.'

'There isn't anything to tell. I don't know anything. But I did think of a possible new motive for the death of poor Mr Hatch.'

'Why was he killed?'

'Suppose he was murdered by the Fists, as their trademark indicates. Why should they kill Hatch for revenge, and not your grandfather? Could killing him have been a device—a step in an elaborate plan? What was the result of Hatch's death?'

'I don't know. We don't know anything about Hatch.'

The nun smiled. 'I realize that. But what is the one result that we know? Something went wrong. The police found out about it too quick. His death brought the Homicide Squad into this house and gave them unlimited access to every room.'

She paused. Liz slowly assimilated the nun's meaning, though her mind was still distracted by earlier thoughts. 'But what was their plan in the first place?'

'I know my theory leaves too much unexplained. It isn't even, I'm afraid, one of my better guesses. But outside enemies must be taken into consideration and guarded against.'

Liz nodded. But she kept thinking, 'Ben and Sherry are alone together. And nothing is irrevocable.'

Roger Garvey came in just then. The secretary had changed even in the brief time since Liz last had seen him. His fine regular features looked drawn and pale, and his fingers were twitching.

Liz looked up and said, 'Hello.'

'Sergeant Verdi said I might come out here.' He seemed nervously anxious to justify himself. 'Your uncle wants a drink and I was the only one who knew where to get the liquor.' He crossed the room to the cellar door and hesitated. 'Did they— have they made certain the cellar is all right?'

'I believe the usual routine is to start at the top of the house,' said Sister Ursula. 'I doubt if they've searched the cellar yet.'

'Oh!' Roger's hand faltered on the door knob. But at last he gathered courage and went clattering down the cellar steps.

'It isn't comfortable, living in a house with murder,' Liz said. 'I've never seen Roger so nervous.'

Sister Ursula frowned. 'That young man isn't nervous. He's mortally afraid.'

Roger Garvey soon came back with a bottle of whisky. 'Would either of you care for some?'

The women shook their heads, so he poured himself a good four ounces and gulped them with a haste that was an insult to the label on the bottle. He stood still a moment and let the shudder run through him. Then he straightened up.

'Sister Ursula,' he said, 'you know a great deal about murder, don't you?'

'I have had a little experience.'

'Then tell me. Tonight, in this house, is there going to be another killing?'

The nun framed her words cautiously. 'It is hard to say. The pattern is thus far so unclear that it's impossible to tell what the murderer's next step must be. It is conceivable, perhaps even possible. Why?'

'I've got to get out of here,' he said, almost to himself. 'Because there will be another. I didn't even need you to tell me. I knew it all the time. But I wanted to hear you say so.'

'What do you mean?' Sister Ursula demanded. 'You assert you know all this?'

'Of course. Because you see I'm to be the victim.' He poured another quick one, gulped it, and hurried from the room, paying no attention to the nun's attempt to detain him.

'I don't understand why he said that,' Liz mused. 'Earlier this evening, Uncle Brian was telling me how anxious Roger seemed to get out of this house. But why should he think he's in danger?'

The kitchen extension of the phone rang. At the second ring, Liz rose to her feet.

'With everybody tied up maybe I'd better answer it,' she said. She crossed the room.

IX

Someone else answered on another extension in the house just as Liz picked up the receiver. She was about to replace it, then curiosity prevented her, for she had heard an official-sounding voice say, 'Latimer?'

'Speaking,' Ben answered.

'We've collared Vitelli,' the voice said. 'Rather, the Feds grabbed him. Jumping parole and sending death-threats don't count for much, but he forgot to notify his draft board of his new address. So the Feds moved in and tracked him down, and he tried to shoot it out. That was a mistake.'

She heard Ben say, 'Dead?' There was disappointment in his voice.

'Dying, maybe. If you want his statement about those notes, you'd better hustle down to the hospital pronto.'

The vocabulary of Ben's comments indicated that the novice Sherry was no longer in the room.

'All right,' he concluded. 'Be there in fifteen minutes.'

Liz heard the wire click and hung up, too. She found Sister Ursula looking at her reproachfully.

'Murder has a shocking effect on the character, as De Quincey pointed out,' the nun said. 'And you're reduced to eavesdropping?'

'I'm glad I did. Now I know what to do next.'

Sister Ursula paused a moment. 'I shan't ask you,' she said. 'But from what I've seen and heard of you, Felicity, I know that inaction is the most unbearable of tortures for you. If you've found something to do—do it and God bless you.'

'Thanks, Sister.' Liz smiled, and felt a little more like herself.

The only way to do this was openly, so openly that nothing could be suspected.

Try to sneak out, and the guards wouldn't appreciate your motives. She calmly walked down the steps of the back porch and approached the uniformed policeman who was on guard.

'Lieutenant Latimer is taking me down to help identify a suspect and I'm to meet him out here. Where's his car?'

Her unofficial standing as the Loot's girl doubtless helped. The cop did not question her story, but pointed the car out to her.

After fifteen minutes and two cigarettes, she began to wonder if her plan had miscarried. Could Ben have gone some other way? But just as she stubbed out the second cigarette, he appeared and climbed in behind the wheel.

'Hello,' she said.

He turned on her. 'Felicity Cain—' he began with formal fury.

'Oh, but please, Ben! I'm going nuts cooped up in that house. Let me ride down with you and talk to you. I've got to do something.'

He turned the ignition switch. 'Who's arguing?' he snorted. 'I've been spending the last fifteen minutes hunting for you. You're the closest of anybody to your grandfather and know most about these Fist notes. I want you with me when I quiz Vitelli. Where've you been hiding?'

'Here,' said Liz meekly. 'And it's a fine thing,' she added ruefully, 'when a girl can't think up a really smart lie without having it turn into the truth!'

Ben didn't answer. He swung the car out of the driveway and pressed down hard on the accelerator. They went humming along the paved road out in front, under the dark, leafy branches of trees.

'It seems so strange to be going at fifty,' Liz observed.

'You cost me fifteen minutes,' Ben grunted. 'Then Ryan decided to tell me you were in this car. Vitelli may not wait for tyre conservation.'

Liz laughed. Already her spirits were beginning to improve.

'Fifty used to be nothing and already it feels like zooming with a Pratt & Whitney,' she said. 'Funny how quickly you get used to things. Like Jeff Carey who just came back from Iowa and said, "And you know what? At night the streets there are *all lit up!*" He sounded awed. But I wonder if you can ever get used to it?'

'Used to what?' Ben prompted.

'Used to murder. If it was murder,' she added hastily.

'It was murder, all right. No bottle was found within possible heaving distance of that window.'

'Oh. You got that report already?'

'Yes.'

'And the other report?'

'What other—oh, yes,' Ben said slowly. 'I got that, too.'

'And nobody was found hiding anywhere in the house?' Liz began to grow frightened. Could someone in the family be a murderer?

Ben surmised what she was thinking and tried to reassure her. 'Of course no search is absolutely conclusive.'

Liz was distressed. 'Don't, Ben. It's kind of you to try to soften the news, but I understand what it means. A killer among those you trust and love—that's horrible!'

Ben's voice was officially dry. 'No one entered or left that house since Hatch arrived. There is no one in it now but the members of the household. And Hatch was murdered.'

'In all the questioning did anything come up that might be useful in finding out who's guilty?'

'Not a thing.'

'Not from Sherry, either?'

'Why Sherry?'

'I just wondered what you discussed.'

'Interesting woman,' Ben mused aloud. 'Damned interesting. She didn't have anything helpful on Hatch, but we talked quite a bit. Somehow she makes me see lots of subjects from a new point of view.'

His voice trailed off. Liz was silent, too, as they drove on through the tree-lined streets. Finally a brightly lighted hospital loomed up before them.

They got out of the car and went in.

'There's nothing we can do to save him,' the intern of the ward said. 'Internal haemorrhage. He's going fast.'

'Can he talk?' Ben demanded.

'I think he can. But he hasn't so far. Lafferty's in there with him.'

Ben greeted the moon-faced FBI man in the ward as an old colleague.

'Hi! Fine service I get from the Government, shooting up the man I need for questioning. What do you think I pay taxes for?'

Lafferty shrugged. 'Don't blame me, Latimer. It was his idea. And one of my men is down the hall, in just about as bad shape.'

'Vitelli won't talk?'

'Try what you can get out of him. I've sent for Belcore to help out.'

'Good.'

Liz kept looking at the man in the bed. This whole terrible night had revolved around men in beds. That was the *leitmotiv*. And they had all smiled—Graffer with the peaceful smile of tired age, Hatch with that frightful contorted smile of strychnine and this man with a blend of cunning and triumph which was fully as horrible.

Ben said, 'Vitelli!'

The man gave no sign of hearing. He just went on smiling.

'You're going to die, Vitelli. And you know why? Because you can't trust the Fists. Because they aren't yours any more. One of them turned you in to the Feds.'

Vitelli lay impassive, content.

'Yes, one of them snitched,' Ben went on. 'Here's your chance to get even. Spill what you know, and they'll all land in prison. And you'll die in peace.'

Vitelli shook his head with slow pleasure.

A dapper long-faced man with keen button eyes came into the room. He was dressed in a single-breasted, rather worn suit of dark clothes. His black eyes sparkled as he saw the man on the bed, and his black moustache twitched happily.

'Lieutenant Belcore, you know Lafferty, don't you?' Ben said. 'And this is Liz Cain.'

For the first time there was a response from the man on the bed. He lifted one feeble hand and made a scornful gesture with his thumb and fingers.

Lieutenant Belcore invoked the body of Bacchus and sketchily outlined the possible ancestry of any man who could make such a gesture to a lady. Vitelli replied briefly, using a few hoarse, laboured words.

His tones were harsh and rasping. He had little breath to give it. But underneath the rasp could be detected a voice which had once been slow and oily and cold.

Liz knew a good deal of the man from her grandfather. She knew how he had perverted the original liberal, revolutionary tendencies of Italian secret societies into a personal racket for himself. It used to be said that Vitelli had tears in his eyes whenever he collected protection money. The payment had robbed him of the pleasure he could have derived in punishing non-payment.

Twenty years in prison had not changed Vitelli. His voice was the vocal horror that was to be expected from a man of his stamp.

'What did Vitelli say?' Ben asked Belcore.

Belcore looked at Liz. 'It was not necessary to translate.'

'Ask him what good he expects to get out of being stubborn?'

But Vitelli had propped himself up on one elbow and was speaking unprompted. His words were a deadly flow of some new acid that froze even as it burned. And the light in his little eyes was that of wicked exultation. The words went on monotonously until a sudden spasm of coughing interrupted them. The blood on his mouth was even redder than his lips.

'What did he say?' Ben asked.

'He said he is glad Miss Cain is here. He says he wants her to know that her grandfather took twenty years out of his life but that payment has been arranged and will be made. He asserts the plans are all perfected and the collection may take place this very night. Now he does not care if he dies; it is all fixed.'

Ben whirled to the bed. 'What plans? Who's doing it? You can talk English if you want to. Spill it, Vitelli, or we'll round up every relative you've got in North Beach and give them the works.'

Another fit of coughing shook Vitelli. Liz turned her eyes away as the blood gushed forth. There was a ghastly rattle in the wounded man's throat, but he managed to speak once more, and for the first time in English.

'Go to hell!' he said.

His defiance still sounded in the room when his breathing finally stopped.

Those were the last words of Angelo Vitelli.

X

It was not until the doctors and nurses had been called and certain formalities were finished that Ben Latimer gave full expression to his inward disgust.

He took a rapid turn up and down the room, his broad shoulders very straight and stiff, his eyes grim and hard, then stopped and spoke tersely to the waiting FBI agent.

'That fellow died like just what he was—a sewer rat,' he said. 'But at least with rats you know exactly where you stand. They don't beat around the bush. They don't pretend.'

'Knowing that doesn't help us,' the FBI man complained. 'It's too bad he didn't talk. I've an idea he might have been able to give us some very useful information. He probably could have told us where to pick up the rest of his mob. Now it'll take months and months of hard digging.'

Lieutenant Belcore twisted his hat around in his hands. He looked a little tired and annoyed. His voice, too, carried a distinct note of weariness.

'Not much you can do with fellows like Vitelli. They usually resent other mobsters muscling in on their people.'

'I just wonder what, if anything, Vitelli knew about the killing of a certain shipyard worker,' Ben mused. 'If the war were still going on you might be tempted to label it as sabotage.'

Belcore frowned. 'I wish we could truthfully say all these rats were fascist tools,' he went on. 'It is hard to realize that some men who helped fight for liberty are as bitterly against the law.'

He paused briefly, then glanced sharply at Latimer.

'You mentioned a shipyard worker, Lieutenant. You remember that homicide case last week in North Beach?'

'I left it up to Verdi,' Ben admitted. 'Nothing much you can do when an unidentified drifter gets his skull cracked. Routine takes its course.'

'Well, he is no longer unidentified. You will get the full report tomorrow, but I thought you might like to know. And he was no drifter. He had a good paying job at Marinship.'

'So?'

'A check-up on fingerprints at all the plants revealed a lot.' Belcore nodded. 'Your unidentified man is named Homer Hatch.'

Ben's face went through contortions such as are seldom seen even in a hospital. 'Homer Hatch!' he repeated. 'And at Marinship. It couldn't be the same!'

He took from his pocket an identification card and handed it to the Italian, who whipped out a notebook and compared its number with what was written there.

'I don't know where you got this card,' Belcore said. 'But it's the same Homer Hatch.'

Ben whistled. 'This is one for the book, boys. I'm investigating two separate murders, and both corpses are the same man!'

Liz tried to talk on the way back, but she was rebuffed by a growl. Not until they were almost home did Ben break his silent pondering.

'I've been trying to find a pattern in this damn thing,' he apologized gruffly. 'Sorry if I barked at you.'

'And have you found a pattern?'

'The hell of it is, I've found at least three. They go like this. The Cain Homer Hatch, our Hatch, the poisoned Hatch, is a phony. So what follows from that? Why should anybody be posing as a murdered shipyard worker? The answer is simple.'

Ben cleared his throat. 'Pattern A. Our Hatch was a labour saboteur. He killed the real Hatch to take over his job and raise hell at Marinship. Someone in the house is his confederate who arranged for him to make his headquarters there. He and the confederate quarrelled and the confederate disposed of him. Objections?'

Liz hotly vented her scorn. 'Plenty. Nobody in our house would be the confederate of such a man!'

'Leave personalities out, Liz. Under the proper circumstances, anyone can be and do anything. That's something you learn on the Force. Can you suggest other objections?'

'Yes. There wasn't time for them to have a quarrel. Hatch was killed almost as soon as he got there.'

'I don't know about that,' Ben said. 'Ten minutes is enough to provide a motive for murder. Suppose he was backing out on the plan, threatening to give it away. That might be plenty to make somebody want to kill him. But let's go on to the next.'

'All right,' said Liz. 'Let's hear it.'

'Pattern B. First part same as before, but no confederate. Instead somebody in the house recognized Hatch for what he is and wipes him out. Objections?'

Liz shook her head. 'That's even weaker. Why murder him?

If someone recognized him as a phony and probably a saboteur, why not just turn him over to the authorities?'

'Suppose you didn't have enough evidence but wanted to keep him from doing damage?'

'His working in a defence plant under false identification would be enough to hold him, wouldn't it?'

'Yes, I guess so. Well, Pattern C. We still have the original Hatch killed by a subversive element for their own dastardly purpose. And our Hatch is a private eye or an undercover Fed taking his place to try to track down his murderers. But they get him instead. Objections?'

'That would still mean that somebody in the house was a fifth columnist. And that isn't possible.'

'Isn't possible? After you've heard Garvey shooting his mouth off about saving the world for the British Empire and the rest of his line?'

'Just because a man talks that way doesn't mean he's a traitor. Roger couldn't really *do* anything that would injure the war effort.'

'Any other objections?'

'Yes. Two that apply to all these ideas. One, they all depend on the mere chance that the Housing Bureau sent Hatch to our house. Isn't that hanging a lot on coincidence?'

'Coincidences happen,' Ben said. 'I've got to work on what might have occurred, Liz, not on what we both would like to be true.'

'All right.' Liz's voice became crisp. 'This is no sentimental objection. How did the murderer give Hatch—I suppose we've got to go on calling him that—how did he give him the strychnine? Under any of your patterns, Hatch would have good reasons for being wary. If Hatch was acquainted with the murderer, he'd know better than to take a drink from him. If the murderer spotted him without being recognized, Hatch would surely become suspicious if a total stranger wandered into his bedroom and said, "Here, have a drink!"'

Ben thought a while. Then he said, 'Thanks.'

'Did I help any?' Liz asked.

'Frankly, no. I'd been making all those objections to myself. But I wanted to see if they were obvious or if I was being professionally over-cautious. They're obvious all right, and valid. Especially the last. Furthermore, until I can figure out how Hatch was persuaded to drink that strychnine, I haven't got a case.'

The car chugged slowly up the cobbled hill. The night was moon-bright and peaceful—the sort of a still night when it is almost impossible to believe that not many months ago shells were falling on distant islands across the sea while the world was locked in a violent war.

Ben must have been thinking along those lines, too.

'War and hate—they seem impossible under such a moon,' he said.

'I know. Peaceful nights like this are too good to last.'

'No more peace in a minute. We'll be back at the house. There's nothing I can really accomplish until I check on Hatch's identity tomorrow. Yet I'd like to get the rest of these stories straightened out tonight if I can. I never saw a case with so few leads of any description.'

The night's peace was indeed too good to last. It was shattered now by a half dozen shots.

The car leaped ahead with a jolt that almost threw Liz from her seat. Then as it swerved to the curb by the house, a black figure darted in front of its headlights. There was a squeal of brakes, another jolt and the car stopped. The person lying on the street in front of it was still, too.

Liz leaped out of the car almost as quickly as Ben did. She was beside him as he bent over the figure.

'Thank God for good brakes,' Latimer muttered. 'I barely nudged him. But he's bleeding badly—and not from what the car did to him either. It's a bullet hole.'

Liz shrank back. 'Who is it?'

Ben turned the figure face up. Roger Garvey's fine handsome features gleamed pallidly in the moonlight.

'Oh!' Liz gasped and shuddered. 'It's the Fist again. He was right. He predicted this. So they got him, too!'

Ben looked up to see Sergeant Verdi approaching. He rose angrily to his feet.

'Well, what goes on here? The house full of police and the murderer still gets away with another try? This one'll live, I think, but that's no thanks to you.'

'Aw, we're doin' our best.'

'Nix on the alibis, Verdi. But I hope to God you've got the killer this time. If you haven't, it's back to a beat for you. All right, Sergeant. Who shot this man?'

'I hate to tell you about it.'

'Come on! Who shot him?'

Sergeant Verdi looked glum. He swallowed. 'Er-ah, I'm sorta afraid it was me.'

Ben stared at him. 'You! *What's that?*'

Verdi gulped again. 'He'd been hitting the bottle pretty hard and he kept carrying on about how he had to get the hell out of this house or they'd bump him next. So at last he tries to make a break for it. Ryan tackles him in the hall, but he wrenches himself loose. Then I yells for him to stop or I'll shoot.'

'So?'

'So he didn't stop.'

Ben leaned over and slipped his hands under Garvey's armpits.

'Take the feet, Verdi,' he said. 'And there's one consolation,' he added. 'At least I know who this is.'

XI

Ryan was standing at the door, keeping the household inside. Dr Frayne stepped forward as they brought in the wounded man.

'I think he'll be okay, Doctor,' Ben said. 'If you'd look him over and give me a report, I'd be obliged. We'll get the police surgeon out here but that bleeding ought to he stopped right away. Verdi, you and McGinnis carry him up to his room. You direct them, will you, Doctor? Thanks. McGinnis! You'll stay there with him.'

Sherry came downstairs. As she passed the men carrying Garvey, she cringed away from them, but Dr Frayne quietly reassured her. When she reached the hall, Sister Ursula asked a question.

'Your grandfather?'

'He slept through it, thank heaven.'

Uncle Brian made a loud noise intended to indicate relief.

'Ben—Lieutenant—I want to talk to you,' he said.

'Fine. With Garvey and the doctor out of the way for the moment, you're the only one left for me to interview. Shall we go into the library?'

'What I've got to say I'd just as soon the women heard.' Brian Cain's voice was hearty and his manner easy, but he wasted no words. Just as Ben had become Lieutenant Latimer after Hatch's death, so Liz now saw her Uncle Brian change into Mr Cain, the executive.

'First to clear up a foolish minor point. We all told you no one saw this Hatch after his arrival. Well, I'm afraid I did. It's not important. After I'd showed him, to his room, I remembered a Hatch who was shop foreman for me some ten years ago. First rate man. Never knew what became of him, and I needed an experienced foreman in the plant. He resembled the Hatch I had known, so I went to see him. If he was related to the fellow I knew, I wanted to ask where to find him. I had no luck, however. He offered me a drink, but I wasn't feeling well and turned the offer down. That's all I know. Everything.

'But when our roomer was murdered and you began your inquisition, I got the jitters—which was idiotic, of course. Since nobody had seen me, I decided just to forget the episode. You can understand why. I was the last man to see him alive and all that. But tonight I thought it over and realized how foolishly I acted.'

Ben's eyes met those of Sister Ursula. 'He offered you a drink?' Ben asked.

The nun waited eagerly for the answer.

'Yes. Seemed a friendly sort of fellow.'

'What sort of a drink?'

'I didn't even notice. Hard liquor of some sort. Bottle was a fifth, I think.' Brian Cain waved his hand. 'But enough of this, Ben. These irrelevant matters may be professional, but they aren't getting us any place. There's something else I wanted to discuss.'

'Yes?' Ben showed curiosity.

'My father is a very sick man,' went on Brian, unheeding. 'Sudden shock could easily kill him. If he should learn that there was a murderer loose in this house tonight—well, he might die. If he does, I'll hold you responsible. Dr Frayne gave him a sedative and I think he'll sleep through tonight. But tomorrow morning he'll be anxious to know what's been going on here. In time he's bound to learn. When that happens, I want him to learn that the case is solved, the murderer arrested, and all danger has departed.'

Ben Latimer nodded. 'I understand how you feel, sir. But it isn't possible to have everything break the way we wish. There's a lot of essential routine work which I can't handle until offices are open tomorrow.'

'I'm not asking you what's possible,' Cain shot back crisply. 'The Government doesn't ask me what's possible when it wants planes. It tells me what must be done, and I see to it that it is done. Now I'm telling you that this case should be solved tonight. You're Liz's friend, Ben, and I respect your professional status. Nevertheless, you've only got tonight. In the morning I'll put the Golden West Agency on the job. They're used to my ways, and they never yet wasted time complaining about bad breaks.'

Ben stared after Brian Cain as he stalked away. He had given Ben his ultimatum.

'The Golden West,' Ben muttered. 'If they could solve murders as well as they can break strikes, everything would be rosy.'

'The trouble with being a giant is that you're forever disappointed with pigmies,' Sister Ursula said. 'Mr Cain is really flattering you, Lieutenant. He expects you to find murderers the way he builds planes.'

'You'd all better go to bed, ladies,' Ben said. 'I think you've told me all you can. And don't be worried. There'll be men in the halls all night.'

Without saying anything more, he walked off, frowning.

'You two go,' Sister Ursula said to Liz and Sherry. 'I want a word with the lieutenant.'

The two girls silently climbed the stairs. As they reached the top, Liz turned to her cousin. She hardly knew what she was going to say— something to convey a little human understanding in this coldly official night. Whatever was on her lips died there when she saw that the novice was crying.

Liz took her hand. 'I know, Sherry,' she said.

Sherry's husky voice was shaky. 'It's so different. I wanted to come home and make Graffer feel good so we'd all be happy for a little while. Now this had to happen.'

'I know,' Liz repeated.

Sherry snuffled and fumbled in her long sleeve for a handkerchief. 'You can leave the world but the world doesn't leave you,' she said. 'Good night, Liz.' She went into her room.

Liz walked down the hall, nodding abstractedly at the guard stationed outside Graffer's room. Further on she met Dr Frayne as he came out of Roger Garvey's bedroom.

'Oh! Hello, Liz.'

'Hello.' Before he shut the door, she caught a glimpse of Roger in bed, pale and still. He was asleep. Men in beds—so many of them!

'Is he all right?' Liz asked.

'He'll be fine in the morning after a sleep. And once I thought I had retired! In all my hectic G.P. days up in the Sierras, I never really spent a night like this. Get some sleep, Liz. You look ragged.'

'I'll try.'

'Would you like a sedative?'

'No, thanks. Oh, Doctor?'

'Yes?'

'Has Ben talked to you yet?'

'Not yet. Why?'

'I was wondering. When we came out from dinner after Mother screamed, you couldn't find your bag for a minute. Remember?'

'I'm old, I guess. Always putting things down and never remembering where they are.'

He lifted his head and glanced sharply at Liz. 'Hum! Could be! But that's nonsense. Ridiculous. But I'll tell your Ben. You're a smart girl, Liz.'

Smart girl? She smiled wryly as she closed herself in her own room. 'I'm so smart I can't even get myself straightened out inside,' she murmured. 'I keep worrying about Ben and about Graffer, and I see that dreadful Vitelli lying there dying, and I hear Roger saying he'll be next. It's awful!'

I'd take a drink now, she thought. I'd even take a drink from that bottle Uncle Brian saw and that's vanished so completely. I wonder if their search was thorough. Of course, they were hunting for a man, not a bottle, and when I get to thinking this way it sets me worrying about Mother. Probably there's no need to worry about her because tomorrow she'll have decided this was all a special persecution devised just to worry her.

Her mind was still working busily an hour after she got into bed. Even her room, that bare narrow room which seemed more nun's cell than boudoir, seemed strange to her. She was lonely and lost and she longed to talk with somebody. She needed human companionship.

She also wanted to cry, she realized suddenly. Not because of any sorrow—she was too confused to feel sorrow—but the satisfactory release of crying, the easing of physical and mental tension. She needed a shoulder for tears.

But Ben had become Detective-Lieutenant Latimer, and Graffer, the best shoulder in the world, must not be disturbed. And Sherry was too closely involved in what troubled Liz. She naturally never thought of her mother, for Mrs Cain's shoulders were not that kind. There was one person in this house who would do. Sister Ursula!

Liz slipped into her plain tailored robe and her mules. It was an absurd nocturnal expedition she had planned. But she had made up her mind and was determined to go through with it. She opened her door.

In the hall Graffer's guard stopped her. 'Okay, lady,' he said. 'What goes?'

Her explanation sounded foolish. 'I just wanted to go down and talk to Sister Ursula for a while.'

'Uh-uh.' The detective was polite enough, but plainly he disapproved. 'We got orders nobody goes prowling around tonight, see?'

'But I won't do any harm.'

'Yep, and I bet if we had run into the duck who was going into Hatch's room, he'd have said the same thing. Not that I mean you're up to anything like that, you understand, but orders is orders.'

The old house was dark and still, and the officer kept his voice to a gruff whisper.

'I'm warning you, officer, I've got to have a shoulder to cry on and, if you keep me here, I'll damned well use yours,' Liz told him.

The officer made a warding movement. 'Keep back, lady. I'm

married. I dunno what this means, but you better get right back to your room.'

'Oh, officer!' Liz almost choked with suppressed mirth. Already she was feeling much better. This argument was so absurd the hysterical symptoms were departing.

At this moment Sergeant Verdi came around the corner from the direction of the stairs. When he caught sight of Liz he quickened his pace.

'Hello, Miss Cain,' he said, stopping near her. 'This is luck. I'm glad you are still up. I was just coming after you. Sister Ursula wants to see you.'

Liz stared at him in surprise. 'That's strange,' she said. 'By an odd coincidence, I was just starting out to see Sister Ursula on my own hook. I couldn't sleep. But this officer halted me.'

Verdi nodded at the detective. 'It's all right. She can go.' He looked at Liz. 'I'll just walk along with you to see that you get there safely. Sister Ursula is in the room near the kitchen.'

'I know.' Liz grinned at the guard. 'Better luck next time.'

XII

There was a light in the library, but Liz knew that Ben would not want to see her now.

When they reached the room which had once been occupied by the cook downstairs, Sergeant Verdi left Liz. She knocked, and Sister Ursula opened the door.

'Come in, my dear,' said Sister Ursula. 'It was nice of you to come.'

'That's all right,' Liz said. 'I've been hoping to see you.'

Suddenly words were pouring out in a confused torrent. Sister Ursula listened quietly, with a tender smile of understanding on her lips. Finally the words stopped and the tears came.

When it was over, Liz found cigarettes in the pocket of her robe and lighted one.

'I didn't know why I acted so silly. You've got a good shoulder, Sister.'

'I need one. Often. But you're a child, Liz. In your own life, you're a woman—no, let us say an adult, with no sex distinction. But since you've been cut off from your chosen career by your arm, you're falling back on your emotions, and there you're a child. You speak of Ben as though he were nobody himself—just a stock figure for women to dispute about. He's not. Lieutenant Latimer is a man who has a very difficult job to do and is doing it well. He can't be your gallant lover every minute of the day.'

Liz nodded. 'But you can't expect me to be sensible tonight, can you? With all that has happened?'

'No.' The nun's quiet voice was grave. 'But someone has to be sensible. I've tried to be. That's why I sent for you.'

'I don't think I understand.'

'I have a certain theory I'd like to test. I believe you heard Lieutenant Latimer mention that this is not my first contact with murder?'

'Yes. And the way you pounced on the point about that bottle was astonishing. It had uncomfortable possibilities. I'm afraid I'm still not being sensible. Anyway, you mean you're still trying to solve the murder?'

'I have solved it. That's why I wanted to talk to you. I wanted to tell you about it and see how the solution sounds.'

Solution to murder! The words rang in Liz's ears. For the first time she perceived their full implication. It had been murder and the nun knew the answer. Suddenly Liz realized that this was it. A quiet scene here. Two women talking in a downstairs room of a silent old house. This was what the events had all been leading up to. This was the crucial moment.

It all seemed so peaceful, so undramatic. Sister Ursula began to speak.

'There are so many things we have to account for, so many

little things,' she said. 'If we can find a pattern embracing all of them, we can be almost sure that that pattern is the truth. We need the truth, and we need it now. Your uncle is right. We must spare your family the pain of a long investigation, and the worry of your uncle's private detectives.'

'Also the danger of another murder,' Liz said. 'Roger was so afraid.'

'Needlessly,' said Sister Ursula. 'Mr Garvey's life is in no danger, unless my answer is shockingly wrong. Not at the moment, at least. But let me try to list what we have to explain:

'The murder of the real Hatch. The presence of the Fist under the body of the false Hatch. The disappearance of the bottle which your uncle saw. The shifting of Dr Frayne's medicine case. Roger Garvey's fear of death in this house. Vitelli's conviction that his plans will be carried out. Your uncle's indisposition when we were all eating together.'

Liz had been listening quietly and nodding as the nun ticked off each point, but now she broke in.

'Uncle Brian. You think that the food poisoning, or whatever happened to him, was maybe a rehearsal?'

'I think your uncle's poisoning is one of the most vital points in this whole case.

'Let us look at the murder of the real Hatch. It seems fruitless to search for motives in his personal history which we don't as yet know. If he were killed for personal reasons and his impersonator happened to be killed for others, that explains much. I think we must assume that he was killed by the impersonator, and for the purposes of imposture. Now why should he be impersonated?'

'Because he worked at Marinship, I guess. That's all we know about him.'

'No, Liz. We know one other thing about him. He worked at Marinship, and the Housing Bureau had assigned him a room here. Now as to the presence of the Fist; the symbol of the Fist has been found often before beside bodies, and always it was left there by the murderer. So we easily assumed that it had been left by the murderer in this case, too. But there is another possibility—it was left by the lodger before he became a corpse. It was in his possession before the murder and fell out of his pocket in his spasms.

'Put those two ideas together. The real Hatch was killed because he had a room here, and the Fist symbol belonged to the false Hatch.'

Liz gasped aloud. 'Then—then the impostor was a Fist. They killed the real Hatch so they could smuggle a man in here for evil purposes! They guessed we'd have a police guard after the threats, but they knew we wouldn't turn away a defence worker from the Housing Bureau. And that's what Vitelli meant. He didn't know his man was dead.'

'Let us try to reconstruct it from there,' the nun said. 'The false Hatch came to this house to kill your grandfather. But instead he was himself murdered. Why? It is next to impossible to assume that he knew anyone in this house. He would be running too great a risk of detection if he did. Or if the person was an ally who would not betray him, then that person could have undertaken the job himself without this elaborate masquerade. The false Hatch did not know anyone here. But he might have recognized someone, or have been recognized.

'Say that he knew something vital about the past of an individual here in this house. He may have attempted blackmail, or the individual may simply have feared that he might and forestalled him. The individual saw his chance in Dr Frayne's case.

'As to Mr Garvey's fright, ask yourself—what happened after he announced that he would be the next victim?' Sister Ursula's voice was insistent and loud. 'What vital fact came to light in the evidence?'

'After Roger was shot, Uncle Brian told us about the bottle.' Sister Ursula smiled. It was a mechanical, unhappy smile.

'The bottle!' she said. 'And there we are at the crux of the whole case. How was that strychnine administered? According to your uncle, Hatch was drinking from the bottle. There was no glass for the murderer to poison. He would have to poison the bottle itself. And yet Hatch would be on his guard. He was here on a dangerous mission. All men were his enemies. Would he accept a drink from a person whom he distrusted?'

'It doesn't seem likely.'

'But there is a way. One way in which that poison could have been administered with complete confidence. If the murderer himself drank from the same bottle.'

'But if you did that, you would poison yourself!' Liz protested.

There was the click of a light switch and the room was in darkness.

XIII

Out of the darkness a voice spoke. Its tones were hollow, almost inhuman.

'There was no policeman in the hall,' it said. 'Such negligence on the part of the authorities is a lucky break for me. I am here to kill you both. No, do not scream. That would force me to fire in the darkness and possibly only maim you. I am giving you this moment of darkness for your prayers.'

The voice was ghastly, unrecognizable. It is what the voice of Death would sound like, Liz thought.

'It will all explain itself,' the voice went on. 'You sent for Liz, Sister. They know that. It will be clear that you wished to confront her with evidence of her guilt. She killed you out of spite, herself from remorse. The picture will be plain.'

There was no sound in the darkness but the tiny clicking of Sister Ursula's rosary beads.

'You are wise to attempt nothing,' the voice went on. 'Since you must die, die in peace.'

The light came on. Liz's blinking eyes saw the figure in the doorway, and her brain whirled. Then she heard the shot.

But it did not come from the automatic pistol in the figure's hand. That automatic fell to the floor as blood spurted from the hand holding it and a look of terrified amazement spread over Uncle Brian's face.

For Liz, the darkness grew and enveloped her . . .

Sister Ursula was sitting by the bed when Liz opened her eyes. She shuddered as memory came back. 'Is it all over? Was it really Uncle Brian?'

Sister Ursula nodded.

'Where is he now? Was he killed?'

'He was only slightly wounded. He's down at Headquarters. Lieutenant Latimer phoned a few minutes ago. Brian Cain is making a complete confession.'

'But how did you know?'

'Two things made me sure,' the nun replied quietly. 'One was the bottle and the other was the food poisoning. You remember I said there was one sure way of allaying Hatch's suspicion?'

'Yes, drinking it yourself. But how was it accomplished?'

'By drinking it himself—and then taking an emetic and an antidote before the poison could begin to work. There was some tincture of iodine missing from Dr Frayne's bag, too. Diluted, that is a specific antidote for strychnine. The murderer drank with Hatch, then left him promptly and visited the bathroom. And of all the people in this house, only your uncle showed the effects of such treatment, though he attributed it to indisposition.

'Also on his word alone depended the evidence of the bottle. There was no bottle. The poisoned liquor was given in Mr Cain's silver flask, relic of the twenties, which would never be noticed by police carefully hunting for a liquor bottle belonging to Hatch.'

'But why should he have made up the bottle scene?'

'To distract us from the important fact that he had admitted being in Hatch's room. Why did he admit that? Because Roger Garvey saw him there. Garvey was afraid the murderer would kill him. Why? Because Garvey knew something dangerous. How did the murderer know he knew? Because Garvey had told the murderer, probably with a threat of blackmail. When the murderer refused to pay for silence, Garvey thought he was scheduled to die.'

'Uncle Brian tried to kill us,' Liz said. 'Why didn't he kill Roger?'

'He was too wise,' Sister Ursula said. 'There was no need of it. Instead, he drew the teeth of the blackmailer by admitting the visit himself and adding a distracting touch with the bottle.'

'Have you seen Roger?'

'Yes. He talked this morning. And his blackmail was not for money. You remember when he was pressing your uncle for a job? After he heard Mr Cain deny returning to Hatch's room, he tried to use his knowledge as a lever to get that job. It never entered his head that Mr Cain might refuse.'

'But he has a good job here.'

'His employer may die soon, ending the job. But that was not the main point. Employed by the Cain aeroplane plant, he might get draft deferment, which he could not hope for here. He risked his life, as he thought, with a murderer and got himself shot by the police, in order that he might not be shot by the enemy.'

'But if you knew all this, why didn't you tell Ben and have him attend to Uncle Brian?'

'I did tell Lieutenant Latimer. That was why we arranged last night's scene. We did not have a case for a jury. We needed more evidence. You remember that your mother's shuffling of rooms ended up with your uncle and me in the servants' quarters? I arranged to explain my theory to you loudly enough so that he would hear it in the next room. I hoped that he would betray himself, and Lieutenant Latimer was ready in the closet when he did.'

At this moment Dr Frayne poked his bearded face in at the door. 'Feeling chipper again, Liz?'

'I guess so. As chipper as I can under the circumstances. How's Graffer?'

'I haven't seen him yet. Overslept this morning myself after last night's strenuous duties.' He withdrew his head.

'Sister Ursula,' Liz said. 'Why on earth did Uncle Brian kill that Fist impostor?'

'Because Hatch recognized him. At least that's what I surmise. Do you remember back during the Sinclair campaign when there was talk about the New Vigilantes? They were going to protect and save the State after it was plunged into Socialistic chaos.

'No one ever knew who the important men in the organization were. The group had fascist connections. The Fists were anti-fascist, and Hatch's assignment then was to study them in North Beach. As an apparent fascist, he got high enough in the New Vigilantes to meet the leaders. When he saw Mr Cain again, he recognized him.

'Revelation of the Vigilante business would ruin the reputation of a hero of modern industry.'

Ben came in, then, to interrupt them. He said nothing until he had kissed Liz.

Then as he started to speak, she said. 'Don't ask me how I am and am I chipper? What do you expect?'

'Ostrich feathers,' said Ben. 'At least I can ask how you are, Sister?'

Sudden realization hit Liz. 'And if I am all right, it isn't much thanks to you, Ben Latimer! You—you used me for bait!'

Before Ben could answer, the door opened. It was Dr Frayne again.

'Don't worry about your grandfather's grieving over the news,' the physician said. 'He won't ever know—here.' They looked at him, and he added, 'Last night. In his sleep.' Frayne shut the door.

'He was a good man,' said Ben.

Liz's eyes were dry with that dryness that stings so much worse than tears.

'Now look, Liz,' Ben went on. 'Don't be sore at me. You say I used you. Okay. Maybe that's even true. I guess it is. But don't you see why I used you? Sister Ursula wanted to call Sherry, but I vetoed it.'

Liz's temper flashed through her grief. 'So you wouldn't risk her precious neck, but with me it was all right?'

'Uh-huh. Because I can use you, you see. Just like I can use my own hand. I wouldn't have the right to go risking a stranger. But you're part of me.'

Liz smiled up at him. Out of the corner of her eye she saw Sister Ursula quietly leaving the room.

ANTHONY BOUCHER

William Anthony Parker White, who would become one of the most important figures in American mystery fiction, was born on 21 August 1911 in Oakland, California. His parents were doctors and after his father's death in 1912, White was raised in the Catholic faith by his mother with the support of his grandfather.

A voracious reader, White soon tried writing himself and at the age of only fifteen sold a supernatural short story to *Weird Tales*. Nevertheless, writing was a hobby; his passion was the theatre. At Pasadena Junior College he became president of the Players' Guild, the college's junior dramatic society for which he acted in numerous productions, such as *Phaedra* (1932), *The Merchant of Venice* (1931) and *The Royal Family* by G. S. Kaufman and Edna Ferber (1930). He also directed and sometimes acted in his own plays, including *Erlkönig*, a translation from Goethe. As well as German, White was or would become fluent in French, Italian, Russian, Spanish and, to a degree, Sanskrit.

After leaving Pasadena in 1928, White went to the University of Southern California to study for a Bachelor of Arts degree, and in 1932 he went up to the University of California in Berkeley to study for a Masters. At UC he wrote plays for the Experimental Theater Company, including the supernatural mystery *To Remember Me* (1933) and two campus comedies, *Kaleidoscope* (1933) and *Second Semester* (1933). It was at Berkeley that White met Phyllis

Price, the daughter of his German professor, and the two bonded over a shared love of opera. While he achieved his masters, with a thesis entitled 'The Duality of Impressionism in Recent German Drama', he shelved his original idea of becoming a teacher and decided instead to pursue a career in journalism.

White's career as a journalist took off quickly with a stint as arts critic for the *United Progressive News*, a short-lived Los Angeles newspaper. The job required him to do what he liked to do anyway—attend theatre and concerts—and it also gave him time to try his hand at writing a novel. Rather than use his own prosaic, and far from uncommon, name, he decided to adopt a pen name, the first of several. He became 'Anthony Boucher', the name by which he is most familiar to crime fiction readers; the pseudonym combines his middle name and his grandmother's maiden name. In June 1937 Simon & Schuster announced that Anthony Boucher's first novel would be *Death of a Publisher* and it would be published that year. Autumn came and White's first book duly appeared, although it had a different title and no publisher was harmed as part of its plot. *The Case of the Seven of Calvary* is a campus mystery, set in Berkeley, and the case is investigated by White's alter ego, Martin Lamb, and Dr John Ashwin. Ashwin also features in an unpublished short story, 'Death on the Bay', and a second novel— as revealed in the most authoritative overview of White's life and achievements, *Anthony Boucher: A Biobibliography* by Jeffrey Marks (2008); the novel, *The Case of the Toad-in-the-Hole*, is due to be published by Wildside Press in 2022.

In 1938, White and Phyllis Price were married. They had two sons and, juggling family life with writing, White published six more novel-length detective stories by 1942. These included two under another pen name, 'H. H. Holmes', itself the pseudonym of an appalling serial killer whose real name, Herman Mudgett, White would also use for short stories and verse.

White's novels are archetypal Golden Age puzzles peppered with impossible crimes, unusual clues and arcane references, which also feature in his shorter fiction published in *Ellery Queen's Mystery Magazine* and elsewhere. White was an innovator and more than any other writer he sought to blend mystery with other genres, particularly horror, espionage and science fiction. By contrast, other than where a campus provides the setting, there is little overtly biographical in his work, although his Catholicism is shared by his best-loved characters, Sister Ursula of the Order of Martha of Bethany, and the California police detective Fergus O'Breen.

Despite—or perhaps because of—never being in full health, White's energy was simply phenomenal: he translated the work of others, including Georges Simenon and Jorge Luis Borges; he edited anthologies, the first of which appeared in 1943; and in collaboration with others, he wrote dozens of radio plays for series such as *The Adventures of Ellery Queen*, for Sherlock Holmes, and for his own creation, *The Casebook of Gregory Hood*. When not at his desk White was gregarious, and as well as helping to set up a California chapter of the Baker Street Irregulars, he was a founding member of the Mystery Writers of America, which awarded him the first of four Edgars in 1945.

Like a number of other writers, White receded from writing fiction when he found that reviewing was less arduous and more remunerative. Over the course of his career, he reviewed for— among others—the *San Francisco Chronicle*, the *Chicago Sunday Times*, the *Los Angeles Daily News*, *Opera News* and, in New York, the *Herald Tribune* and the *Times*. He also became increasingly active in local politics, and in 1947 was elected chair of the Berkeley Democratic Club. A year later, he was elected to serve as the member for Alameda County and as a representative for the Democrats on the party's state central committee. A passionate libertarian, White was one of the many who campaigned—successfully—against Richard Nixon and Karl Mundt's infamous bill to 'protect the United States against un-American and subversive activities'.

In 1951, with White as its President, the Mystery Writers of America published a collaborative novel on similar lines to *The*

Floating Admiral, published twenty years earlier by the MWA's British counterpart, the Detection Club. As often with such round-robin novels, the majority of the contributors to *The Marble Forest* by 'Theo Durrant' (named for another infamous murderer) were lesser lights and other than White are largely unknown today.

During the 1950s, White also edited *Fantasy and Science Fiction Magazine* and *True Crime Detective* while continuing to review books, write stories and edit anthologies and even appear on the radio. But, despite a formidable work ethic he remained a strong family man and found time to relax with Phyllis and the boys, to listen to his extensive collection of early opera recordings, and to cook and play poker with friends.

White's life was to be cut short at the age of 56. After a very late diagnosis, he died from lung cancer on 29 April 1968 at Kaiser Foundation Hospital in Oakland, California. He lives on, in reputation and in the annual crime and mystery fiction convention 'Bouchercon', established in his honour in 1970.

'Vacancy with Corpse' was first published in *Mystery Book Magazine*, February 1946, as by 'H. H. Holmes'.

WHERE DO WE GO FROM HERE?

Dorothy L. Sayers

(*A clock chimes the half hour*)

GEORGE: I say, Laura. Half-past eight. You'll be late for your bridge.

LAURA: I think I'll give it a miss tonight. I'm tired, and it's raining.

GEORGE: (*sharply*) Nonsense. It's only just round the corner. You know they always expect you on Tuesdays. You'll leave them one short and spoil their whole evening for them.

LAURA: Gracious, George! It's not like you to be so considerate of other people. Usually you say: 'Can't you stay at home for once, instead of wasting your time on those old tabbies?'

GEORGE: Well, they are old tabbies. But if you undertake to do a thing, you should do it.

LAURA: Here endeth the First Lesson. I don't suppose the Temperleys will be going either—

GEORGE: All the more reason—

LAURA: And I feel as if I had a headache coming on.

GEORGE: Oh, have you, dear? Well, why don't you go upstairs and lie down? Run along now, and I'll bring you up some hot milk and an aspirin. Nothing like taking things in time.

LAURA: You seem to be in a great hurry to get rid of me. What's the matter? Got a date with a girl?

GEORGE: Really, Laura! Why on earth you should think—

LAURA: Why not? After all, *we* had to meet on the sly in Elizabeth's time, and what's happened once may happen again.

GEORGE: Certainly not. You're not Elizabeth. Very different, thank heaven!

LAURA: Thank you, George. Though personally I rather liked Elizabeth. Of course she was a bit over life-size, and not *quite* the right sort of wife for somebody making his way up to be works manager. A trifle too loud and hearty and fond of bangles and boys—

GEORGE: And pink gins.

LAURA: It must really have been quite a relief when she ran away to London—quite apart from *us*, I mean.

GEORGE: *Must* we discuss Elizabeth?

LAURA: No, dear. She's dead now, poor thing, and it's an ill wind that blows nobody any good. But she wasn't a bad sort in her way.

GEORGE: You didn't have to live with her.

LAURA: No. But we both had to live with *you*—so she and I have something in common.

GEORGE: Are you trying to work up a row, Laura?

LAURA: No, dear. But when you were in love with Elizabeth, I expect she found you just as romantic as *I* found you when you were married to Elizabeth and in love with *me*. She couldn't know, and I couldn't know, that you were the sort of person who goes all pompous the minute he's signed the register.

GEORGE: Look here, my girl, you're trying to irritate me. I won't be irritated. I refuse to discuss my failings, or Elizabeth's failings—

LAURA: Or even *my* failings?

GEORGE: Or even yours. If you're not feeling well, go upstairs and to bed. If you're merely being awkward, go and play bridge with your tabbies.

LAURA: As long as I go.

GEORGE: (*firmly*) Yes. If you once get into this mood you'll go on till midnight. And I will not oblige you by having a scene.

LAURA: Not even for the fun of making it up at the end?

GEORGE: No. You are a baggage, aren't you?

LAURA: Am I? Well, if you won't play, I suppose we'd better make it up now. All over.

(*They kiss*)

I'll go and do my duty at the bridge-table.

GEORGE: Shall I get your coat?

LAURA: It's in the hall. And my umbrella. Is it still raining?

GEORGE: I'll have a look . . . No, it's stopped.

LAURA: Oh, good. (*at door*) Don't wait up for me. Cheerio!

GEORGE: Cheerio!

(*Door shuts behind her. A second or two later, the front-door bangs and Laura's steps go down the path*)

GEORGE: Good Lord! That was a near shave. Usually she's out of the house before we've washed up the dinner-things. This year of grace and victory 1945!—Raining all day, no food, no coal, no servants—

(*Telephone rings*)

Now what the hell's that? (*at receiver*) Hallo! Yes? Who? . . . No, this is Tadbury 462 . . . No, this is Mr George Wilson's house . . . You've got the wrong number. (*slams down receiver*) Silly ass! I thought it was going to be—

(*Doorbell rings*)

There! Now for it!

(*Opening of door and front-door*)

Is that you, Walter? . . . Well, come in, man, come in and let's get the door shut. It's beastly cold. You can put your things on the chest.

WALTER: (*in the hall*) How are you, George? You look much the same.

GEORGE: (*shortly*) I'm all right.

WALTER: Not too delighted at the return of the prodigal cousin? . . . In here?

GEORGE: No, in the dining-room. (*as they enter*) Can't keep on more than one fire these days.

WALTER: What price victory? Looks cosy enough, all the same.

GEORGE: I daresay it does—compared with a cell in—whatever prison you have been adorning with your presence.

WALTER: Of course, you *would* have to get that one in. And anyhow, it was all a frame up by those ruddy police.

GEORGE: Of course; it always is.

WALTER: Three years hard for looting! After doing A.R.P. and salvage ever since the war started, and getting a medal for rescue work. And it wasn't looting. I only put the things in my pocket to keep 'em safe and forget about 'em. It was pure accident.

GEORGE: (*drily*) Quite a common sort of accident, I'm sure. Well, since you are here, you may as well sit down.

WALTER: (*ironically*) That's very friendly of you, George. More than I had the right to expect. Would it run to a drink as well?

GEORGE: I suppose so. (*pouring out a drink*) Laura is very sorry to have missed you, but she has an engagement.

WALTER: Meaning that you knew beforehand she had an engagement and took damned good care not to tell her I was coming.

GEORGE: If you like. As a matter of fact, she's only this minute gone. I wonder you didn't run into her in the street.

WALTER: Just as well I didn't, perhaps. Well, cheers!

GEORGE: Cheers! . . . Now, look here. Let's get down to brass tacks. What are you after? And why the devil didn't you stay in London?

WALTER: There's not much opening in London for anybody that's been put in gaol on a trumped-up charge of looting.

GEORGE: There is still less in Tadbury, I assure you.

WALTER: Besides, I thought my affectionate cousins might be pleased to see me after all these years. Elizabeth was always pleased to see me.

GEORGE: Never mind Elizabeth. What you're doing is cadging for money.

WALTER: You've no right to say 'cadging'. It's a very offensive word. I've just looked in to ask for a little more on account.

GEORGE: On account of what?

WALTER: Come off it! On account of that little service I had the honour and privilege of doing for my dear cousin in 1942. And don't say 'What little service?' because that only wastes time.

GEORGE: My dear Walter, I have never for one moment denied that I was greatly obliged to you for the trouble you took to advise the authorities of the discovery of poor Elizabeth's body, and to assemble the—er—evidence of identity and so on, at a good deal of risk to yourself. And you must admit that I made full acknowledgement at the time, and treated you very generously—

WALTER: Generously! A measly hundred quid. I suppose you thought it was an easy job. All very well for you, sitting here on your backside in a safe area and reserved occupation. You have no idea what an air-raid was like. Besides, it meant a lot of work. I had to get all the things properly fire-marked, and then wait about for a suitable 'incident'—that wasn't as simple in '42 as it would have been earlier on. There weren't so many of them and everything was much better organized. And even then I had to crawl about looking for the right sort of stiff and plant the evidence properly and see there wasn't anything else to give the show away. That bracelet. How'd you like to try sticking a bracelet on the arm of somebody who's been roasted to a cinder? It would turn your fat tummy up. You wouldn't do it for twenty hundred quid. Bah! Give me another drink.

GEORGE: What in the world are you trying to insinuate?

WALTER: I'm saying that I was grossly underpaid for the risk and trouble of faking that body to look like Bessie.

GEORGE: I haven't the faintest idea what you're talking about.

WALTER: (*slight pause*) Oh! So that's your line, is it? Play the innocent, eh? Are you going to deny that six months after Bessie disappeared, you wrote to me to say that you were in a very awkward position, that you couldn't imagine why she hadn't written, that you thought she must have been killed in an air-raid, and that you'd give me a hundred pounds to know for certain?

GEORGE: No, I don't deny that. It wasn't a very nice letter, and I'm sorry I wrote it. But naturally it's very worrying, not knowing whether you're married or not; and if Elizabeth *was* dead, I wanted to do the right thing by Laura—

WALTER: And to cash in on Bessie's bit of capital she left you in her will.

GEORGE: That never entered my head. But I was anxious and upset, and I admit writing the letter.

WALTER: That's just as well, because I've got it here in my pocket. Are you going to deny that I wrote back saying I'd look out for Bessie, but if I found her I'd have to do something to identify her?

GEORGE: Certainly I deny it. You never answered my letter at all. I thought it very callous of you.

WALTER: Then I suppose you'll deny sending me a parcel with a gold-topped umbrella with her initials, and an inscribed bracelet and a locket with your own precious picture inside.

GEORGE: I deny that absolutely. She took the things away with her, and you found them on her, and I identified them afterwards. Are you going to say that you can produce the wrapping-paper and a label in my handwriting with the date and the Tadbury postmark and a schedule of contents?

WALTER: No, I'm not. Because you were cunning enough to type the address and post the things from Manchester.

GEORGE: Was I? (*sarcastically*) I am glad to know you credit me with so much sense.

WALTER: And if I were to show that letter of yours to Laura— or to the police—wouldn't they think it a very odd coincidence that after you'd heard nothing of Bessie for six months, I should happen on her body only a few weeks *after* you'd offered me a hundred quid for proof of her death?

GEORGE: Very odd indeed. Coincidences sometimes are very odd. But you're surely not going to the police to inform them—quite gratuitously—that you practised a heartless fraud on your unsuspecting cousin in the hope that he might—from a pure sense of honour—give you the hundred pounds he had thoughtlessly mentioned in a casual way in a letter?

WALTER: I might go to Laura.

GEORGE: Go to Laura by all means. She's not likely to believe you.

WALTER: Laura's got sense. She'd want to know, if it was me that planned the fraud, how did I get hold of Bessie's things?

GEORGE: She'd think you stole them. Or looted them, if you prefer the word. Elizabeth took them with her to London. If, as you say, the body you found them on wasn't Elizabeth's, you must have pinched them from her. Was that it? Was Elizabeth with *you* all the time, while I was going half-potty and writing you distracted letters? You damned twister! You— my God! I see the whole thing. It *was* Elizabeth's body. *You* were the lover she ran off to in London. You murdered Elizabeth and threw her into a burning building. And now you have the infernal cheek to come here blackmailing me with this fantastic story about a fraud! Get out of the house— get out before I ring up the police!

WALTER: So that's the game, is it? That's the game! And what would you say if I proved to you that Bessie was still alive—?

GEORGE: That's a damned lie!

(*Momentary pause and a crash of crockery off*)

WALTER: Hell's bells, what's that?

GEORGE: It came from the kitchen.

WALTER: Probably the cat.

GEORGE: We don't keep a cat. (*opening door of hatch with slight click*) Laura! How long have you been snooping there with your head in the serving-hatch?

LAURA: Practically all the time. The story got *so* exciting I upset the coffee pot. Good evening, Walter.

WALTER: Hallo, Laura. George said you'd gone out.

LAURA: I went out by the front and came in by the back. George was so keen to get rid of me that I thought you must be his fancy girl or something. You're looking very well. How did you like being a guest of Royalty, so to speak? Did you get the same lousy rations as we do?

GEORGE: For God's sake, Laura—

LAURA: Yes, dear! It is *too* absurd to stand chattering through a wall like Pyramus and Thisbe, isn't it? I'll come round.

(*She shuts the serving hatch*)

GEORGE: (*with gloomy triumph*) Well, you can't demand hush-money now to keep things from Laura.

WALTER: I suppose you planted her there on purpose.

GEORGE: I did not. You heard what she said.

WALTER: Then, if you hadn't anything to conceal from her, why did you hustle her out of the house?

GEORGE: Because I don't choose that my wife should associate with gaol-birds.

LAURA: (*entering*) Now then, darlings, let's get this straight. Sit down, everybody, and, George, give me a drink. It was awfully cold in that kitchen. George, we simply must have those loose boards seen to. They creak like fury. Rotten for detective-work. And the lino's getting awful. What's the good of being in the building trade if you can't wangle yourself some priority lino?

Thanks, angel. Cheers! Well, now. *You* say Elizabeth went up to Town on one of her usual jaunts—which day was it again?

GEORGE: Third of December 1941.

LAURA: So it was. She went away saying she'd be back in a week or so, and that was the last you heard of her.

GEORGE: I had one postcard.

LAURA: I had forgotten the postcard.

WALTER: Where from?

GEORGE: There wasn't any address. I imagined she was staying at Pettibank's Hotel as usual. She just said she'd had a good journey and I wasn't to worry about air-raids.

LAURA: Elizabeth was always very brave about air-raids. She never let *them* stop her going up to Town.

GEORGE: *Nothing* would stop her going up to Town every three months or so. She said she got the hump in Tadbury.

LAURA: I do sympathise. Sorry, George, but I do. Well, after that—

GEORGE: After about ten days I got the wind up

LAURA: She hardly ever stayed in London more than a week.

GEORGE: I wrote to her twice and got no answer. And then I wrote to Pettibank's and they said she hadn't been there. So I didn't know what to think. At least, I thought I *did* know what to think. But Walter knows all this. I told him.

LAURA: Yes, darling. But I like to get things clear. Weeks grew into months, as it says in the penny novelettes, and then you got worried and wrote Walter a silly letter.

GEORGE: And about a month after *that*, Walter announced that he had found Elizabeth's body in the wreck of a bombed cinema. And produced proof. And now he says—

LAURA: Yes, I know. I heard him. *You* say, Walter, that you wrote to George offering to fake up the body of some total stranger and pretend it was Elizabeth if he would send you the wherewithal. And that he sent you an umbrella and a bangle and a locket—

GEORGE: I deny that.

LAURA: George denies it, and you can't prove it.

WALTER: No.

LAURA: No. But you say you did the fake and he gave you a hundred pounds on the strength of it.

WALTER: Quite right.

LAURA: And now *you* say, George, that Walter is making all this up, under the impression that you would pay him more money for not letting *me* know that Elizabeth was—or might have been—alive after you and I got married. It's a bit late for that now, isn't it? Because I do know. There's the police, of course—but you didn't really mean to go to them, did you Walter? You must have had about enough of the police.

GEORGE:
WALTER: } Yes—but look here, Laura—

LAURA: Wait a bit; I'm coming to that. George says that *either* it was Elizabeth's body you found in the cinema *or* that if it wasn't you must have gone to see Elizabeth in Town and pinched her belongings (in which case, what's become of Elizabeth?), or *else* that you . . . George! You didn't really mean to suggest that Walter had done away with poor Elizabeth?

GEORGE: Well—I don't know what I did. I think, and I've always thought, that she died in the air-raid. But if—as *he* says—she didn't, then, as *you* say, what's become of her?

LAURA: That's the point. Because Walter says she's still alive.

WALTER: No I don't. I was saying, when George called me a liar, that she *was* alive last autumn. And I've got a letter from her to prove it.

GEORGE: Nonsense.

LAURA: Why is it nonsense, George? Walter may be telling the truth.

GEORGE: I tell you he isn't.

LAURA: I mean about the fake. Not, of course, about your being a party to it.

GEORGE: He couldn't tell the truth if he tried. Besides, last autumn he was in Wormwood Scrubs or somewhere.

LAURA: I daresay they deliver letters to Wormwood Scrubs. Don't they, Walter?

WALTER: It wasn't Wormwood Scrubs.

LAURA: What a pity. It's such a lovely name. *Do* they deliver letters wherever it was?

WALTER: Sometimes. But as a matter of fact this was sent to my old digs, and I got it when I came out. My landlady kept all my stuff for me.

LAURA: Sweet of her. Well, let's have the letter. It'll be nice to get a real bit of evidence, instead of all this argument and calling names.

WALTER: All right. Here you are . . . Now then, George, don't snatch. You might burn it or swallow it or something. I'll read it to you: 'Pettibank's Hotel, Judd Street, Bloomsbury, 12 September 1944. Cheerio Walter! Here we are, back again at the old stand. Come round and see us if you're on the loose. This is a good pub, and we'll rustle you a drink, war or no war. Here's hoping—Bessie' . . . Well, George, what about it? Of course, she didn't know I wasn't in a position to take advantage of her invitation.

GEORGE: (*slowly*) You wrote that yourself.

WALTER: Me? Now, look here, Laura; I won't trust George but I'll trust *you*. Catch hold. Is that, or is it not, Bessie's writing?

LAURA: Yes.

(*George gives a faint yelp*)

Yes, George, it is. One simply couldn't mistake Elizabeth's writing, even in pencil. She wrote that, all right. Well, I always thought she was rather a remarkable woman.

WALTER: What's remarkable about it?

LAURA: She was so faithful to old friends. 'This is a good pub and we'll rustle you a drink.' Written on a perfectly clean bit of hotel notepaper, on 12 September 1944. And on the *seventh* of September 1944, Pettibank's Hotel got a direct hit from a doodlebug, and was gutted from roof to basement.

GEORGE: ⎫
⎬ What?!
WALTER: ⎭

LAURA: But Elizabeth still calls it 'a good pub' and is completely confident that it can furnish Walter with a drink . . . No, Walter, I'm sorry, but it won't wash. The story wasn't in the papers, of course, even if the papers penetrate to Wormwood Scrubs.

(*Walter utters a protesting snort*)

But you really ought to have had a look at the place before you came up to Tadbury.

WALTER: It may be burnt down now. That doesn't say it was *then*. Your damn pat with your seventh of September. How do you come to know such a lot about it?

LAURA: Because I was in Judd Street on the 8th of September and it was still smoking then. You remember, George? That was the day I went up to London to visit an old friend who was ill and wanted to see me before he died. He lived in Doughty Street, and my taxi went through Judd Street on the way from King's Cross. You've probably got it in your diary—but anyhow, they'll be a record of the 'incident' somewhere, and you could easily verify it . . . That letter was written in September 'forty-*one*, wasn't it, Walter? Elizabeth's last trip *before* the last one? And you just put in a couple of extra pencil strokes and turned the one into a four.

WALTER: Oh, hell! . . . Here, give me the letter back.

LAURA: No, I think not.

GEORGE: I should jolly well think not. You get out, and be thankful I don't charge you with forgery and attempted blackmail.

WALTER: Oh, well! I thought it was worth trying. You never know your luck. Laura was too smart for me, that's all. Because the blinking hotel. It might have picked some other night to be burnt down . . . All the same, I still say you were dammed mean. Because you know damn well you did send me those things.

GEORGE: That's quite enough about it. Don't start all over again.

WALTER: Or if it wasn't you, it was Laura. Same thing. Don't try to hide behind a silly quibble. Did you send them, Laura?

LAURA: I most certainly did not. Nobody sent them. You found them on the body.

GEORGE: Your whole story's a bluffing blackmail trick.

LAURA: That letter gives the game right away.

WALTER: All right, all right. I've chucked the game. You've won. You've got me into a position where you can deny everything and I can't prove anything, and nobody's going to believe what I say. I agree, and it's my own damned fault. But that doesn't prevent my knowing what I do now. Why the blazes can't you admit it, just between ourselves? It's not as though we'd done anybody any harm. If it's Laura you're thinking of—

LAURA: Don't anybody mind *me*.

WALTER: You needn't worry, Laura. Even if Bessie is alive—

GEORGE: I tell you she's not alive.

LAURA: I really don't think she can be, or she'd have turned up by now.

GEORGE: Laura! You're not pretending to believe this preposterous story of Walter's?

LAURA: (*evenly*) I'm not pretending to believe it for a moment. Though of course, speaking quite impartially, and overlooking Walter's rather amateur effort at forgery, it's simply your word against his. I'm only agreeing with Walter that no harm would have been done even if his story were true. If Elizabeth is alive she's obviously in no hurry to reclaim George, and if she's dead, all anybody has done is to provide her with a body and a marble tombstone. There'd be a trifle of bigamy, of course; but only technical. I mean, we could always take shelter from the police behind the tombstone. So where's the harm?

WALTER: That's what I say. Always supposing Bessie is alive— or that she died fair.

GEORGE: What the hell do you mean by that?

WALTER: Well, if Bessie went to London and died, or was killed in an air-raid, O.K. No harm's done, and you're sitting pretty. But suppose she never went to London at all.

GEORGE: I absolutely refuse to suppose anything of the kind. Here! What are you getting at?

LAURA: Come, Walter, everybody knows Elizabeth went to London. She told lots of people she was going. And George's charlady said at the inquiry how she had helped her pack two suitcases and left her having tea. And Elizabeth told her she was catching the 5.35. Don't you remember?

WALTER: I know Bessie meant to go to London. But what's to prove she ever got there? What's to prove she ever started, eh?

GEORGE: Nonsense!

WALTER: You never found the taxi that took her to the station, did you?

GEORGE: We never looked for it. Nobody was fool enough to suggest she hadn't gone to London. Besides, she might have taken a bus.

WALTER: Bessie take a bus? With two suitcases? She'd rather have missed the train. Did anybody see her leave the house?

GEORGE: It was a November evening. Rather foggy. And no street-lamps.

WALTER: And she was never actually traced to London. Now, was she?

GEORGE: Trace one middle-aged woman on a crowded main-line train in the middle of a war in the black-out? Don't be an ass. Besides, why should we try to trace her?

WALTER: But you *know* she never arrived at Pettibank's Hotel.

GEORGE: (*stiffly*) We thought there was a reason for that.

WALTER: And if so there might be. A damn good reason. Bessie was alone in the house, wasn't she, after the char left?

GEORGE: I suppose so. But—

WALTER: So if you'd come back early from the office and said 'Pop into the car, darling, and I'll run you up to the station', you could have carried her off and disposed of her in some handy place—

GEORGE: (*triumphantly*) There's where you're mistaken. I hadn't got a car. Put it down in 1940. Couldn't afford one.

WALTER: (*slightly disconcerted*) Oh! (*recovering*) Well, there are other ways to dispose of people. You'd got all night.

GEORGE: (*explosively*) Now, see here!

LAURA: (*quietly*) No, Walter, he hadn't . . . You may as well tell him, George.

GEORGE: I don't see why.

LAURA: I don't mind. We may as well get this silly idea out of his head.

GEORGE: As you like. I got home from the office at 5:15, found that Elizabeth had gone, and went straight round to Laura's place.

LAURA: George dined with me, and stayed all night—if you really must know.

GEORGE: So you can put that in your pipe and smoke it.

LAURA: (*reasonably*) George could hardly have disposed of a corpse and two suitcases all in five minutes, could he?

GEORGE: And the daily woman came in at eight in the morning to get my breakfast. She'd probably have noticed if she'd seen Elizabeth lying about. (*with heavy sarcasm*) Unless she swept her up and threw her away accidentally. You'd better ask her.

WALTER: Did she notice that *you* weren't there?

GEORGE: (*grimly*) She did. And it cost me a fiver.

WALTER: Well, Laura, it's all very well for you to alibi George. But who's to say you didn't do the job between you?

LAURA: Why, of course, Walter! How brilliant of you! George disposes of Elizabeth in the back garden, while I hold the torch and warn him if I hear the Air-Raid Warden coming. Or, alternatively, I do the digging and George holds the torch. And we swear, quite truly, that we were together the whole time. Only, why on earth should I want to do away with Elizabeth?

WALTER: To marry George, of course.

LAURA: There! What a tangled web we weave when first we practise to deceive! I couldn't have wanted to marry George.

WALTER: George said—

LAURA: *George* wanted to marry *me*. But I knew I couldn't marry George. In fact, I'm not married to him now.

GEORGE: } What?!
WALTER: }

LAURA: No. I'm sorry, George. I suppose I ought to have told you before. The sick friend I went to see in London wasn't exactly a friend. He was my husband.

GEORGE: Good God! You always said you were a widow.

LAURA: (*sweetly*) A grass-widow, darling. Poor Harry was always rather unreliable. He deserted me ages before I ever met you. So I pretended he was dead. It sounded more respectable.

GEORGE: Upon my word!

LAURA: So you see, Walter, I had really nothing to gain by Elizabeth's death. In fact, it was rather jollier on the whole having George without having to look after him. Nothing cools down romance so much has looking after people. Naturally, after you'd found poor Elizabeth, I felt I *ought* to look after him, and I couldn't very well live in his house unless we were supposed to be married. But I must say I often wish Elizabeth was back—yes, I do, George, when you're fussy and pompous and grumble about the rations. And then poor Harry—he was *rather* sweet when the end came—sending for me and apologising for having treated me so badly. It's extraordinary how charming men can be when you hardly ever see them . . . So there it is, Walter. I didn't spend that night burying Elizabeth. As a matter of fact you can prove I was at home, because the police came round about a light showing in the scullery and I had to go down and let them in—don't you remember, George, how agitated you got for fear they should find out you were there?

GEORGE: What? Oh, yes—yes, of course. *Need* we go into all this?

LAURA: Only to set Walter's mind at rest, dear . . . The policeman was quite horrid and wouldn't believe that the light went on of its own accord, and I was fined three pounds.

WALTER: Seems to have been an expensive night for both of you.

LAURA: It was, really. So I thought on the whole it would come cheaper to pretend to marry George. Anyway, I do hope you're quite satisfied now. Unless, of course, you would like to blackmail *me* about the bigamy—Harry, I mean, and all that.

WALTER: I don't believe a single word you say. Either of you.

LAURA: And we don't believe a single word *you* say. Either of us. So that makes it quite fair all round. Especially as George looks as though he didn't believe a word *I* say.

GEORGE: I don't know what to think. I suppose I've got to believe you.

LAURA: Don't let any of us believe anybody. Let's leave the whole thing a mystery. Either Walter killed Elizabeth and he's trying to put it on George; or George killed Elizabeth and is trying to put it on Walter; or I killed Elizabeth and am, most considerately, not trying to put it on anybody; or George and I both killed Elizabeth and she vanished into thin air; or Elizabeth isn't dead at all and George and I have committed a double bigamy, or—which is much the most convenient and comfortable thing to believe—Elizabeth was really killed in the air-raid, and Walter really found her, and he's only trying now to push up the price a little by telling a not-very-convincing story backed up by a totally unconvincing forgery. Don't you think you'd better leave it at that, Walter? Especially as it's the only story there is any evidence for at all? Or is ever likely to be? Unless, of course, one of these days Elizabeth were to come walking in as large as life—

GEORGE: She won't do that. I mean—

LAURA: I agree it's not likely, after all this time. Even if Walter were telling the truth.

GEORGE: Which he isn't.

LAURA: So you see, Walter; your only hope of making anything more out of this little transaction is to produce Elizabeth alive—

WALTER: Or dead.

GEORGE: Damnation! I'm not going to stand any more of this. First Walter comes along trying to get money out of me with a preposterous story accusing me of a heartless fraud. Then my wife spies on me, lacerates my most sacred feelings and says she isn't my wife after all. Then I'm accused of murder—

WALTER: You accused me of murder first.

GEORGE: I shouldn't put it past you.

LAURA: George, please—

GEORGE: Shut up! And Walter, you can go to hell. Belle's dead, and you won't find her body—

WALTER: You sound damn sure of it.

GEORGE: Of course I'm sure.

LAURA: Naturally. You've found it already. You can't make a career of finding Elizabeth's body. Now, run along, Walter. Here's a fiver for you to get a bed for the night—

GEORGE: I forbid you to give him money.

LAURA: I'm not your wife, George, and you can't forbid me. Here's the money, Walter, and that's all you'll get. I'm keeping this letter of yours, and if ever you come here again I shall know what to do with it.

WALTER: Thanks, Laura. I like you. You've got guts.

GEORGE: And now clear out before I put you out.

WALTER: Right-oh! Good night, Laura.

LAURA: Good night. George will see you to the door.

GEORGE: I most certainly will.

(*They go out to the hall*)

LAURA: My God! I need a drink after that. (*pours one*)

GEORGE: (*in the hall*) *Now* what do you want?

WALTER: My hat.

GEORGE: Take your damned hat. *And* your coat. And get out.

(*Front-door slams. Laura pours out another drink*)

GEORGE: (*entering*) Look here, Laura, why on earth did you give that swine anything? You only come back for more.

LAURA: I thought it was the least we could do, after brazenly denying his perfectly true story.

GEORGE: True? (*warily*) You don't mean to say you fell for that letter of his? *Wasn't* that hotel burnt down?

LAURA: Oh, yes. The letter was a forgery all right. So I took advantage of it and backed you up in contradicting the whole thing. But the rest of the story was true . . . Don't bother to tell lies about it. I saw Elizabeth's umbrella in this house ages after she—disappeared.

GEORGE: You did, did you? . . . Well . . . Well, as you said yourself, even if we did fake up a little bit of evidence, there's no harm done. You don't really believe that Elizabeth's still alive, do you?

LAURA: I am sure she's not.

GEORGE: Then that's alright. I'm sorry I had to be rough with Walter, but once you give way to a blackmailer you never get rid of him. And I paid him quite well. Perhaps I ought to have told you. But it seemed a simple way out of it. If we'd waited to presume death in the ordinary legal way, it might have taken years. And there was the will to be proved. And we wanted to get married, didn't we? . . .

(*Laura does not answer*)

Laura! You stood by me like a brick. I'm very grateful. That *was* all a story for Walter's benefit, wasn't it? About your husband, I mean?

LAURA: No. That was perfectly true. I can show you the marriage certificate, and the death certificate if you like.

GEORGE: Good heavens! . . . But he *is* dead. There's nothing to prevent us from getting married *now*.

LAURA: Nothing—provided I agree.

GEORGE: Provided you agree? But my dear girl, why shouldn't you agree? We've been very happy together, haven't we? You say you don't feel romantic any more, but one can't expect romance to last for ever. I'm very fond of you; you always said you were fond of me. What have you got against me? Surely not that little bit of harmless fabrication about the evidence? Anyway, you've accepted that. You've been on my side all through. You—you're not going to desert me now. I can't believe it. Laura, you *will* marry me, won't you?

LAURA: Is it worth while? Everybody thinks we are married already.

GEORGE: Yes; but naturally I want us to be properly married. After all you've done for me, it's only right.

LAURA: Not only right, but necessary. Isn't it? From your point of view.

GEORGE: Why do you say, from *my* point of view?

LAURA: Because a wife cannot in law give evidence against her husband.

GEORGE: (*hoarsely*) You're mad. What evidence?

LAURA: That at six o'clock in the morning after Elizabeth— vanished, you came round to my house, looking extremely hot and agitated, and asked me, if anybody made enquiries, to pretend you had been with me all night.

GEORGE: I explained that at the time.

LAURA: You told me a rather thin story about having had a lot of drinks and got into a row with some American soldiers. And thinking you might have been recognized and that it wouldn't do you any good at the office. You'd have done better to stay at home and sit tight. Because nobody ever did make any inquiry. But you made the usual mistake of trying to cover up. And then, after all, you couldn't trust me, and thought you'd better marry me and shut my mouth. So Elizabeth's body *had* to be found—in London . . . Just as a matter of interest, what did you use? For the real body, I mean? Quick-lime? Or concrete?

GEORGE: This is fantastic—

LAURA: You could easily get them, I suppose, being in the building trade. They both make a nice airtight grave. But they both preserve the body.

GEORGE: Once and for all I emphatically deny this monstrous accusation which you and Walter seem to be conspiring to—

LAURA: It's no good, George. I know where the body is.

GEORGE: You know *what*?

LAURA: You gave yourself away. Didn't you notice? Don't you know what you said to Walter? You said 'Belle's dead and you won't find her body'. Belle! Why did you call her Belle? What put that name into your head? Belle Elmore was Crippen's wife, wasn't she? Where did Crippen put his wife? What was the link between Elizabeth and Belle Elmore?

GEORGE: You're hysterical, Laura. It was a slip of the tongue. And anyhow, I can't believe I ever said any such thing.

LAURA: Very well. I must have been mistaken. Yes, George; we'll *prove* I'm mistaken. We'll send for a man tomorrow *to take up those boards in the kitchen.*

GEORGE: (*beaten*) No. No.

LAURA: I thought not . . . I sometimes wondered—but I never

knew, till tonight. And I've stood in that kitchen, cooking your dinner. On those creaky boards. I explained of the creaky boards! I said (*laughing convulsively*), I said they were rotten for detective-work!

GEORGE: Stop it! Stop it! (*he smacks her face*) Pull yourself together.

LAURA: Leave me alone! (*she recovers herself*) George, I can't forgive that.

GEORGE: What are you going to do about it?

LAURA: Nothing. So long as I walk straight out of this house and never set foot—*there*—again.

GEORGE: How do I know you won't go to the police?

LAURA: You'll have to trust me. After all, I didn't let you on to Walter.

GEORGE: I suppose you thought you could make more out of it yourself. See here, my girl, I'm not going to put up with being blackmailed by *you*. You'll damn well marry me and sit tight and hold your tongue. Get that. If not—

LAURA: Let go. You're breaking my wrist.

GEORGE: If not, you can go and join Elizabeth. D'you hear?

LAURA: You can't do that twice and get away with it.

GEORGE: We'd see about that. And if I'm going to be hanged I may as well be hanged for the two of you. Two can die as cheaply as one. So that's where *you* come unstuck.

LAURA: (*slowly*) I see. I suppose we're more or less both in the same boat by now. All right, George. I'll stay put. And I'll marry you, if you like—

GEORGE: (*immensely relieved, and laying on the emotion with a trowel*) You will! That's my good girl. That's my dear, faithful Laura. I knew you wouldn't let me down. Forgive those dreadful things I said. I've been under such a strain. I didn't know what I was doing. And I only did it because I loved you. Darling! You do mean it? You will marry me?

LAURA: I've told you I will. (*with a complete change of tone—*

very hard, bright and quick) Though of course it's not the sort of murder I like to be associated with. So dreadfully amateurish. Such a mistake to have alibis and accomplices. So silly and impatient to fake unnecessary evidence and get blackmailed. So stupid to saddle yourself with a body, so that you don't even let your house. One should always aim for a *natural*-looking death and a nice, presentable body. Still—I've said I'll marry you, and I will—if you like to take the risk.

GEORGE: What risk?

LAURA: (*very brisk and bright indeed*) Well, dear, husbands can be a nuisance just as much as wives. I didn't finish telling you about Harry. It's true that he was my husband. And it's true that he didn't die till last year. But he wasn't apologetic and repentant. He made himself very unpleasant. And he didn't die of his own accord. I killed him. And the body was *quite* presentable . . .

DOROTHY L. SAYERS

Dorothy Leigh Sayers was born on 13 June 1893 in Oxford where her father was chaplain at the cathedral and headmaster of the choristers' school. By 1901, the Reverend Henry Sayers and his family moved to Huntingdsonshire, where he had been appointed rector of Bluntisham-cum-Earith, a village whose people and landscape would echo in Sayers' most celebrated crime novel, *The Nine Tailors* (1934).

From 1909 to 1912 Sayers attended the Godolphin School in Salisbury as a boarder. A model pupil, she excelled in all subjects, achieving distinctions in her higher certificate examinations in French, German and English. She was also active in school life, including playing the violin in the school orchestra, appearing as the Princess Graciosa in a play presented by her house in 1910, *The Ten Dancing Princesses*, and reciting a poem, 'Panache', at a school celebration.

In 1911, Sayers achieved the highest mark in the whole of England in the Cambridge Higher Local Examinations. And in 1912 the Gilchrist Educational Trust awarded her a scholarship in modern languages and medieval literature at Somerville College, Oxford. Sayers graduated with a first-class honours degree in 1915. In parallel with her studies, she formed the women-only Mutual Admiration Society with a small number of other female students, including the historian Muriel St Clare Byrne, with whom she would collaborate on the play that became her final novel, *Busman's Honeymoon* (1937). While at Somerville, Sayers also sang in the choir and wrote, directed and acted in several dramatic productions including *Pied Pipings*, the 'Going Down' play for 1915, as well as contributing to several editions of the annual anthology of *Oxford Poetry* and publishing a collection of her own verse.

In line with the antediluvian attitudes of the times, Sayers did not receive her university degrees formally until 1920, one of the first women to do so. While opinions vary as to how far Sayers can be regarded as a feminist, she was throughout her life a humanist, albeit one with strong religious beliefs. Her libertarian outlook is exemplified by her decision to contribute a sapphic ode and another poem to the sole issue of *The Quorum*, a discreet 'magazine of friendship' produced by the British Society for the Study of Sex Psychology, which campaigned against discrimination, and the Order of Chaeronea, a secret society with similar aims. While sympathetic to the mission of these organizations, Sayers had affairs with two married men. In 1924 she gave birth to a son, John Anthony Sayers, who was raised by her aunt and cousin but eventually adopted by Sayers and her husband 'Mac' Fleming, whom she had married in 1926.

On coming down from Oxford, Sayers joined the London advertising agency, S. H. Benson. It was while working for Benson's as a copywriter on campaigns for Guinness and Colman's Mustard, and authoring *The Recipe Book of the Mustard Club* (1926), that Sayers wrote her first novel, *Whose Body?* (1923). It features the Oxford-educated Lord Peter Wimsey, who would go on to become one of the best-loved detectives of the Golden Age of crime and detective fiction. He appears in eleven novels by Sayers, including *Murder Must Advertise* (1933) which was inspired by the author's time at Benson's, 21 collected short stories as well as 'The Locked Room' (which was published for the first time in 2019 in *Bodies from the Library 2*) and a handful of unfinished stories.

In addition to chronicling Wimsey's life and investigations, Sayers was an active member of the Detection Club, a dining club for crime writers not wholly dissimilar to the Mutual Admiration Society, and she edited three superb volumes of *Great Stories of Mystery, Detection and Horror*. Together with her insightful reviews for the *Sunday Times* newspaper and elsewhere, Sayers played a major part in countering the damage done to the reputation of crime writers by the tsunami of badly written and poorly plotted mysteries in the 1920s and 1930s.

However, although Sayers is rightly regarded as a giant of the crime and mystery genre, she is also respected as a religious thinker. She was widely praised for her Christian radio plays, *He That Should Come* (1938), the twelve plays that comprise *The Man Born to be King* (1941–1942) and *The Just Vengeance* (1947), all of which have been broadcast many times. A formidable linguist, she also produced a remarkably accurate but highly accessible translation of Dante's *Divine Comedy*, which was completed after her death by her god-daughter Barbara Reynolds, author of the definitive biography, *Dorothy L. Sayers: Her Life and Soul* (1993).

Dorothy L. Sayers—one must never forget the 'L'—died at 24 Newland Street in Witham, Essex on 17 December 1957. Today a fine statue of the author stands opposite the house; it was erected by the Dorothy L. Sayers Society (www.sayers.org.uk), formed in 1976 to promote appreciation of the many aspects of Sayers' life and work. At her death, she left unfinished a final Lord Peter Wimsey novel, *Thrones, Dominations*. Many years later this was completed by Jill Paton Walsh, who went on to publish three more continuation novels and was working on a fourth when she died on 18 October 2020.

'Where Do We Go from Here?' was first broadcast on the BBC Light Programme on 24 February 1948 for *Mystery Playhouse*, a series of six plays written by members of the Detection Club in order to raise funds for the Club. The script is published here for the first time.

BENEFIT OF THE DOUBT

Anthony Berkeley

I have based the following story upon facts related to me by an elderly medical man who declared that the experience actually befell him in the early days of practice.

It has been necessary, of course, to alter the names of the persons concerned and to make certain changes in locality; but the doctor who furnished me with this story is no longer alive.

If Dr Charles Harvey had not been so young a man, the course of several lives might have been very different.

In the first place, had he had more experience of general practice, he would probably not have turned out at midnight to go to see a patient who appeared, so far as he could make out, to be suffering from nothing worse than a mild stomach ache.

He would have lulled the man's wife, when she came to fetch him, with fair words, made up a bottle of something soothing with a little bismuth and a lot of sodium bicarbonate, and promised to call the next morning.

But that is just what he did not do.

The summons came when he was half undressed, the night-bell shrilling its impatience in the corner of his bedroom. Huddling a dressing-gown round him, he went down to the front door.

A woman's form, indistinct in the darkness, confronted him.

'Is that you, doctor? Will you please come round and see my husband, Mr Spately, 63, Westdean Road? He's been taken very queer.'

Her voice was calm and well modulated. If she felt agitated she certainly did not show it.

Harvey took her into his consulting-room, and asked the usual questions.

She sat, a slim, almost prim figure, dressed in neat black, her cotton-gloved hands folded in her lap, and answered his questions in a voice so low as to be almost toneless.

Harvey was quite young enough to notice with interest that her face, though curiously pale, was distinctly pretty. He set her age at about twenty-six.

She seemed vague about her husband's symptoms, but Harvey was not surprised at that; most people were vague about the symptoms of others.

All he could really make out was that her husband had been taken queer not long after supper with pains in the stomach, and she thought a doctor ought to see him.

Harvey did try to demur, but with a quiet firmness in odd contrast to her demure manner she persisted.

She was very worried about her husband; he had been taken very queer; the doctor must please come back with her at once.

Harvey allowed himself to be overridden.

He was helped to his decision by a surreptitious consulting of his index of panel patients. The name of Spately did not appear on it. They must be private patients, therefore—and Harvey could not neglect private patients.

Old Dr Jamieson, from whom he had bought the practice five months before, had neglected it terribly during the last few years; Harvey was having an anxious time working it up again; and if panel patients mean bread-and-butter, private ones mean the jam on it.

He hurried upstairs, dressed again, and went down to get out his ancient car

Westdean Road was one of the new streets on the outskirts of the town, neither a pleasant road nor an unpleasant one, just nondescript.

But the lace curtains in all the windows looked clean, and each house had a strip of garden in front of it. There was nothing to distinguish No. 63 from any of the others.

Mrs Spately hurried out of the car before he could reach over and open the door for her, and almost ran up the three yards of garden-path, latchkey already in hand.

A most devoted wife, thought Harvey annoyingly; in spite of that repressed manner of hers, she must be really upset. He was glad he had come.

Following her along the tiny hall and up the stairs, he noted with approval, too, the really beautiful lines of her figure, which her long black coat did not altogether hide, and the silky, almost feline grace with which she moved.

Her eyes, he had noticed, were a peculiarly vivid shade of light blue, and had nothing of the usual rather doll-like effect of blue eyes. Without doubt the girl had character.

In the room into which she led him a man was lying in the big bed—a large, fat, jovial man, with a red face and a large bald patch on the top of his head, who must have been forty-five if he was a day.

'Mr Spately?' queried Harvey. The man's appearance had come as a surprise to him, in contrast to the woman's youth.

The man waved a podgy, white hand. 'Ha, doctor! Afraid you've had a journey for nothing, but you know what these women are.' He winked largely.

Dr Harvey smiled professionally and, setting his bag on the chair by the bed, prepared to make his examination. 'Well, Mr Spately, what is it you complain of?'

'Me? Why, nothing,' laughed the man, apparently much amused. 'It's the wife who's been doing the complaining.'

'But you've had some pain?'

'Well, just a touch of indigestion after supper, but nothing to make a fuss about. But off she packed me to bed, with a hot--water bottle on me tummy and Lord knows what, and wouldn't be satisfied till she had brought you along too.

'Fact is, doctor,' said the man, with another large wink, 'the ladies enjoy a bit of fussing, eh?

'They like to get a chap on his back in bed, out of mischief, and then pretend they're saving his life with hot-water bottles and things, eh? Bless their hearts!'

He laughed again, enormously.

'But you must have felt bad?'

Harvey's irritation at having been brought out on such an apparently purposeless errand was gradually overcoming even his satisfaction over the Spateleys being private patients.

'My husband has really been much worse than he pretends,' said the woman's level monotone behind him. 'He never was one to make a fuss. Please examine him, doctor.'

Harvey complied, to a running accompaniment of jests from the patient. The result bore out completely Mr Spateley's own diagnosis.

So far as Harvey could make out (though certainly his examination was somewhat perfunctory), there was absolutely nothing the matter with him.

But for all that, one does not tell a patient that he is in bed on false pretences—at least, not when one has been in practice such a short time.

'Humph!' said Harvey, stroking his chin and looking his most professional. 'Nothing very serious, Mr Spately. Slight acidity. I'll send you round a bottle of medicine tomorrow morning.'

'Not ready to be measured for my little coffin yet, then?' grinned the patient.

'Certainly not. And there's no need for you to stay in bed.'

'Hear that, Millie? There's nothing wrong with me. Tell her again, doctor. Though even then I doubt whether she'll believe you.'

Harvey took his leave.

In the hall downstairs Mrs Spately caught his arm. 'Well, doctor?'

'Well?'

'I mean, of course he's worse than you said. Is it—serious?'

'My dear Mrs Spately,' answered Harvey, as courteously as he could, 'there is practically nothing the matter with him. A little bicarbonate of soda, if you've got any in the house, is all he needs. You've been alarming yourself unnecessarily.'

She looked at him stolidly, her pretty face quite wooden. 'I'm sorry if I've bothered you for nothing. I thought he was very ill. He was very bad before you came, I'm sure.'

'Well, if he gets worse, send for me again,' Harvey said impatiently. 'But there's nothing for you to alarm yourself about. I'll send round the medicine first thing.'

As he shut the front gate he glanced back to look at her. She was standing in the lighted doorway, gazing after him stonily. Harvey shrugged his shoulders. Wifely devotion is all very well, but it has its irritating sides.

But the next morning Harvey received a severe shock. Scarcely had he begun his breakfast when his housekeeper appeared to announce that a lady was in the waiting-room and wished to see him at once, urgently; a Mrs Spately.

'Good heavens!' Harvey groaned to himself. 'Isn't she ever going to leave me in peace?'

He gulped down some coffee and finished his bacon in two mouthfuls.

'You've come for the medicine?' he said, almost curtly, as the black-clad figure rose to meet him. 'I said I'd send it, but if you—'

'No, doctor, I haven't come for the medicine,' she interrupted him quietly. 'That's too late—now.'

'What do you mean?' Harvey stared at her.

'My husband died an hour ago.' She returned his look as steadily as ever.

'What!' Harvey exclaimed. 'He—he's dead?'

'An hour ago.'

Harvey's jaw dropped as he continued to stare at her. This was terrible.

'He was in very great pain at the end,' the woman's level voice continued: 'but I didn't like to send for you, in case it wasn't serious. You thought it wasn't serious.'

'Yes, but good heavens, Mrs Spately, you should have sent for me at once. I never dreamt that—' He broke off.

The ghastly fact that the man must have been at the point of death the previous night and he had never realised it stared him in the face. 'I'll come round at once.'

While he got out the car, his dismay grew. Negligence; culpable negligence; criminal negligence—this might well be the end of his career as a doctor.

The mere thought of what the coroner would almost certainly say at the inquest made him shiver.

There was no doubt that Spately was dead; very dead indeed. But beyond that one overwhelming fact, there was nothing to be learned from an examination of the body.

Harvey knew he was wasting his time as he pored over what had been that jovial man.

'Have you finished, doctor? I had better come back with you, hadn't I?'

'Come back with me?' Harvey repeated stupidly.

'For the certificate. The death certificate.'

'But I—I can't very well issue a death certificate, you see. I haven't been attending him. I—I can't say for certain what caused death. I shall have to report to the coroner,' Harvey said miserably.

She looked at him steadily. 'Will that mean an inquest, and them cutting him open?'

'I'm very much afraid so.'

'And won't they say you might have—saved him?'

Harvey did not answer. There was a short silence.

'I know myself, of course,' said Mrs Spately quietly, 'that you did everything for him that could be done, doctor, whatever others might say. And least said, soonest mended. I think you examined him well enough to give a certificate.'

'Well—perhaps I did,' Harvey mumbled.

He took her back to his consulting-room, and drew his book of death certificates from the table-drawer.

At 'Cause of death' he hesitated for a moment, and then wrote rapidly 'Gastric ulcer'. After all, a gastric ulcer was about the only explanation.

Mrs Spately took the certificate and folded it carefully away in her bag, thanking him with what seemed to him even at the time something of an enigmatic expression in her blue eyes.

'Poor Will always wanted to be cremated,' she said as she did so, 'and I wouldn't like to go against his wishes. I'll need another certificate for that, won't I, doctor?'

Harvey shifted uneasily. That meant that a colleague would have to examine the body. Would not his own negligence be inevitably discovered? He tried to dissuade the woman from the notion.

Giving way at last to her determination, he lifted his telephone receiver, and, calling the doctor in the town whom he knew best, explained the need.

'Gastric ulcer?' repeated the other cheerfully. 'And you're satisfied? Right-ho! I'll give her a second certificate. Send her round to me right away. Oh, no; I shan't bother to make an examination. Take your word for it, Harvey.'

Harvey sighed with relief. There would be no scandal after all.

It was perhaps, speaking strictly, not altogether correct on his part to have given a certificate with such small knowledge of the case; but, anyhow, as the woman herself had said, the man was dead now, and 'least said, soonest mended'.

And his career was saved. But, by Jove, he would be a bit more careful next time. Poor woman, though! She had taken it all extraordinarily well; hadn't seemed to blame him a bit. Young Dr Harvey felt excessively grateful to Mrs Spately.

The sequel came three months later, when Harvey's professional conscience had almost ceased to prick him.

His housekeeper, a garrulous female, threw out an item of gossip one morning as she brought in his breakfast.

'That Mrs Spately, sir, of Westdean Road, her as came to see you that morning her 'usband died. She was married yesterday to the lodger, young Bateson.

'Bin their lodger for two years, he had, and people always said he'd be her next if ever Spately was took. Though it's not hardly decent, to my way of thinking, to be in such a hurry about it, before her first 'usband's properly cold in his grave, as you might say.

'Will you have boiled cod for dinner tonight, sir, or shall I make you a nice bit of Irish stoo?'

Harvey sat for some time after she had gone, staring at the table-cloth. He realised then that a gastric ulcer was not the only explanation; another one was poison!

Harvey never did anything further in the matter. There was no body to exhume. Mrs Spately had been too clever for that.

ANTHONY BERKELEY

Anthony Berkeley Cox (1893–1971) was born on 5 July 1893, the son of a North London doctor. While Cox's career as a writer was short-lived, his reputation has endured, reflecting in particular his highly influential contribution to the evolution of crime fiction and his role in creating the Detection Club, the dining society for writers of mysteries and thriller fiction which will celebrate its centenary towards the end of the 2020s.

More than a century ago, after coming down from Oxford, and following a spell in the British Army which left him with permanently damaged lungs, Tony Cox tried his hand at various forms of business. He soon discovered that he had an astonishing facility for writing comic vignettes, producing dozens and dozens of them, many featuring a winsome child called Brenda. However, always an opportunist, Cox was quick to register the burgeoning appetite of the public for crime and detective stories. His first, *The Layton Court Mystery* (1925) was published anonymously and in many ways it set the tone for his career as a crime novelist. There was an ingenious problem, a surprising solution and—in the form of Roger Sheringham—a surprisingly fallible detective. In just under ten years, Sheringham appeared in ten novels published as by 'Anthony Berkeley', and these included one of the true masterpieces of the Golden Age of crime and detection, *The Poisoned Chocolates Case* (1929). In this novel, inspired by real events and based, loosely, on a satirical short story published in 1922, Cox turned the process of writing a detective story on its head: where other writers devised clues that would confuse the reader by suggesting different solutions, Cox made the construction—and deconstruction—of multiple solutions the heart of the story.

In parallel with chronicling the cases of Roger Sheringham in novels and short stories, Cox also produced a couple of collections of comic pieces and a novel-length comic fantasy, *The Professor on Paws* (1926), which is in some ways a feline antecedent of George Langelaan's horrific short story *The Fly* (1986). Cox also wrote a few non-series novels including *Not to Be Taken* (1938) and *Death in the House* (1939), which were initially published as competitions in *John o'London's Weekly*. Rarest of these, until it was reprinted by Collins Crime Club in 2021, is *The Wintringham Mystery*, a Wodehousian comedy thriller published originally in 1926 as a competition in the British newspaper, the *Daily Mirror*.

While detective stories earned him a good living, Cox wanted to try something new, and for this he needed a new pseudonym. The first of three novels written as 'Francis Iles' was *Malice Aforethought* (1931), an astonishing novel which kickstarted the transition away from puzzles of plot to puzzles of character. As 'Iles', Cox also wrote some short stories as well as articles for the London *Daily News* about criminal psychology—pieces like 'Coward's Crime' (1935) about poison pen writers, and 'Accidental Murder' (1934) about murder in what he styled 'mitigating circumstances'.

In addition to writing about crimes and criminals, real and fictional, Cox was a committed campaigner, albeit largely on paper. *O England* (1934) is a diatribe against red tape. And in 1936, when it was announced that the heir to the British throne, Edward Prince of Wales, had fallen in love with an American woman, Wallis Simpson, Cox was outraged. Anticipating the birther conspiracy, he made a detailed analysis of the legitimacy of her divorce and then tried to persuade Buckingham Palace to take it seriously. He was not successful. Nonetheless, he remained an ardent monarchist and in 1936, after Edward's short-lived reign and abdication, Cox and his second wife, Helen, marked the coronation of King George VI by presenting chocolate, a mug and a medal to every child in the parish of Welcombe in Devon, where they lived.

In 1937, emulating the plot of his most recent book, Cox attempted to get himself sent to prison for a crime he did not commit. The central character in *Trial and Error* (1937), Lawrence Todhunter, was arrested for murder, whereas Cox was charged with failing to obey a stop sign. He explained to Okehampton Police Court that his 'ideas of what safe driving constitutes requires conflict with those of the local authority which put up the stop sign'. Perhaps unsurprisingly, his protestations—and an attempt to read out a twelve-page statement in court—were ignored and the magistrates imposed a fine. In 1940 he established Civil Liaison, which aimed to increase civilian engagement in supporting Britain's war effort. While the organization was short-lived, its ethos was carried over into other organizations, including the volunteer Air Raid Protection wardens and Britain's volunteer Home Guard, for which Cox composed a march.

Towards the end of the 1930s, Cox all but abandoned writing fiction. The final titles by 'Anthony Berkeley' and 'Francis Iles' appeared in 1939 and, other than some radio plays and short stories, Cox limited himself to reviewing crime fiction and composing waltzes, some of which he self-published in 1960.

Tony Cox died on 9 March 1971, leaving nearly £180,000, equivalent to more than £2 million ($2,700,000) in today's money.

Long forgotten, 'Benefit of the Doubt' was first published in the magazine *John Bull* on 23 January 1932. It was subtitled 'The real life story of a young doctor's dilemma'. That might even be true—perhaps the young doctor was Cox's father?

SCANDAL OF THE LOUVRE

S. S. Van Dine

One soft summer day, when the walnuts were casting fluttering embroideries of light and shadow over the parks and streets of the French capital, and the rich green grass had reached its height of vividness in the lawn stretches of the *Cour du Carrousel* of the ancient palace of the Louvre, a trio of what appeared to be tourists alighted from a swaying *fiacre* before the entrance to the great picture museum. Two of them seemed more than eager to proceed to the *Salon Carré* where hung the masterpieces of Veronese, da Vinci, Titian and many other world-renowned masters. But the third lagged behind muttering and grumbling as though performing a most unpleasant duty.

He was a large, florid man of about forty-five. His clothes were baggy and of a loud check. His cravat was of a lurid blue-green with red stripes; and his hands were adorned with expensive but ill-chosen rings. A large diamond shone aggressively from his shirt front, and there was a feather—an adornment in vogue at the time—protruding from the ribbon of his hat. All in all, he looked the part of a sluggish German of the working class, who had lately come into a fortune, and was 'doing' Europe.

His companions' looks served to accentuate the eccentricities of the other. There was a quietness and good taste displayed in their well-fitting and simple garments, and they possessed an undeniable air of good breeding. One was a man of about thirty, whose every movement betrayed his social culture, and whose restraint and delicacy of feature showed the man of inherent refinement.

His companion was a girl, eight or ten years his junior. About her hung a sense of appealing and happy melancholy—a something from which emanated affection and tenderness, a potent charm of both appearance and character. Her hair was as black and alive as a starling's wing; and her eyes, bright from beneath long lashes, had a vitality and alertness seldom seen in brunettes.

This girl was Lilly Franklin, *née* Dinan, wife of Harry Franklin, who was one of the cleverest, 'squarest' and most intelligent crooks then operating. The heavy man of German appearance was Red Bernheim, a New York Jew, erstwhile leader of a band of organized crooks, but now the devoted and ardent admirer of Harry Franklin, as well as his absolutely reliable henchman.

The three went slowly through the long gallery, down the short flight of steps into the Rubens rooms, then back through the galleries of the French school, and at last stood once again in the *Salon Carré*, tired and satiated with art for the day.

There were few visitors about at the time, it being an admission day, and the trio strolled about looking at the copies of the hung work being made by the students. They were astonished at the exactitude of the imitative work and watched the busy students with intense interest. They were particularly wonder-struck when they stopped in front of da Vinci's 'Gioconda' and saw a picture, nearly finished, which in every detail, down to the very cracks in the paint, the tint and drawing, was a perfect duplicate of the, original. In silence they marvelled for some time at the closeness of the work and at the infinite patience with which the student lay in the details. Then Red, bursting forth at last, fairly cried:

'There you are! D'you see? Do you fine art lovers think you could tell one from the other? If not, which is the best? I'm asking you: which is the best—the work of the old gink what made that one?'—pointing to the wall—'or the guy what's putting the finishing strokes on this one?'—indicating the one on the easel.

Red laughed triumphantly and turned away while Harry Franklin stood in deep thought. Lilly looked up anxiously into his eyes, her arm through his. His mind was not altogether on art, however. He was thinking of a subject more relative to his wife's and his own welfare. He stood perhaps five minutes thus, unseeing. Then he turned to Red Bernheim.

'Do you know,' he commented, 'that picture of Leonardo's is one of the most talked-of paintings in the world? It is probably one of the most valuable works of art in existence, for it has a tremendous sentimental interest, as well as an artistic one. There isn't a great collector in the world who wouldn't give his last dollar for it. If we owned that, Red, we could live in luxury for the rest of our lives.'

'Sure!' agreed the other. 'The same goes about Brooklyn Bridge. Let's slip up New York harbour some night and run away with it.'

Franklin ignored his partner's good-natured sarcasm, and hurried out of the Louvre without a word, Lilly and Red following him. He called a taxicab, and the three climbed in and were driven to their apartments in the Hôtel Lutetia on the Boulevard Raspail.

For a while Harry sat in thought. Then he turned to Lilly.

'How's your French, kid?' he asked. 'Do you find you still remember your native tongue after all your years in America?'

'Oh, I get along like a Parisienne,' the girl replied proudly. 'Mother and Father always used to make me talk in French. My accent's fine. All I need is to pick up some of the current slang— then no one would know I'd ever left France.'

'Good!' commented Harry, kissing her.

'Now brush up on your slang. You'll need it.'

Red rubbed his hands together. He scented a new adventure.

A week later Henry E. Ostrander was surprised from a sound slumber at eleven o'clock in the morning by an urgent call on the telephone in his luxurious rooms at the Grand Hotel. At first he was for letting it ring. His head still ached from the champagne and dancing of the night before when, in company of two friends and a guide, he had attempted to exhaust the ribald pleasures of Montmartre. But the ringing was so persistent that at last he arose to stop it. He jerked down the receiver angrily and grunted 'Hello.' A voice, vibrant and masculine, asked if he were the Mr Ostrander whose fame was world-wide as a picture collector. He answered affirmatively in a curt voice, and was about to cut off his unknown inquisitor when what he heard made him change his mind. His tone altered and he consented to a *rendezvous* with the stranger for twelve o'clock.

At the appointed hour he met Harry Franklin on the enclosed veranda at the rear of the hotel. The two men shook hands and sat down. No time was lost in preliminaries. Franklin told him immediately and in a business-like way that he could secure the greatest picture in Paris for the other's collection if he, Ostrander, would pay the price and see to its shipment out of the country. The millionaire was eager to know what work it was, hoping it might be some small canvas from a private collection. He was ready to pay liberally for such a work. He was in Europe at the time hoping to pick up something valuable.

In his collection were many ill-gotten works. There was a Gothic angel from the Cathedral at Rouen, an altar piece from Notre-Dame, a very old prie-Dieu from Milan, and many smaller works, each representing a sacrilege committed by one of those bands of thieves who are organized for the one purpose of stealing *objets d'art* from public and private collections, only to sell them to avid and unscrupulous collectors who care more for the object than for a clear conscience. Ostrander was acquainted with the leaders of several such bands, and had made purchases through them. He knew they were fearless and daring, but he was carried wholly off his feet when Franklin announced his intention.

'I shall steal the *Mona Lisa* of da Vinci and sell it to the highest bidder!'

If Franklin had said he was to steal the Venus of Milo or Napoleon's tomb itself, he would scarcely have made more of an impression. Ostrander nearly fell from his chair: his eyes bulged from his head. The enormity of the deed!

'Man, you're raving crazy!' he managed to say at last. 'What kind of a fool are you, anyway? Don't you know that, besides being priceless, that work stands supreme as the best-preserved example of Italian art?' Then he smiled. The thing was preposterous. 'Say, don't joke about such things. Come down to earth.' Then he asked more calmly: 'What's your proposition?'

'I have told you, Mr Ostrander,' Franklin returned quietly, 'I intend to steal the *Mona Lisa*, and if you don't care to make a bid, I shall say good-day.'

Ostrander raised his hand.

'Wait!' he said. 'Let me think a minute.'

Franklin resumed his seat.

The great collector was trembling slightly.

'My God!' he exclaimed, as if to himself. 'If I really thought I could get the *Mona Lisa*—to have it for my own, personally, privately!' He gloated over the thought. 'But it's incredible—utterly preposterous! It can't be done.' He looked at Franklin sharply. He suspected some hoax.

The other devined his suspicions, and smiled.

'You need not pay one cent till you are satisfied—till the picture is in your hands,' he said. 'You will know it has been stolen some time before I will present you with it.'

'You fellows are slick,' Ostrander admitted. 'You've gotten me things before I didn't think possible . . . But this—' He whistled, and strode up and down excitedly. 'It would be the great scandal of the century!'

'Do you want the picture?' the younger man asked, rising and putting on his hat.

'Sit down—sit down!' Ostrander urged. 'Let's talk the matter over.'

The conversation was resumed on a business basis. Fifteen minutes later Franklin departed after having secured an offer which meant riches if he would deliver the picture to Ostrander before a certain date.

Ostrander, however, did not expect to get it. The idea was too fantastic. Steal the *Mona Lisa*! Impossible! The dream of a crazy man! The man must be drunk to hold the belief that he could outwit the police of the world.

'Well, anyway,' he mused, 'the picture is priceless, worth millions, ungettable: and the sum I offered would be indeed small if I really got possession of this famous masterpiece.'

Chuckling, he strolled out upon the Boulevard and took a seat on the terrace of the Café de la Paix.

Everyone interested in art who has been to Paris knows that the picture museum of the Louvre is closed every Monday and Thursday morning for the purpose of cleaning and dusting the statuary, pictures, frames, cases and floors. Early on these two mornings are to be seen groups of men and women going into the small entrances which lead, by devious and dark, narrow stone stairways, to the big, light galleries above.

The Monday after Franklin's talk with Ostrander, Lilly, dressed in the manner of the other workers and carrying a bundle in which were threads, fine wire, *savon noir* and rags (all for cleaning) entered the Louvre with the others. It had not been an easy task for her to secure employment. It had first been necessary to find out who was the head of the cleaning squad. Later Lilly was brought to his notice; and then, by her charming ways and intimate beauty, she ingratiated herself in his good graces in a manner he could not resist. She had taken a room in the boarding house where he lived, and had made it a point to be constantly passing him in the hall with a smile. After he had spoken to her once she felt assured of obtaining her end.

Today was her first chance; and the man who employed her, himself a workman and one of the museum guards, was on the point of acknowledging to himself that she was a very desirable and charming young woman to know. But on this particular day she kept him at a distance and worked hard—so hard, in fact, that her heretofore well-kept and dainty hands became red and blistered. The man, however, hovered about her, joking and laughing; but she, though seeming to enter whole-heartedly into the innocent fun, was, in reality, making mental notes of the conditions which obtained in the gallery on closed days.

She noted that there was no formality necessary to go in and out of the many rooms. The restorers and workmen were continually coming and going unchallenged through this storehouse of treasures, as freely as if there was not a thing of value to tempt them. Often whole rooms were left entirely unguarded for as long as ten minutes at a time.

At noon she departed, happy in her knowledge, to report to Harry every detail of what she had seen. He was greatly pleased. He gave her some further instructions, and sent her back to her lodgings.

The following Monday was the day fixed upon for the *coup*. The magnitude of the undertaking appalled Red Bernheim and Lilly. Though outwardly calm, Lilly at heart was in a terrible panic of fear, not so much for herself as for Harry, whose love and companionship had made of her an ideal wife and had raised her from the dregs of the underworld to what seemed to her a paradise.

Harry himself was not so easy in his mind as he had been on other occasions. A certain restlessness could be noted in his actions. The worry he was undergoing showed in an occasional slight drawing of his features. It was to be the big 'job' of his life. Indeed, he was half inclined to promise himself he would settle down and live quietly if he carried it through successfully.

To Red, Harry seemed to have gone back on his original ideas of taking money only from those who richly deserved a lesson. 'What do you call this?' he would ask sarcastically. 'Is there some ethical reason for lifting the dame from this here nation to America? Don't tell me you're as patriotic as that! It's just what I tole you before: when the big money calls, those who can, goes! But I'm fer letting it slip by. It's too much chance. It can't be done; and you know what these here wrist-watch frog-eaters'll do to us if we're caught. Stealin' the Monny Lisy! Gosh! I'd rather rob the Turks or the Japs than these boys. They're small, but they're cute. You never know what they've got up their sleeve . . . What do you say?'

'You know I never give up a thing I have started to do, Red,' Franklin would answer. 'And as for your jibes about my waning principles—well, I shall answer for them later. Besides, there is a very good reason why France should lose many of her treasures. You are, perhaps, not aware that the great Napoleon carried about in the wake of his armies art experts who saw to the selecting and shipment to Paris of the great art works of his conquered territories . . . This was eminently evil—not morally, understand, but artistically. Those countries that can produce no art, deserve none. Napoleon had a right to despoil his enemies of money and goods; but the thought and flower of a nation should be inviolate. His divinity I could question on many points. At present I must ask you, for your own good, to be patient. Mourn my loss of self-respect if you will, but never believe that anyone can make of me a man who gives up the fight.'

And this was all Red could extract from the admired partner who had made him rich through the play of his nimble wit.

'As I have told you before, Red,' Franklin philosophized, 'men who can swindle and steal in such a way that the law is power-less to punish them, deserve punishment even more than smaller and less subtle offenders. The judges on the bench receive a salary for dealing out justice, do they not? Very well. I have appointed myself a judge superior to the men of the Supreme Court. I handle cases beyond their scope—insidious and dastardly cases whose gangrene honeycombs the social fabric.

Why should I not receive a living? My efforts are bent to punish the guilty and to attain happiness at one and the same time. Would that I could train others to the task!'

The time passed more than slowly, but finally the great day arrived. There was little sleep in that household the night before, but early Lilly was on her way across the river from the *Rive Gauche*, on the top of the omnibus. With her was her ardent admirer—the Louvre guard—who had gone so far as to pinch her cheek while she was looking the other way.

As she began her duties she thought once more carefully over her plans. The minutes dragged while she had to cajole the workman and keep him about her. As the clock neared eleven she let him become more familiar. She brushed against him coquettishly, put her face close to his, and playfully pushed him about. All the time her heart was beating like a trip hammer. As the minutes rolled by she began to loathe this creature whom she had to deceive. All her love for Harry came up to choke her and to moisten her eyes; and it was an Herculean task to laugh and sing under the circumstances.

At five minutes of the hour she stopped, and said with an exaggerated seriousness which made her companion thrill:

'You say you love me, don't you? How do I know if you tell the truth? You've never even kissed me.'

Then springing lightly to her feet, she tripped across the room, laughing aloud. The man sprang to his feet, a large smile on his heavy face, and ran after her.

'If that's all the proof you want,' he exclaimed, 'you shall have it now, *ma petite môme!*'

She easily eluded his arms until her watch pointed to one minute of the hour. When the great clock outside sounded eleven, she ran between two long curtains in a passage that led to another gallery. This passage was where old frames and students' easels and copies were kept, and it was always empty.

Here she led him a merry chase about the table until she was out of breath. At last he caught her and put his arms about her, she struggling and on the point of tears all the time. The tears he took for surrender, little dreaming they were for worry for another man to whom her very life would have been willingly given. She was very tired now, and putting on a serious face, she pushed him away, saying:

'Listen, Auguste, they'll miss us out here, and you see you can't get a kiss unless I want you to. So promise me only to take one—and it's yours. But lie to me, and I swear I'll never speak to you again.'

The man laughed and promised, for a given kiss in France would mean that she loved him. She patted his cheek tenderly, and at last let him lean down and kiss her forehead . . .

In the meantime much had happened. As these two left the room, a small door at the rear had been noiselessly opened and a workman, with the blouse of a plasterer, a dark head of long hair and a black moustache, had come in quickly. With him he carried a large cloth and a screwdriver. Hastening across the room he quickly jerked the frame of the *Mona Lisa* from the wall. Next, he loosened the nails which held it in place, and, covering it with the cloth, ran out of the same little door through which he had come, and disappeared. He jumped into a waiting machine, which straightaway sped from the grounds and across the bridge. At last it stopped, and its occupant alighted and was soon lost in the crowd of the *Rue du Bac*.

The machine had already left the Museum door with its sacred prize before Lilly let her pretended admirer come back, and it was ten minutes before they were back in the *Salle Carré*. The *Mona Lisa* is not a large picture, and its absence was not discovered. The workmen and guards were all too busy in their preparations for going home.

Lilly was trembling violently as she walked out of the door with the other cleaners. Her knees were shaking so that she could scarcely stand; and her face was very pale. She had eluded her would-be lover: when he had gone to secure his hat and coat, she had hurried away. Once in the street, she almost ran to the Metro station. When she was seated, she burst out crying from sheer reaction, and the subway guard took it upon himself to comfort her.

Lilly alighted at the *Gare Montparnasse*. There Red awaited her. She quickly changed her clothes, which were awaiting her under the seat, and was driven to the hotel. She found Harry indolently smoking a cigarette with a sage smile on his face, and threw herself, sobbing, into his ready arms.

'When do we leave, Harry?' she asked. 'Soon? . . . When will you see Ostrander? Is everything all right? . . . What will happen when they discover that the picture's gone? They're sure to notice it tomorrow . . . Oh, Harry, I was so afraid you'd get caught. Tell me how you did it.'

Franklin answered all her questions and soothed her as best he could, admonishing her that all was not over yet and that some still very risky work was still to be accomplished.

Red strolled in and grasped Harry's hand.

'I'll hand it to you again, Harry. You're there! Where's the money? Have you got the cash?'

'No.' Franklin smiled. 'I have neither the picture nor the cash. We'll have to give Ostrander a day or two to be sufficiently pleased with the excitement which will start tomorrow. We must make him feel that he is getting his money's worth. It's a big price he's paying, and he could hold me up easily if he wanted to lose the picture. The picture, by the way, I left in the tool box of the machine. Under the circumstances that is about the safest place. An auto is also about the safest place for a money transaction when you want to be sure nobody is listening. It is also a good trunk for the smuggling of contraband goods to a foreign country . . . Let me see, we rented the machine by the week. I'm afraid we're going to be obliged to pay a large price for it, because to all intents and purposes it will have to be wrecked.'

The next morning, August the twenty-second, 1911, the storm broke forth. The theft of da Vinci's great masterpiece was discovered by one of the guards. In an hour the newsboys were dashing up the boulevards crying the extras at the top of their voices. Paris went nearly insane. Everyone ceased their duties to discuss the great tragedy. The city was hysterical with excitement. All the officials were blaming the curator, Dujardin-Beaumetz, who, in turn, was blaming the administration for not supplying him with sufficient guards. Investigations were called. Recriminations were hurled back and forth. The police announced clues, and the papers teemed with interviews and explanations. But despite the uproar and confusion of the entire capital, everyone felt that the picture would be returned or found very soon. One impression which gained considerable headway was that some accident had befallen it, which the government was endeavouring to hush up by saying it was lost. '

The next morning—Wednesday—Ostrander did not keep the telephone ringing so long as on the first occasion when Franklin called up. A proud and self-satisfied smile lit up his features as Harry's name was announced. He hurried downstairs immediately.

The two men shook hands and retired to a secluded corner of the American bar.

'You did it, man!' exclaimed the collector in an awed voice. 'By God, you're a wonder! Left no clue, and fooled 'em all! . . . Well, I'm ready with my end. When can I get hold of it?'

'Mr Ostrander, here is my advice,' Harry answered. 'You know the difficulty of the American port authorities. The best thing to do is to buy the machine which I'll point out to you; then ship it at once to your home in New York. The picture will be in the tool box carefully wrapped up and concealed. In order to buy the machine without the painting being discovered, we'll pretend to wreck it, and I'll go and pay the claim. You know, if you purchased it in the ordinary way some salesman might open the tool box by way of demonstration; and again, suspicion might be aroused. The car is below. If you'll come for a ride, we'll have a look.'

That night Franklin took the machine out by himself, and early in the morning returned with it to the hotel. He left his car at the door, went to the owner's and, after telling of the imaginative accident, bought the car and brought away a bill of sale.

He lost no time in going to Ostrander to collect. That man, still suspicious, demanded to see that the picture was still in the car before paying. After another long drive and a careful scrutiny of the masterpiece in the early light of dawn, they returned in time for the bank opening. A half hour later Franklin and Red were traversing the Pont Saint-Michel with over $150,000 in American banknotes safely tucked away in their wallets. Ostrander was elated over his possession of the stolen picture and the bill of sale of the automobile. He kept his eye on the machine until it was safely under way for Calais, from where it would be put aboard a fast boat for America.

That night Franklin, Lilly and Red took the train for Florence by way of Marseilles and Milan—happy to be free of the encumbrance of the dangerous art treasure and rejoicing in their possession of a new fortune.

Once in Florence the warm and balmy air of the most beautiful city in the world made dreamers of them all. They settled down for a well-deserved rest on a high hill overlooking the Arno in a villa surrounded by flowers and tall cypress trees. There the days flew by as though on magic wings. Even Red forgot his lust for gold and seemed to become part of that wonderful southland.

Every day or so they would hear echoes of that famous theft, and at sight of these bits of news or new clues Franklin would smile, and Red would gloat over the fact that the largest amount they had ever made was a downright steal and not an idealized lesson in decency for the benefit of some erring brother. He had always scoffed at Franklin's idealism; and now he felt that in some way he had won a sort of immoral victory over his partner.

Nearly three years of pure happiness passed thus, and the memory of that thrilling day in Paris had nearly faded from their minds when one day a bellowing and stamping was heard on the walk leading to their little house. Red Bernheim, scarlet in the face, rushed in, waving a paper.

'Look here!' he cried angrily. 'What in hell does this mean? . . . Read! "The *Mona Lisa* restored to its place on the walls of the Louvre. Thief a patriotic madman, caught in Italy. His name is Vincenzo Peruggia. Says he stole it to restore it to the Italian Government.""

And Red went on to tell how this Italian, imbued with zeal, becoming depressed over the thought of the great Napoleon's vandalism while in Italy, walked into the gallery one day, took the masterpiece and escaped.

'Well, Red, what's the matter?' he asked pleasantly. 'All is well; the picture has been restored to its rightful owners.'

'What's that!' shrieked Red. 'How about Ostrander? Did he give it back again? . . . Say, Harry, let's have the dope.'

'Sit down, Red, and I'll give you the story.' Franklin was grinning. 'Ostrander had the picture. He only saw it once in his life, and that was the day you drove us to Robeson. The next drive was, if you remember, made in the early morning, and his view was not as microscopic as it might have been. You may well wonder how I avoided giving it to him . . . Well, you remember the day we arrived in Paris and saw that poor fellow copying the picture? You tried to kid me about the duplicate's perfection. Well, I bought that finished copy, and it was that copy, which cost me three hundred francs, which I sold to Ostrander for $150,000. I *did* leave it in the tool box until the old scoundrel had seen it. But when I took out the car the same night I changed the copy for the original, bought a trunk on my way home, nailed the original in the bottom, and checked it at the Gare de Lyons. Ostrander bought a machine in which to smuggle a copy to America!' Harry laughed.

'I brought the original here to Florence. As you see, I could have deprived the French nation—the most capable of appreciating and loving art—of that picture. But I didn't want to. Six weeks ago I hired a reliable Milanese to take the picture back and clumsily expose the shape and size to some custom house man so he would be detected. Of course, I paid the man well for taking the chances . . . Just as I thought, the *beau geste* is highly appreciated by the French; and this man's story of taking the work as an act of patriotism will set him free in Italy and be indulgently regarded by the French. He has done his work well.'

He paused a moment. Then he went on: 'Everyone, I believe, is happy. We ourselves have no complaint to make, nor has M. Dujardin-Beaumetz, the curator of the Louvre. My man will be well paid, and, as I see it, everyone but Ostrander has been squarely treated. For him I have little sympathy. He is a thief by nature. He would hide a transcendent piece of art from the eyes of the deserving in order to gratify his own vanity by hanging it in a dark gallery. The lesson I have given him is . . .'

'Oh, Hell!' growled Red, casting an indignant look over his shoulder, and stamping out of the room.

Lilly snuggled close to her husband; and Franklin looked after the retreating form of Bernheim with a facial expression somewhat akin to the *Mona Lisa*'s enigmatic smile.

S. S. VAN DINE

Willard Huntington Wright was born on 15 October 1888 in Charlottesville, Virginia, the son of hoteliers Archibald Davenport Wright and Annie Van Vranken. In a 1929 interview, the man who would become 'S. S. Van Dine' claimed to 'have written since the age of four, when a poem of mine was printed in my home paper. I wrote a full-length novel at nine, and illustrated it myself. Luckily it was never published—it was worse than the poem.'

In 1899, Wright's parents moved to in the Californian seaside resort of Santa Monica where they ran the Arcadia Hotel. Wright attended Pomona College and Saint Vincent's College where he was known as a prankster, once faking a student's death. From college, Wright attended Harvard in 1906–1907 but left without graduating. In 1906, *The Pacific Monthly* published his first short story, 'No Story at All', and on 13 July 1907 he married Katherine Belle Boynton, and a year later their daughter, Beverley, was born.

In the same year, Wright joined the *Los Angeles Times*, where his first article was published under the by-line 'Wilbur Huntington Wright' and other articles appeared anonymously. Wright was appointed literary editor in 1909, reviewing books and—frankly—pontificating on all sorts of literary subjects in a long-running column entitled 'New Books and Book News'. After leaving the newspaper, Wright 'went east' to New York, becoming literary critic of *Town Topics* and forming an association with the journalists

George Jean Nathan and Henry L. Mencken. This led to Wright's becoming an editor of *Smart Set* magazine from 1912 to 1914 alongside Julian Johnson, a colleague from his days on the *Times*. Wright was also at different times literary editor of the *New York Evening Mail*, music editor and art critic of *Forum and International Studio*, a columnist on the *San Francisco Bulletin*, and art critic of *Hearst's International Magazine*.

While working as a journalist, Wright also produced nine books, including a guide to *The Paintings of the Metropolitan Museum* (1915), *Songs of Youth* (1913) and *The Creative Will: Studies in the Philosophy and Syntax of Aesthetics* (1916). While he was—in his own words—'a highbrow', Wright was also writing mystery stories for *Pearson's Magazine* as 'Albert Otis', named for the president and general manager of the *Los Angeles Times*.

Around this time the Wrights separated. He was in poor health and in 1923 suffered a complete physical breakdown, leaving him bedridden for around two years during which he read detective fiction and trial reports. Never uncertain of his own abilities, Wright decided that he could do better. He wrote a 30,000-word synopsis of three murder mysteries and sent them to Maxwell E. Perkins, a former classmate at Harvard who was working for the publisher Scribner's. Perkins and his colleagues were very impressed and offered an advance of $3,000 (equivalent today to $50,000 or £40,000). Wright was delighted, and set to work on the novels, which would be published as *The Benson Murder Case* (1926), *The Canary Murder Case* (1927) and *The Greene Murder Case* (1928). Conscious of his reputation, Wright decided that they should appear under a pseudonym. Rejecting the idea of using 'Albert Otis' again, he chose 'S. S. Van Dine'. Van Dyne [*sic*] was an old family name and the initials were selected simply for their distinctiveness. As a disguise it was none too effective and by 1927 'S. S. Van Dine' had been identified as Willard Huntington Wright. More books followed—*The Bishop Murder Case* (1929) and *The Scarab Murder Case* (1930), both featuring, like the first three, Philo Vance, a detective very much in the mould of the aristocratic amateurs of British detective fiction at that time.

The public's response was astonishing, and the recognition—and income—that Wright gained far overshadowed his work as a journalist. Initially he had intended to write only six crime novels but he soon changed his mind. As he would often say in interviews, 'S. S. Van Dine' made more money in six months than Willard Huntington Wright in fifteen years. And as well as appearing on the page, the Philo Vance mysteries were soon optioned for the cinema. Wright's transition from highbrow to mystery-monger had gone extraordinarily well, and things were about to get even better.

After a trip to Europe in the late 1920s, Wright was sailing back to America when he found himself on deck, seated next to a woman who was reading *The Greene Murder Case* while her daughter, an art student called Eleanor Rulapaugh, was engrossed in Wright's *Modern Painting, Its Tendency and Meaning* (1915). The three fell into conversation, in the course of which Wright was disparaging about 'trash' mysteries. When later he revealed himself to be the author of both books, the younger woman felt he had been mocking her, and they parted on cool terms.

A year or so earlier Wright had bought a holiday home in Bradley Beach, New Jersey, where, as something of a celebrity, he sponsored a local chess tournament. This led to Wright's being invited to serve a term as the town's police commissioner, which ended embarrassingly when he failed to solve a real murder and had to seek help from Inspector John Coughlin, formerly of the New York Police Department. While the press made fun of the failure of the masterly 'S. S. Van Dine', Eleanor Rulapaugh was one of many to send Wright a supportive letter; however, she didn't provide her address . . . On his return to California, a neighbour showed Wright a portrait of his child made by a local artist, Claire de Lisle. Wright was entranced, and when he met the painter he was astonished to discover her to be none other than

Eleanor Rulapaugh. Willard and Katherine Wright were separated, and in 1930 he and Eleanor were free to marry.

The popularity of 'S. S. Van Dine' continued to grow, with more and more films, but Wright's health was in decline. He died of a coronary thrombosis on 11 April 1939 at his penthouse flat on Central Park West in New York, where, among other things, he kept a collection of shaved dice, weighted tables and other devices used by fraudulent casinos to cheat the public.

'The Scandal of the Louvre' was first published in *Pearson's Magazine* in June 1916 as by 'Albert Otis'. A collection of Wright's 'Albert Otis' stories is scheduled for publication in 2022 by the American small press, Crippen & Landru.

THE PRESSURE OF CIRCUMSTANCE

J. J. Connington

I

Norris Lessingham glanced across at his son, and a touch of wistfulness flickered momentarily over his rather grim features. 'Time's getting short,' he said, abruptly. Jack glanced up at the clock on the mantelpiece.

'Yes. Nuisance, this hanging about at the last moment, waiting for train time.'

The older man, grudging the passing of every minute which brought parting nearer, could still appreciate the feelings of the younger generation. This Amazonian expedition was a big thing for Jack. With luck, it might make him a marked man in his chosen line; and even the invitation to join it had been no inconsiderable compliment to his entomological ability. At his age, naturally, the opportunity bulked far larger than the risks.

'You can't stay over till tomorrow and take the boat-train?' he asked, in the tone of one who expects nothing but a negative answer.

Jack shook his head.

'I promised Forester I'd stay the night with him, if he'd motor me down to the boat. Get there before the crowd from the boat express, that way. Much easier.'

Norris Lessingham nodded. A promise was a promise, to be

kept at any cost. He had taught Jack that from his boyhood. Only he wished that Jack had not made the promise, since it meant cutting into the time they still had together. Things seem so different when one recognises that one may be looking on one's son for the last time. What he had heard about that Brazilian country from his expert friends had not reassured him much.

There was so much that he wanted to say, at this last hour; but strong though his feelings were, his natural reserve kept them from his tongue. It was almost with relief that he saw the door open and his married daughter, Monica, came into the room.

'Well, Jack? All ready, are you? I'm coming down to the station with you.'

'Good. Heavy luggage, including a consignment of spare collar-studs, went off yesterday, so I expect we can tuck you into the car all right. Where's Basil?'

'He sent his apologies. He's got a consultation—an urgent case—or he'd have come with me. But he'll be on the platform at the station in time for the train without fail.'

'Nice of him, that. I know how busy he is. Could never have stood the rush of Harley Street myself.'

After kissing her father, Monica sat down, putting her handbag on a table beside her. Though not demonstrative, they were a closely united family with a fund of mutual understanding which had no need for verbal expression

When Monica had married Estcourt, she had not left the inner circle. Instead, her husband had been brought into it. Norris Lessingham approved of his son-in-law, who had a kindred nature and similar tastes in many respects. If one were in a tight corner, Basil would be a good man to have beside one: quick, cool, and unflinching when it came to the test.

'Where's Claire?' Monica inquired.

'Gone to a bridge party at the Foresters,' Jack informed her curtly. 'She had to go, she said. They were short at one table.'

Monica's fine eyebrows arched slightly and then came suddenly back to normal as her brother glanced in her direction. Really, she reflected, her sister-in-law might for once have made it convenient to fit her arrangements to theirs.

When Jack had married, old Lessingham had bought for the young couple the second half of the big semi-detached house in which he lived. For convenience, communication doorways had been driven through on each storey and closed by heavy draught-curtains; but in practice the two households ran in complete independence of each other. Though taciturn, Norris Lessingham was not unsociable; and his daughter-in-law was supposed to act as hostess for him when he gave dinners to his friends; but in recent times Claire's haphazard way of making her arrangements had made her so unreliable that Monica had to be called in, more often than not, to take her place.

Monica, whom only illness could dispense from a given engagement, simply failed to understand the methods of her sister-in-law. Nor could she fathom her brother's reaction to Claire's ways. He seemed to see everything, and yet never to draw the conclusions which were obvious to herself and her father.

Jack seemed to have married the wrong woman without having the wit to find out how unsuitable she was, even after a year in double harness. But where Jack was concerned, Monica was prepared to make any excuses. After all, he seemed just as much in love with Claire as ever, though he got little enough in return, so far as an outsider could see.

Jack rose from his chair with a clouded face.

'Going to ring up Claire at the Foresters,' he explained, as he left the room.

When the door closed behind him, Monica crossed over and took a chair close to her father.

'She's hurt Jack by this last caper,' she said, dropping her voice. 'It's too bad of her, the very evening that he's leaving us.'

Her father's only response was an inarticulate sound in which disgust and contempt seemed to be mingled.

'I can't make her out,' Monica went on. 'She seems to have no sense; never got beyond the flapper stage, somehow. That phrase of hers irritates me like an advertisement slogan.'

'What phrase?' demanded old Lessingham.

'Oh, what she's always saying: "Anything for a good time, short of the limit!"'

'So she has a limit, has she?' Lessingham commented coldly. 'So have I. I won't have her making Jack ridiculous behind his back while he's away. It's his own affair while he's here. Once he's gone, it's our business, Monica. You'll need to keep an eye on her.'

'I hardly ever see her,' Monica protested. 'She's not in my set, and I'm not in hers.'

'Well, I won't have Jack made to look a fool.'

Surprised by the cold anger behind the words, Monica made no reply and they waited in silence till Jack returned. Monica glanced at the clock.

'Is she on the way home?' she asked.

Jack shook his head.

'She hasn't been to the Foresters. Mrs F. was a shade frosty over the phone. Claire's let her down badly. You know how Mrs Forester hates any cutting-in business at her shows. Likes to have her tables full. Very polite, of course, but I could hear her voice trembling a bit. Terrible temper that woman has.'

'But where has she gone to?' Monica queried.

'Try Scotland Yard. How should I know?' Jack answered brusquely.

Monica, though puzzled, refrained from rubbing the thing in. Old Lessingham made no comment, but his face showed plainly enough what he thought of the affair. If the bridge-- party had been important enough to take Claire away from Jack this afternoon, how came it that she could drop out at the last moment and go off elsewhere without a word to her hostess?

'It's about time we were starting, isn't it?' he suggested, rising to his feet. 'Basil will be at the train. No use keeping him hanging about, waiting for us.'

The drive to the station was a silent one. Neither Monica nor her father cared to make conversation, and Jack seemed deep in his own reflections. Obviously he was disappointed by Claire's failing to come back and give him a chance of saying goodbye to her, alone, in their own house.

As they came on to the platform, Monica's quick glance picked out a figure standing further up the train.

'There's Basil!'

In response to her signal, he came towards them; a keen-- eyed, lightly moving man in the early thirties, with that stamp of neatness which marks out the good surgeon. Monica, to whom marriage was still fresh, looked him up and down with approval as he approached. Basil never let one down, she reflected thankfully.

'Your seat's up yonder, next the dining-car; corner away from the corridor,' he explained to Jack.

They reached Jack's carriage and dismissed the porter. Jack moved over to the bookstall to buy something to read on the journey, but his gaze kept wandering to the ticket-barrier. Suddenly his whole attitude changed; he set off down the plat- form eagerly, and Monica caught sight of her sister-in-law, just passing the collector.

'So she's managed to get here in time, after all. Better late than never,' she reflected, half in relief and half in contempt.

Then she saw that Claire was not alone. She came up the platform chattering to a man at her side, without a glance to see where her husband might be. Just like Claire, Monica reflected, to drag after her to this parting a man who was next door to a stranger.

Owen Langler was no favourite of Monica. He had good looks of a kind, plenty of money, and no discoverable morals. He was the sort of man who cannot be left alone with a girl for ten minutes without making love to her.

'I've just dropped in to see the happy dispatch,' he explained, adroitly frustrating Jack's attempt to get Claire aside to himself. 'I'm always an eager member of the See-'em-off Club. So you're going to the Amazon to collect blackbeetles, or something, Claire tells me. Extraordinary taste. Amazing really. But it takes all kinds to make a world.'

Jack gave him a curt nod and turned to Claire.

'Glad you came, dear.'

There was no vexation or irony in his tone. He simply meant what he said; and Monica's irritation gave place to a faint surprise. Was he really as fond of Claire as all that? He must be very much in love with her when he could take behaviour of this kind without showing the slightest resentment.

Everything forgiven, so long as she turned up to say good-bye at the last moment. Well, as Langler had said, it takes all kinds to make a world, and she had no call to criticise Jack if he chose to take the thing in that spirit.

Claire seemed to feel that some explanation was needed.

'I had a bit of a headache, Jack, and I simply couldn't face that bridge-party when it came to the pinch; so when Owe rang up and asked me to have tea with him, I simply had to go. And then, somehow, the time simply *flew*; and when I looked at my watch there was just time to get here in a taxi; and then we got into a traffic jam and I thought we'd miss you after all.

'But luckily we had a simply perfect taxi-driver and he got us here in time through a lot of back streets, simply ghastly places, but he could go quicker that way, I suppose . . .'

She ran on, chattering of the infinitely unimportant, as was her way. At least she was telling the truth, Monica noted, since she made no attempt to conceal the fact that she had cut the bridge-party to go with Langler.

The clock hands were almost on train time. People were getting into their carriages all along the platform. Jack turned to his sister.

'Goodbye, Monica. Wish me luck.'

'The very best, dear.'

Estcourt shook hands in silence. His smile said all that was necessary.

Jack turned to his father.

'Goodbye, father. You'll see that Claire comes to no harm while I'm away?'

A rather bleak look crossed old Lessingham's face.

'Of course. That's a promise,' he answered, using the old family formula for a binding engagement. Then an affectionate smile altered his features. 'Goodbye, Jack. Don't take more risks than you need to, and be sure to cable us just before you leave civilized parts.'

'Right!'

Quite naturally, Claire stepped forward, pulled down Jack's head and kissed him.

'Goodbye, Jack dear. Home soon.'

The guard's whistle blew, and Jack had just time to gain his carriage as the train began to move out.

The self-elected member of the See-'em-off Club turned to Claire with a sigh of relief which he did not think it worthwhile to suppress.

'Well, that's over, thank goodness. These partings are dismal rites, aren't they? One needs cheering up afterwards. What about a little dinner somewhere? And a spot of dancing later on? That's the best cure for the ultramarines. Make it so?'

Claire hesitated for just a moment. Then, apparently, her slogan carried the day. 'Anything for a good time.' It would make no real difference to Jack, no matter how she spent her evening.

And it would be a dreary business to while away the time after dinner in that big, empty house. She gave a nod of assent.

'You'll come?' said Langler. 'Splendid! I'll pick you up in time for dinner.'

II

As old Lessingham put the final touch to his black tie, his quick ear caught the trill of a bell, and he glanced at his wrist-watch. One of his guests had arrived well in advance of time. Lessingham made no effort to hurry on that account

He had guessed the identity of this premature comer, and he was sure that someone else would be there to entertain the visitor. He finished his dressing in a leisurely way, picked up from the dressing-table his cigar-case, lighter and his laboratory key. Then, switching off the light, he went slowly downstairs to the drawing-room.

It was two months since Jack had vanished into the unexplored fastnesses of Brazil, and things had not stood still during his absence. Claire had found Langler amusing. They had been about together continually, and the girl seemed to have let her husband slip from her mind in the excitement of her aimless life. Nor had Lessingham been idle. He had laid his plans: and in a few hours, perhaps, the time might come to put them to the test.

At this last moment, luck had served him well. Monica had proposed that she and Estcourt should come to dinner that night and afterwards take Claire on to a dance. A sudden emergency in his practice had prevented Estcourt from dining with them, though he could pick up the girls after dinner.

To balance the table, Claire had invited Langler. Lessingham, rather to her surprise, had made no objection, despite his obvious dislike of the man. It suited his plans perfectly. Over their wine, with the girls out of the way, he could draw Langler out, take him off his guard, and learn something of him at first hand, something which would fill in the last blank spaces in the picture he had slowly built up since Jack left him in charge.

He opened the door, noiselessly, into the big L-shaped drawing-room. The angle of the wall cut off the direct view into the room, but in an old-fashioned ornamental mirror on the wall he caught a glimpse of two figures on the settee starting swiftly apart in the twilight. An amused expression crossed his face as he switched on the lights. His trouble in buying that mirror and rehanging his pictures to suit had not been altogether wasted. Every piece of evidence was important at this juncture.

When he turned the corner of the L, he was grimly amused to find Langler in a chair some feet away from the settee. As he had foreseen, neither of them had noticed the mirror in the dusk.

His cordial greeting banished any suspicion they might have had, and talk flowed pleasantly enough until Monica arrived. She was evidently looking forward to an enjoyable evening, though Langler's presence had evidently struck a jarring note.

'And what are you going to do with yourself when you've got us off your hands?' she demanded after a moment or two. 'Go down to that laboratory as usual, I suppose? You couldn't tear yourself away from it?'

Lessingham shook his grey head with a faint smile.

'No, I can't,' he answered, taking the others into his confidence intentionally. 'Each night at ten o'clock I have to take a series of photographs. It's a kind of slow-motion cinema-film and a break in the run of it would ruin the work of some weeks. That's why I've had no one to dinner for the last month or so.'

'Rather a slow affair,' Langler commented, with a trace of contempt in his tone. 'Is it worth all the trouble?'

'To me, yes,' Lessingham replied indifferently. 'And with these scientific affairs, one never knows what the ultimate result may be. They ramify amazingly, sometimes. When Cross and Bevan started to work on cellulose, nobody could have foreseen that half the girls in the country would be wearing artificial silk as a result.'

'Ah, now you're talking about something that touches the spot,' Langler interrupted. 'If you could find some way of making the faces at one end as pretty as the stockings at the other, you'd be building a brighter world for us all. Any chance of it?'

Lessingham's smile was quite unforced.

'Well, even there, science does its bit, you know. Lipsticks, skin-foods, face-powder: they all come out of the laboratory. What more do you want?'

'Something in that,' Langler admitted reflectively, as though the idea was new to him

'Even my present line of work might touch a life or two by the time it's finished,' Lessingham volunteered carelessly.

'You must tell me about it some other time,' Langler proposed, without enthusiasm. Then he seemed suddenly to remember an oversight, and turned to Claire. 'Do you mind if I write a note? It's something that's slipped my mind. Rather important. Perhaps you could get it posted for me?'

Taking permission for granted, he went down the room to a writing-table, pulled out a fountain-pen, and began to scribble. Lessingham, chatting to the two girls in an undertone, kept an eye on his guest's proceedings.

Langler selected two single sheets, wrote what seemed to be a short note, and then picked up an envelope. But only one of the written sheets went into the envelope before he sealed and addressed it. The second sheet, with a line or two on it, went furtively into his pocket, folded small. Lessingham's thin lips curved in a quickly-repressed smile. He had laid his trap, and it amused him to see Langler walking into it so easily. Evidently Mr Owen Langler was no very formidable opponent in this game which was being forced upon him.

'That's that,' said Langler, rising from the table and coming towards them with the envelope displayed in his hand. 'I've taken one of your stamps. You don't mind? And may I ring to have it posted? It's rather important.'

Claire made a gesture towards the bell, and Langler pressed the button. When the maid had taken the letter, Monica turned to Langler.

'It's a pity to leave you to your own resources after dinner. We're going on to a small dance at the Shards. My husband's calling for us. You don't know the Shards?'

'No,' Langler admitted. 'But don't worry about me. I shall find something to fill in the evening easily enough. I never live by a timetable. Claire and I are rather alike in that way,' he added, shooting a glance across at the girl on the settee. 'It's a mistake to have things planned to the last dot, I think. Takes away from the pleasure of them when you know for certain they're going to happen. Half the sport's in not knowing just what's coming next.'

'Very amusing,' Lessingham commented with a smile. 'Sometimes I feel inclined to look on things that way myself.'

Monica, who was not amused, began to wonder if her father was losing his sense of humour.

Dinner was announced at this moment. They passed into the dining-room. Lessingham, lingering momentarily to switch off the lights in the drawing-room, saw Langler's hand go to his pocket. Then, as if by accident, he brushed against Claire, and Lessingham saw a scrap of paper changing hands. He smiled again, but this time there was no geniality but merely contempt. Really, Langler was a very easy mark. Finesse was hardly necessary in dealing with a person of his mental equipment.

During the meal Lessingham contented himself with stimulating the conversation if it showed signs of flagging. He was reserving himself for his interview with Langler when they were alone together, and for the present he cast himself for the role of an attentive but self-effacing host. During the first two courses, Claire chattered vivaciously as usual, flitting from one triviality to another with no traceable continuity.

Monica made little effort to be more than courteous, so that Langler was left to fill in the gaps in the loquacity of his hostess. He was not averse from this, but he was careful to talk briefly and to end up always with a question which gave Claire a fresh starting-point.

Lessingham, though apparently unobservant, kept a close watch on his daughter-in-law. How was she going to read the note? The safest way would be to wait until the girls had left the room, when she could make some excuse to go off by herself for a moment or two.

But could anyone of her character show the patience necessary to wait for this opportunity? No, she would want to know the contents at once. And when she at last succeeded, under cover of fumbling to extract a handkerchief from her evening bag below the table-level, Lessingham knew exactly what she was about.

Monica, who had not seen the manoeuvre, was more surprised than Lessingham by the next move. Suddenly the flow of words slackened. Langler was left to bear a larger share of the conversation, which he was by no means unwilling to do, as it seemed. Soon Claire was reduced to monosyllables, and at that point Langler affected to notice something amiss.

'What's wrong?' he asked, sympathetically. 'Feeling under the weather tonight?'

Lessingham, behind his mask, put this down as an artistic blunder on Langler's part. He should have waited and allowed one of the others to ask that question. Obviously the man was so eager that he could not keep himself in hand. Well, all the better from Lessingham's point of view. That lack of self-restraint was just what he had been hoping for in Langler's character.

Claire rubbed her eyes with a childish gesture which seemed natural for her.

'I've got the beginning of a headache,' she complained, as though she had received a deliberate injury. 'It'll pass off, perhaps.'

She was not much of an actress, however, and from time to time the old vivacity broke through her pretence. But at last, as the girls rose to leave the room, she turned to Monica.

'I'm not going to that dance tonight. I don't feel up to it. It doesn't matter, really. And if I went, I'd be only a nuisance, moping about like a sick cat.'

She passed her hand over her brow as though to soothe the pain. Monica thought little of this last-moment change in plan. It was so like Claire to scrap an engagement in this way, without considering other people. And in this case little harm would be done. A dance was not the same as a bridge party.

'Shall I get you some aspirin?' she asked. 'You'd better take it at once. It might check the headache before it gets really bad.'

Claire shook her head.

'No, thanks. Perhaps I'll take some later on. I'll go into the drawing-room with you until Basil turns up. Then I'll slip off to bed and try to get to sleep. That's the best way.'

Langler came forward.

'Mr Estcourt is coming almost at once, isn't he? Then perhaps I'd better say goodnight now, to both of you. I'm going to ask Mr Lessingham to show me some of the wonderful things he was telling us about in his laboratory.'

Lessingham almost chuckled at this speech. That bit of soft soap about 'wonderful things' amused him intensely, for he had a very good idea of what Langler's interest in laboratories amounted to. It was so obvious what the man was driving at. 'Get the old fool into his laboratory. Come away as soon as possible. She'll be waiting for me in the drawing-room when the coast's clear. And Lessingham has to take these photographs at half past ten, and that won't be a matter of a minute or two.'

One did not need to be a mind-reader to fathom people like

Langler. But what deepened his enjoyment of the situation was the fact that Langler, of his own accord, had blundered straight into the trap, without waiting for it to be baited. He wanted to visit the laboratory? Well, no one would be more pleased than his host, if he insisted.

Lessingham opened the door for the girls to pass out. Then, closing it, he returned to his seat, inviting Langler to take his own chair. Now they had come to the decisive stage of the evening.

III

As Lessingham pushed the decanter across the table to Langler, he reflected comfortably that he knew just how matters stood. Wholly disregardful of conventional niceties where Jack's interests were concerned, he had employed private detectives to watch over his daughter-in-law; and their reports showed that hitherto Claire had not overstepped the 'limit' of her slogan. Fool though she was, she had been just sufficiently cautious.

But with Langler, anything might happen. Lessingham had gathered information about the man's past history, and it was all of a piece. Believing himself irresistible, his vanity was involved as soon as he fixed his choice on a woman, and he was ruthless to his victims.

For the most part, his affairs were furtive, ending obscurely; but Lessingham's researches had unearthed one ugly business which had finished in a suicide. At the inquest Langler had been technically cleared but the Coroner had left him with little credit.

Now Lessingham, knowing the man's weakness, deliberately led the talk by slow degrees to his guest's favourite subject—and Langler rose to the bait. Making love was his speciality; failing that, he liked best to talk about it.

'I'm afraid I know very little about women,' the older man said diffidently at last, as though bowing to a superior's knowledge 'I suppose there's some definite technique in these affairs?'

There was an encouraging twinkle in his grey eyes as he spoke, and about his mouth the trace of a sardonic smile which seemed to say, 'Come, we're both men of the world. I'm not a shockable type.'

'Technique?' Langler echoed, reflectively. 'Well, I suppose you can call it that, just as you talk about artists' technique. But in practice, each case stands by itself. That's what makes it so fascinating to me, Lessingham.'

'Oh, there must be some general rules,' said Lessingham, impatiently. 'You don't mean to tell me that a man of your experience is no better than a boy in his teens when it comes to sizing up a girl who interests you? You must have learned something from practice. You can't be much of an artist in the business if you haven't got beyond the pot-hooks, at your age.'

The faint sneer in Lessingham's tone flicked Langler's vanity, as his host intended; and he reacted precisely as the older man had foreseen. For a moment or two he was silent, as though reviewing some of his many affairs in order to find pegs on which to hang his ideas. Then, apparently baffled, he made a gesture of irritation.

'You can't classify things like these,' he said, crossly. 'Each is a special case, as I told you. If it's a shop-girl, you might buy her a musquash coat. If it's a lonely girl, homesick perhaps, you can take her about a bit till she gets a taste for company and bright lights. Then she can't bear to lose that.'

'Or a married girl may have got bored with a dull husband and wants something more interesting. Or a grass-widow may be pining for someone to amuse her. Or, maybe, a girl's just bored with things in general and jumps at the chance of a little risk and excitement.'

Lessingham betrayed more interest.

'Well, after all,' he pointed out, 'you've got the basis of a classification there. You trade on poverty, and loneliness, and unhappiness, and the irk for excitement. Is that the whole recipe? It seems simpler than I had supposed.'

'It's not so simple as you make out,' Langler protested.

He hesitated again, rather longer than the last time, before continuing.

'Look here. I'll give you an instance or two, just to convince you that you can't lay down rules. No names, of course.'

Lessingham agreed with a nod; and Langler, now really enjoying himself, proceeded to quote case after case, glancing at his host to see the effect of each anecdote. These quiet old birds might not do that sort of thing themselves, he reflected, but they did love to hear about it. He found Lessingham's attention very flattering.

One or two of the stories were so thinly disguised that Lessingham, from his private information, had no difficulty in identifying the women involved. And from the fact that Langler told these tales accurately enough, his host inferred that the other narratives were no mere inventions.

He listened with obvious interest as the catalogue was unfolded, now sordid, occasionally tragic; and when Langler seemed doubtful, Lessingham was always ready with some curt cynicism which encouraged the narrator to further efforts.

But in the pleasure of his reminiscences, Langler had forgotten the passing of time. He glanced at his watch, and the position of its hands seemed to cut off his autobiographical flow. Lessingham rose from his chair. If he had any doubts, Langler's reminiscences had completely dispelled them. Things should take the course he had planned. As his guest got to his feet, Lessingham put a question.

'You've convinced me that it's a fascinating amusement,' he admitted. 'But what about the other side? What do these girls get out of it?'

'Why, I give them a better time than they're having.'

'For how long?'

Langler laughed knowingly. He had taken rather more wine than he ought to have done.

'Till the gilt wears off the gingerbread, I suppose.'

'And then? You salve your conscience by providing for them in some way or other?'

Langler stared at him in genuine surprise.

'Far from it. When you buy a box of cigars, do you pay the shopkeeper a pension for the rest of his life? Not much! He's got to find fresh customers when you've gone. So have the girls.'

'That's a very neat analogy,' Lessingham admitted, without disapproval. 'And sometimes the shopkeeper closes down, doesn't he, without bothering about fresh customers? Like Lettice Stannary?'

'Lettice Stannary?' repeated Langler. 'Oh, she was a little fool, if you want one. Fancy taking sleep-stuff over a thing of that sort! I suppose she thought I meant to marry her. Good Lord!'

He halted for a moment, and Lessingham wondered if he had felt a pang of conscience. But Langler's next words satisfied him on that score.

'She was one of these fluffy, clinging little things, you know. Very affectionate and with no brains to worry her when she shook her head. A week of her chatter bored me stiff, once the thing was done, but she was one of the sort who think it's going on for ever, like the brook.

'When she found I was tired of her, she cried all day long, as if that would do any good. Girls of her type shouldn't cry; it ruins their looks and then bang goes their last chance. She'd no sense of realities, Lettice. She'd have got over it in no time, if she'd been sensible, instead of letting me in for no end of trouble, as she did.'

Lessingham reflected that Claire might be called a 'fluffy, clinging little thing'; and in some curious way that description softened his heart slightly towards his daughter-in-law just as it hardened him towards Langler.

By Lessingham's standards, Claire was a mere empty-headed little fool; but in the normal course of things, that was the worst one could say about her. The real danger was not from her, but from Langler. If he were out of the way, she would revert to type again, and the risk would be over.

Lessingham saw that his guest was now only too anxious to be rid of him; but he meant to delay him further and make him still more eager.

'Try some of this, before you go,' he said, hospitably, turning to the sideboard. 'It's out of the common, and I don't offer it to everybody. But you've given me an amusing evening. I picked it up in Italy.'

Langler had not the courtesy to treat it as it deserved. He tossed it down at one gulp, and it made him no soberer. He glanced round the room as he put down his glass.

'Good stuff,' he commented. 'By the way, that's a copy of a Fragonard, over there, isn't it?'

'No, it's a real one,' Lessingham corrected.

'You do yourself well,' Langler opined as the wine got the better of his manners. 'You made a pile out of the war, didn't you? Blood money, some people call it; but it seems to spend just as well as the ordinary kind.'

'It never troubled my conscience,' Lessingham assured him with a smile. 'As a matter of fact, I made it by saving life: gas-- masks and a submarine gadget. It was the submarine side of it that led me on to this high-pressure work, in a way; and luckily I had enough money to fit up a laboratory to my liking.'

'Yes, yes, this scientific stuff,' Langler interrupted impatiently. 'Not much use in trying to explain it to me, I'm afraid. Still, I'd like to see your place. It'll be a fresh experience for me. Daniel in the lions' den, eh? Between ourselves, is there anything in all this research and so forth, or is it all my eye? It doesn't seem the sort of thing one could get a kick out of.'

'I'm afraid it won't interest you,' Lessingham admitted. 'I don't want to bore you, so perhaps we'd better not bother about the laboratory tonight. I'll let you out before I shut myself up for the rest of the evening.'

It was a safe enough offer, for if Langler accepted it then he lost his chance of furtively rejoining Claire, with his host 'shut up for the rest of the evening'. To leave the house meant ringing the bell and making a public re-entry on some excuse or other, which might arouse suspicion.

'Not at all. I'd like to see what you have on show.'

'It's not very exciting,' Lessingham admitted with perfect frankness. 'All you'll see will be some apparatus and a few plants. I'm studying the effect of high pressures on plant growth. Vegetables are more sensitive than you'd think to slight changes in their environment.

'It's interesting to see what happens when one changes the pressure. Animals are outside my bounds. One can photograph a plant day by day since it's fixed in the same spot; and that gives a permanent record of what's been happening week by week.

'But animals are more troublesome. Even the daily weighing and measuring of a guinea-pig might be more trouble than it was worth. So I prefer to stick to vegetables.'

'Quite so. Well, what about getting a move on?' Langler suggested. 'I understand as much as I'm likely ever to do, now, so I may as well see what's to be seen '

Lessingham gave him a second or two to change his mind, if he wished to do so. Then he opened the door and led the way past the drawing-room to the passage which communicated with the laboratory outside the main building.

IV

Lessingham halted before a heavy steel door and pointed to a house-telephone on a bracket beside it.

'That links me up with the outside world if necessary, when

I'm busy inside,' he explained, as he swung the door open. 'Now we'll go through.'

Langler, stepping over the threshold, found himself in a compartment hardly larger than a small lift.

'This isn't my laboratory,' Lessingham pointed out. 'It's merely an intermediate space with two doors, one into the laboratory and the other into the passage. Just now, it's at atmospheric pressure, naturally. I shut the outer door and start the pumps by this switch.'

Langler heard the dull heavy thud of some pumping machinery, and a current of air gushed intermittently through an orifice in the wall.

'Now this is the point you must note carefully,' Lessingham continued. 'See this control-handle? When it's turned, it opens communication with the outside and the high-pressure air can escape from here, bringing the pressure down to normal. You see the gauge beside it, with 'NORMAL' marked on the red line. When you come out again, you must let the pressure down *slowly*, remember. That's important. Delicate machinery isn't built to stand sudden jerks. You realise that, don't you?'

Langler nodded in response. He seemed slightly unsteady on his feet and put out his hand to the wall of the compartment.

'You feel a bit dizzy?' Lessingham asked. 'One's apt to feel like that for a moment or two. It's due to the change of pressure in the middle ear, I believe. Swallow, once or twice; that may help to cure it.'

'My ears are ringing,' Langler complained.

'There's nothing in that. It will soon pass off.'

For some time longer Lessingham allowed his pumps to work and the pressure in the compartment rose rapidly. At last an examination of a second gauge showed him that there was equality between the entrance-room and the inner chamber. He threw open the connecting door and ushered his guest into the laboratory.

'Not very exciting,' Langler commented, staring owlishly

about him at the unfamiliar environment. If Lessingham had brought a gorilla into his laboratory, it would have shown as much intelligent interest.

'I didn't promise you much,' Lessingham pointed out. 'You can't look at the view, since there aren't any windows. The whole thing is built of ferro-concrete, made to stand far higher pressures than I'm ever likely to use.'

Despite his guest's obvious lack of curiosity, he insisted on explaining in rather wearisome detail the functions of the various pieces of apparatus: the row of cinema-cameras which recorded daily the growth of the plants under examination, the ultra-violet lights which took the place of the sun, the arrangement which kept the humidity constant, the temperature regulator, the electric fans which kept the air well mixed and prevented the heavy carbon dioxide gas from accumulating at floor level.

He made no effort to be interesting or even lucid; and he watched with a certain sardonic amusement the growing fidgetiness of Langler, who was obviously only too anxious to find some excuse for terminating the lecture.

Lessingham had little difficulty in guessing what was in the man's mind. He wanted to get out of this place as soon as he could. His glances at his watch showed that he feared Claire might tire of waiting alone if he delayed too long.

Once with her in the drawing-room, it would be easy enough to feign interest in something, a piece of jewellery, a book, or a picture, anything which would form an excuse for visiting her side of the house. He could pick up his hat and coat as he went, so that it would seem as though he had gone home after quitting the laboratory.

Then, past those curtains, he would be alone with Claire in a part of the premises which Lessingham never entered. That was the opportunity for which he had been scheming since he came to the house that evening.

At last Lessingham seemed to take pity on his reluctant listener.

'I think that's really all I have to show you,' he said. 'And now, if you don't mind, I'll have to turn you out and get on with my work. I've a lot to do before I can get to bed.'

Langler, in evident fear lest something might lead to further delay, bade his host a hasty farewell. As he was going towards the exit, Lessingham stopped him with a gesture.

'Don't forget to let down the pressure very slowly with that control handle,' he said. 'These high pressures set up all sorts of unexpected strains, and fragile apparatus is apt to suffer if you run down the scale too quick. But I told you that before, didn't I? Gently does it. By the way, you needn't trouble about closing the outer door. A special automatic gadget drives it home into its bed after you've gone out. I'll say goodbye now.'

He opened the laboratory door and ushered Langler into the small compartment. Then, closing the door, he studied the gauge for a short time, while a faint smile curved his lips. After that he turned back to his research apparatus, humming an air under his breath as though quite satisfied and care-free.

In their sitting-room, the housemaid was chatting with Mrs Greenhill, the cook-housekeeper.

'Mrs Jack's headache must have got better. She said at dinner she was going straight off to bed, but she's still sitting up in the drawing-room.'

'With this Langler man you were telling me about?' queried Mrs Greenhill.

Freda shook her head. She was gifted with exceptionally acute hearing; and without being specially prying, she generally had a fair knowledge of what was happening in the house.

'No, he went down to the laboratory after dinner. He's there yet. And that's surprising, for anyone can see with half an eye that he's . . . Well, if Mr Jack hadn't been there first, he could have clicked with Mrs Jack quick enough. And not much wonder, I say.

'He's like one of these men you see at the talkies, but never have the luck to come across except on the screen. Sort of looks at you with these liquid eyes at his . . . *you* know. If he was to offer me an engagement ring I wouldn't be long in taking it.'

'If he offers you an engagement ring, my lass,' said Mrs Greenhill, who was old-fashioned and cynical, 'you take my advice and run straight to the jeweller's and see if it's the genuine article. It won't be. These talkies put all sorts of silly notions into young girls' heads, to my mind. Now there's the greengrocer's man. Not a bad-looking young fellow, and steady. Gets a good wage. Why don't you . . . What's that?'

The sound of a heavy body falling in the hall. The choking cry of a man in agony. Then Freda's sharp ears caught a quick patter of feet from the drawing-room, and a woman's shriek echoed through the house.

Mrs Greenhill wasted no time. Before the second outcry came from the hall, she was out of her sitting-room, followed by the trembling Freda. When they came round the corner they saw Langler writhing on the floor, his clothes in the horrible disarray of a death agony, while Claire knelt beside him, hiding her face in her hands. As they looked, the body gave one last convulsion, rolled over, and lay still.

There was a stolid streak in Mrs Greenhill's character which served them well at this moment. She had seen death more than once in her family circle, though never in this ghastly form, and she kept her head. Her first thought was for Claire, whom she half-persuaded, half-forced back into the drawing-room, soothing her as best she could.

'Just sit there a moment, ma'am,' she adjured her, 'and I'll get Mr Lessingham. He's in his laboratory.'

And in her retreat she thoughtfully turned the key in the lock lest Claire should attempt to return to the hall. Freda, with staring eyes, had retreated into one corner of the hall, away from the body. Mrs Greenhill pounced on her at once. A girl in that state needed something to do, before she went off the handle, the housekeeper surmised.

'You, Freda. You go and ring up Mr Estcourt. You know where he is—where Mrs Jack was going tonight. Tell him to come here at once. Understand me? At once, tell him. And go now. I'm going to get Mr Lessingham from the laboratory.'

It was an understood rule in the house that the telephone at the laboratory door was not to be used except in emergencies, but this was obviously no time to stand on ceremony. Mrs Greenhill rang, and after a few seconds Lessingham's voice inquired what brought her there. Breathlessly she gave an account of what had just happened.

'Is he dead? You're quite sure?' Lessingham demanded when she had told her tale.

'Oh, yes, sir. There's no doubt about it. I know what dead people look like. Terrible pain he was suffering before the end, sir. I've told Freda to ring up Mr Estcourt. That was right. wasn't it?'

Lessingham seemed to consider for a moment, before answering.

'Quite right. He'll be here shortly, I expect. In the meantime, since Mr Langler is dead, there's nothing to be done. I can't come myself just now. Mr Estcourt will look after things.'

The click of the replaced receiver came through to Mrs Greenhill, ending the conversation decisively. The housekeeper mechanically hung up her own receiver. This incident staggered her even more than Langler's death had done. Lessingham had always been, to her mind, the kindest and most sympathetic of employers and his behaviour now seemed wholly unnatural.

'Well, I never!' she ejaculated to herself. 'Here's a friend of his, dead in his own hall, and all he's got to say is to ask if he's quite dead and that he'll come out by-and-by and see about it!

I didn't think he was that sort, by a long chalk. It just shows one can't tell what people are really like.'

Thoroughly shocked by Lessingham's callousness, she returned to the hall and sought out Freda, who was on the verge of hysterics in the cloak-room.

'Did you do that telephoning?' Mrs Greenhill demanded, severely, for she had little sympathy with what she called 'nerves'.

'Yes. Mr Estcourt's coming. He'll be here in a minute or two. And I rang up the police station, too, and they're sending someone up at once.'

'The police? What did you want to ring them up for? The man's had a fit or else he's died of heart disease, same as my uncle did. A doctor's all that's wanted.'

Freda might reasonably have objected that if a doctor was required, then a surgeon was hardly the best person to summon; but her knowledge of these niceties was sketchy. She made no defence, but Mrs Greenhill's reproof seemed to have brought her nearer to normal, and she managed to keep herself in hand.

From the drawing-room came the sound of Claire crying, with an occasional outburst of disjointed words. Mrs Greenhill decided it was best, in that case, to let things alone. She settled down grimly to wait for Estcourt's arrival, puzzling meanwhile over the mystery of Lessingham's behaviour.

V

When Estcourt, hurrying from his interrupted dance, was challenged by a uniformed constable at Lessingham's door, he may well have felt surprise, but he was too cool-headed to show it. On giving his name, he was ushered in and received by the officer in charge.

Inspector Wyndcliffe had not been long on the premises, but he had spent his time well. He had taken the evidence, such as it was, of the three women and had tactfully induced them to remain in the drawing-room. From Mrs Greenhill, he learned of the summons to Estcourt, whose name was familiar to him.

Up to that stage, he had felt that the police had been called in on a false alarm. But the next incident aroused suspicions that all was not as it should be. He made an attempt to induce Lessingham to leave the laboratory and met with a blunt refusal.

Lessingham declared that Estcourt could explain matters when he arrived. And when the inspector persisted, Lessingham had simply hung up his receiver and left Wyndcliffe helpless and fuming on the other side of the steel door.

Estcourt, on his arrival, was quick to note a certain hostility and suspiciousness in the inspector's manner; but he ignored it completely. He made what seemed to Wyndcliffe a very superficial examination of Langler's body, merely as if to satisfy himself that the man was dead. Then he rose to his feet and put a question to the inspector.

'Was this man in the laboratory with Mr Lessingham tonight?'

'He was, sir.' Wyndcliffe consulted his notes. 'The housemaid says they left the dining-room at about a quarter to ten. She heard them in the hall, then, evidently on the way to this laboratory.'

'When did death occur?'

'We were rung up at 10.10,' the inspector answered him cautiously.

Estcourt pondered for some seconds, as though calculating something. Then he took the inspector by surprise.

'I'll sign a certificate giving it as "Death by misadventure",' he volunteered. 'That will save you any further trouble, won't it?'

Wyndcliffe's eyes narrowed slightly. He remembered that Estcourt was Lessingham's son-in-law and therefore had a strong motive for shielding the older man, if there had been any foul play. The suspicion roused by Lessingham's peculiar behaviour now blazed up actively.

'I'm afraid that will hardly do, sir,' he declared bluntly. 'We shall have to get the police surgeon's opinion. I may as well tell you, sir, that I once had to do with an arsenic-poisoning case. The symptoms here—as described by the two maids—look to me very much like arsenic.

'He was very sick. You can see that yourself. He had intense pain in the stomach region, "writhing in agony, cramps," they told me, just before he died. I'm not pitting my knowledge against yours, of course; but we must have a second opinion. Personally, I can't take "misadventure" as a proper explanation.

'Perfectly sound,' Estcourt agreed, equably. 'I've no objection to what you say. Since you've been called in, the responsibility's yours.'

'One further point, sir. We must have Mr Lessingham's evidence, obviously. Why didn't he come out of his laboratory when I called on him to do so?'

'Because he couldn't,' said Estcourt concisely.

'But . . .'

'I see what you're driving at,' continued the surgeon. 'It's a mare's nest, if you don't mind my putting it so. I'm not sneering, Mr Wyndcliffe. It's merely that this case is rather out of the normal, and nine doctors out of ten would be puzzled by it. I happen to have seen a similar case when I was attached to an anti-submarine business in the war. Ever hear of "caisson sickness"?'

Wyndcliffe shook his head. Estcourt's matter-of-fact manner was making him wonder if he had not been rather too hasty in what he had said.

'I'll explain,' Estcourt volunteered. 'And I daresay I can find some books in the library here which will let you check what I say. First of all, Mr Lessingham is a scientific man carrying out some research work in his laboratory on the effects of high pressures. The laboratory has been specially built for the work. It's designed like this.'

He took a notebook and pencil from his pocket and by means of a rough sketch explained the plan of the laboratory and the intermediate chamber.

'Now, here is the point,' be continued. 'You know that air is a mixture of oxygen and nitrogen mainly, with some other things like carbon dioxide and argon in minor percentages. Very good.

'When you breathe normally, you inhale the mixture. The oxygen dissolves in your blood and is carried through your system, cleaning up things in general, and oxidising carbon compounds to carbon dioxide, which you breathe out. The nitrogen also dissolves in your blood, but as it's chemically inert it plays no part in your vital machinery and you breathe it out again unchanged. See that?'

'I follow you so far,' the inspector admitted, 'but I don't see it gets us any further.'

'Not immediately,' agreed Estcourt. 'But now suppose you double the air-pressure. Then the blood takes up twice as much oxygen as before and twice as much nitrogen. The extra oxygen does no harm. It simply speeds up your vital processes a bit, because now there's twice as much of the oxidising agent present. The nitrogen, being inactive, does no harm either, so long as you keep the pressure up.

'You breathe it out again twice as fast, that's all. But notice, the blood has been able, owing to the doubled pressure, to dissolve twice as much nitrogen as it does normally; and it can only hold that quantity in solution so long as the outside pressure is maintained. What will happen if you suddenly reduce the pressure?'

'I shouldn't like to say,' confessed Wyndcliffe cautiously.

'Well, here's something from daily life. Soda-water has been bottled under three or four atmospheres pressure of carbon dioxide. What happens when you unscrew the stopper?'

'The gas bubbles off with a fizz, of course.'

'And suppose you had blood in the bottle and you saturated it with nitrogen gas under three or four atmospheres pressure, what would happen when you loosened the stopper?'

'I suppose it would bubble off just the same, would it?'

'Exactly. And the result will be gas bubbles forming in all your veins and arteries, giving rise to air-locks in your circulatory system. If you're a motor-cyclist, and ever had an airlock in your petrol feed, you'll know what I mean.'

As it chanced, the inspector had a vivid recollection of just such an airlock.

'I know what you mean, sir. The blood would stop circulating?'

'And that means death, of course. A rather uncomfortable form of it, too. I once saw a diver go out that way after he'd been pulled up too quick from a deep dive to investigate a sunk submarine. The symptoms were just the same as in this case here. So probably the cause is the same in the two cases: too quick a release of pressure.

'If a diver has gone deep, the only way is to pull him up very gradually so as to let the dissolved nitrogen come out of solution in very small quantities at a time, so that it's breathed out instead of forming big bubbles in the system. If you have a post-mortem in this case, see that the pathologist looks for these bubbles, round about the spine especially. I'd advise a post-mortem, Mr Wyndcliffe. We don't want any grounds left for suspicion about arsenic or anything of that sort, you know.'

The inspector's suspicions were clearing away, but they had not entirely gone.

'But how did he come into this state?' he demanded.

'Isn't it obvious? He went into the laboratory with Mr Lessingham, under high pressure. Mr Lessingham works in the laboratory at night, I know. He would have his work to do; so after he had shown Langler round, he would explain to him how to get outside through the intermediate trap-chamber; and, knowing Mr Lessingham I'm sure he would caution Langler to be slow in the matter of lowering the pressure. Langler must have disregarded his instructions and come out far too quick. And so . . .'

He pointed down to the body at their feet. Wyndcliffe thought for a moment or two. Then he smiled rather sheepishly.

'And that's why Mr Lessingham wouldn't come out when I asked him to?'

'Of course. It would have killed him, if he had. And I think you'll admit that a telephone was hardly a suitable means for giving you this little scientific lecture on the properties of gas solutions under pressure. He left it to me, naturally. Satisfied?'

The inspector made a gesture of assent.

'He seems to have brought it on himself, if your account's correct, sir. "Misadventure" describes it accurately enough, though it didn't look like it at first.'

'Now let's see what's still to be done,' Estcourt proposed. 'First of all, we'd better get these women off to bed, out of the way. Then your police surgeon will want a look round, I expect, and a talk with me won't do him any harm.

'Meanwhile, you might do worse than check what I've told you from the monographs in the library here, while you're waiting for Mr Lessingham to come out. He's longer than usual, tonight. I expect that after this affair he's inclined to be extra cautious.'

'I shouldn't blame him myself,' the inspector commented rather grimly. 'We shall have to remove the body tonight, of course. I expect you'll be glad to have it taken away.'

An examination of passages in the technical works in the library satisfied the inspector completely, and he began to feel slightly ashamed of the way he had betrayed his suspicions earlier in the evening.

When Lessingham at last ventured out of his laboratory Wyndcliffe merely made some almost formal inquiries as to the events of the past few hours. The verdict of the police surgeon, after consultation with Estcourt, completed the conversion.

When the officials had gone Estcourt spent a few minutes in telephoning to his wife, to explain what had occurred. Then, before going home, he thought it well to have a word or two with his father-in-law. Lessingham was smoking in the drawing-room, and Estcourt noticed that the smoke spirals rose straight from the cigar. The hand that held it was steady as a rock.

Estcourt came and leaned against the mantelpiece instead of sitting down, to show that he did not mean to stay long. They understood each other well enough to need no explicit statements. A hint was enough; and Estcourt, in the present affair, had no wish to have things put too definitely.

'Langler's no great loss,' he said bluntly. 'I never heard anything good of him.'

Lessingham gave him a keen glance

'Some people will be safer, now he's gone,' he commented. 'He gave me some of his autobiography after dinner. A wholly worthless creature, I found him, by his own showing. I gather that he took me for an old fool who couldn't see what was going on under his own nose.'

Estcourt nodded. At times he had wondered just how much the older man knew about Langler and Claire.

'No harm done?' he asked.

'Yes, a lot,' Lessingham retorted unexpectedly. 'I've lost three months' work tonight. I put the laboratory up to thrice its usual pressure this evening. That's ruined the whole of the results in this series. I'll have to scrap the lot. Still, I suppose it's cheap at the price.'

Estcourt understood what lay behind the words. Even under normal working conditions, a careless exit from the laboratory was fraught with danger. When the pressure was trebled, the thing became practically a certainty.

'You cautioned him, of course?'

'Naturally,' Lessingham assured him with a wintry smile. 'I warned him that high pressures played tricks with delicate machinery. Anyone knows that the body's a delicate machine. But he didn't listen. He was thinking of something else, something that made him eager to get away from the laboratory as soon as he could.'

He paused and then added, as by an afterthought:

'Claire was waiting in the drawing-room.'

Estcourt did not even profess to be shocked. He knew Jack; he had some understanding of Claire; and his feelings for Langler had been a mixture of dislike and contempt. Evidently Lessingham had stepped in at the very last moment to avert a real tragedy, much more important than the elimination of Langler.

Lessingham smoked in silence for a while. Then he added reflectively:

'It will be a lesson to her. One hopes she'll profit by it. I rather think so.'

J. J. CONNINGTON

Alfred Walter Stewart, whose pseudonym was 'J. J. Connington', was born in Glasgow on 5 September 1880. Stewart was the son of the Dean of Faculties at the city's university where, after leaving school, he studied Chemistry, supported by a scholarship. It was the start of a long and prestigious academic career. Further scholarships followed, and in 1905 he was appointed a Carnegie Research Fellow. In 1909, after failing the previous year to become Chair of Chemistry at Dundee University, Stewart took up a role as Lecturer on Organic Chemistry at Queen's University, Belfast. In 1914 he was appointed Lecturer on Physical Chemistry and Radioactivity at Glasgow, where in 1916 he married Jessie Lily Coats. Three years later he returned to Queen's as Professor of Chemistry, a position he held until 1944, shortly before his death.

While Alfred Stewart would write many academic papers and several chemistry textbooks, he was also renowned for his lectures, during which he performed experiments. These included series for the Belfast Natural History and Philosophical Society on 'The Rise of Radioactivity' (1920) and for the Belfast Workers' Educational Association on 'The Foundation Stones of the Universe (1925) and 'Chemistry in Everyday Life' (1926). He also ran an open course for Queens on 'Light, Flames and Explosions' (1924) and lectured on 'Scientific Evidence' (1929) for the Chemical Society of Ulster. In 1937, Stewart was part of the team that claimed to have photographed the Loch Ness Monster, chronicled in Commander Rupert Gould's *The Loch Ness Monster and Others* (1934).

As well as chemistry and radioactivity, Stewart was fascinated by the study of forgery in handwriting, on which he lectured to the University Law Society. It led to his giving evidence in a trial where, in the judge's words, he established himself as 'an obvious expert', and this experience led him to consider writing crime fiction. Over twenty years he wrote seventeen novels featuring the fearsomely intelligent Sir Clinton Driffield: mysteries like the double puzzle of *Murder in the Maze* (1927), in which two brothers are poisoned by curare, and *The Sweepstake Murders* (1931), where members of a syndicate are killed one by one. In other cases, Driffield unravelled the machinations of a 'poison pen' in *For Murder Will Speak* (1938) and investigated the death of a money-lender in *No Past Is Dead* (1942). His final case was *Common Sense Is All You Need* (1947), the plot of which encompasses air raids, paper salvage and the killing of a treasure hunter.

Stewart also created two less well-known detectives: a police superintendent called Ross, and Max Brand, a one-man 'Brains Trust' for Radio Ardennes, whose first case, *The Counsellor* (1939), involved the kidnapping of a young woman and her father's apparent suicide.

As well as detective stories, Stewart wrote science fiction. The novel *Nordenholt's Million* (1923) depicts a global famine resulting from the accidental release of denitrifying bacilli, echoing the works of H. G. Wells and anticipating those of J. G. Ballard, and in an uncollected short story, 'Danger in the Dark Cave' (1938), he speculates about a source of infinite energy.

Alfred Stewart died at his home in Belfast on 1 July 1947. He had been ill for some time. His final work, published posthumously under his own name, was 'an escape book', an eclectic volume of essays entitled *Alias J. J. Connington* (1947), whose original title had been the somewhat opaque *Elephants in Place of Towns*.

'The Pressure of Circumstance' was first published as a serial in the London *Daily News* between 10 and 14 February 1936. Stewart later adapted the story into an 'original' radio play, broadcast on the BBC Home Service in two parts on 23 and 30 August 1943 as the last of the series *Mystery Playhouse* by members of the Detection Club.

THE RIDDLE OF
THE CABIN CRUISER

John Dickson Carr

JOHN DICKSON CARR: This is the story of a curious crime—
and an even more curious mistake. You perhaps read, in the
newspapers last August, of the death of Mr George Randolph,
that very wealthy stockbroker, who was found stabbed to
death in his cabin cruiser—a sort of glorified motor-boat—a
quarter of a mile off the coast of Brecon, in North Wales.
The full story behind that death belongs to Dr Carteret, who
at the time was deputising as Coroner in Brecon for his old
friend Mr Malloy. And so, in the seaside town on that hot
August afternoon . . . (*Fade out*)

(*Fade in*)

CARTARET: Members of the Jury, you have just heard formal
identification of the body by the widow of the deceased, Mrs
Mary Randolph. Will you take the witness-chair again, Mrs
Randolph?

MARIE: (*apparently suffering from shock, in a suppressed voice*)
Yes. Of course, Dr Carteret.

CARTERET: I don't want to distress you, Mrs Randolph. Do
you feel well enough for this?

MARIE: Yes, thanks. I'm all right.

CARTERET: I believe, Mrs Randolph, it was you who discovered
your husband's body?

MARIE: Yes. I and—Mr Hurst. That gentleman who's sitting over there.

CARTERET: Thank you. And the date of this was . . . ?

MARIE: August third. The Bank Holiday.

CARTERET: (*agreeable*) Ah, yes: the Bank Holiday! I well remember it. A brilliant, hot day: not a breath of wind; ideal for swimming. I believe you and Mr Hurst *had* gone bathing?

MARIE: Yes. George—my husband—owns a private beach at Nelson's Cove.

CARTERET: Will the Jury please look at the map in front of them? Thank you. And then, Mrs Randolph?

MARIE: Well! We saw the cabin cruiser.

CARTERET: You saw it where?

MARIE: About three or four hundred yards out at sea. With nobody at the wheel. Just—drifting. And Mr Hurst said . . . (*Hurst interjects*)

HURST: (*in a strong, sharp, impetuous voice*) I said, Dr Carteret, that . . .

CARTERET: (*smoothly*) One moment, Mr Hurst. I shall be happy to call you to the witness-chair presently.

MARIE: Mr Hurst said, 'Hullo! That's George's boat!'

CARTERET: And then?

MARIE: We thought it must have got loose, or been drifting out to sea.

CARTERET: Go on, Mrs Randolph.

MARIE: Naturally, we didn't want *that* to happen. So we swam out to it.

CARTERET: Three or four hundred yards?

MARIE: (*almost amused*) That's nothing. We're both good swimmers.

CARTERET: I see. And then . . . ?

MARIE: When we got to the boat, we gave a hail in case there should be someone aboard. Nobody answered. So we climbed aboard. And . . . (*signs of hysteria*)

CARTERET: Take it gently, Mrs Randolph.

MARIE: In the little cabin, we found George's body on one of the bunks. He was dead. There was a knife in his chest, with both his hands pressed to the hilt. He had killed himself because—oh, I don't *know* why! But he'd cut the boat adrift, and then killed himself.

CARTERET: You will presently hear, members of the Jury, medical evidence to the effect that Mr George Randolph's death is perfectly consistent with the theory that he killed himself.

HURST: (*bursting out*) Of course he killed himself!

CARTERET: Please, Mr Hurst!

HURST: I'm sorry, sir.

CARTERET: There is just one thing, Mrs Randolph, on which I am not quite clear.

MARIE: Yes?

CARTERET: You tell us that Mr Hurst said to you, 'Hullo! That's George's boat!'

MARIE: Yes. Of course he did!

CARTERET: Could Mr Hurst—or you yourself, for that matter—recognise Mr Randolph's cabin cruiser at that distance? Could you read the name, for instance?

MARIE: Good heavens, no!

CARTERET: Or recognise the markings?

MARIE: No. All those boats look a good deal alike.

CARTERET: Then—forgive me—how did you know it *was* your husband's boat?

MARIE: (*impatiently*) Because of the flag.

CARTERET: Flag?

MARIE: George used to belong to a little yachting club on the East Coast. They had a terribly fancy flag. When we came here, George kept the flag and always ran it up on the little rod mast of the cabin cruiser. When I saw that red-and-gold striped flag, with the words 'NIMROD

YACHTING CLUB' across it, I knew it couldn't be anybody else. So did Mr Hurst.

CARTERET: (*enlightened*) I see, Mrs Randolph. For the moment, I think, we may excuse you. Will Mr Huntley Hurst please take the witness-chair?

HURST: (*grimly*) With the greatest pleasure.

CARTERET: You recognise, sir, that you are under oath here?

HURST: I do.

CARTERET: You were well acquainted with the late Mr George Randolph?

HURST: I knew George very well, yes. He was much older than I am, of course.

CARTERET: Then I can ask you questions, Mr Hurst, which might prove (*coughs*) . . . shall we say? . . . more embarrassing to Mrs Randolph.

HURST: Ask anything you like.

CARTERET: When you found that Mr Randolph had apparently committed suicide . . .

HURST: (*sharply*) Why 'apparently'?

CARTERET: When you found that Mr Randolph was dead, did it surprise you?

HURST: (*slight pause*) No.

CARTERET: May I ask why not?

HURST: Must I answer that question?

CARTERET: This is not a Court of Law, sir. It is an enquiry. But I think you'd be well advised to answer.

HURST: (*fiercely*) Why not? The whole town knows about it. There'd been . . . rumours.

CARTERET: Rumours? About what?

HURST: If you must know, about Mrs Randolph and me.

CARTERET: (*suavely*) I see. Were these rumours true?

MARIE: No! They were foul lies!

HURST: What's more, you've got no right to ask that question!

CARTERET: Forgive me. We are trying to establish motive. If

Mr Randolph were depressed—overcome in his mind—and therefore liable to take his own life . . . ?

HURST: It's no use denying, he *was* depressed.

CARTERET: Enough, in your opinion, to take his own life?

HURST: (*reluctantly*) In my opinion, yes. It was the first thing I thought of when I saw his body.

CARTERET: Who was the first to see the body? You or Mrs Randolph?

HURST: I was.

CARTERET: The dead man's hands, we have heard, were still on the hilt of the knife?

HURST: That's right.

CARTERET: Left hand over the right, Mr Hurst; or right hand over the left?

HURST: Right over the left. Pressing the blade in. Like this!

CARTERET: Thank you, Mr Hurst. That will be all.

HURST: (*amazed*) That will be all? You don't want to ask any more questions?

CARTERET: Not for the present. (*Slowly*) Members of the Jury, much more evidence will be brought before you prior to the end of this inquest. This evidence will include a statement that, despite the fine weather which prevailed on the afternoon of the death, the barometer at Mr Randolph's house home showed the indications of the storm which later burst with great violence along that part of the coast.

(*Slight pause*)

But this is by the way. You are here to determine whether the death of Mr George Randolph was accident, suicide, or murder. And you are the sole judges of the facts; not I. Yet it will surely be obvious to you that—within the past few minutes—there has been told in this court a falsehood so plain, a lie so easily proved, as strongly to suggest the probability of murder. Come, gentlemen!—you needn't look so surprised as all that! Surely it must be plain, even to a somewhat doddering person like myself, that . . . (*The voice fades*)

JOHN DICKSON CARR: Well? You are the judges. Was it accident, suicide, or murder? What was the provable falsehood which roused the suspicions of Dr Carteret; and which, I might tell you, ultimately betrayed the whole plot?

SOLUTION

If it was a brilliant, hot day 'not a breath of wind', Mrs Hirst would not have been able to read the flag on Mr Randolph's cabin cruiser. Therefore she was lying. As to whether she or Mr Hurst had murdered her husband, that would be for a criminal court to decide.

JOHN DICKSON CARR

John Dickson Carr was born on 30 November 1906 in Uniontown, Pennsylvania, the son of Julia Kisinger and Wooda Carr, a prominent attorney and onetime Democratic Congressman. Carr Senior had edited the *Uniontown Daily Herald* where—not coincidentally—his son got his first break, writing regular columns and providing sporting and theatrical reviews. Carr Junior wrote in the evenings after school, where he excelled in the literary arts, finishing his first year's work with two distinctions: second prize in the school poetry competition and the gold medal in the countrywide Theodore Roosevelt competition conducted by the Colonial Dames of America.

When Carr moved to Haverford College he started writing for the college magazine, *The Haverfordian*, eventually becoming its editor. His juvenilia covers many genres but Carr most enjoyed writing—and reading—detective stories. At college he created Henri Bencolin, a Parisian investigator who would go on to appear in his first novel, *It Walks by Night* (1930), based on a story which had appeared a year earlier in *The Haverfordian* and can be found in *Bodies from the Library 3* (2020).

Carr's favourite kind of detective story involved the literary equivalent of a magic trick. They are commonly styled locked-room mysteries, an often misused term that is shorthand for a situation that seems impossible but for which there is a possible (if sometimes implausible) explanation; there may be a closed circle of suspects with respect to a locked-room murder, but the terms are not synonymous. Countless writers—from Arthur Conan Doyle and Agatha Christie to Soji Shimadi and Paul Halter—have written impossible crime stories. Many openly credit Carr as an influence, and it is also certain that without him there would have been no *Banacek*, no *Monk* and no *Death in Paradise*. He was, quite simply, *The Man Who Explained Miracles* (1995), to quote the title of the excellent biography by Douglas G. Greene, *the* authority on Carr's life and work.

Over 50 years, Carr presented almost every kind of impossible crime there is—from invisible assailants and vanishing murderers to cases that feature baffling clues and bizarre weapons—and he shares the distinction with Agatha Christie of creating *two* 'great detectives': as 'Carter Dickson' he wrote 22 novels with the rumbustious Sir Henry Merrivale, a barrister, spymaster and physician partially inspired by Carr's own father; and writing under his own name there is the gargantuan academic, Dr Gideon Fell, based on the creator of Father J. Paul Brown, G. K. Chesterton whose influence—and sometimes plots—can be seen throughout Carr's work.

As well as writing many books and short stories, Carr also produced dozens of radio plays, writing for the long-running CBS series *Suspense* and *Cabin B13* in the United States. After he moved to Britain in 1932, he worked for the BBC, for which he created the influential *Appointment with Fear* series. During the Second World War, he also played his part in the Allied war effort by writing semi-fictional propaganda plays. These aside, the majority of Carr's scripts are captivating and concise, pulling the listener in and playing with sound effects and dialogue to create atmosphere and intrigue, exemplified in *The Island of Coffins*, a collection of Carr's *Cabin B13* scripts published in 2021 by Crippen & Landru.

As well as the ability to create entrancing problems and memorable characters, Carr also developed the crime novel in two important ways. While he did not invent the historical detective story—that honour probably goes to Melville Davisson Post—Carr did much to popularise it after the Second World War, laying a trail for other writers like Anne Perry and Ellis Peters, as well as the modern master, Paul Doherty. Carr was also pioneering in his use of the supernatural and science fiction in novel-length detective stories like *Fire, Burn!* (1957), which features something very like time travel, and *The Burning Court* (1937), in which he provides a witchly solution as well as a rational one. Today Carr is recognised as a giant of the Golden Age of crime and detective fiction, and probably always will be the only writer to serve as secretary of the Detection Club and president of the Mystery Writers of America, which awarded him Edgars in 1949 and 1962.

After suffering for some years from the legacy of heavy smoking, John Dickson Carr died from lung cancer at Greenville, South Carolina, on 27 February 1977.

'The Riddle of the Cabin Cruiser' was first broadcast on 18 November 1943 on the BBC's General Forces service. It was the third in a series of mystery plays entitled 'A Corner in Crime', a feature of the long-running variety programme *Here's Wishing You Well Again*. The solution was broadcast on 2 December. This is its first publication.

Skeleton in the Cupboard

Ianthe Jerrold

At the time Corney Dew buried his brother-in-law in the Celtic barrow—locally called the tump—hardly anybody had heard of the Aymesley Antiquarian Club.

But when Gwyn Griffith became the club's secretary he started hiking round the countryside looking for Roman or Celtic remains or anything else he could find to make Saturday outings for his members: and he soon started pestering Corney to let him open the tump and see if what was inside was a Druid or a Roman.

Corney could have told him what was inside—his brother-in-law, Davy—but, of course, he just put on a wooden face and said the tump was nothing but an old heap of road-clearings, and he remembered his grandfather heaping them there.

Gwyn Griffith said that in that case there surely to goodness would be no harm in the Antiquarian Club having a look! When Corney went on looking wooden, Gwyn Griffith concluded that his reluctance must be due to superstition, and assured him that if they found any bones in the tump they'd treat them reverently, just photograph them and put them back.

Corney could hardly keep a straight face at the notion of Davy being reverently photographed and put back, but at least he had an idea now of what to say. He told Gwyn confidentially that the fact was, there was a tradition in his family that a curse would come on any Dew who tampered with the tump or let anybody else tamper with it.

Gwyn Griffith gave it up for the time being, and Corney was left in a fine state of perturbation. Suppose it should occur to Gwyn Griffith to come poking round in the tump while Corney was asleep? Davy, being only about two feet down, could hardly escape notice, and although Corney had very little respect for antiquarians, he doubted if Gwyn Griffith would be soft enough to take Davy for a Druid.

Corney had buried his brother-in-law in the tump because it was a place he'd never want to plough up, where digging was quick and easy, and where the brambles and thorns conveniently hid both his operations and the scar left by them.

He'd tucked Davy away in the early hours of the morning and gone home to make a hearty meal of fried bacon and strong tea, for he'd never liked Davy—a poor sort of chap who'd driven Corney's sister Marion to her grave with his shiftlessness—and he was not going to pretend to himself that he was sorry the chap was dead.

His only regret had been that he still didn't know where his Aunt Ann's gold ring was. He'd searched all Davy's pockets through and through, and the lining of his jacket, and inside his shoes.

But although Davy had been wearing the ring when he first arrived that evening—it was just like the silly beggar to come trying to borrow money wearing a gold ring that didn't belong to him, but had been loaned to him years ago to marry his wife with, on condition he gave it back after the honeymoon—it was nowhere to be found.

After the tea and bacon, Corney had gone all over the floor with a bicycle lamp, but it was no use. Davy must have hidden the ring somewhere when they started quarrelling about it.

At any rate, if Corney hadn't the ring, neither had Davy, and there was some satisfaction in that!

Corney was not the man to be depressed for long, and until the visit of Gwyn Griffith he had scarcely given a thought to Davy, except to wonder sometimes when he was out rabbiting, how the rabbits got on with him. After all, his conscience was clear—pretty clear. Goodness knew why the chap had died! His head had hit the flags a bit hard, maybe: but if he'd handed over Corney's property when Corney asked for it, Corney wouldn't have hit him.

Corney was well aware, though, that it would look bad for him if anybody ever found out about Davy, for people don't usually bury their relations secretly in old heathen tumps, and Corney wouldn't have done it, very likely, if he hadn't been too busy with his harvest and a cow with mastitis to spare time for inquests and that kind of thing.

Yes, it would look bad if anybody found Davy: and after Gwyn had gone, Corney felt quite depressed, for he didn't trust him at all—a roaming, inquisitive chap like that, with all his time on his hands.

Corney went quite off his food thinking about it, and Mrs Thomas the Cwm started telling the neighbours that old bachelors never made old bones, and trying to reckon to herself how much Corney's grandfather clock would fetch in an auction sale and whether she'd have enough saved up when the time came.

And when, one evening, Gwyn Griffith came back again, Corney only wished he could put Gwyn in with Davy and have been done with him. But it was no use thinking of that; for, apart from it being sinful, Gwyn Griffith was a man with a place in the world and people would inquire after him whereas nobody had inquired after poor Davy for fear of seeing him again.

Gwyn started all his persuasions once more, telling Corney how the owners of such old ancient things only held them in trust for humanity, and so on. But Corney, having found a good line, stuck to it, and just went on saying that he was sorry, but he couldn't go against the curse, until Gwyn had to give it up again.

But just as Gwyn was going, he said something that threw Corney into quite a panic. He said that as far as he could see, the only way to get the tump opened would be to get a police order to do it.

'What?' gasped Corney, hardly believing his ears.

'Only a joke, man!' said Gwyn Griffith. 'But Lloyd the policeman is one of our new members, look you! Sure you haven't got somebody tucked away in there the police ought to know about?'

He went off laughing like anything at his own jocosity, but it was no joke to Corney, who spent all that night cutting faggots and lugging them into his back kitchen. And the next evening, after dark, he went out to the tump with a wheelbarrow and a spade.

It was a moonlight night, so though he took a lantern he didn't need to use it except at the end, to make sure he hadn't left any bits behind. For there was nothing of Davy now but bones.

However, Corney got home without meeting anybody, and only had to stop once to pick up some fingerbones which had come loose and had dropped over the edge of the barrow. He had lit the fire in the bread-oven early in the evening, and when he opened the little door the dome-shaped oven was full of swirling flame, so he made no delay and got Davy in as best he could, feet-end first, shovelling the loose pieces in after him. He didn't at all like the look on Davy's face as it went in—but then he never had liked the look on Davy's face.

He shut the oven door, put the kettle on for a cup of tea, and sat there thinking about his sister's wedding-day and how everybody had said the marriage would come to no good, and wishing he hadn't been such a softie as to loan Davy his Aunt Ann's gold ring, for he might have known he'd never get it back.

It was when he went out to the back kitchen to get last week's newspaper from the top of the copper to see how much a gold sovereign was worth now, that he realised that Davy was ending up as he'd lived—in a stink. 'My goodness!' said Corney to himself, 'what'll I do now? The neighbours will be thinking my place is on fire!'

And he opened the oven door, though the smell nearly choked him, and bundled in as much more brushwood as would go, hoping to hurry matters up.

Sure enough, before long there was Thomas the Cwm at the door wanting to know what was the matter, and his missus sticking her sharp nose forward as usual. But Corney was ready for them, and said his week's batch of bread had caught fire owing to him not having raked the oven out properly. Mrs Thomas squeaked with glee at that, as a woman always does at a man's mistakes, and said she'd rake the lot out on to the floor if she was Corney, and pour cold water over it.

'What, and crack the flags?' said Corney, looking astounded, although goodness knew the flags around his oven had been cracked to atoms since his great-grandmother's day. 'Let them bide!' said he, but before he could prevent her, Mrs Thomas had the oven door open a crack and her nose poking in.

'My Goddie, what was the matter with your yeast?' she squeaked. 'The batch has run all over the place!' and she shut the door quick and started telling Corney about how the same thing had happened at her sister's three winters ago, and it was all owing to some yeast they'd got from the new baker in Huntingly.

This set Corney laughing like anything, when they'd gone, thinking of Mrs Thomas's sister with her brother-in-law in the bread-oven. And then he went on to consider how little neighbours and relations knew of one another, when you came to think of it, and how, after all, if Mrs Thomas's sister *had* had a relation in her bread-oven. Mrs Thomas need not have known anything about it, any more than she knew about Davy, even after smelling and seeing him. And he cut himself a slice of fat bacon, and sat enjoying his own sentiments.

Well, now that the tump has been cleared of his property, Corney felt it would be un-neighbourly to go on denying Gwyn Griffith the treat of digging for a Druid. So after a few months' delay, to be respectful to Davy and give his grave time to heal over, he withdrew his objections to having the tump opened.

And Gwyn brought all his Antiquarian Club over on a Saturday morning early, with spades and sieves and picks and a book he'd picked up second-hand in Presteign about how to open tumps and what you might expect to find in them.

They started by clearing away the brushwood and brambles, and then Gwyn made a very nice speech about Corney, saying what a public-spirited man he was, and after a lot of argument about where to start, they began digging, putting all the earth through sieves, because that was what the book said they ought to do.

They didn't start at the side, though, as the book said, cutting a bit out of the tump as if it were a cake, because the tump was a lot harder than any cake. So they started at the top, where it was crumbly and easy, and before long there was a great outcry and everybody was gathering round one of the sieves. And there—would you believe it?—was Aunt Ann's gold ring!

'My goodness!' thought Corney. 'The dirty blackguard must have swallowed it!' And he started forwards to grab his property.

But then he stopped, because for the life of him he couldn't see how he was going to explain his Aunt Ann's ring without encouraging people to ask a lot of silly questions.

So before he could think of anything to say, there was Gwyn Griffith locking it up in a tin case and everybody discussing whether it belonged to the Bronze Age or the Roman.

Well, they didn't find anything more that day, and all the next week it rained, so the digging had to wait, and Corney didn't see anything of Gwyn. He was often on the point of going over to Aymesley to get his ring back, but he couldn't see how to explain his Aunt Ann's ring being in the tump, without getting a lot too near the truth.

The ring went up to the Crown as treasure-trove, and the Crown was very polite about it, but returned it, saying the owner of the ground could have it, for all it cared.

You would think the matter would have been settled then. But not a bit of it. Gwyn Griffith took it for granted that Corney wanted nothing better than to loan the ring to the new Folk Museum he was starting in Aymesley, where he already had a lot of queerly-shaped flints, and old ox-plough, and three patten-irons; and Corney thought about Davy, and didn't know how to refuse.

The Antiquarian Club didn't find anything else in the tump, except some large flat stones, which Gwyn said were the remains of a cist. He said there had been bones in them, right enough, but somebody must have lifted them out a long while ago. Corney reflected that he was not the only man in history who'd found it convenient to alter his mind about the best place for his brother-in-law.

But when, a year or so afterwards, the Ancient Monuments Act was passed, and he had a paper sent him with the Government's seal at the top of it, telling him that if he so much as touched the tump with the side of a spade he'd be sent to prison or fined, it gave Corney the worst turn he'd ever had in his life, and he was a more serious man from that day forward, and took to paying very nearly as much income tax as he owed, and made a will leaving his Aunt Ann's gold ring to the Aymesley Museum for ever.

He had had no idea the Government had means of knowing so much about him.

IANTHE JERROLD

Ianthe Bridgeman Jerrold (1898–1977) had *a lot* to live up to. Her father, Walter Jerrold, was a historian, playwright, biographer, novelist and journalist; and her mother, Clara Armstrong Jerrold, was a historian and poet. Her grandfather, Thomas Jerrold, was an actor and a writer on gardening. And her *great* grandfather, was Douglas Jerrold, a successful novelist, journalist and playwright who, at the age of fourteen, had written a two-act comic burletta . . . not long after his return from service in the British Navy.

It is perhaps not so surprising then to learn that Ianthe Jerrold first appeared in print at the age of only nine when one of her poems was published in *Thrush* magazine. As Jerrold put it in an interview in 1952, she had been 'put on the tramlines' by her parents and, although she claimed not to have read any of their books until she was an adult, the pull of her forebears was irresistible. In 1913, when she was still a teenager, a collection of Jerrold's verse, *XVI Poems*, was published in a limited edition of 29 copies. Other poems appeared in national newspapers as well as in prominent British magazines like *Country Life* and *The Spectator*—and she also wrote short stories, including some for children which were accompanied by illustrations by her younger sister Daphne.

1923 saw the publication of Ianthe Jerrold's first novel, *Young Richard Mast*. Her lyrical style and vivid characterization was widely praised and three more novels followed, including the partly autobiographical *Hangingstone Farm* (1924). Her father had made one now long-forgotten contribution to the mystery genre, *The Disappearance of Arthur Dale* (1901), and in 1929 his daughter published the first of two gently paced detective stories featuring John Christmas, a genial amateur detective. In *The Studio Crime* (1929), Christmas investigates the apparent impossibility of a dead-and-alive man, and *Dead Man's Quarry* (1930) sees him investigating the murder of a cyclist. While neither was in any way influential or a classic of the genre, the novels are entertaining and earned Jerrold membership of the prestigious Detection Club founded by Anthony Berkeley.

Despite the success of the Christmas cases, Ianthe Jerrold decided to stick to 'straight' fiction and during the 1930s she produced several characterful romances like *Summer's Day* (1933) and *The Dogs Do Bark* (1936). However, she remained keen on crime fiction and eventually wrote two more novels, disguising herself as Geraldine Bridgman—a homophonic version of her middle name and surname. If John Christmas's investigations owe something to Margery Allingham and others, the Bridgman novels seem to owe rather a lot to Gladys Mitchell. In *Let Him Lie* (1940), the detective is a young woman, based in part on Jerrold's sisters Daphne and Phyllis, who had both attended the Slade School of Art. Murder and archaeology collide in a plot inspired by the ban on excavations at Cwmma Tump, a medieval earthwork located near the seventeenth-century farmhouse in Brilley, Herefordshire, which Jerrold had bought in 1934 with her husband George Menges, a wealthy Lloyds underwriter.

The second Bridgman novel, *There May Be Danger* (1948), is an atmospheric but slightly Blytonesque thriller in which an out-of-work actress investigates the disappearance of a child but ends up uncovering something else entirely. While *Let Him Lie* had been reviewed positively, the poor reception received by *There May Be Danger* led Jerrold to abandon crime fiction altogether and return to romances, some dealing with modern life and others having a historical setting, but almost all focused on strong female central characters. Throughout her life, Ianthe Jerrold loved the theatre and, again channeling her forebears, she decided to write a play. *An Untender Passion* (1945) is a romance set in 1811, and it was successful enough to inspire her to write a second, a domestic drama called *A House in Notting Hill* (1951). However, in her own words, neither play 'did any good' and for the rest of her career Jerrold concentrated on writing novels including the extraordinary *My Angel* (1960), in which another of her many heroines, Emma Tryst, encounters a young man who is growing wings!

In 1965, George Menges died and Cwmmau Farmhouse was accepted in lieu of tax by the British heritage conservation charity, the National Trust. The transfer was subject to a right of residence for Ianthe Jerrold who lived there until the late 1970s. She died in a London nursing home on 31 May 1977.

'Skeleton in the Cupboard' was published in the *Brisbane Telegraph* on 2 August 1952, although there might have been an earlier, as yet untraced appearance.

THE YEAR AND THE DAY

Edmund Crispin

When he came into the Venturers' Club that Saturday afternoon, he had the look of a man going slumming. Also, he was very slightly drunk—not drunk enough to have lost caution, but drunk enough to want to tell someone, anyone, about something he was proud of. At ten to three in the dead London weekend, there was only me there.

Through the dingy windows of the bar I saw his Rolls and his chauffeur waiting. I don't know how I was so sure they were both *his*, and not just hired. Twelve years after being called to the Bar I still couldn't have dreamed of having a Rolls and a chauffeur myself, whether I'd hired them or whether I'd bought them. I just did know, that's all.

I knew it from the way he walked and from the way he talked to the barman, as well as from the clothes he wore and the gold-strapped Omega watch and the little-finger ring on his immaculately manicured hand. I knew it, too, from the self-assurance with which he ordered champagne. Members of the Venturers' didn't do that very often, they couldn't afford to. But I'd had enough experience of the Courts to know when people can't really afford to buy champagne and when they can. He could.

As we were alone there, of course he asked me to join him, and of course I did. After all, we had been up at Oxford together, even though we'd completely lost touch since.

He was good about the courtesies, I'll say that for him.

We'd been at the same College; he'd been reading medicine while I'd been reading law. In the eighteen years since then I suppose his income as a brain surgeon had been on average twenty times mine as a barrister.

It occurred to me to wonder why he hadn't got his knighthood yet; and then I remembered. A year or so previously he'd retired; brain surgeons, I thought, must earn a hell of a lot of money to be able to retire in such obvious prosperity at the age of forty or thereabouts.

He said to me, 'You remember Harvester?'

I said yes, of course I did—though but for the fact of Harvester's death two years ago and the particularly nasty circumstances which led up to it, I'm not sure that I should have done, much. Harvester had been contemporary at Oxford with me and with—well, let's call him 'X'. I mean the distinguished medical man I've been talking about so far. And the reason I mightn't otherwise have remembered Harvester was that even as an undergraduate he'd been a shy, retiring man who didn't make many friends, or acquaintances, either, for that matter.

Of the friends, 'X' had certainly been the most important.

'I was always a bit brash, dear boy,' 'X' said now. 'Pushing, you know; quite the opposite type to him. Can't think why he should have taken to me, but somehow he did. And somehow,' he smiled affably at me over the rim of his glass, 'I took to him, too.'

Money? Had it been money? 'X' had been an undergraduate no better off than I had been. Harvester, on the other hand, had inherited three million at the age of twenty-one.

'We kept in touch,' 'X' told me. "Even after we went down from Oxford, we kept in touch quite a lot. He'd have financed me in the early stages—offered to, in fact—but there wasn't any real need. By the way, did you ever meet his wife?'

I said no.

'Wretched business, really, her dying bringing that ghastly boy into the world.'

I said yes.

He poured more champagne for us both, then leaned back comfortably in his chair.

'Nasty piece of work, that boy was,' he said. 'Spoilt, of course, but there was something wrong in his heredity, too. Must have come from the mother, because Harvester himself wasn't any fool.' The faintest flicker of a smile appeared on his face. 'Not until after the boy had tried to brain him, I mean. After that, of course, his skull was in such a mess that no one could have expected him to think clearly.'

I said, 'You treated him yourself, did you?'

'Good Lord, no. Sir Henry did all the operating and so forth. I was just flagged in as consultant. Never touched him myself, thank God.'

I put my glass down carefully. 'Why "thank God"?' I asked.

'Too tricky, dear boy. Look, you know the circumstances?'

I did know them. Harvester's teenage son had made a deliberate, cold-blooded attempt on his father's life, purely for the sake of getting his hands on his father's money, and had messed it up in every conceivable way. For one thing, Harvester hadn't died; not then, anyway. On top of that, the boy's attempts to cover up his guilt had been so babyish that the C.I.D. laboratories had disposed of them conclusively inside twenty-four hours.

'Seriously,' he said, "one's quite thankful that poor old Harvester was in that coma for six months, so that he never knew his son had been arrested, tried and convicted for attempted murder, and popped into prison.'

'*Never* knew?'

'X' smiled again, a little pityingly this time.

'My dear boy, even after he was conscious again, we wouldn't

have dreamed of telling him. He was still very bad, you understand. *He* lingered on and lingered on. But we all knew it was
a hopeless case. He was fairly clear-headed sometimes, but you
couldn't rely on it. *He* didn't say anything about the boy, and
even if he'd wanted to, in the state he was in we couldn't possibly
have let a copper with a notebook squat down by the side of
his bed and pester him with questions.'

It was then, I think, that a premonition stealthily began to
scratch at my spine. I'd never done much criminal practice. On
the other hand, to get to be a barrister you do have to know a
bit about criminal law, and it wouldn't be in human nature not
to be specially interested in murder. And there were one or two
things about the law relating to murder which I was now dimly
beginning to remember.

'X' sighed. 'Yes, he lingered on, and the months went by,
and . . . Well, anyway, poor old Harvester. Such a nice chap.
He—'

'Wait!' I interrupted abruptly. 'As it happened, I was out of
the country when Harvester died. After his son tried to kill him
with that poker, just *how* long did he last?'

'More champagne? No? Ah well, I suppose it's closing time
anyway. And I must get back down to Sussex. Incidentally, dear
boy, I've got rather a nice place down there; small, but pleasant.
Why not come down sometime and stay for a weekend? For
longer, if you like. I'm one of the idle rich now, you know. So
there's always a party of some kind going on.'

'Harvester,' I said.

He emptied the last of the bottle into his own glass, and eyed
it complacently without for the moment picking it up.

'Ah, yes, you were wanting to know exactly when he died.
Interesting, that. As it happened, he pegged out just a year and
three hours almost to the minute after that bloody son of his
wounded him on the head.'

Now I was remembering a lot more about my law studies.

Remembering, too, the second trial which Harvester's son had been dragged from prison to be subjected to, and the verdict. And yet, why was 'X' so pleased about it all? There he sat, in the armchair opposite to mine, clever, balding, tight, self-satisfied, fascinated with his own cleverness, obviously longing to tell someone about it, and equally obviously confident that the telling could never put him in any possible sort of danger. Now it was my cue. Even then I knew that I ought just to have got up and left. That I should never have given him the satisfaction of saying the things he wanted said, was waiting for me to say. But, you understand, I still wasn't *sure*, and if what I suspected was true, there just *might* be something I could do about it . . .

'A year and three hours,' I said. 'Harvester died a year and three hours after the act which killed him. If it had been a year and twenty-five hours, what then?'

'X' called for the barman, asking for his overcoat to be brought.

'Dear boy,' he murmured, "you're the legal expert, aren't you? I'm just a simple medical man. The real trouble was, you see, that Harvester knew perfectly well he was going to die, and he didn't want to die in the nursing-home. He wanted to die in his own bed.'

'Even though moving him would have been dangerous?'

'Not just dangerous. Miracles apart, it was pretty certain to be fatal.'

'And yet you allowed it?'

'X' raised his eyebrows.

'Allowed it, dear boy? I advised very strongly against it. Very strongly indeed. But then, as I told you, I wasn't in charge of the case. By the way, have you ever met Sir Henry? Nice old boy. Very good at his job, but a bit woolly-minded about other things. Anyway, Sir Henry's idea was that since there was nothing more anyone could do for Harvester, and since he was bound to hand in his chips within a few weeks regardless, there couldn't be any real harm in humouring him. Particularly as he'd made that crazy attempt to get up and—'

'To *get up*?'

'X''s overcoat came. He fished in his wallet, tipped the barman handsomely, and with a charming smile asked him to leave the thing ready in the porter's lodge downstairs. At once gratified and thoroughly unwilling to show it, the barman nodded curtly and took himself off.

'Yes, he actually got himself out of bed,' said 'X' , shaking his head sadly. 'God knows how. I can tell you, from the medical point of view it set him back quite a bit. I'd had a few words with him a little before that—it was one of his lucid intervals— but of course he'd seemed quite passive then.'

I said, '"A few words"? Anything interesting?'

'No, no, dear boy. Just the usual placebo. And I oughtn't to have done it, I realise that now. On account of our being old friends, there's a chance it may have got him over-excited.'

He shrugged.

'One just can't tell. Anyway, it was soon after that that he took it into his head to try and get up. Of course, the nursing staff pushed him back into bed pretty sharpish, but by that time, his cerebral circulation had taken a lot of punishment. It didn't show at first, so they went ahead with Sir Henry's idea of shifting him back to his house in Eaton Square. As a result of which he died in the ambulance on the way there.'

Outside I could see the Rolls and the chauffeur still waiting, and I could hear that the London traffic was beginning to build up to its usual Saturday evening flurry.

'Convenient,' I said.

'Convenient, dear boy? Oh, yes, certainly. In this country the murder law requires that a victim shall die within a year and a day of the act which caused his death. Harvester just managed that, didn't he? So his son was brought out of prison and stuck up in the dock at the Old Bailey and convicted of murder. Not just attempted murder, as it would have been if Harvester had survived a few hours longer.'

'X' drained his glass. 'These legal forms,' he murmured. 'Too silly. And in this case, very tragic, too.' He heaved himself to his feet.

'Well now, this has been extraordinarily pleasant, but I'm afraid I really do have to be getting down to Sussex. Some silly cocktail-party which my wife has arranged. I—'

'Just one more thing.'

'Of course, of course.'

'Here we are, all alone,' I said. 'And there are you, and you haven't got to the point even yet, have you?'

'The point, dear boy?'

'You see, there's something else about criminal law which I've just remembered. A murderer if convicted can't profit financially or in any other way from his crime.'

'Quite right, dear boy, quite right. Shocking if he could. What I mean is, he'd be able to inherit and pass the money on to anyone he chose—'

'Too shocking to contemplate,' I said. 'I take it that Harvester's son is without his fortune?'

'X' looked at me with what I can only describe as real pleasure.

'Very acute, that,' he said. 'While I'm lazing away down in the country, believe me I'm still going to be watching your career with a lot of interest and enthusiasm—and a lot of affection, too.'

'Yes, Harvester's son was his sole heir. No other family, actually. So of course when Harvester died within the year and the day and Harvester's son was convicted of the killing, all the Harvester fortune went elsewhere, to the residuary legatee, in fact.'

He gave me a light, pleasant wave of the hand, and started to move out of the room.

'In fact, as there was no other family,' he said, 'Harvester in his will named an old friend as residuary legatee. And the old friend got the lot.

'Don't forget about coming to see me in Sussex, dear boy, will you? We're really quite comfortable down there.'

EDMUND CRISPIN

Robert Bruce Montgomery was born on 2 October 1921 at Chesham Bois in Buckinghamshire. Montgomery's Scottish mother, Marion Blackwood Jarvie, was an amateur musician and his Irish father, Robert Ernest Montgomery, a civil servant who in 1938 received the Order of the British Empire for his service in the India Department.

Although a deformity of the feet affected Montgomery's ability to take part in most physical activities at school, he excelled academically. His first school was Heatherton House in Amersham, where he received the Form Prize in 1930 and in the same year appeared in a production of *The Pied Piper of Hamelin*, happily not playing the lame lone survivor. At Merchant Taylors' School he developed as a musician and as a composer, largely self-taught. In his authoritative biography, *Bruce Montgomery/Edmund Crispin: A Life in Music and Books* (2007), David Whittle described Montgomery's concert performances at Merchant Taylors' where he played the organ and piano and how, despite his lameness, he developed an interest in ballet, challenging those who considered it effeminate.

Away from school, Montgomery gave piano recitals at Amersham-on-the-Hill Free Church and at Chorley Wood Baptists' Church. He was also interested in the theatre, writing and appearing in a sketch, long lost, entitled 'Murder in an Antique Shop' and acting in another called 'Broadcast Play', which were both presented in February 1939 at St Leonard's Church Hall in Chesham Bois in aid of the local refugee fund. Montgomery's liberal sentiments are reflected in an impassioned letter he wrote at the age of eighteen to the London *Daily News*, in which he criticised the impact of conscription, particularly on performers, and questioned what Britain was 'fighting for unless it be our culture (freedom is not worth much without it)'.

At Merchant Taylors', according to one of his pupils, Julian Critchley, Montgomery had 'won many prizes but was none too popular', although 'at Oxford, he blossomed' as a scholarship student in St John's College. He read Modern Languages, but it was his extracurricular activities that gave him greatest pleasure. He was appointed as organist and choir master at St John's, and he wrote and played music, went to the cinema, attended choral evensong, and spent many hours in pubs in conversation with friends like the poet and jazz-lover Philip Larkin, for whom he wrote 'Embers', an unpublished, mildly pornographic short story.

Montgomery also read books, and in his final year John Maxwell—then artistic director at the Oxford Playhouse—lent him his copy of John Dickson Carr's *The Crooked Hinge* (1938), and Montgomery stayed up all night to finish reading it. Carr's book, and the conviviality of the friends who had also read it, inspired him to write his own detective novel, *The Case of the Gilded Fly* (1944), in which he introduced the professor detective, Gervase Fen, whose initials consciously replicated those of Carr's Gideon Fell.

At that time Montgomery had an ambition one day to write a mainstream novel, so he decided to adopt a pseudonym for what he thought would be a short-lived venture into detective fiction. In later life, he offered more than one explanation for the origin of the pen name: it might have been taken from a character in one of Michael Innes's detective stories, *Hamlet: Revenge!* (1937); or it might have been intended to be 'Rufus Crispin', picking up on the colour of his hair, had he not discovered the existence of the writer Rufus King; and he opted for 'Edmund' because he happened to be reading *King Lear* and was drawn to Lear's son 'because he was a bastard'.

On coming down in 1943, Montgomery taught at Shrewsbury School for two years. He was not a conventional schoolmaster, and his favourite idea for an English lesson was to read a ghost story by M. R. James, whom Montgomery would later pastiche in the novel *Holy Disorders* (1945) and in the uncollected short story 'St Bartholomew's Day'. The experience was rewarding in more than one sense, for he said in later years that 'teaching small boys at Shrewsbury taught me more about crime than I ever needed to know'.

After Shrewsbury, Montgomery went to live in Abingdon, where he continued to write books and would entertain friends from Oxford. There he also fell in something like love with Jeni Turnball, the daughter of the local publican, another in a long line of women with whom Crispin would become mildly infatuated.

From Abingdon, Montgomery moved to Rockhill House, Heath Road, Brixham, which his parents had bought in 1940. He loved Devon, and it would provide the setting for several of his later books, including *Buried for Pleasure* (1948), in which Fen runs for Parliament. While his career as a crime writer moved forward at a gentle pace, Montgomery's career as a composer took off, and he would go on to score more than 30 films, including the *Doctor* series based on the books of Richard Gordon and many of the early *Carry On* comedies. Montgomery also composed church music, carols and concert works, and his work was performed at London's Wigmore Hall and the Sheldonian Theatre in Oxford, where his masterpiece, *Oxford Requiem*, was first performed in 1951.

Although he had been something of an outsider at school, the older Montgomery was gregarious. As well as taking an active part in many community groups in Brixham, he was elected a member of the Detection Club in 1947, having been proposed by Carr.

Montgomery took his membership seriously, travelling regularly to London meetings often with his near neighbour in Devon, Agatha Christie. He used to tell the tale of how, when giving Christie a lift home after a Club meeting, she had pulled his leg about his failure to write a book for some time; when he complained that he couldn't think of a plot, Christie smiled and said that she was surprised that that would worry him! The criticism was not unfamiliar. Montgomery's books *do* have plots, of course, but the emphasis is not on detection, nor do his mysteries have the structural precision of Christie, Carr or Queen. Sometimes, they are overwhelmed by Marxian humour, which he took from Carr, along with a tendency for Gervase Fen periodically to break the fourth wall with the reader.

In the 1950s Montgomery made several efforts to complete a novel, variously called *Timor Mortis* and *Judgement at Paris*, but he found the convolutions of the plot, involving the partial dismemberment of a beauty queen and impersonation, too complicated to resolve. After multiple false starts, he abandoned the idea of writing more novels, preferring instead to focus on his music, which was proving far more rewarding financially. He did continue to write, albeit only short stories, the majority of which appeared in the London *Evening Standard*, and he appeared from time to time on BBC radio programmes. He also reviewed books for the *Sunday Times* and compiled anthologies of science fiction, which he felt had 'taken over the rationalism of the puzzle story where crime fiction has abandoned it'.

Montgomery suffered from ill health—the legacy of years of smoking and drinking to excess were catching up with him. To make matters considerably worse, his right hand became crippled by Dupuytren's contracture, affecting his ability to play and therefore his ability to compose. The end was in sight, and shortly before his death Montgomery married his long-time secretary and nurse, Ann Clements. With her encouragement, he produced a final case for Gervase Fen, *The Glimpses of the Moon* (1977), a novel which owes a debt to Gladys Mitchell, who, along with Carr and Michael Innes, had been Montgomery's favourite writers. While the novel had been extrapolated from the debris of the two books he had begun in the 1950s, its unevenness gives the impression that more than one person had a hand in the writing.

A year later, on 15 September 1976, Bruce Montgomery died at home of heart failure. In the words of the obituarist for *The Times*, he 'could easily have become Britain's most successful post-war writer of detective stories. He could have made a busy and lucrative career composing film music. His music was agreeable. His books are elegant, literate and funny. He might have done a great deal more, but what he did produce get much pleasure to many people.'

This is the first publication of the undated manuscript 'The Year and the Day'.

MURDER IN MONTPARNASSE

John Bude

I

CAFÉ VAVIN

The door of Number 44, Rue Delambre slowly opened and a little hunchback emerged from the murky hallway and peered up and down the street. A nearby clock had just struck ten. Beyond the roofs to the north, the night sky glowed with the reflected lights of the Boulevard du Montparnasse and although the year had just moved into September it was hot and airless between the tall houses. Having paused on the doorstep long enough to light a cheroot, the hunchback went back into the darkened passage and reappeared wheeling an invalid chair. To reach the handles of this contraption the little fellow was forced to raise his hands above his head, but by the easy manner in which he manoeuvred the chair it was obvious that he was perfectly used to his job.

Prosper, in fact, had been chaperoning old Pierre Lebrun for nearly ten years. He knew the invalid's idiosyncrasies so well that they exchanged no more than a dozen words a day. From the moment Lebrun had been worked into his clothes, the day, or rather the night, followed an unbroken routine. Lebrun never rose until seven in the evening and never went to bed until the small hours. He only existed at night. The daytime was something to be got through as quickly as possible and for the most part he dozed the hours away with his strange dreams overlapping his waking thoughts which were even stranger. Prosper looked after him as a nurse looks after a child. The hunchback did the shopping, prepared their scanty meals, cleaned up the single room in which they lived and pushed the wheelchair on its nightly journey to the Café Vavin.

Pierre Lebrun was a curious looking man and, although he was known the length and breadth of Montparnasse, nobody really knew how old he was, or what he looked like, for Lebrun suffered with failing eyesight and for years had looked upon a gloomy world through tinted spectacles. The whole of his left side was paralysed and, for reasons of economy, his own teeth, which had long been extracted, had never been replaced. It gave his cheeks a sunken look and put a downward twist to his mouth. But his lack of molars had ceased to worry Lebrun, for he ate no more than was needed to keep him upright in his wheelchair and looked upon conversation as an unnecessary luxury. Yet for all his dour, uncompromising, melancholic personality, the *habitués* of the Montparnasse cafés had a real affection for this broken-down bit of humanity. They knew his tragedy and were sorry for him.

Absinthe was the poison which had undermined his moral and physical health. And when the Government stepped in and made the sale of absinthe illegal, Lebrun, like thousands of others, became a *Pernod* fiend.

Two years before this particular September night he had attempted to commit suicide by slipping a dose of arsenic into his *Pernod*. Only the quick-wittedness of Monsieur Bonnard, the proprietor of the Café Vavin, had saved him from a very uncomfortable death. Thereafter Prosper kept a watch on his master and went through his pockets every night before they set out on their little pilgrimage.

Proceeding rapidly down the Rue Delambre, they turned into the blazing river of the Boulevard Montparnasse. Prosper was forced to peer round the side of the wheelchair in order to steer it through the crowd of idiots which drifted ceaselessly up and down the broad pavements. They passed the Dôme and the Coupole and eventually came abreast of the Café Vavin. Lebrun's table was never occupied. He had long ago staked his claim in the corner under the glass screen, where Prosper could park his wheelchair without it being in the way.

Several people nodded or waved a hand as the couple moved up between the tables. Leaving the hunchback to bow his grotesque acknowledgments from side to side, Lebrun made no sign. The chair was wheeled up to the table and Monsieur Bonnard himself came forward and flicked a napkin under the old man's nose.

'Good evening, M'sieur. Henri! M'sieur Lebrun is waiting for his *Pernod. Vite! Vite!* You will pardon any delay, but our old clients are returning from their holidays and each night we grow more crowded. But it is good to see the familiar faces back again.'

Lebrun nodded.

'M'sieur Blake is back,' he croaked in a barely audible voice. 'I see him there under his usual box-tree.' He shook his head sadly. 'He did not treat that little girl at all well. You remember Madeleine? Ah—she was a beauty! He was cruel to her.'

Lebrun turned slightly and looked through his black glasses at the hunchback, who was standing beside the chair picking his teeth.

'Dismiss, Prosper!'

The hunchback grinned, saluted, slunk off among the tables and disappeared up the boulevard to his favourite *bistro*. There he would stay until the early hours drinking *bock* and playing dominoes, until the spirit moved him to collect his master and return him to the Rue Delambre. Pierre was never impatient.

After all—wasn't he Emperor of the Café Vavin? He had sat at his corner table when most of the faces round him had been buried in school-books. He remembered the first day when Noel Blake, the English painter, had sat beneath the third box-tree from the right. He remembered the April night, when the braziers had been glowing . . . the night when little Picôt had brought the news of Madeleine's suicide. Only an hour before, close to the Pont d'Austerlitz, Picôt had seen the *gendarmes* fishing the dripping figure out of the Seine. Blake had not shown up for many nights after that and the rumour was adrift that the little model had taken her life because of the Englishman. It made Lebrun very angry because he knew that Madeleine had been Blake's mistress and he still had enough moral integrity to realise that a man who discards a mistress when she is in love with him is not exactly a *bon garçon*. Madeleine had given up everything for her Englishman. She had even refused to sit for any other painter because she believed Blake would be jealous. She had been the mistress of other artists before, but she had never been in love until she met Noel Blake. Old Lebrun sighed. Was it yesterday or years ago that little Picôt had run white-faced to the café? Now the lovely Madeleine was merely a memory, another legend drifting up and down the boulevard like a ghost.

Prosper leant against the *zinc* of his favourite *bistro* in the Rue de la Gaîté and chatted with the blue-chinned proprietor. He was not drunk, just happy and benevolent. Suddenly the big kitchen clock above the rows of multi-coloured bottles whirred frantically and struck three. Prosper set down his empty glass, settled his *billet* and solemnly shook hands with Jean Dancourt as if setting off on a very long journey. Then with a quick bow or two to the few habitués still seated in the tiny café, he passed out into the street.

There were few people about as the hunchback sidled along

the shuttered walls of the houses and crossed the Boulevard Edgar Quinet, but just as he was about to turn into the Boulevard Montparnasse a figure detached itself from a shadowy doorway and caught him by the arm. Prosper stopped dead and began to tremble. The man's face was hidden beneath a broad-brimmed hat and it was not until the figure spoke that the hunchback recognised his companion. He let out a sigh of relief.

'I am sorry. M'sieur. In the dark I did not recognise. And how should I know—?'

'Don't worry about that. I've been waiting to see you—on your own. Understand, Prosper? You can spare me a few minutes, eh?'

The hunchback chuckled thickly.

'I do not think the master will worry his head off if I do not collect him before dawn. You know him, M'sieur?'

'Quite. Well, we can't talk here. Follow me to Rue Auguste Comte—the house with the yellow shutters—the second floor studios. I have friends there who wish to meet you. A little business discussion, my good fellow. But I think it would be best if we don't arrive together. You must remain some hundred metres behind me. You will find the street door open. I will be waiting for you at the top of the stairs.'

'Very good, M'sieur.'

'And Prosper.'

'Yes, M'sieur?'

'I must warn you that your silence over this meeting is essential. A single word to your master or anybody else and—'

The tall, thin figure made a significant gesture, the import of which the hunchback did not fail to understand. Some ten minutes later the couple were reunited at the head of the stairs which led up from the level of the Rue Auguste Comte.

Only a few belated drinkers drowsed at the tables of the Café Vavin. Lebrun was fast asleep with his face hanging down in the folds of his big, black coat and his incongruous *képi*, which had once seen service in the Foreign Legion, comically askew on his head. A yawning waiter lounged in the doorway of the restaurant, idly turning the pages of a week-old pictorial. Under his special bay-tree Noel Blake stared owlishly at the pile of saucers which served as a tally for the drinks he had knocked back during the course of the evening. A half-empty glass of *Cinzano* and soda-water, in which floated a lump of ice, stood ready at his elbow. He was thirty-six but any man surprising him at that moment would have allowed him another twenty years and wagered on his good judgment! With his ragged black beard, his brightly patterned 'sportings' and his small, black *béret*, Blake looked more French than a Frenchman. He had not set foot in England for fifteen years.

Summoning the waiter, he paid his bill, lit a cigarette and wandered off slowly down the deserted boulevard. Some few hundred yards along he turned right into the Rue Campagne--Première and presently, drawing level with a wrought-iron gate, drew out a key and let himself into the courtyard of the Ateliers Daubigny. His own studio lay directly ahead through a little arched passage, the entrance flanked by two badly-chipped Tritons blowing on conch-shells. Two or three steps led up from the passage to the level of his studio-door. He went in and switched on the lights.

II

MURDER IN MONTPARNASSE

It was on September 10th that a strange phenomenon was noticed at the Café Vavin. Ten o'clock, eleven, twelve—the hours struck—and the table of Monsieur Pierre Lebrun remained unoccupied! It was something that had not happened for years during the warmer months. Bonnard was bombarded with enquiries as the tables filled and his clients noticed the vacant space under the glass-screen.

'Oh, but it is nothing to worry about, *messieurs*. M'sieur Lebrun is not ill. It is an unexpected visit he is paying to the country.'

'But Lebrun said nothing about it himself when I spoke to him last night,' objected M. Mabille. 'It is curious that he should fail to let us know of such an important event. Why, for all the years that I have known him, I have never known him to leave Montparnasse, let alone Paris. We can only hope that he will get his *Pernod* bottle wherever he may be! Without it I think he would have nothing to live for.'

'That's true enough,' broke in a fresh voice from a nearby table. 'Several times I have stopped to chat with Lebrun and each time he has spoken of his unhappiness. "Why did they not let me die before?" That's what he asked me. He holds you responsible for that failure, Bonnard. You were only just in time.'

The others nodded. Ever since the night when Lebrun had put arsenic in his *Pernod*, the Café Vavin had anticipated his suicide. They put down his continued existence in a harsh and ungenerous world to the hunchback's unfailing watchfulness.

And then, ten days later, on the night of September 20th, old Lebrun suddenly reappeared. It was nearing midnight when Prosper wheeled his master into the Café Vavin. Lebrun seemed to be asleep and when Bonnard came forward, beaming with delight, to welcome back his oldest customer, the hunchback raised a finger to his lips and quickly shook his head.

'Pardon, M'sieur—but the journey. Only late this evening we arrived in the Rue Delambre. The master is worn out with so much excitement. I insist that he go to bed. But no—he is as obstinate as a she-mule. "Prosper—we will hold court at the Café Vavin tonight," he said, "Or I will get another fool to take your place." So you see, M'sieur, I get him into the chair and now he is fast asleep.'

'Well, my friend, he is perfectly safe with us. Henri—a *Pernod* in case M'sieur Lebrun should wake. That is all right, Prosper. See that M'sieur's cloak is wrapped well around him. Even in his corner it is a little chilly in this wind.'

As Prosper wrapped the cloak closer round his master's huddled body, Henri whisked forward his tray and set the glass on the table. Then with a bow to the proprietor, the hunchback, buttoning his own ill-fitting coat, passed out into the windy funnel of the boulevard.

Prosper quickened his step until he reached the Boulevard Edgar Quinet. A group of three men stood talking in a doorway and, as the hunchback drew level, he caught the eye of the man facing him and nodded. The other two men did not turn their heads but continued earnestly with the discussion. As soon as Prosper was out of sight, the group broke up suddenly and melted away in different directions. An observant onlooker would have noticed a certain hurried anxiety in their walk. They seemed to huddle into the upturned collars of their coats. For all their seeming disinterest in each other's destinations, it was curious that this trio, some three-quarters of an hour later, should be pacing the platforms of the Gare du Nord. No sign of recognition passed between them. They merely prowled up and down with their noses in their newspapers like all impatient travellers who find they have time to kill.

Prosper did not stay long at the *bistro* in the Rue de la Gaîté. Just long enough for a couple of *demis* and a talk with the proprietor about his stay in the country. Dancourt enquired which district he had visited.

'Perhaps,' said the proprietor in a wistful voice, 'it was my own beloved Burgundy? I was born there in Dijon, but I have not been out of Paris for forty years. Except, of course, for the war.'

'You do not know Normandy?' enquired Prosper.

'No, *mon ami.*'

'It was there that we stayed,' said Prosper promptly. 'In a little village. It was so small that I do not even remember if it had a name. It had a *bistro*. But it was no good. In Normandy they don't understand the art of drinking as they do in Paris.'

Presently, Prosper glanced at the clock. Twelve-thirty. It was time he returned to the Café Vavin.

Only a handful of customers remained in the café, although Bonnard himself had not yet retired to his bed. The hunchback's glance sped swiftly to the figure seated in the wheelchair. It looked as if Lebrun had not yet awakened, for an untouched glass of *Pernod* still stood at his elbow, and his face was still half-sunk in the folds of his voluminous cloak.

Bonnard made a gesture towards Prosper's master and shrugged his shoulders. Prosper nodded.

'It is as I thought, M'sieur. He is exhausted. He would have done better to have stayed on his couch.'

'He has not raised an eyelid since he arrived,' said Bonnard. 'But I will leave the drink in case he should wake. I am sorry not to have greeted your master on his return. Tell him from me, when he wakes, that Monsieur Bonnard offers his felicitations.'

Prosper bowed and hitched himself up like a child on to a chair which he had drawn up beside Lebrun's table. Bonnard went into the restaurant, above which he lived with his family. Henri dozed at the cash-desk. The few customers murmured sleepily over their final drinks in a far corner of the café.

Some twenty minutes later the Café Vavin was deserted save for Prosper, his master and the nodding Henri. The hunchback rose stealthily, crossed to the restaurant entrance and glanced at the clock. It was ten minutes past one. Then, on tip-toe, he returned to his seat at Lebrun's table and called for Henri. The waiter awoke with a start, snatched up his napkin, flung it over his arm and hurried out on to the pavement. Instinctively he glanced at Lebrun's glass and was surprised to see it half-empty.

'Your master has awakened, eh?'

Prosper nodded and winked.

'But he seems to have fallen asleep again. You can guess his fatigue, Henri, that he should fall asleep before his glass is empty.' Prosper lowered his voice and added in confidential tones: 'Listen, Henri, I want you to watch over the master for a few minutes. There is a very special letter of his which I have forgotten to post. He will be full of fury if he finds out that it has not gone tonight. If he should wake, bring another *Pernod*. You cannot be wrong in doing that!'

Henri chuckled and winked in turn, and the hunchback scuttled off down the boulevard in the direction of the nearest post-box. For some time Henri gazed stupidly at the figure humped in the invalid-chair. At the back of his mind he wondered what it must be like to be paralysed and half-blind. The poor old chap must be frozen to the bone, dozing away in the chill of the September evening. His cloak, too, seemed to have half-slipped from his shoulders. Prosper should have noticed that and set it right. Very cautiously Henri leant forward and twitched the cloak a little higher. It seems to be caught in the back of the wheelchair. He tugged a little harder and suddenly, to his horror, the body of Lebrun toppled forward and his head hit the table with a resounding thump. Even in the excitement of the moment the waiter in Henri was upper-most, for shooting out an arm he snatched up the half-empty glass of *Pernod* before the old man fell and set it aside on the adjacent table. Then, trembling with anxiety, he tried to raise him to a sitting posture. The body seemed strangely heavy and limp. Had that unexpected contact with the table-top knocked the old fellow unconscious? Certain it was that the head would not remain upright on the neck. It lolled forward in the most grotesque fashion with the faded *képi* jammed down over the forehead. What should he do? Rouse Monsieur Bonnard? Wait until Prosper should return? Perhaps brandy . . . but how was he to force the spirit between the old man's lips single-handed? Henri's alarm increased. Suppose the blow on the forehead had killed Monsieur Lebrun? Mightn't he, Henri, be arrested on a charge of murder? After all, if he hadn't fiddled with that cloak . . . *Mon Dieu! Mon Dieu!* This was terrible . . . terrible!

For a moment the bewildered waiter did not move, then coming to a sudden decision, he rushed into the café and ran up the staircase to his master's apartments. In less than thirty seconds, in answer to Henri's frantic knockings, Bonnard appeared in the doorway.

'Well—idiot—what does it mean? Have you gone mad?'

'It is Monsieur Lebrun,' gasped Henri.

'Lebrun? He is still here?'

'He has fallen, M'sieur—hit his head against the table. I think he is dead!'

'Dead? Here—out of my way!'

Bonnard flapped down the stairs in his nightgown and out on to the pavement. Lebrun still lay where he had toppled, his forehead resting against the table, his two arms hanging down like the flippers of a seal. Bonnard groped for his pulse. There was no response—not a flutter of blood in the veins! As Bonnard straightened up, Prosper appeared and ran with a cry toward the table.

'M'sieur—what is the matter? Why are you here in your nightgown?'

Bonnard ignored the question.

'The police. We must get on to the police. We cannot afford a scandal in the Café Vavin.'

'But the master, M'sieur?'

'Dead,' replied Bonnard curtly as he gathered up the trailing hem of his nightgown and rushed inside to the 'phone.

The hunchback let out a sharp wail and collapsed, weeping, on the steps of the restaurant.

'Now,' said Inspector Moreau, 'let's get this in order. When you tried to arrange the cloak round Monsieur Lebrun's shoulders, he fell forward and struck his head sharply on the table, eh? Was he asleep when you first touched him?'

'But how can I say? How should I know?' wailed the unfortunate waiter. 'In any other man—yes. But in the case of Monsieur Lebrun—'

'You mean the dark glasses? You were unable to see whether his eyes were open or closed? *Eh, bien*—so much for that. But you say he had been awake just previously?'

'Indeed, M'sieur, he must have been, for his glass of *Pernod* was half empty.'

'That is right,' broke in Prosper quickly. 'I arrive here some time about a quarter to one and a little after that time the master awake and ask what time it is. I tell him and—'

'A minute,' cut in Moreau incisively. 'Who do you happen to be? Why should you be sitting beside Monsieur Lebrun?'

In a torrent of words Prosper explained his position in the Lebrun household. Moreau nodded.

'Go on.'

'Well, M'sieur, after he had asked the time, the master notice the *Pernod* and he threw back half the glass in one big gulp—so!' The hunchback made a descriptive gesture. 'Then he say "Bon!" and keep silent and after a time he seem to be asleep. Then I remember a letter which I should have posted for the master and I leave Henri to watch him while I go to the postbox.'

'I see.' Moreau got up and walked to the doorway of the restaurant in which he had been conducting his preliminary enquiries. A group of *gendarmes* was gathered about the body, which was still slumping forward from the wheelchair.

The Inspector took a quick glance round and suddenly his eye alighted on the object he was seeking. He stepped forward and picked up the half-glass of *Pernod* from the table where Henri had placed it just before Lebrun had toppled forward. This Moreau carried back carefully into the café, sniffing it as he went. Henri identified it as the glass from which the dead man had been drinking.

'Tell me, *Monsieur l'Inspecteur*,' broke in Bonnard, who had been watching Moreau's movements with interest, 'do you think that Monsieur Lebrun may have poisoned himself?'

'Why should I think that?'

'Then you have not heard!' exclaimed Bonnard. 'Two years ago, in this very café, Lebrun attempted to kill himself with arsenic. If I had not seen him place the powder in his glass—'

'He has seemed depressed of late?'

'But very much so, M'sieur. Often he has spoken of taking his life. *Hélas*—what had he to live for? Paralysed, half-blind, with no real friends, slowly going mad through continual drinking . . . perhaps this is the kindest thing that could have happened.'

Moreau nodded but made no comment. Already he was beginning to see daylight—the same old story, the hopeless despair of the dipsomaniac, the quick way out, the opportunity seized and . . . another commonplace suicide! He turned to greet a little man with a black beard who came hurrying between the tables.

'Ah M'sieur, I have been waiting for you. I think it is a simple case, but perhaps when you have viewed the body—'

The doctor nodded and followed Moreau over to the wheel-chair, where he made a cursory examination. As he was doing so the Inspector primed him up with the facts of the case.

'Umph,' said the doctor as he straightened up, 'it's quite certain that he didn't die from the blow on the forehead. I think he was dead before he fell forward. You say he attempted suicide two years ago? Arsenic, eh? Well this time, if it is poison, then it is not arsenic we shall find. There would have been vomiting, perhaps, convulsions, which his servant could not have failed to notice. Well, Inspector, I think if you get the body to the mortuary I could perform a post-mortem at once. I should like, too, the glass from which he was drinking and its contents. I do not think the case will prove to be very troublesome where you are concerned. I will ring through to the *Sûreté* when I have made the necessary tests.'

Four hours later, as dawn was coming up over the jumbled roofs of the city, the doctor's unemotional voice was speeding over the wires to the Inspector.

'Morphine—the hydrochloride—at least two grains in the residue of the *Pernod*. I tested the saliva and found strong traces of morphine. The pupil of the eye was contracted—a typical result of morphine poisoning. No doubt about it, Inspector— Lebrun committed suicide. He must have smuggled the morphine salts into his drink when nobody was looking.'

'As I anticipated, M'sieur, I shall have to make further enquiries naturally, but I don't think there will be any unexpected evidence to upset your verdict.'

For the remainder of that day Inspector Moreau was busy collecting various depositions. Prosper was closely questioned in the Rue Delambre concerning the morphine, but he could not say how his master had been able to obtain the fatal dose. Through Bonnard, the Inspector got in touch with several habitués of the Café Vavin and they all agreed that Lebrun suffered, and had suffered for years, from acute melancholia. More than one had heard him speak quite openly of suicide and recently at that.

For once it seemed, his usual routine upset by the journey up to Paris, Prosper had failed to search his master's pockets before they left the Rue Delambre. There was only one factor in the case which surprised Inspector Moreau. When, in the

mortuary, he had removed Lebrun's dark glasses he was astonished to find him far younger than the general evidence led
him to believe. Forty, fifty—certainly not more. It seemed tragic
that a man with a future still ahead of him should have fallen
victim to a vice which, though slow in its devastating results,
has but one inevitable end.

III

THE MISSING ARTIST

For a day or two Lebrun's suicide was the chief topic of conversation among the pavement-tables of Montparnasse. Prosper
was seen about the streets mournfully shopping, a long loaf
under one arm, a litre of red wine cuddled in the other. His
eyes had a fluttering, nervous expression, as if at any corner he
expected to encounter the ghost of his dead master.

There was a vacancy also at the table under the third bay-tree
from the right. It was nearly a fortnight since Noel Blake had
shown up at the Café Vavin. His absence caused no comment,
because his friends knew well enough that Blake would shut
himself away for days when his brush was running sweetly.
Nobody made enquiries for him at his studio, for it was an
unspoken rule that those who wished to chat with him could
always do so at Bonnard's.

But less than a week after the Lebrun tragedy a rumour
concerning Blake was going round the cafés. He had been
arrested as a spy. He had forged a cheque and made a get-away
over the Belgian frontier. He had stolen a jewel-case from a
woman's flat and succeeded in crossing the channel with some
eighty thousand francs worth of diamonds in his possession.
The later the rumour, the more fantastic the details. But there
was one drop of truth to be distilled from all this wild hearsay—
Noel Blake had undoubtedly disappeared.

*

It was Madame Mollien who first got in touch with the police. She had waited four nights for Blake to return and when on the fifth day his bed still remained unslept in, she rang up the *Sûreté*. Twenty minutes later Inspector Moreau was at the Ateliers Daubigny.

Wasn't it possible that Monsieur Blake might be staying with friends? Madame Mollien shook her head. Never before had Monsieur slept away from his studio without first informing her. He was most regular in his habits. 'A woman perhaps?' suggested Moreau. Madame disagreed. Monsieur had an eye to economy and if he wished to sleep with a woman he brought her back with him to the studio. What more natural? It was a sensible arrangement.

'When did he first disappear?'

'It was a Friday—the Friday before last. That would be—'

'The twentieth,' broke in Moreau, adding to himself: 'The night of the Lebrun affair, eh? A coincidence.' Aloud he went on: 'Tell me, Madame, what time on Friday was it when you last saw Monsieur Blake?'

'Eleven o'clock that morning, M'sieur. Always at eleven o'clock I take up Monsieur's coffee and brioche.'

'He sleeps late?'

'Indeed, M'sieur—often he does not come in from the cafés until the early hours.'

'You take up all his meals to him?'

'Oh no, M'sieur—only his *petit déjeuner*. His other meals he has on the Boulevard.'

'I see. And on this particular Friday did he seem strange or upset in any way?'

'No, M'sieur. He seemed to be quite himself. He spoke, I remember, of a picture which he was anxious to finish—that picture there which you see on the easel.'

'And you did not see him for the rest of the day?'

'No, M'sieur. And the next morning when I take up his coffee I find the door unlocked and the bed still made as I had left it.'

'But on Friday morning wasn't Monsieur Blake still in bed when you took up his tray? When did you have time to make the bed?'

'Oh, as usual, M'sieur. M'sieur Blake always has his *petit déjeuner* seated at the table and while he is drinking his coffee I make the bed and clear up the rest of his apartment.'

'I see. Did you notice anything unusual about the room on Saturday morning?'

Madame Mollien hesitated, then she took the Inspector by the arm and led him to the easel.

'Do you notice anything strange about this picture, M'sieur?'

Moreau peered at it and then laughed lightly: 'To me, Madame, it is not so much strange as incomprehensible!'

'But you notice nothing unusual?'

'*Mon Dieu!*—yes! The sail of this boat—it is smudged across the sky, as if something had been brushed against it when the paint was wet.'

'Yes. M'sieur, and on Saturday morning the paint *was* still wet. It is curious that M'sieur Blake should have been so care-less, for he had been working many weeks on this picture.'

'You heard no sounds from the studio during the day or night of that particular Friday?'

'I cannot be sure of that, M'sieur. It is curious. I have my apartment in one wing of the courtyard. It was a little before midnight when I think I hear—'

'Well?'

'Squeaks, M'sieur.'

'Squeaks?'

'Exactly, M'sieur—as of something squeaking in the court-yard. For a moment I was frightened, then I think it is nothing to worry about and I go to sleep again.'

'One more little point, Madame. During the five days that Monsieur Blake has been away, has this room remained undisturbed?'

'Oh yes, M'sieur. I have kept the door locked. I have a master-key, you understand? So that I can get into the studios to dust or make the beds when the occupants are out.'

'Exactly. And have you dusted or in any way disturbed any of the furniture or objects in this room since Monsieur Blake has been absent?'

'No, M'sieur.'

Moreau was puzzled. The strange disappearance of this Englishman seemed to bear with it the outlines of a first-class mystery. Why should he vanish so abruptly and leave behind him a room full of pictures? Blake must have been in a queer frame of mind to have smudged that wet paint across the middle of his latest canvas.

Moreau gave a little snort of impatience and, turning aside from theory, got down to a practical examination of the studio.

It was really a self-contained flat, for through one door Moreau found a kitchenette and through another, a minute bathroom. His first interest lay in the kitchenette and almost directly Moreau found something new to perplex him. On a small, enamel-topped table stood a half-empty cup of coffee and a half-eaten slice of bread-and-butter capped with thin slices of Dutch cheese. On the edge of the draining-board was the burnt-out stub of a *Gitane* cigarette from which drooped a long cylinder of ash. From these little scraps of evidence he tried to reconstruct the events which had taken place in that kitchen. One thing was obvious—some time during the course of Friday evening, Blake had come into the kitchen, brewed himself a cup of coffee, cut himself a slice of bread and cheese and then, in the midst of this snack, something, or somebody, had interrupted him. He had not expected to be disturbed, for when he had entered the kitchen to pour out his coffee, which he had heated in a saucepan over the gas stove, Blake had been smoking a *Gitane*. Realising that he could not eat and smoke at the same time, he had set the lighted cigarette aside, intending to finish it after he had eaten his bread and cheese. The interruption had come and this man of precise and careful habits had left the burning cigarette on the draining-board! What or who had drawn him so abruptly from that casual, little meal? Was it too much to suppose that almost directly after Noel Blake had walked out of the kitchenette, he had walked out of the studio, out of the Rue Campagne-Première, out of, the district Montparnasse, and thus into oblivion?

'Walked?' thought Inspector Moreau dubiously. 'By his own free-will? No, no—somehow, I think not. If that were so, why did he not return to finish his coffee and cigarette? It seems more possible that he left because he was *forced* to leave, perhaps even under physical pressure. Might there have been a struggle, chloroform perhaps and—'

Moreau clicked his fingers and broke into a smile. The picture! The smudge! A struggle? Surely that was a feasible explanation? In the course of such a struggle it would be quite possible for an arm or shoulder to brush against the wet paint. He moved quickly to the easel and fixed in his mind's-eye the exact colour of the boat's sail. It was a vivid russet—no, not quite, it was a shade brighter. Tangerine. Ah, that was it precisely! And if his theory were correct, somewhere there was a sleeve, a shoulder, a lapel, belonging either to Blake or his assumed assailants, which would reveal a similar smudge of colour. Maybe the coat had since been sent to the cleaners. *Ça fait rien!* Moreau chuckled. The all-seeing eye of the ultra-microscope was profoundly difficult to fool. Many a criminal had forgotten this little fact and suffered accordingly.

Moreau passed into the bathroom. The wash-basin, closet, the wall-cabinet and the bath itself occupied so much space that there was barely room to turn round in the place. The bath had obviously received the recent attentions of Madame Mollien, for it glistened a pristine white. But the same could not be said for the wash-basin. A thin rime of dried soap was clearly evident, suggesting that the basin had been used after Madame had cleaned up the flat on Friday morning. *Eh bien*—there was nothing unusual about that. Moreau was just about to turn aside for an examination of the cabinet when his eye was suddenly arrested by a detail which he had nearly overlooked The rime of dirt round the basin did not consist solely of dried soap. Here and there minute scraps of stubbly, black hairs had been caught in the rime. Somebody had been shaving in the basin. And since this was Blake's bathroom was it absurd to suppose that the shaver was Blake? But *mon Dieu!* It was impossible! Moreau drew his enlarged photo of the missing man from his pocket—a photo which Madame Mollien had cut from a recent art magazine. The chief feature of Noel Blake's physiognomy was the untidy black beard which encircled it. And a man with a beard does not leave a stubble of hair among the dried soap in his wash-basin!

A new thought struck Moreau. He reached out and clicked open the mirrored door of the cabinet. The usual bathroom paraphernalia was ranged on the glass shelves—hair lotion, comb, denture brushes and fixative. a bottle of mouthwash and so forth—but the one thing which Moreau failed to find was the very thing which he had anticipated would not be there. Shaving tackle. Exactly. In Noel Blake's bathroom cabinet one would not expect to find a shaving brush or razor. Then how, in the name of thunder, had that characteristic hair stubble got into the wash-basin? Whose hair was it? Blake's? If so he must have removed his beard by the usual process, first by trimming it as short as possible with scissors, then finishing the job off with a razor. But, *sacré nom d'un nom*, Blake had no razor! He had no reason to have one in the flat. Unless— Moreau suddenly recognised the possibility—unless Blake had deliberately intended to remove his beard before he disappeared, bought the necessary shaving-tackle and taken it with him. An attempt at disguise, eh? Did it mean that Blake's reason for disappearing was of a criminal nature?

But how did this shape up with the half-eaten meal, the suggestion of a struggle? These factors hinted at a totally unexpected flight from the Rue Campagne-Première. The second factor argued deliberate forethought. Moreau was for the moment flummoxed!

Drawing out a powerful magnifying glass he returned to a more detailed examination of the rime in the wash-basin. At once he was struck by a new detail. The tiny hairs caught in the dried soap were of abnormal length when compared with those resulting from the process of a normal shave. Moreover, the hairs were of varying lengths. Wasn't this exactly what one would expect to find if Blake had shaved off his beard? After the trim with the scissors, which could not be particularly close, the razor would remove a forest of fairly long hairs, some longer than others because of the varying configurations of the face—a wrinkle or a hollow, for example, where the scissors could not do their work so thoroughly.

The more Moreau thought about it, the more certain he felt that before Blake had left the studio, either willingly or under compulsion, he had first shaved off his beard. So now it was essential that a police broadcast should be made for the missing man, with this new descriptive feature included in it. *Bon!* This was progress. Slight perhaps, but decidedly encouraging.

IV

THE SQUEAKING CHAIR

Madame Mollien had heard strange noises in the Courtyard of the Ateliers Daubigny a little before midnight. Was it not possible, thought Moreau, that somebody living in or around the Rue Campagne-Première had seen Blake come out of the courtyard about that time? Either Blake alone or accompanied? The street would be fairly deserted at that hour and in a deserted street little events are more noticeable.

But after two days' exhaustive enquiries his spirits slipped back into a pit of the darkest depression. Old Papa Picôt, who had been zig-zagging down the street about midnight, had seen three men passing up the Rue Campagne-Première in the direction of the Boulevard Raspail, but after a fervid cross-examination the only details he could recall in connection with the group were that one of the men was carrying a big parcel under his arm and another was talking very quickly in a foreign language. Was it English? 'Possibly,' said Papa Picôt. Was it German? 'Equally possibly,' said Papa Picôt. Or Dutch? 'It is well within the bounds of possibility,' asserted Papa Picôt with a bland smile. Exasperated, the Inspector shouted: 'And possibly, *mon ami*, you were drunk.'

'Oh no, M'sieur,' replied Père Picôt, 'there is no possibility about that—it is a certainty!'

Moreau felt disheartened.

And then the Inspector came across some new and startling information. At the end of his second day's investigation around the Ateliers Daubigny, he turned into a little café in the Rue Campagne-Première to replenish his stock of cigars. The proprietor, recognising Moreau, began to chat with him about the Lebrun case, airing his opinions about the inevitable end of all confirmed *Pernod* drinkers.

'It is strange, *M'sieur l'Inspecteur*, but only an hour before the poor fellow took poison I saw him go by this very café in his wheelchair. The little hunchback, his servant, was pushing him. *Mon Dieu*, but it is a true saying that Death lies round the next corner—in this case, *mon ami*, the Montparnasse boulevard.'

Moreau pricked up his ears.

'But Lebrun lived in the Rue Delambre. He would not come down this street on his way to the Café Vavin. You must have been mistaken.'

'Oh no, M'sieur—my wife, too, she saw him right enough. There is no mistake.'

'At what time was this?' demanded Moreau, now on the alert.

The proprietor shrugged and threw out his hands.

'Midnight, perhaps. Perhaps just after midnight. I cannot be sure. But somewhere about then.'

The Inspector, who was in plain clothes, accepted a light for his cigar and strolled off in a pensive mood towards the Boulevard Montparnasse. He turned into the Coupole and ordered a half-bottle of burgundy. Why should Prosper have been pushing his master down the Rue Campagne-Première at midnight on September 20th instead of down the Rue Delambre? These streets entered the Boulevard Montparnasse from exactly opposite directions. Why the detour? Had Lebrun's suicide any connection with Noel Blake's disappearance? Did Blake know Lebrun? *Mon Dieu!* Was it possible that the police had been too casual in assuming that Lebrun had taken his own life, merely because the doctor had found morphine in the residue of the *Pernod* and in the saliva of the deceased? Yes. Yes. Lebrun had taken an overdose of morphine, but had the poison been administered by some other hand? Blake's, *par exemple*? Moreau's eager mind began to reel out an immediate hypothesis.

Suppose Lebrun had been lured in some way to the Ateliers Daubigny. Suppose Prosper were in the pay of Noel Blake, a partner in a deliberately planned crime? The hunchback wheels his master from the Rue Delambre into Blake's studio. There Blake offers Lebrun a glass of his beloved *Pernod*—but a glass heavily impregnated with the hydrochloride of morphine. Lebrun drinks. The poison has its inevitable effect *and the dead body of the dipsomaniac is wheeled to the Café Vavin by the hunchback*. There, another glass of *Pernod* is set, as usual, before Lebrun. Prosper smuggles a second fatal dose of the morphine into the glass and when nobody is looking pours half the drink away, perhaps into the tub of one of the many bay-trees set among the tables of the Café Vavin. What more simple? Blake hastily shaves off his beard and vanishes, obviously intending to reappear with some glib explanation, when all chance of suspicion concerning the cause of Lebrun's death has died out. Two points at once occurred to the Inspector. First, that unfinished snack in the kitchenette. Prosper must have turned up sooner than was arranged and, in his natural excitement, Blake had forgotten about the cigarette. Moreover, he might easily have brushed against the wet paint for the same reason. Second—those peculiar squeaks which Madame Mollien swore she had heard about midnight of the twentieth. *Was it not perhaps Lebrun's wheelchair which needed oiling?*

There were, decided Moreau, three things to be done at once. He must slip along to the Café Vavin and see Bonnard. He must see if it were possible for Lebrun to have sat at his table, unspeaking and obviously not spoken to, during the course of the hour that he had remained in his chair before Henri had made the discovery. Then he must cross-question Prosper. Finally, the wheelchair. He must find it. He must make sure about that singular squeak.

Moreau drained his glass, slapped down a note on the table, and rose briskly. His volatile spirits were soaring heavens-high again!

Monsieur Bonnard was shocked by the implications of Moreau's swift questions. But he could not deny that such a theory were possible. Lebrun had appeared to be sleeping when Prosper first wheeled him to his usual table. The hunchback, in fact, had warned Bonnard himself that his master was tired after the train journey up to Paris and begged that he should not be disturbed.

'And then?' snapped Moreau.

'Well, M'sieur, I signed to Henri that he should serve Lebrun with a *Pernod* in case he should wake.'

'The glass was brought at once?'

'Yes, M'sieur.'

'And then Prosper left the café to go to his favourite *bistro*, eh?'

'As usual, M'sieur.'

'And he was back—how soon?'

'In about half an hour, M'sieur—just after twelve-thirty.'

'And during that time Lebrun had not awakened?'

'No, M'sieur. His glass still remained untouched. I then went, myself, to bed and left Henri in charge. Prosper drew up a chair to the table and sat for a time, I understand, with his master. But it would be better that Henri should tell about the rest.' Bonnard raised a hand. 'Henri!'

The waiter approached and gave a short bow. Moreau explained in a few words what he wanted to know. Henri considered the questions for a moment and then said: 'No, M'sieur—I did not see M'sieur Lebrun awake myself, for I was inside at the cash-desk. There were only a few customers left outside, at a far table. When Prosper called to me that he wished to post a letter, perhaps some twenty minutes later, I went out and found that half the *Pernod* had been drunk by Monsieur Lebrun. I remarked, naturally, that M'sieur must have awakened and Prosper agreed. Then Prosper explained about the letter and left me with M'sieur—'

'All right! All right!' cut in Moreau. 'The rest we know. Tell me—near Lebrun's usual table—is there a tub?'

Henri led Moreau to the entrance of the restaurant and pointed.

'*Voilà*, M'sieur—you can see for yourself.'

'And it would be the same tub that was beside the table on the night of the tragedy?'

Bonnard, who had followed the others out on to the pavement, nodded.

'I am certain, since they are heavy, that the tubs have not been changed.'

'M'sieur Bonnard,' said Moreau solemnly, 'I shall want that tub.'

'The tub, M'sieur? But why?'

Moreau smiled.

'I have an idea that it may whisper a secret about the events of that Friday night, which you or Henri have never suspected. Sometimes, M'sieur Bonnard, we can make the inanimate talk more sense than a dozen human beings. Yes, perhaps your innocent little bay-tree—'

And again Moreau smiled.

When the inspector left the Café Vavin, he made his way direct to Number 44, Rue Delambre. He had a feeling that the place was deserted and, after pulling twice at the bell, he was about to turn away, when the door opened and three inches of pointed nose appeared round the end of it. Beyond the nose was a very bent, very dishevelled old crone.

'Well? Well?' she demanded in a querulous voice. 'What do you want? You must have come to the wrong house. I have never seen you before.'

'Nor I you, Madame,' said Moreau with a little salute. 'But now that we have met, may I introduce myself? Inspector Moreau of the *Sûreté*, Madame.' He bowed. 'I am an old friend of poor M'sieur Lebrun and I wish to see his servant, Prosper.'

The old lady cackled.

'Ah indeed—he was a sly one—the hunchback. But you won't find him here any longer. Oh no, indeed! Indeed no, *mon ami*. Since his master died he has been busy here. Never has there been such bargaining in this street before. He sell everything and tuck the money inside his vest. Oh—ho—he is indeed a clever rascal. He has made a lot of money, for people were ready to pay high prices for something which belonged to poor Monsieur Lebrun.'

The old lady wiped a rheumy eye and drew her shawl tighter across her sunken breast.

'And where is Prosper now, Madame? At the Hôtel Crillon, perhaps?'

'That is not what he told me,' answered the old lady, on whom Moreau's touch of irony was wasted. 'He has taken his baggage to the *bistro* of Monsieur Jean Dancourt in the Rue de la Gaité. Indeed I saw him go. It was very droll. He carted away all his baggage in the wheelchair of poor Monsieur Lebrun. I understand him to say that he will stay there until he is so poor that he must find another job.'

'The Rue de la Gaité, eh?' Moreau knew the *bistro* well enough. He bade the old lady goodnight and walked briskly back into the Boulevard Montparnasse.

In a few minutes Jean Dancourt was breathing gusty wafts of garlic into his face across the *zinc* of the little café. The hunchback had stayed for a few nights in the *bistro*. But only the day before he had packed up his bags and departed, so Dancourt believed, to a little village in Normandy. No, he did not know the name of the village. The invalid-chair? Yes—Prosper had brought it to the *bistro* the first day, but the next morning he had sold it to old Phillipe Troyon, whose second--hand store was, as M'sieur Moreau probably recollected, in the Rue de Vaugirard.

Moreau thanked the proprietor and hurried off to the *Sûreté*. He wanted a description of Prosper to be broadcast without delay. It should not be difficult to track down the missing man. After all, a hunchback is always conspicuous. As for that nameless little village in Normandy—well that, thought Moreau, was just a pretty fairy-tale.

*

Moreau had early abroad the following morning. Already the necessary police mechanism had been set in motion in an effort to apprehend the missing hunchback. A police car had set off through the early morning streets to collect the all-important tub from the Café Vavin—the tub which might send sensational headlines streaming across the pages of the daily Press. Moreau had arranged with the laboratory staff of the *Sûreté* to make an immediate analysis of the earth in which the bay-tree was potted. As for himself, he was determined to track down the whereabouts of Lebrun's wheelchair.

But when Moreau arrived in the longest street of Paris, the Rue de Vaugirard, his optimism received a check. Only a day or two before, Troyon had had a customer for the chair—a M'sieur Pigalle, of 14, Rue Raynouard. Could Troyon recollect if the wheels of the chair needed oiling? Had the chair a decided squeak? *Hélas!* Troyon could not remember. Moreau then jotted down the name and address of the purchaser and, in an irritable mood, left the shop.

Presently he dived into the Pasteur station of the *Métro* which was nearby. At Passy he got out and in a few minutes he was opposite Monsieur Pigalle's house.

A maid opened the door and in answer to Moreau's enquiry she explained that Monsieur Pigalle himself was out, but if M'sieur Moreau cared to stay, there was no doubt that the master would be back in a very short time. Moreau thanked the girl and settled himself in a comfortable armchair to wait.

About five minutes later the Inspector sat up with a start. He listened intently, holding his breath. Surely his hearing had not played him false? He jumped up, crossed to the window and looked out. *Mon Dieu!* There was no mistake about it! That rhythmic squeak, squeak, squeak was emanating from a wheelchair, which a long slab of a fellow in funereal black was pushing with great dignity along the pavement.

Two minutes later this same fellow was standing respectfully beside Monsieur Pigalle, who was shaking hands with the Inspector in the drawing-room. Pigalle waved his servant away with an irritable gesture. When the imperturbable fellow had withdrawn, the cripple turned to Moreau with a wry grimace.

'That idiot—he will drive me mad! He is obstinate! Never will he do what I tell him. Never! Never! Twenty times I have told him to oil my wheelchair and twenty times he has taken care to forget! But pardon, M'sieur, I am digressing. What do you wish to talk about, eh?'

Moreau smiled.

'I have no need to ask any questions now, M'sieur. They were answered for me before you came into the house!'

At midnight or thereabouts, Madame Mollien had heard peculiar squeaks crossing the courtyard. She was mystified. But this, surely, was the answer to the mystery? At midnight on September the 20th, the night that Lebrun was found dead in the Café Vavin, Prosper had wheeled his master out of Blake's studio and down the Rue Campagne-Première.

'My theory,' thought Moreau, 'seems less like a theory now than a fact. If Blake killed Lebrun as I imagine, so much is explained away. We know now why Prosper approached the Boulevard Montparnasse from such an unusual direction. We have a reason for Blake's disappearance, the shaving of his beard. Perhaps, too, we can assume the reason why the little hunchback has run away as well. Perhaps if we find Blake we shall find Prosper or *vice versa*. Perhaps, on the other hand, I am a fool. And yet, somehow, I think not.'

And when Moreau got back to the *Sûreté* he felt even more certain about it. Everything seemed to be pointing one way now: *Pierre Lebrun on the night of September 20th had been murdered with malice, aforethought.* The hunt was on!

V

LES TROIS MOUSQUETAIRES

Moreau's ever-increasing conviction was based mainly on the results obtained by the experts at the *Sûreté*. More and more, during the course of his long professional career, he had learnt to rely on the help of the scientists. In the early days the unfortunate gropings and blunderings of these pioneers had shown them up in a somewhat ridiculous light; but with the increase of precision in instruments and methods of analysis, in micro-photography, ballistics and all the paraphernalia of the scientific detective, these men had proved their worth twice over. In this case—later to be known as the Lebrun Mystery—what had they been able to tell the Inspector?

First and foremost, capping his deductions with a perfect piece of proof, the earth taken from the tub proved to contain the hydrochloride salts of morphine. In short, it now appeared certain that the hunchback had acted exactly as Moreau imagined. This being so, it seemed equally certain that Blake's disappearance was the direct result of Lebrun's poisoning.

The results of further tests made by the experts in Blake's studio were of a similarly clarifying nature. Under the ultra-microscope the hair stubble collected from the wash-basin revealed the fact that, at one end, each hair had been severed with scissors. Scissors, so the experts contended, that were none too sharp. Whereas the opposite end of each hair showed the characteristic clean cut of a very sharp razor. Again it seemed that Moreau's assumption was undeniably the truth.

New evidence came to light. Adhering to the wet paint which had been smudged across Blake's seascape were several minute strands of dark blue material, which might have come from a rough tweed coat of that particular colour. These infinitesimal wisps of unravelled wool perplexed Moreau, for Madame

Mollien had declared that she had never seen Blake in a dark blue tweed coat. Lebrun wore black and Prosper, as far as could be gathered, had never been seen about in tweeds. Was there, demanded Moreau, a fourth person present in the studio that night?

Even more did he postulate this question after his talk with the fingerprint experts, who had shown enormous industry in 'lifting' some scores of specimens from various surfaces in the room. The fingerprints on the coffee cup corresponded to those found on the oily surface of Blake's palette. So far so good. Moreau now had an unquestionable specimen of Blake's own prints. They were to be found all over the place—on the mirror of the wall-cabinet, on the wash-basin, on the polished handle of a paper-knife, on the handles of drawers. But why, in the name of all that was sacred, should no less than two other sets of prints be 'lifted' from the wash-basin and the chromium-plated taps belonging to it? Prosper's? Indeed no! It had been simple to eradicate the hunchback's prints. They were clear as crystal on the half-glass of *Pernod* which the doctor had analysed. Granted, Henri had touched the glass and the doctor himself, but when their particular prints had been taken, a third set was still to be found on the glass surface. These, *ipso facto*, *must* have been those of Prosper, since he handled the glass to pour half the *Pernod* into the tub. Nor were the prints on the wash-basin those of Madame Mollien. Then to whom did those two unknown sets of prints belong? Who had had access to Blake's bathroom? According to Madame she had thoroughly polished and cleaned the basin on Friday morning and during the course of the day, as far as she could say, M'sieur Blake had had no visitors. And yet two different sets of prints had been left on that wash-basin before Madame had locked the studio door on the following morning. Moreover, these prints appeared on other objects in the room. One set on the back of a highly-polished chair. The other on the supports of Blake's easel. And then, confounding Moreau even further, the experts upheld that a third uncatalogued set were visible on the top of a small mahogany table. So no less than six people must have been present—Blake, Prosper, Lebrun and three unknown men or women!

'You see now,' exclaimed Moreau, as the conference broke up, 'what you scientists have done for me! With one hand you help, with the other you confound. What am I to think now? Did Blake kill Lebrun? Is it not possible, now, that one of these three unknown visitors might have done so? And who are they—eh? You experts tell me comfortably that they are there, but you do not say who they are. For you, this part of the case is finished, but for me, *hélas*, it is only just going to begin, But perhaps in the files you will find the counterpart of these prints and then it will be made easier. An old criminal, perhaps, that has been through our hands. Well, *messieurs*, I can only pray that it is so!'

But unfortunately for the Inspector it was *not* so. The three men or women were unknown to the *Sûreté*. Then who? Who? Why were they there? What motive had Blake and these three unknown persons for killing Lebrun? Their victim had no money. A murder of revenge? Perhaps. A murder for a life insurance? But Moreau ascertained that Lebrun's life was not insured. Jealousy? Of what? A poor, miserable, half-dead drunkard? *Cherchez la femme?* But certainly there could be no woman in the case. Lebrun had only one love in his later life! Five people to kill one helpless, half-mad dipsomaniac! It seemed incredible. And these three people who now appeared to have been present when the ghoulish piece of work was being done—who the devil could they be?

Suddenly Moreau remembered Papa Picôt. Hadn't the old reprobate seen three men walking down the Rue Campagne-- Première about midnight on the twentieth? Walking away, in this case, from the Boulevard Montparnasse, the direction which the hunchback had taken. One of the men, so Papa Picôt upheld, had been speaking in a foreign tongue. Information slender enough, but something upon which to work, thought Moreau. Was it too much to suppose that these three men were friends? If so, it was more than probable that they might be seen about together in the cafés of Montparnasse. *Mon Dieu*—yes! That was the line of investigation to take. These men, if they followed the example of Blake and Prosper, might have likewise vanished from their usual haunts. Enquiries must be set on foot in every likely café and *bistro* in the district. A check-up on every *habitué* must be made. And if the men *were* missing then the chances were that they would be known by name and repute by the proprietor of their particular *rendezvous*. It was strange how conservative the typical Parisian was in this matter of *rendez-vous*—six nights out of seven he would sit at the same table in the same café and talk with the same friends. Strange, yes, but also a lucky habit for an overworked member of the Paris *Sûreté*!

One of the first moves Moreau had naturally made in his effort to trace the missing Prosper was to instigate careful inquiries at all the chief stations of the city. It was shortly after his talk with the fingerprint experts that a Sergeant came through on the 'phone to the Inspector's office. He was speaking, he explained, from a call-box in the Gare Montparnasse.

'I have been in touch with most of the station's personnel, Inspector, and I've got good news for you. The booking-clerk, who was on duty two days ago on the Alençon-Brest section of the line, swears that he has seen our friend. He particularly noticed him because he had to stand on tip-toe in order to ask for his ticket. There seems to be no doubt that it was the hunch-back.'

'And his destination? Does he remember?' demanded Moreau anxiously.

'Yes, M'sieur. A single ticket to Brest.'

'And the time of the train—did you think of that?'

'Naturally, Inspector. It left the Gare Montparnasse at—'

'No, no!' cut in Moreau briskly. 'That does not interest me—what I need to know is the time of the train's arrival at Brest.'

'That, too, I have,' said the Sergeant smugly. 'It would be at 18.10, M'sieur.'

'Good—that is all I want to know,' said Moreau in tones of great satisfaction. 'You have done well, *mon ami!*'

Some ten minutes later Moreau was on a long-distance call to the *commissariat de police* at Brest. Would the Inspector find out if a hunchback had left the Paris train which reached Brest at 18.10? A description of the wanted man followed. It was possible that this man was staying at one of the hotels in the town. If this were so, would the Inspector kindly apprehend the gentleman in question and return him, *à l'instant*, to Paris.

'And now,' thought Moreau, when he had rung off, 'for the three unknown gentlemen whom Papa Picôt saw walking down the Rue Campagne-Première.'

Wasting only enough time to collect a small posse of subordinates, Moreau bundled the constables into a car and drove to the Boulevard Montparnasse. There he portioned out various sections of the street to his helpers and loosed them, like a pack of bloodhounds, on their search for information. A time and place was fixed for their reassembly and Moreau, himself, plunged energetically into his section of the work.

Two hours later he returned in a dejected mood to the *rendez-vous*, where many of his helpers had already assembled. Their reports were equally negative and it was not until Sergeant Morny returned that Moreau's tension lifted. Morny had gleaned, in fact, some very interesting information. The proprietor of the Café Junot in the Place de Rentes believed that the wanted men were *habitués* of his establishment. The men, he declared, were inseparables and had earned the sobriquet in the district Montparnasse of *Les Trois Mousquetaires*. He had not seen these three most regular customers for some few days. He had been puzzled since they had made no mention of going away.

'*Bon!*' snapped Moreau. 'You, Morny, will come with me in the car to the Café Junot. We will cross-question this excellent fellow and squeeze him like a lemon, eh? You others can return by *métro* to the *Sûreté*.'

But René Besnard proved a very unyielding lemon to squeeze. His head was about as much use to him or anybody else as a turnip and a hard, green turnip at that! Moreau shot question after question at him, but at the end of an hour he had only collected a very meagre handful of answers. The known facts could be tabulated thus:

Unknown Number 1. Name—Elmer Pike, of foreign nationality, perhaps American.

Unknown Number 2. Name—Courtenay. Nationality—English.

Unknown Number 3. Name—Lemâtre, a portrait painter. Nationality—French.

So far so good. But Besnard had no idea of their habits, their circle of friends, their addresses, their social standing. He could not remember when they had first absented themselves from his café. It *might* have been after September 20th. He would not trust himself to say. Nor could he say with any exactitude how they normally dressed or what they looked like. Lemâtre was tall, very tall. He was sure of that. He believed that Pike wore glasses when he was reading the newspaper. Courteney smoked a pipe and drank quantities of *bock*, which was, of course, an excellent thing for the fortunes of the café.

'They spoke French when talking together?' demanded Moreau patiently.

'So I believe, M'sieur.'

'But, *mon Dieu*, you must *know*!' exclaimed Moreau. 'Yes or no?'

'Then, yes, M'sieur . . . sometimes.'

'Sometimes! Sometimes! What the devil do you mean?'

'Well, M'sieur, sometimes, when either of the foreign gentlemen got excited they spoke in English.'

'But when they spoke French, they spoke good French, eh? Fluent French?'

'*Hélas*, M'sieur, I have not the education to know that. Perhaps it was good. Perhaps it was not so good. How can a simple fellow like myself decide what is good French and what is not good French?'

Moreau gesticulated wildly.

'Tell me this, M'sieur, just this—how long had Pike and Courteney lived in Paris? How long have they been *habitués* of your café, *par exemple*?'

'Six months, perhaps. Perhaps a year.'

'Perhaps twelve, twenty, thirty, forty years, eh? You can remember nothing, idiot!'

'Precisely, M'sieur. But I have been told that the gentlemen at one time patronised the Café Vavin on the Boulevard. Perhaps M'sieur Bonnard, who owns the Café Vavin, can tell you more about these gentlemen than I can.'

Moreau let out a yelp of despair.

'For a whole hour I've been questioning you and you have taken all this time to give me one really useful piece of information! Believe me, *mon ami*, M'sieur Bonnard will certainly be able to tell me more about these gentlemen, for he certainly could not tell me less. *Bon jour, stupide!*'

In this last estimate Moreau proved himself right, for Bonnard was as generous with his information as Besnard had been miserly. Most certainly he knew all about *Les Trois Mousquetaires*. He had made it a habit to put himself *au fait* with his customers' interests and doings. It was quite true that at one time these three very intimate friends had collected each evening at the Café Vavin.

John Courteney, the Englishman, was quite a well-known critic on art matters, on both sides of the Channel. He had lived in Paris since 1920, mostly in hotels on the *Rive Gauche*. Elmer Pike, an American, had come to the city some two or three years later and struck up a friendship with Courteney. Pike was an author, though Bonnard did not think he had to rely on his profession for a living. He always seemed to have plenty of money. Lemâtre, the third member of the trio, was a portrait painter, a true Parisian—it was he who had first suggested that they should take a large studio-flat in the district and work together at the various jobs.

'At one time,' went on Bonnard, 'there was a fourth member in this *ménage*. They were always together on the boulevards and often they spent long weekends away from Paris down on the coast, where, I understand, they had bought a small sailing-boat. But, *hélas*, as is so often the case, M'sieur, a woman came into their lives. After that, things, perhaps, were not so comfortable. You remember Little Madeleine Rameau?'

Moreau nodded.

'She was a model, eh? I have an idea that she committed suicide some six months ago. The dead body was taken from the Seine, *n'est ce pas*?'

'But you do not recall the suspected reason for her suicide, inspector?'

'An *affaire du cœur*, I imagine.'

'Precisely, M'sieur. And the men that she loved was the fourth member of this *ménage* of which I was speaking. Somebody you know—at least by name. The man that has vanished from the Ateliers Daubigny.'

'Noel Blake!' exclaimed Moreau.

'Yes, M'sieur. It was well known along the boulevards that a curious situation had arisen when Madeline entered the lives of these four friends. Ah!' Bonnard blew a gusty kiss with his fingertips. 'She was a beauty, M'sieur. A rare loveliness that it is difficult to describe. Wherever that little lady went she cast a spell of enchantment over the men. Was it strange that these four should fall in love with her? But in the end it was Blake that she chose to live with—she adored him as she has never adored any other man. So Blake moved into the Ateliers Daubigny and the others stayed on in their place in the Rue St Jacques. But often they would still meet here—yes, the four men and poor Madeleine. At that time Pike, Courteney and Lemâtre were still *habitués* of the Café Vavin.'

'Then what was the trouble which drove them to take shelter under the wing of that stupid fellow Besnard?' asked Moreau, who has been deeply interested in Bonnard's recital.

'It was after the poor girl had thrown herself off the Pont d'Austerlitz. Blake grew tired of his mistress, M'sieur, as even the best of us will. But in his case, perhaps, it was more than that. He was callous, even brutally indifferent to Madeleine's trouble, though he, himself, had been the cause of it. *Eh bien*— the old story. When he learnt that she was *enceinte*, when her figure was no longer possible to paint or, for that matter, M'sieur . . . no longer beautiful, Blake wished to get rid of her. An embarrassment, you understand? But if he turned her out, how was she to make a living? A model who is *enceinte* is naturally a drag on the market. And so, when the tragic moment arrived, and Madeleine found herself on the streets, she took the inevitable way out. It is not far, M'sieur, from the embrace of a lover who is growing cold, to the even colder embrace of the river.' Bonnard sighed. 'If I had only recognised her tragedy sooner, M'sieur, my wife and I might have given her refuge here. But we did not know the true facts until it was too late'

'And after her suicide, Blake's three friends no longer met him here at the café?'

'That is true, M'sieur. From that day, so I understand, they have never acknowledged their old friend by so much as a nod. Remember that they loved the poor girl. They looked upon Blake as her murderer.'

Moreau nodded slowly. Although the story had moved him, he was already searching for its implications, rather than dwelling on its tragedy.

'And all this happened?' he asked.

'Last April, M'sieur—about six months ago.'

'And the number of their studio in the Rue St Jacques?'

Bonnard shook his head.

'That I do not know, M'sieur, but I understand that the knocker of their front door is fashioned in the form of a naked woman. Some say that the face of the woman is the face of Madeleine and that it was an order specially executed for the three friends.'

'*Eh bien*,' thought Moreau as he drove slowly in the direction of the Rue St Jacques with Sergeant Morny. 'Where am I now?'

Bonnard's story had confused rather than clarified the Lebrun case. Why should Courteney, Pike and Lemâtre have foregathered in the studio of their sworn enemy and committed murder, when the chief essential of a criminal conspiracy of this magnitude was perfect mutual trust? Was he off on a false scent?

But when they eventually drew up opposite the house with the distinctive door-knocker, Sergeant Morny pointed excitedly to one of the lower windows.

'See there, M'sieur—we are too late!'

'*Á Louer*,' read Moreau. '*Merde!*'

He jumped hastily out of the car and sounded the knocker. Almost at once, the door opened and a tall, business-like woman in the inevitable black of the petite *Parisienne* appeared. Moreau saluted and, after introducing himself, explained his mission in the Rue St Jacques.

'I am sorry, M'sieur, but the gentlemen in question are no longer living here. It was a great blow to me when they left, since I rely on the rents from my lower flats for a living. It was very sudden and unexpected, their decision to leave.'

'Tell me, Madame—the exact date that they left—do you remember?'

'Yes. M'sieur. It was September 9th. The van called that day for the furniture which was to be put in store.'

'September 9th,' repeated Moreau reflectively, then added: 'Have you any idea where they were going?'

'Into the country, I think, M'sieur. They made some mention of a little village in Normandy, but I do not recall hearing the exact name of the place.'

Moreau nodded. He had heard that phrase before—'A little village in Normandy'. That was what Jean Dancourt had said when speaking of Prosper's destination after he had left the *bistro* in the Rue de la Gaité. Was it a coincidence? Or did it mean that, after all, he was on the right track and that *Les Trois Mousquetaires* were linked up in some mysterious way with the doings of the hunchback?

'May we see their flat, Madame? Just a matter of routine investigation.'

The landlady conducted the two officials down the passage, drew out a key and unlocked a door. They passed into a long and lofty room, now as bare as a picked bone. Moreau's eye suddenly alighted on the big marble fireplace.

'Has that fireplace been dusted or in any way cleaned, Madame, since September 9th?'

'I am afraid, M'sieur—'

'No. No. There is no need to apologise.'

Moreau took out the three photographic enlargements of the uncatalogued fingerprints found in the Ateliers Daubigny. He set them up carefully in a row on the mantelshelf. Then, taking out a bottle of mercury powder, he dusted it lightly along the polished surface of the marble and then carefully blew away the excess. As if by magic, the faint outlines of several fingerprints appeared on the white marble. Taking out a magnifying-glass Moreau eagerly examined them. For nearly fifteen minutes he pored over the prints, constantly referring to the photographs. At the end of that time he pocketed the photographs and thanking the landlady, who had watched the scene in utter bewilderment, he and Morny went out to the car.

For the first few hundred yards Morny controlled his curiosity, then he turned eagerly to his superior.

'*Eh bien*, M'sieur?'

Moreau smiled.

'Morny,' he said impressively, 'I am right! One of those three men was present when Lebrun was poisoned. And if one, is it too much to suppose that all three helped our friend Blake in the murder? And what is more, *mon ami*, there may be just one further little atom of proof waiting for me when I get back to the *Sûreté*. Let us pray that my lucky star stays exactly where providence has fixed it!'

And in this case Inspector Moreau's lucky star behaved itself. On the note found in Lebrun's pocket after his death, purporting to have been written at that little station in Normandy whilst waiting for the Paris train—on that note, the experts had 'developed' two sets of prints. One set was unquestionably that of the murdered man. The other corresponded in every detail to the set which Moreau had just 'lifted' off the mantelpiece in the deserted studio!

VI

THE MYSTERY OF THE *MARIE JEANNE*

Now that Moreau had been able to link up *Les Trois Mousquetaires* with the murder of the dipsomaniac, the case, as he saw it, was not without its humorous side. Here he was faced with the job of discovering the whereabouts of no less than five different individuals. Three of these *seemed* to have vanished on September 9th; Blake on the night of the 20th, and Prosper some few days later; or, to be precise, on October 2nd. Actually Courteney, Pike and Lemâtre could not have left Paris until the 20th and the chances were that, although these various individuals might have left Paris by different routes, Blake included, they would eventually come together at some prearranged hide-out. Prosper, it seemed, had been left as a sort of rear-guard on the scene of the crime, perhaps to find out which way the wind was blowing and whether it was tinged with the odour of suspicion. The hunchback had made for Brest. Did it mean that the others were also to be found at the famous Breton port?

Early the next morning, October 5th, the eagerly awaited report came through from the police at Brest. Some of the hunchback's activities had been traced. It had been definitely established that he had stayed a night in a cheap waterside hotel under an assumed name. He had told the proprietor, who naturally had no cause to be suspicious, that he was a commercial traveller. About three o'clock in the morning the landlord had been awakened by his wife, who swore she had heard noises in the courtyard under the window. But after having looked out of the window and seen nothing, the couple imagined they had been mistaken and went to sleep again.

'Shortly after three o'clock of that morning, October 3rd,' went on the Inspector, 'some fishermen who had just put in with a late catch saw our friend skulking about on the quay. The little fellow, they explained, had a pretty wit but he did not seem ready to give any reason for his presence down by the harbour. They naturally imagined that he was off one of the many boats moored to the quayside. And that,' concluded the Inspector, 'is all'

'But it is enough,' replied Moreau, 'to bring me down to Brest without a moment's delay. I want to find out something about the shipping which was lying in the harbour during the night and early morning of the third.'

*

It was then that Moreau recalled Bonnard's remark about the boat which the wanted men apparently used for weekend pleasure cruises somewhere down on the coast. Moreau felt certain that they would not have used Brest as the normal harbourage for their boat. Their plan would have been, perhaps, to meander down the coast and pick up the hunch-back on the prearranged date, at the prearranged time. Perhaps Blake had been picked up at some other port in the same way, in order to avert suspicion should the police be on their track. Their destination he could only assume—some lonely spot on the Spanish coast, perhaps, where they could get ashore without an examination of the ship's papers or their own *cartes d'identité*.

Further than this, Moreau suspected than the boat must be of small tonnage, probably of the small yacht class, such as many people use for pleasure cruises along the coast. An examination of the official harbour records showed that such a boat had put into Brest late on the evening of October 2nd. Furthermore, to Moreau's enormous delight, this particular boat had put out to sea during the early hours of October 3rd. He turned to the harbour-master.

'This boat, M'sieur—the *Marie Jeanne*—it would, of course, be registered?'

'Ah, of course, M'sieur. As you know, every vessel over fifteen tons must have a certificate of registry before it can put to sea.'

'You examined the ship's papers when she put into the harbour here?'

'A mere formality, M'sieur. I made no special note of the particulars the moment I saw the necessary papers were in order. Might I suggest, M'sieur, that you go into the town and have lunch and then return here? In the meantime I will put through a call to the Ministry of Shipping in Paris and see if they can give me her particulars.'

When Moreau returned to the harbour after an excellent

lunch, the harbour-master ran towards him waving a paper excitedly above his head.

'I have it, M'sieur. She was registered at Boulogne in the autumn of last year. She is here described as a yawl of twenty-two tons and is privately and jointly owned in the names of Messieurs Pike and Courteney.'

Moreau let out an exclamation of pleasure.

'Pike! Courteney! *Mon Dieu!* Then I was not barking up the wrong tree.' He glanced at the perplexed harbour-master. 'Tell me, *mon ami*—in your office, have you a time-table? I want to catch the very next train to Boulogne.'

In the train Moreau had plenty of time to put his mind to the various problems which occupied so great a part of his thoughts.

He was convinced that Blake had cleared out because of Lebrun's death and that he was, at this moment, safe aboard the *Marie Jeanne*. But not one single jot of information had been obtained to suggest that Blake had had any connection with Lebrun or Prosper before the dipsomaniac had been put away. This was the most puzzling factor in the ease. The murder seemed motiveless, a casual, out-of-the-blue sort of crime like some ghastly practical joke. And why, why had Blake perpetrated this joke with the help of the three men who most hated him?

Pike, Courteney, Blake and Lemâtre could easily board the boat at Boulogne without arousing the least suspicion. Prosper, of course. was a different pair of shoes. The hunchback was distinctive. Should any suspicion arise surrounding Lebrun's death, it would have been fatal for Prosper to have been seen near the *Marie Jeanne*. Hence this sly trip down to Brest.

What now? An immediate broadcast to all French ports, a warning to coastguards, a wireless message to all ships in the probable vicinity of the *Marie Jeanne*.

*

The harbour authorities at Boulogne, as officials of a big channel port, were familiar with the ways and needs of the police. Sergeant Hirondelle was one good man among many and Moreau realised at once that all information proceeding from that broad and humorous mouth would be perfectly reliable.

'The *Marie Jeanne*, eh, M'sieur? Let's see now—Elmer Pike and John Courteney are the joint owners. Tubby little craft to look at, but seaworthy enough. Twenty tons or so.'

In a few succinct sentences Moreau explained his interest in the *Marie Jeanne*.

'But before we talk about the boat, Sergeant, I should very much value your description of Pike and Courteney.'

'M'sieur Pike, the American—how can I best describe him? Medium height, broad-shouldered, with sandy hair and many freckles, Inspector. Horn-rimmed glasses and very fastidiously dressed. He speaks French well, but with a nasal accent. Courteney, the Englishman, also speaks fluent French and in his case the accent is scarcely noticeable. A great pipe-smoker, M'sieur, with the result that his moustache is stained always with nicotine. Red face, blue eyes, fair hair and an unusually deep voice. He walks—and this may prove invaluable, Inspector— with a slight limp. Both these men, as you probably know, are naturalised Frenchmen. Lemâtre—you have heard of Lemâtre, M'sieur?' Moreau nodded. 'Ah, so I imagined, for the three men are inseparable. Tall, dark, rather saturnine expression, with an olive complexion and brown eyes that should have belonged to woman—that is Lemâtre, M'sieur. Does that, more or less, explain what you desire to know?'

'Perfectly,' said Moreau. 'And now to more important matters. When did you last see these three men?'

'That is difficult, M'sieur—offhand. But wait —I can lay my finger on the exact date without great trouble. It was on the same day that fifty thousand pounds' worth of bullion was loaded on the night-boat for Folkstone. I and many others were on special duty. M'sieur, whilst the boxes were being loaded into the hold.' Hirondelle looked up and hailed another official who was crossing the maze of railway lines which spread out like so many fingers pointed towards the sea. 'Tell me, Gaston— that consignment of gold for Folkestone which was dispatched toward the end of last month—what was the exact date?'

Gaston spat neatly over a bollard and sucked at his cigarette; then: 'The 20th, Sergeant—September 20th.'

'The 20th,' echoed Moreau excitedly. 'You are sure that this was the night when you last saw the three men?'

'But certainly, M'sieur—there can be no mistake about it. Except that, to be more accurate, it was the early hours of the 21st—about three or four of the morning.'

'Surely that was an extraordinary time for them to board their boat, Sergeant?'

'No! No! They had explained on a previous visit that they would shortly be taking a trip down the coast. It seemed that Courteney, who is a journalist, had to be present at an evening concert in Paris, so they could not travel until he had put in his report at the newspaper office that night.'

'And they put out of harbour at once?'

'Shortly after dawn, M'sieur.'

'Tell me, Sergeant, you are quite sure that there was not a fourth individual on board the boat?'

'There most decidedly was, M'sieur—they would not put to sea without old Louis Raymond.'

'He is part of the crew, I take it?'

'According to old Louis himself, M'sieur, he is the *whole* crew. Helmsman, deck-hand, master-mariner, cook and chief mate.'

'And he was on board when the others arrived on the 21st?'

'Yes, M'sieur. When Pike and Lemâtre came down on their previous visit to victual the boat, Louis had orders to stay aboard until the 21st.'

'This previous visit,' asked Moreau incisively, 'when was it?'

Hirondelle beamed expansively.

'My birthday, M'sieur—the tenth of September.'

'And they came down, you say, to put some stores and so forth on board?'

'Exactly, M'sieur. Pike and Lemâtre drove down from Paris with a large crate of provisions in the back seat. I happened to be present when the excise official made his examination—that is how I know what the crate contained.'

'*Eh bien*, Sergeant,' said Moreau suddenly, extending his hand, 'this has been a most felicitous task for me. Thanks, *mon ami*!'

Moreau had to wait exactly twenty-four hours for news of the *Marie Jeanne*. The broadcast had gone out from the French radio stations shortly after his talk with Hirondelle. At noon on the following day, October 6th, a fishing-boat put into the harbour of La Rochelle with a second, smaller boat in tow. They had found the boat, drifting, so they explained, a few miles out from the shore. It had evidently been abandoned since, when they put out a dinghy and boarded her, they found the yawl deserted. There seemed to be no sign of disorder or no reason for this sudden departure of the crew. Twenty minutes after the boat had been towed into harbour, Inspector Moreau knew that the search for the missing *Marie Jeanne* had come to a full-stop. But, *mon Dieu*, of what use was the boat to him without the crew? Where, in heaven's name, were Pike, Courteney, Lemâtre, Blake, Prosper and old Louis? Drowned? Marooned? Adrift in the ship's dinghy? Moreau shook his head. Somewhere along the stretch of coastline the whole gang had got ashore (hadn't the authorities at La Rochelle stated that the ship's dinghy was missing?) and were now snugly hidden away in some deserted farmhouse or cottage. Pike must have had a wireless set on board and had picked up the broadcast message asking for information concerning the whereabouts of the yawl. Moreau smiled. He was thinking of the detailed descriptions be had obtained from

Hirondelle. That evening the radio stations would again carry an appeal from the *Sûreté*. Wireless had turned the world into a tennis ball—a word could encompass it in a second!

VII

THE LONELY HUT

But for all Moreau's faith in the wonders of radio, silence alone answered the nightly appeals issued from the police headquarters. The newspapers, too, were doing their part. Moreau himself had gone down to La Rochelle and had spent several hours on the *Marie Jeanne*. On board he found . . . nothing! Nothing, that was, of real value. The only thing gained by his careful examination was something which he had always anticipated. Three sets of fingerprints lifted from various objects on the boat corresponded to the three previously uncatalogued sets in Blake's studio. One set, as to be expected, tallied with the set which Moreau had found on the mantle-piece in the Rue St Jacques. But which set belonged to Pike and which to Lemâtre or Courteney, Moreau was unable to say. One thing only puzzled him—Blake, for some inexplicable reason, seemed to have gone about the *Marie Jeanne* in rubber-gloves, for nowhere did he appear to have left a single print! The Inspector could only assume that over this point he had been mistaken—Noel Blake was *not*, after all, one of the men on board. The artist must have slipped away to some refuge of his own, thinking, perhaps, that this was the one case in which safety did not lie in numbers!

It was obvious from the vast array of 'empties' scattered about the roomy cabin of the boat that the fugitives had been drinking pretty heavily. The crate, which Hirondelle had mentioned, must have been emptied of all provisions and thrown overboard, for there was no sign of it on the boat.

*

Moreau had been directing the local operations from La Rochelle for four days, when the first hopeful scrap of news drifted in. A small boy playing on a deserted stretch of the foreshore, some six miles south of the town, had found a small boat wedged in some rocks. There was no name on the boat, but it appeared to be in good condition.

Moreau at once motored down and, after a mile's walk, came to the spot where the dinghy was wedged. He was not able to satisfy himself, however, that the dinghy was without question that of the *Marie Jeanne*. All he found by way of a clue were two or three small splinters of blue glass which seemed to have slipped down between the bilgeboards. A perfectly meaningless clue and, on that account, useless.

But, *mon Dieu*, here was evidence of the right kind! A clutter of footprints on a little sandy path which led up from the shore. The local men could not account for them. The path was never used by the inhabitants of the nearby village.

'Then *ipso facto*,' thought Moreau in triumph. '*Ipso facto!*'

When this jumble of prints reached the top of the cliffs, they were obligingly thinned out into an individual track, which made off in a straight line inland, across a large stretch of arable. Luckily the earth was still moist from fairly recent rains and Moreau was able to get down to some very satisfactory mensuration. For some inexplicable reason, instead of the six sets of prints that he expected to find, there were only four! *Eh bien*— even allowing for the fact that he was wrong about Blake (witness the lack of fingerprints on the boat), there should have still been five people in that dinghy—Lemâtre, Pike, Courteney, old Louis and the hunchback. He believed, moreover, that the unusually small footprint, which made up one of the four discernible, was that of the hunchback, Prosper. Wasn't it sensible to suppose that the remaining three must be those of *Les Trois Mousquetaires*? Wouldn't they naturally stick together? Then where was Louis? Surely they hadn't thrown the poor devil overboard in order to ensure his silence? Were these men really capable of such an inhuman act?

He turned to Sergeant Morny, whom he had brought down from Paris as his aide-de-camp, and explained his fears.

Morny said slowly: 'There is just one other possibility, M'sieur. I have here a fairly large-scale map of this locality. Perhaps, M'sieur, if you glance at it—' The Inspector took the proffered map and looked at it for some moments. Morny went on, obviously delighted by the puzzled frown on the forehead of his superior. 'Might I suggest, M'sieur, that you carry your eye out a little from La Rochelle. There is a—ah! You have realised my meaning! The Île de Ré! And a little further south the somewhat larger island of Oléron! Isn't it possible, M'sieur, that Louis was marooned at some lonely point on one of these islands?'

'Marooned!' exclaimed Moreau. 'It is a good suggestion. We will first see where these tracks condescend to lead us, then you and I, *mon ami*, will charter a motor launch and run out to these islands. *Alors, allons!*'

But the tracks proved a dead-end investigation. Beyond the arable lay acres of pasturage, which had naturally taken no impression of those fugitive feet. The few hovels in the locality were also visited and their peasant owners interrogated, but they, like the three famous apes, had seen nothing, heard nothing and could say nothing. Moreau felt more and more certain that, once clear of the coast, the four men would split up and travel individually toward the Pyrenees, in the hope of crossing the frontiers into Spain.

The Île de Ré is small, a mere matter of some twenty-eight square miles, but on to that flourishing island are crowded some fourteen thousand inhabitants. It seemed strange to Moreau that, should Morny's theory be correct, some news of the castaway had not reached the mainland. After all, the distance between the isle and the coast was only six miles and many of the inhabitants would have radios. Perhaps Louis himself was lying low, fearing to be mixed up in the trouble which had obviously beset his masters. Had Louis realised why the *Marie Jeanne* had been abandoned? What excuse had Pike given him for setting him ashore on the island? (If this were actually the case.)

Moreau pondered these questions and many others, as the powerful motor-launch drummed its course through a welter of spray toward the distant smudge of the island. In a short time the launch was made fast in the lee of a small, stone jetty and Moreau sprang eagerly ashore. Several fishermen, engaged chiefly in oyster-catching, were lounging about the little quay-side and, without delay, Moreau began to question them. But he drew a blank. If the *Marie Jeanne* had put in at the island, then they had seen nothing of her. But most probably, if she had been running down the Bay, she had made for the far side of the island. Moreau nodded. This seemed a very reasonable explanation. Moreover, he anticipated that if Louis had been set ashore, it would have been done at night by means of the ship's dinghy.

At St Martin he got in touch with the local police and a car was put at his disposal. Following Moreau's instructions, the uniformed chauffeur headed for the most western point of the island, the tip of which pushed well out into the Bay. There Moreau instigated a further series of enquiries, particularly among the scattered houses and hovels by the shore. But again the evidence was disappointing. One man imagined he had heard the sound of oars creaking in their rowlocks sometime during the early hours of October 6th. But he had seen nothing. For all that Moreau made him point out where he had been standing when he had imagined the sound. The man in question, a vine-grower, directed them to a lonely stretch of sand, where, it appeared, he had been trying his hand at a little night-fishing. It was about a mile from where Moreau had interrogated the witness and when he and Morny reached the spot dusk had already fallen. This stretch of the foreshore was desolate enough and, at first glance, seemingly without habitation.

'We will take a careful look along these sands before the light fails us completely,' said Moreau. 'You, Morny, to the right—I to the left. We will work for half a kilometre from either side of this spot and meet here afterwards. Remember—it is that stretch of sand which is unwashed by the sea which interests us.'

Without further discussion they separated, heads well down, eyes roving, like a couple of beachcombers on the lookout for some unexpected scrap of flotsam. And in this case Moreau found what he was looking for! He had only traversed some two or three hundred metres when he let out an exclamation of delight. A clearly defined set of prints scored the virgin spread of sand. The toes pointed inland. Toward the sea the tracks petered out at the high-tide mark and, although the Inspector cast around in a big circle, no outward prints were visible. Beside, or rather mingled with, the normal footprints were two curious parallel furrows, which every now and then vanished, to reappear some little distance further on. A shout to Morny brought the latter running along the shore. When the breathless Sergeant drew level, Moreau pointed out his discovery.

'You see, *mon vieux*! We must follow these tracks as far as we can inland.'

'But these other lines, M'sieur—they come and go. *Pourquoi?*' Moreau shrugged.

'It is possible that Louis was dragging something heavy behind him. Maybe he was forced to carry ashore some evidence which our friends did not want us to discover on the abandoned boat. But we will not worry about that now. Advance, Morny, advance!'

Luckily for Moreau the sand continued in a gently shelving slope away from the sea. The footprints, despite the fact that only a silvery glimmer of light now lit the desolation of the foreshore, were quite easy to follow. The weight on the fellow's back had caused his feet to bunk heavily into the rain-wet sand. They came to the crest of the little rise and immediately Morny let out a sharp cry.

'Look, M'sieur—a light! Down there, in that hollow!'

Moreau peered forward into the gloom. He seemed to discern the faint outlines of a broken-down hut crouching like a wounded beast in the very bottom of this unexpected crater. He signed for Morny to follow and plunged rapidly down the steep bank. He had not been mistaken—the light was coming from an oil-lamp set in the single window of a low, ramshackle hut, from the roof of which projected a tall, iron chimney. Let into the tarred and weather-boarded face of this uninspired domicile was an ill-made door, at the moment half open. Even as Moreau approached, the door swung wide and a figure appeared silhouetted against the light within.

'*Bonsoir, mon ami*,' said Moreau in casual tones. 'May I come in and have a word with you?'

The man, in a filthy blue blouse and baggy trousers, advanced suspiciously and stood staring wide-eyed at the Inspector. He appeared from his hesitant gestures to be uneasy.

'But why have you come here, M'sieur? We have nothing to offer. A little wine, perhaps, but nothing—'

Moreau laughed.

'No. No. You mistake me. We do not want food or drink, my friend. I am in search of something far more precious to me. Information. You understand?'

The man started and recoiled a step.

'But what can I tell—?'

Moreau broke in curtly. 'You own this hut, eh? You live here?'

'No, M'sieur.'

'I see. Then I should like to see the owner at once. I am a member of the *Sûreté*. You have heard of the *Sûreté*, perhaps?'

'Indeed . . . yes, M'sieur,' answered the man in an unsteady voice. 'But the owner—you cannot see him. He is asleep.'

'*Eh bien*—then perhaps you can answer my questions for him. First and foremost, *mon ami*, what is your own name?' The man remained silent. 'Come! Come! It is a very simple question, Your name, *stupide*? You may not know much, but you must know that!'

'It is Raymond, M'sieur,' said the man in sullen tones. 'Louis Raymond.'

'Louis!' exclaimed Moreau. '*Mon Dieu*, I had not expected to find myself so lucky! You, my friend, are the very man I want. You have been put ashore from the *Marie Jeanne*, *n'est ce pas*? Louis Raymond from Boulogne! I am delighted to meet you.'

'But . . . but . . ?'

'No. No. I understand all that has happened. M'sieur Pike no longer required your services, eh? You were surprised, perhaps, when he suddenly decided to put you ashore on the Île de Ré.' Moreau laid a friendly hand on the man's uneasy shoulder. 'Now suppose we go inside, friend Louis, and have a talk about these strange happenings, eh? Lead the way, *mon ami*!'

Suddenly the unfortunate Louis seemed to come alive. Throwing out his arms, he clutched the door-frame, barring the Inspector's passage.

He protested at the top of his voice: 'You cannot come in! The owner—he is asleep! He must not be upset! You hear? He will be angry. You must go away!'

Moreau smiled and gripped the trembling Louis by the arm. Morny advanced a couple of paces and stood threateningly over the protesting man.

'Listen,' said Moreau in a harsher voice. 'If your host, as you say, is asleep, I do not think your shouting will improve his night's rest. Be sensible, *mon ami*. You do not want the Sergeant here to put on the handcuffs, eh? That is not a dignified proce-dure, eh? Now—will you let us enter quietly?'

The poor fellow seemed to shrink inside his loose-fitting clothes, and with a few muttered imprecations and a faint shrug, he stood aside. Moreau with a polite bow passed through the door.

Inspector Moreau, during the course of his professional career, had received many outstanding surprises. He was convinced that his nervous system had become inured to shock. Yet here, confronting him in this dilapidated and desolate little shack, was the biggest, most startling surprise that had ever come his way!

The lamplit room was almost destitute of furniture, thick with dust and cobwebs. A rough mattress of straw and sacking occupied one corner, an unpainted cupboard with a broken door stood in another. A pile of empty tins and bottles was heaped under the window, close to which a few coarse blankets had been carelessly thrown aside from the mattress. In the centre of the room was an old wheel-back chair, perhaps the only really sound piece of furniture in the room.

But all these details did not impress themselves on the Inspector's eye until later. At that moment all his interest was centred upon the huddled figure asleep in the chair. He had never actually set eyes on this man before and yet, from the enlarged photograph which he had so often studied at head-quarters, he had no doubt as to the sleeper's identity. Confounding every logical aspect of the case, in opposition to every natural law, he was confronted by a macabre and singular miracle! *For the man in the wheel-back chair was the self-same man who had been murdered in the Café Vavin on the night of September 20th. A few paces from him, doubtless in a drunken stupor, sat Monsieur Pierre Lebrun!*

The Sergeant appeared in the room, gripping the reluctant sailor by the shoulder. Moreau pointed to the sleeping man.

'That, Morny,' he said impressively, 'is M'sieur Pierre Lebrun, the man for whose murderers we are at this very moment searching. No, no—do not interrupt, *stupide*! Look round this very room. Bottles! *Pernod* bottles! Think of those curious furrows in the sand which puzzled us. Lebrun was paralysed. Those furrows were made by the tips of his toes as he was carried from the dinghy to the hut. Am I right, Louis?' The unfortunate man nodded, far too frightened now to open his mouth. 'And finally,' went on Moreau, 'when I examined the dinghy which had come ashore I found a few pieces of blue glass under the bilge-boards. Lebrun, you may recall, always wore dark glasses. He is still wearing them, you observe, but the left-hand lens has been filled in with brown paper.'

'But . . . but . . . it is impossible, M'sieur,' stammered the bewildered Sergeant. 'If this is M'sieur Lebrun, then whose body was in the coffin which was taken to the Cimetière du Montparnasse? Was it empty, M'sieur?'

'That, my friend. I cannot say . . . yet. But, *mon Dieu*, you may be sure that it is the one thing which I am going to find out! And now, let us wake the old man and see if he can help us to explain away this astonishing situation!'

VIII

WHOSE CORPSE?

The old man seemed dazed and dazzled by the light, as he sat there blinking, with a blanket over his shoulders. Moreau, at his elbow, was saying quietly: '*Alors*, M'sieur, there is no cause for alarm. Doubtless you have been through a number of bewildering experiences, but I can promise you, M'sieur, that your troubles are at an end.'

Lebrun waved a vague hand.

'It is very difficult,' he muttered. 'I cannot yet quite grasp . . . I have been taken here and there . . . but against my will, M'sieur.

I protested. I told Prosper I did not want to leave the Rue Delambre . . . but . . . somehow . . . yes . . . yes . . . I went into a deep sleep that night . . .'

'The night you were taken away from your *appartement*, M'sieur?'

'Yes . . . yes . . . I don't remember just how they took me away . . . I only know that . . . that . .' His head nodded again. He seemed to be falling once more into a drunken doze. Moreau gave him a gentle shake.

'Please, M'sieur—for your own sake, you must tell us all you know. I am Inspector Moreau of the Paris *Sûreté*. Do you understand?'

'Give me a drink,' demanded Lebrun with sudden petulance. 'You wake me up . . . I am not yet clear in the head. But, perhaps, after a drink . . .'

Morny poured out a glass of *Pernod* and handed it to the huddled figure. Lebrun took it eagerly. Moreau waited.

'It was a long time ago,' said Lebrun at length, 'when I was taken away from the Rue Delambre. Weeks, months—I cannot say. At one moment I seemed to be sitting in my wheelchair waiting for Prosper to push me to the Café Vavin, and at the next—I was in the cabin of a boat.' Lebrun pointed a quivering finger at Louis. 'He was there. He will tell you that I am not lying.'

'All right, M'sieur,' broke in Moreau impatiently. 'We will deal with him in due course. But tell me—after you arrived on the boat, you left it again and returned to Paris?'

'No! That is what I cannot understand. Nobody would tell me—even Louis here—why I was on the boat and why the door of the cabin was kept locked. There was food and drink enough—I do not deny that—but when I demanded of this fellow that Prosper should be fetched to take me back to the Rue Delambre, he argued that he had his orders and he must obey them. How long I was on the boat before the others arrived

I cannot say. Most of the time I seemed to sleep. Perhaps I was drugged. But one night the door opened and three men came into the cabin. I recognised them. M'sieur, for like me they were old *habitués* of the Boulevard Montparnasse.'

'Pike?' said Moreau.

Lebrun nodded 'Pike, Courteney and Lemâtre. Naturally I asked for the reason of the trick which had been played on me, but they would tell me nothing. They only assured me that I had nothing to fear. Later, they promised, Prosper was to come aboard and look after me.'

'And he did?'

'Yes, M'sieur. But I think it was some days later. One morning I noticed that the motion of the ship had increased and I was told that we were now in open water. You see, Inspector, I did not even know where the boat had been moored, for the portholes were too high up for me to see out of and, as you may realise, I cannot walk without assistance.'

'And later you saw Prosper?'

Lebrun nodded. 'I think to myself: "When my good Prosper comes aboard I shall learn a lot of things. He will see that I am set ashore." But *hélas*, M'sieur, I was mistaken in this. Prosper could tell me nothing. He seemed strange and different. It struck me that he was afraid of something.'

'And then?'

'Well, M'sieur, it was, I believe, the following night that further peculiar things began to happen. We were sitting in the cabin— Pike, Courteney, Lemâtre and myself. The radio was on and, suddenly, we heard mention of the name "*Marie Jeanne*". The others seemed considerably agitated, M'sieur. They talked among themselves quickly in English. They seem to be having a great argument. I heard my own name mentioned and that of Louis here; also, more than once, they spoke of the Île de Ré. I may have moments when my intelligence, *hélas*, is not very acute, but I guessed that the police broadcast referred to the boat I was on. But, as always, nobody would tell me anything. And then, later that same night, I was wrapped in a blanket, M'sieur, carried up on deck and lowered into a little boat. Pike and Courteney were also in the boat and, of course, Louis. I remember, too, that there were bottles and tins and blankets. Presently the boat ran aground and I was carried out on to the shore and left there with Louis. And that, M'sieur, is all that I know of these strange happenings.'

At the conclusion of his lengthy statement, the old man seemed exhausted. In a few minutes he was fast asleep.

Moreau turned sharply on the woebegone Louis.

'What do you know of all this, eh?'

'But very little, I swear, M'sieur. The master came to my lodgings late one night in Boulogne and ordered me to get up and go aboard the *Marie Jeanne* at once. I was to stay aboard her until they returned from Paris to take a trip down the coast.'

'You remember the date of this visit?'

'Yes, M'sieur—it was the tenth of September.'

'And when you got aboard that night, did you find anything unusual?'

'Indeed, yes. M'sieur Lebrun himself.'

'You knew then that it was M'sieur Lebrun?'

'No, M'sieur. I was told that the old gentleman's name was Delahay, that he was not quite right in the head and that I was to stay aboard and look after him until the master came back from Paris with his friends. On no account was I to let him out of the cabin or tell anybody that he was aboard the boat.'

'I suppose it didn't occur to you,' went on Moreau, after a moment's pause, 'that the harbour officials must have known of his presence on the Marie Jeanne, seeing that nobody can get on to the actual quaysides without their knowledge?'

'I did not think of it, M'sieur. When I am well paid to do my duty, I do not bother my head about such things.'

'And what precise tale did your master tell you when he decided to set you and M'sieur Lebrun ashore?'

'*Tiens!* But it was simple enough. I was to make for this hut, which the master seemed to know about. Here I was to stay for ten days looking after the old gentleman, but taking care that nobody should guess we were on the island. At the end of that time I was to go to the police at St Martin and make a report.'

'And the reason your master put forward for all this?'

'Oh-ho! I was not to be deceived this time! No. M'sieur. He told me that the police were on the track of the *Marie Jeanne*. That they had contraband on board. He claimed that the old gentleman was his uncle, a very respectable citizen except that he was a little mad, and that on no account must he fall into the hands of the police. For his own sake he was to be set ashore on the Île de Ré. But for myself, M'sieur, I think that story is as full of holes as a fishing-net. But then, I am a poor man and M'sieur Pike was always very generous!'

Leaving Morny to sit with the old man until a stretcher could be sent over for him in the morning, Moreau returned with Louis to the *estaminet* where he had ordered the police car to await his return. Hounding the man from the cosy interior, he directed him to drive at once to his headquarters at St Martin. With Louis safely handcuffed in the front seat, Moreau settled down in the back of the old tourer and gave himself up to thought.

With this amazing discovery of a man who was supposed to be a corpse, all his previous assumptions must necessarily be brushed aside. Where should he start? *Eh bien*, why not the night of September 20th?—for on that night *somebody* was poisoned in the Café Vavin or in the Ateliers Daubigny. It was obvious that the victim had been made to impersonate the dipsomaniac and that Prosper had been bribed by the murderers to lend colour to the trick. The hunchback had been necessary at the Café Vavin, firstly to explain his supposed master's drowsiness after his illusionary journey up from the country, and secondly to place the morphia in the drink and, later, to pour half of it away into the tub. It was essential that a natural explanation was forthcoming to explain away the silence of the false Lebrun, and for this purpose Prosper had been ordered to spread the rumour that his employer had been staying at that 'little village in Normandy'. Another important factor in the scheme was the real Lebrun's removal from Paris. This, as Moreau now realised, had been cleverly accomplished by planting the poor fellow aboard the *Marie Jeanne* on the night of September 10th; ten days, in fact, before the actual murder was committed. But how had this been done without the knowledge of the port authorities at Boulogne? Pike and Lemâtre had ostensibly driven down from Paris on the tenth to victual and make ready the boat for their intended trip.

Moreau laughed softly. Precisely! They had a large crate of provisions in the back seat of their tourer. 'Hirondelle had seen this crate opened by the authorities and then taken aboard the *Marie Jeanne*. The port officials knew Pike and Lemâtre. Wasn't it possible that their examination of that crate had been, to say the least of it, casual? A false top, perhaps, packed with a layer of typical provisions and below that faked shelf, the drugged body of poor M'sieur Lebrun! Prosper must have drugged his master's drink earlier that same evening in the Rue Delambre. Pike and Lemâtre had called round in the car with the trick crate. They had waited, no doubt, until the street was deserted and then smuggled the unconscious man into it. So much for Lebrun.

Pike, Courteney, Lemâtre and Blake—they were still the murderers. Of that Moreau was convinced. Some time during the night of September 20th, almost certainly in the Ateliers Daubigny, they had poisoned their selected victim. Their elaborate hoax at the Café Vavin had been devilishly conceived.

Hadn't the police until that very moment believed that Lebrun had been the victim of foul play? Granted the murderers wanted more than this. Their intention was to suggest (a) that the figure in the wheelchair was undeniably that of the dipsomaniac and (b) that he had committed suicide by putting morphine in his drink. Unfortunately this latter assumption on the part of the police had been quickly squashed when certain clues, all of them of a suspicious nature, had been picked up in Blake's studio. Prosper, too, had approached the Café Vavin that night with the invalid-chair from the wrong direction. This curious fact had been noticed by a casual witness in the Rue Campagne-Première. The wheelchair had needed oiling. A little thing—but dangerous to men whose work must be done in deadly silence.

'Yes,' thought Moreau, 'the victim may not be the one we first suspected, but the *modus operandi* of the murder is probably the same. The figure which Prosper wheeled into the Café Vavin was dead before it left Blake's studio. The killing dose of poison had been administered in the studio itself. Indeed yes—in the light of what we now know, this was an essential part of the impersonation trick, for if that figure had been in a fit state to open its mouth, the game would have been up. Bonnard, Henri, the *habitués* of the café might have been deceived by the outward appearance of Lebrun's substitute, but his voice would have let the cat out of the bag immediately.'

Moreau marvelled at the cleverness of the plot. There were certain marked characteristics about the dipsomaniac's appearance which it would be easy to simulate. First there was his unusual attire—the old *képi* and the voluminous black cloak. Prosper had obviously obtained these after his master had been smuggled into the crate. Then there was the very important fact that Lebrun could not walk—a fact which enabled Prosper to wheel a corpse in among the café tables without rousing comment. Finally those black glasses and that gaping, toothless mouth. Didn't it suggest that the real victim of the crime might have had false-teeth? The removal of these would considerably alter a man's appearance and, at the same time, bring his physiognomy more into line with the features of Lebrun. And the one really difficult feature to disguise—the colour, formation and expression of a man's eyes—well, these were invisible behind those black glasses! *Mon Dieu*—but it was devilish clever! The more so since Lebrun had once actually attempted to poison himself with arsenic and was always hinting at suicide.

Maybe it was true that a corpse had graced the Café Vavin on the night of the twentieth, but the question remained—whose corpse?

Moreau thought back to the clues which had come to hand in that fateful room. The fingerprints, the unfinished meal, the burnt-out cigarette, the smudge on the picture, the hairs in the—Suddenly Moreau's mind was illuminated by a blinding flash of realisation as a brilliant idea occurred to him!

By the time he stepped out of the car at St Martin, he had a very good idea as to whose body lay in the Cimetière du Montparnasse!

Early the next morning Moreau left La Rochelle for Paris, the news of his discovery having preceded him to the higher officials of the *Sûreté*. By the time the Inspector arrived in the city, an order for the exhumation of the body had already been drawn up and the necessary arrangements made for the corpse to be uncoffined that same evening after the gates of the cemetery had been closed to the public. The moment Moreau reached the *Sûreté* he was summoned to the office of his immediate chief, the redoubtable Claude Colbert, whose activities for over half a century had so often flared across the front pages of the dailies.

He waved his subordinate into a chair and adjusted his famous gold pince-nez.

'Well, Moreau, a most unexpected twist, eh? But I have an idea that already you have new theories up your voluminous sleeve.'

'Indeed, M'sieur, I think the evidence in the case has been clarified considerably by the discovery that Pierre Lebrun is still alive.'

'Ah-ha! So I imagined! But before you give me a detailed explanation of the reason for your new theories, perhaps you can tell me who we shall find in the coffin which was prematurely designed for M'sieur Lebrun?'

'I may be wrong, M'sieur, but somehow I think not. It is my personal opinion that when we exhume that body this evening, we shall find that the remains are those of a man whom Pike, Courteney and Lemâtre had good cause to hate. In my opinion the man who was made to impersonate Lebrun *was none other than Noel Blake!*'

IX

MOREAU EXPLAINS

Colbert nodded his agreement. When the news had come through from La Rochelle that Lebrun had been found alive, he himself had studied the dossier of the case and come to just such a conclusion. Blake alone, of the five men suspected of having murdered Lebrun, had surrendered no clue as to his possible whereabouts. But Colbert knew the Inspector too well to believe that his opinion had been founded solely on such negative evidence. Just because a man vanishes, it does not follow that he has been murdered.

'And what makes you think this?' demanded Colbert.

'Firstly, M'sieur, it was the lack of Blake's fingerprints on the *Marie Jeanne*. If he had been one of the murderers, as I originally suspected, then I felt sure he would have joined his fellow conspirators on the boat. As they had picked up the hunchback at Brest, so I imagined would they put into some little place in order to pick up Blake. But it was certain from this fingerprint evidence that Blake had not boarded the *Marie Jeanne* previous to her abandonment off La Rochelle. Once my curiosity was aroused concerning Blake's whereabouts, I returned naturally in thought to the Ateliers Daubigny on the night of the twentieth. But before I touch on the actual happenings of this particular night, I would wish to point out, M'sieur, that Pike, Courteney and Lemâtre had a very good motive for wanting to do away with their friend. You have read, perhaps, the signed deposition of M'sieur Bonnard concerning the relationship existing between Blake and the other three men? The tragic story of poor little Madeleine Rameau? *Alors*—I said to myself, "Here is the obvious motive for the murder." It was to be a murder of revenge.

'And at the Ateliers Daubigny—what did we find, M'sieur? An interrupted meal, a burnt-out cigarette. Suggestive is it not? M'sieur Blake did not expect to receive visitors on the night of the twentieth. Hadn't he told Madame Mollien, that very morning, that he did not want to be interrupted in his work? And yet, *hélas*, he *was* interrupted. By Pike, Courteney and Lemâtre, with Prosper, perhaps, concealed in the courtyard with the wheelchair. What actually happened we can only assume, M'sieur. A gentle tap on the door, no doubt. Blake, in the kitchenette, puts down the bread and cheese which he has been eating. His cigarette is left burning on the edge of the draining-board. After all, it is only some casual visitor—he does not expect to be long in sending them away on the plea of his work. He opens the door, M'sieur. He is startled. Pike, Courteney, Lemâtre—the friends that have cut him dead since the day of poor Madeleine's suicide. *Mon Dieu!*—what does it mean? I suggest, M'sieur, that his visitors give him little time to ponder that question. They are on him in a flash, each man to his appointed task—a gag in Blake's mouth, *à l'instant*, for there must be no noise! In a few seconds the unsuspecting man is overpowered. But in the course of the silent struggle, M'sieur, the group has come near to the easel. A sleeve, a shoulder, an elbow brushes against the wet paint.

'Then Prosper is called upon the scene with his wheelchair. There is a point here which rather puzzles me. Madame Mollien swears that she heard strange squeaks in the courtyard about midnight. *Bon!* That is understandable. We know now that the invalid-chair needed oiling and that it must have been pushed out of the courtyard about that time. But why didn't Madame Mollien hear those strange squeaks when the chair was pushed *into* the courtyard?'

'Tell me, Moreau,' Colbert asked, 'that last question—was it merely rhetorical?'

'No, M'sieur,' protested the Inspector. 'I really desire an explanation for this curious hiatus in Madame Mollien's hearing.'

'Then I will give you my own opinion, my friend, for what it is worth. I think, perhaps, that your three conspirators realised at the last minute that the chair might give them away. It was too late then to remedy the squeak. So Prosper was ordered to remain just inside the courtyard with the chair, until Blake was bound and gagged. Then they helped the hunchback to *carry* the chair into the studio. Yes! Yes! Give me a moment, I know what you are about to say. Why was the chair not carried *out* as well? After all, four men could have done so easily, even with the artist's dead body sitting in it. But that is just the sort of slip which occurs in a carefully planned crime. After all, that squeak—it was a stupid little factor in the case. But it was forgotten. And on account of that single little slip you were able to deduce the fact that the wheelchair had been in the courtyard at midnight on the 20th. That clue forged the link joining Lebrun with Blake's studio—or rather the figure which you supposed was Lebrun.'

'It is a very brilliant explanation, M'sieur,' said Moreau tactfully. The wheelchair is *carried* across the court and taken into the studio. A specially prepared solution of the morphine salts was ready in a bottle. Quickly Blake was ungagged and the poison forced down his throat while they held his nose. In a short time there was no more movement—he was dead!

'Now for the impersonation. Prosper had the clothes ready to hand, the *képi*, too, and the black cloak. The body is stripped and redressed in Lebrun's attire. Blake's own clothes are wrapped in a parcel to be taken away from the scene of the crime and destroyed. Of this probability I have evidence. For when Papa Picôt saw those three men walking away down the Rue Campagne-Première just after midnight, he declared that one of them was carrying just such a parcel as we should expect.

We must turn now to the bathroom for our further evidence. I come now to the curious fact of the hairs which had adhered to the rim of dried soap. They were of uneven lengths and it was proved under the ultra-microscope that one end of each hair had been cut with scissors and the other with a razor. *Bon!* As I first saw it, the explanation was simple. Blake, who wore a beard, wished to remove it after murdering Lebrun. Precisely! And in my opinion the explanation in the light of the new facts is equally simple. Blake did not remove his beard himself. It was removed for him *after he was dead*! I found no shaving utensils in the flat. *Pourquoi?* Because, M'sieur, they had been brought to the studio that night for the express purpose of shaving the dead man. Doubtless the hair removed by the scissors was carefully collected, to be carried away and burnt with Blake's clothes. But once again there occurred, M'sieur, one of your "little slips". The murderers did not think of the dried soap which might leave a rim in the basin or the tiny hairs that might be caught in it.

'There was just one other thing which the three men removed and carried away with them for destruction—Blake's false teeth.

We must assume that he had no teeth of his own since it would have been impossible for them to have been extracted on the spot. Moreover, I recall that in the bathroom cabinet I saw a tin of denture fixative.

'So much for that, M'sieur. The impersonation is now complete save for the most important factor in the artist's "make-up". I refer, of course, to those black glasses, which not only concealed Blake's eyes from the world, but those of Lebrun himself. I doubt if Bonnard, who probably knew Lebrun as well as any man save Prosper, would have recognised his old customer if he had been dressed in different attire and minus those glasses. This was a strong point in favour of the deception proving successful.'

'Yes. Yes—that is true enough,' agreed Colbert. 'Otherwise, Moreau, what excuse could there be for the police surgeon in the case?'

'I trust, M'sieur, that you feel no inclination to censure Doctor Lecourbe over this matter?'

Colbert suddenly jabbed his pince-nez in the Inspector's direction and said forcibly: 'Indeed, Moreau, I do! I think his examination was too cursory. Because you and he thought that this was an obvious case of self-poisoning by morphine, you were satisfied with a superficial corroboration of your belief. I will allow the fact that Lecourbe could not he expected to tell from the man's features that he was not Lebrun. But had Lecourbe been less offhand, he should have noticed one or two rather singular things during the course of his post--mortem. Tell me, my friend, did he remove the clothes from the body?'

'No, M'sieur,' admitted Moreau. 'But was it necessary in the circumstances?'

'Very,' barked Colbert, with another accusing jab of the pince-nez. 'The real Lebrun was paralysed, a fact which Lecourbe must have known. Paralysis leaves physical traces, often a certain wastage or torsion of the limbs. Chronic alcoholism does the same, if it has continued over a long enough period. Most certainly, *mon ami*, if Lecourbe *had* stripped the body he would have received an emphatic shock. He *should* have done, Moreau. His action in this case showed gross negligence. He might have saved you and your staff weeks of trouble and the *Sûreté* a lot of expense. As it happened, I suppose the undertaker was the only one to view the body *as* a body and he, M'sieur, would only take the usual professional interest in the length and breadth of the corpse! *Eh bien*—it is no good crying over spilt milk. But doesn't it strike you that Lecourbe was equally uncurious about two other little points? You are forgetting what Prosper had said about his master's movements before he arrived at the café. Hadn't he, according to the hunchback, travelled up to Paris from the country and come straight on to Bonnard's? Then how about that shave? It was a very recent affair, remember. And Lebrun would have shaved *before* he left for Paris in the train! But, as I said before, that is a small point. But this, my friend, is not! When Lecourbe tested the saliva he must have seen the inside of the dead man's mouth. Now I do not profess to know much about dentistry, but I do know this—the condition of the gums in a man who wears a denture and one who does not is very different. In the second case the gums harden considerably and the irregular contours become flattened out. Lecourbe should have been more alert and noticed this fact.'

Moreau nodded dolefully.

'Who,' went on Colbert, after a second's pause, 'identified the body at the coroner's inquest?'

'Prosper, M'sieur.'

'Umph—as I thought. A simple piece of perjury, eh? For your new reconstruction of the crime I have nothing but admiration. I think that we shall identify that exhumed unfortunate as Noel Blake. I think he was murdered just as you say he was. I think he was murdered because of his unmannerly treatment of that poor girl. I think that—' Colbert stopped dead and glanced up quickly at the door. '*Entrez!*'

His secretary entered with a message, which he handed over to the waiting Colbert.

'By radio, M'sieur—from Bayonne.'

Colbert glanced at the message and dismissed the man with a nod.

'It is good news, my friend. The hunchback was discovered at noon today asleep in a barn a few minutes inland from Bayonne itself. He has been taken in charge and will be brought to Paris as soon as possible.'

It was not difficult once the gruesome job of exhuming the body had been accomplished to prove the identity of the murdered man. The artist's suits had been made by a little tailor in the Rue de Vaugirard. The exact measurements were available. It was not difficult to measure up the body and compare results with the tailor's reference book. And in every case the measurements tallied. From beneath the fingernails was scraped a minute pile of dirt, which proved, on analysis, to contain infinitesimal amounts of white lead and oxide of iron, both constituents of ordinary oil paints. There was no suggestion of paralysis but every suggestion that the dead man had been fitted with an upper and lower denture plate. And it was on account of this last very commonplace fact that the absolute identity was made possible. Moreau, determined to vindicate himself over the matter of the original post-mortem, decided that it might be worth getting in touch with Blake's dentist. A few enquiries in the district were sufficient to run the man to earth. And here, for the first time, Moreau gained more information than he had dared in his wildest moments of optimism to expect. Blake's teeth had been extracted only a few months previously. A temporary set had been made to tide him over that period when the gums would be shrinking to their final configurations. Only the week previous to his death Blake had called on the dentist to be fitted for his permanent set of dentures. The teeth had been ready for some weeks, but when the dentist learnt that Blake was missing, he had set them aside until his client should reappear. *Eh bien*—his client had reappeared. The teeth, declared Moreau, should be fitted. They *were* fitted and, what was more, they fitted *perfectly!* The identification was complete.

Prosper's statement inculpated the three friends and eventually Pike, Courteney and Lemâtre were arrested at different times close to the Franco-Spanish frontier. From the imperfectly cleaned sleeve of Pike's coat was extracted a grain of pigment which under the microscope proved to be of an orange colour or, as Moreau insisted at the trial . . . the colour of a tangerine. Prosper's confession, combined with the evidence of the fingerprint experts, did the rest. Pike, Courteney and Lemâtre were found guilty of murder, the hunchback as an accessory both before and after the fact. *Eh bien*—the guillotine? wondered Paris, agog with the customary morbid excitement produced by murder trials. But it is as well to remember that good Gallic blood flowed in the veins of the judge and jury. Was there not a woman in the case? And had not this poor child committed suicide on account of the unpardonable and ungallant behaviour of the murdered man? Pike, Courteney and Lemâtre had been in love with little Madeleine Rameau. In the heart they had been made to suffer, for their love was not returned. After all, was it not a murder of revenge, a *crime passionnel*? They had vindicated the wasted life of a woman—that was all!

'Deportation for fifteen years,' said the judge in the case of *Les Trois Mousquetaires*. The hunchback was to serve ten years penal servitude in a home prison. It came out that Pike had bribed him with a cool two hundred thousand francs. It seems that little Madeleine Rameau must have been a very lovely and a very exceptional girl!

As for M'sieur Pierre Lebrun, he is now wheeled as of old to his favourite table at the Café Vavin, and the man who wheels him is that incorrigible rascal, Louis Raymond! It is an ill wind—

JOHN BUDE

Ernest Carpenter Elmore was born in Maidstone, Kent, on 4 November 1901 to Annie Jane and Thomas Alexander Elmore, a builder and undertaker.

Elmore went to a local school and later boarded at Mill Hill in North London. He decided against following his father into the family business and studied at a secretarial college in Cheltenham. In later years he claimed to have been a games master at St Christopher School in Letchworth where his younger brother Alex was a pupil, but other than helping to train the senior football squad, Elmore's main role appears to have been stage manager for the school's dramatic society. In 1923 he directed a ballet, *The Wanderer*, with music composed by his cousin Hubert Foster Clark (who later conducted for Ballet Rambert) and he wrote and directed *Pharoah the Man* (1924), which received a mixed review from the local paper. He also directed productions for the St Christopher Fellowship Players for former pupils, including Gertrude Jennings' *Five Birds in a Cage* and Shaw's comedy *You Never Can Tell*, in which his brother had a leading role. The school supported Elmore to undertake formal training in stage management at the Everyman Theatre in London, but in December 1926 he was barred from entering 'the school or school grounds at any time', possibly because he joined a professional theatre company despite having had his training subsidised by the school.

With the Lena Ashwell Players one of Elmore's first jobs was working on a production of Ibsen's *Lady Inger of Ostrat*. As well as stage managing, he sometimes appeared on stage, for example as the comical Dr Yellowlees in the Players' 1928 production at Bath of J. M. Barrie's *The Professor's Love Story*. Elmore's experiences 'in rep.' would inform several of his most memorable novels, including the semi-autobiographical romance *The Baboon and the Fiddle* (1932), published under his real name, and three of his pseudonymous detective stories: *Death of a Cad* (1940), *Death in White Pyjamas* (1944) and *Death Steals the Show* (1950).

After leaving the Players Elmore joined The Little Company, appearing in—among other productions—an evening of short plays at a church hall in Lewes in November 1928. It was while he was with the company that he met his future wife, Betty Sharp, whom he would marry in 1933.

In parallel with his theatrical career, Elmore took up writing. His first novel, *The Steel Grubs* (1928), was an apocalyptic fantasy in which the future of humanity is threatened by ferrophagous alien insects which 'nothing known to science' can kill; and despite a second novel, *This Siren Song* (1930), not selling well, he decided to become a full-time writer. Elmore and his wife moved to Crooked Cottage, a fifteenth-century building in the Sussex village of Beckley, and he began writing crime fiction. As 'John Bude', named for the Cornish town, he published 30 full-length novels in less than 25 years, as well as a handful of other pieces, including two short stories under his own name for the *Novel Magazine*.

His principal detective would be the rather arch William Meredith, who appears in around a dozen 'John Bude' novels, but not the first, *The Cornish Coast Murder* (1935), in which Inspector Taunton solves a shooting in the fishing village of Boscawen. Meredith's first case is a poisoning in *The Lake District Murder* (1935), and in his second, *The Sussex Downs Murder* (1936), he investigates a crime that has something in common with one of Conan Doyle's best-known Sherlock Holmes stories. Elmore often drew on his own experiences: in *The Cheltenham Murder Case* (1937) an assassination by arrow takes place in the town's Regency Square, where the author had lived while at the secretarial college; *Loss of a Head* (1938) recalls his time at Mill Hill; and *Death Makes a Prophet* (1947) draws some parallels with his time at St Christopher's.

While continuing to write crime fiction, Elmore wrote a delightful illustrated book for children, *The Tale of the Snuffly Snorty Dog* (1946), and still wrote non-genre novels from time to time, the last of which—*The Lumpton Gobbelings* (1954)—was a bizarre invasion fantasy. He also continued sporadically to be involved in theatre and in 1951 produced *In Victorian Days*, a mime, for a carnival in Beckley in aid of Buxshalls House, a nursing home.

Away from writing, Elmore was a competent tennis player and became a keen gardener. A father of two, he was very much a family man, and in the summer of 1956, harking back to the plot of *A Glut of Red Herrings* (1949), he organized a pirate fancy dress party for the twenty-first birthday of his daughter Jennifer. The location was St Clement's Caves in Hastings, a setting Elmore planned to use for a mystery. In October of the same year he took part in an event organized by Northiam Women's Institute based on the popular BBC radio programme *Any Questions*. As part of a panel of local celebrities, he fielded questions about poltergeists, fox-hunting, rock-and-roll music, the Duchess of Windsor's memoirs, school uniforms, equal pay and Liberace!

In 1953, 'John Bude' was one of the nine writers to accept an invitation from John Creasey and Nigel Morland to become a founder member of the Crime Writers' Association. He joined the Association's main committee, on which he continued to serve until his death on 8 November 1957, two days after being admitted to hospital.

Ernest Elmore's only novella, 'Murder in Montparnasse', was first published by Brown, Watson in October 1949.

THE THISTLE DOWN

H. C. Bailey

'This is Max Tollis speaking,' said the telephone angrily, 'Sir Max Tollis.'

'I am sorry,' the parlourmaid answered, 'Mr Fortune has a consultation.'

'Put me through to him,' the telephone commanded. 'It's a matter of life and death.'

Mr Fortune was building a theatre of his own design for the small girl whom he liked best. He set up the proscenium arch before he listened to this appeal. Then he asked, 'Whose life? Whose death?' For Sir Max Tollis, though known to and knowing everybody, was immensely uninteresting to him.

'Bob Dale has been shot,' Tollis responded with vehemence. 'My secretary, Fortune, a dear boy. God knows how it happened. I can't believe it was suicide. I have the police here, but they're all at sea. I'd give my soul to get the truth clear. Would you come down, like a good fellow? If there's a man alive can work the thing out, it's you, Fortune. Bob never killed himself.'

'When the police want me, they'll tell me so,' said Reggie.

'Damn the police! I'm thinking of the boy's good name. I was fond of him.'

'Where is he?' Reggie asked.

'What? He was found here, my little place, Frith House, just beyond King's Walton. It's only fifteen miles.'

'In an hour,' said Reggie, and rang off.

He took much less, for, curdling the blood of his chauffeur, he drove himself through London. When he swung round the last curves of the drive which led to the white concrete lump of Frith House a man came out of the door and stopped to wait for him and met him with a puzzled smile.

'Good morning, Mr Fortune.'

'Well, well!' Reggie sighed satisfaction. 'So you're in charge. Splendid.'

'The same to you, sir,' Inspector Underwood answered. 'I know you're quick, but this beats all. I've only just 'phoned to ask the Yard for you.'

'I am wonderful. Yes. But not now. Tollis asked first. Sayin' the police were all at sea.'

'They haven't had much time to make land. Tollis is taking it very hard. I don't blame him.'

Tollis came bustling from the house, a large, imposing, florid person. 'Fortune, I'm deeply grateful to you.' He shook hands impressively. 'You know Inspector Underwood? Perhaps you will explain to him—'

'I have. Yes. Anything been moved?'

'No, sir,' said Underwood. 'The body and the car are still as they were when the local police got here at ten o'clock.'

'And nothing done!' Tollis cried. 'Now, Fortune, will you come and examine the poor fellow?'

'One moment. Where was the dead man previous to bein' dead?'

'God knows,' Tollis answered. 'This is the position. My wife and I spend practically all our time here. But yesterday we were both at our flat in town for the Derwent wedding and the Charities Ball. After that was over we drove straight down here and arrived about four in the morning. Bob's car was in the garage then, the chauffeur says, but, of course, it didn't occur to him to look inside. When he opened the garage again after breakfast he saw Bob lying in the back of his car dead and cold. There was a wound in his head and a pistol on the car floor. We got the doctor and the police, and they said he'd been shot. That's all they could say!'

'Not bein' magicians,' Reggie murmured. 'Nor am I, Tollis. However. Anything known of the movements of the dead man yesterday?'

'I wish there was,' said Tollis.

'And there is,' said Underwood. 'A footman here took a telephone message for him at three o'clock from a Mrs Meryon—just to tell Mr Dale "Same place. Same time." He did tell Mr Dale and after that nobody saw Dale again. The servants didn't think anything of his being out to dinner—he often went off when Sir Max wasn't here.'

'It's the first I've heard of this,' Tollis exclaimed.

'You haven't been in much of a state to ask things, sir,' said Underwood.

'I suppose I'm not.' Tollis looked from one man to the other. 'Mrs Meryon—and Bob. I don't understand.'

'Lady known to you?' Reggie asked.

'My wife calls. The Meryons are newcomers; they've taken a cottage for the summer. I believe Mrs Meryon was on the stage, a striking figure of a woman. It's news to me Bob was on any terms with her.'

'We'll work that out,' said Underwood.

'Whatever you want to do, do it.' Tollis was impatient. 'But you'd better show Mr Fortune everything here.'

'I will,' said Underwood, and Reggie took a case from his car and went with them to the garage, which was concealed from the house by a bank of rhododendrons.

Two cars stood in it, a resplendent limousine and a much-used ten which had shed some oil on the floor. Underwood opened the off-side back door of the smaller car.

Reggie saw a body slumped down in a heap as if he had slid

from the back seat, the body of a young and dapper man. His face had been rather too pretty for manhood before the mouth sagged loose, before blood clotted across his cheek. The blood came down from a wound, which darkened the fair wavy hair above his right ear.

'Photograph and fingerprints and all that?' Reggie asked, and Underwood nodded. 'What did the doctor say?'

'Time of death uncertain, but not less than twelve hours ago. Cause of death, shot from a weapon held close to his ear, which might have been that pistol by his legs on the mat. And taking all things together, it was quite possibly suicide.'

'Nonsense,' Tollis exploded. 'I'll never believe that. I knew Bob. He was the last man in the world to kill himself. He never had a grouse. He didn't know what worry was. He enjoyed every minute he lived.'

'And then—this.' Reggie waved a hand at the huddled body. 'Well, well.' He picked up the pistol. 'Webley self-loading. About .455.' He looked at the wound. 'It could be.'

'You say suicide, Fortune?' Tollis demanded. 'Damn it, man, you haven't examined him yet. You can't jump at suicide, like the local doctor, because you find a pistol with him.'

'I never jump,' said Reggie.

'I don't believe Bob ever had a pistol—or knew one end from the other,' Tollis retorted. 'He wasn't that kind of fellow.'

'Don't look it. No. However.' Reggie put the pistol in his pocket. 'We will now have a nearer view. Give me a hand, Underwood.' They lifted the stiff body from the car and Reggie knelt down and opened his case . . . He pored over the wound and his round face was plaintive. 'Well, well,' he sighed and smiled awry. With a pair of tiny forceps he detached from the congealed blood something filmy, fluffy, and put it into a metal box.

'What the devil's that?' Tollis cried.

Reggie did not answer. He was extracting another feathery

tuft and another. He picked yet more from the dead man's hair, but those he put in a second box.

Then he rose and displayed them to Tollis. 'There you are.'

'What is the stuff?' Tollis asked angrily.

'You don't know it? Fruit of *carlina vulgaris*. The common thistle.'

'Thistle down!' Tollis muttered.

'As you say.'

'Are you sure?'

Reggie laughed. 'Oh yes, yes,' as Underwood gave him a questioning stare.

'Thistle down on him,' Tollis cried, 'in the wound! Why, then, he couldn't have been shot here in the garage!'

'But where thistle down was blowin' about. Yes. That is the natural inference. That bein' thus, go along with Underwood and see if any of your servants can tell him the places Dale frequented when he went off in your absence. And I'll take another look at the wound.'

After they had gone, his attention was transferred from the wound to the pistol. Years old, he decided, seen a lot of service, fired recently, one cartridge gone from the magazine. He pocketed the pistol again and proceeded to search the car. 'Case of cartridge not here,' he murmured with a crooked smile, but he went on hands and knees to pore over the mats again. He found tufts of thistle down upon the mat at the back, flattened out by the pressure of a foot which had left spots of damp dust. Beside them was a smeared bloodstain.

Having taken Dale's keys, he locked the car doors, then wandered about the garage, peering into every corner. 'No cartridge case,' he purred, and went back to the house. A butler of irritated visage answered the bell. 'Inspector Underwood engaged with Sir Max?' Reggie enquired. 'All right, I'll carry on.' He crossed the hall and shut himself into the telephone box . . .

When he came out the butler, hovering by another door, turned with a start. 'In there, are they?' Reggie smiled.

'If you please, sir,' the butler ushered him into a room half-study more than half-lounge.

Tollis and Underwood sat there with a woman standing before them.

'Just telephoned 'em to take the body away,' said Reggie. 'Well?'

'This is Miss Benn,' said Underwood, 'Lady Tollis's maid. She tells me she's seen Dale's car on Longley Common more than once and him round about there with Mrs Meryon.'

'Oh.' Reggie surveyed the woman. 'As if they were—friends?'

She pursed her prim lips. 'They looked like it.'

'Thank you. That's all.' He dismissed her. 'You didn't know that, Tollis?'

'She'd never told me.'

'Nor your wife?'

Tollis flushed. 'Of course not. She's a decent woman. My wife loathes scandal.'

'I hope Lady Tollis hasn't been too much distressed by Dale's death.'

'Naturally she's upset. She was fond of the boy. We both were. This story of Mrs Meryon is staggering. I should never have thought Dale would care for a woman of her type, and a married woman too.'

'You believe the story?'

'I believe what Benn said, absolutely. She's no scandalmonger.'

'I had to drag it out of her,' said Underwood, 'and it fits with the 'phone message from Mrs Meryon telling Dale to come to the same place, same time.'

'That is so,' Reggie agreed. 'Yes. By the way, did you find a cartridge case?'

'No, sir.' Underwood's sagacious eyes watched him steadily like a dog's. 'I couldn't see one in the car or in the garage.'

'What's that?' Tollis broke in. 'Dale was shot, wasn't he?'

'Oh yes. Yes. But the pistol found with him would eject a cartridge when fired. It was fired. And the cartridge isn't there.'

'Why, then,' Tollis cried—'then Dale didn't commit suicide.'

'That is the obvious inference,' Reggie murmured.

'That's what you meant when you showed me the thistle down in the wound. He was killed somewhere else and brought back with the pistol to get the murder taken for suicide. You're marvellous, Fortune.'

'Not me. No. Only see what there is. And believe evidence. We haven't finished. Murderer not yet found. Nor the place of murder. Where do thistles grow round here, Tollis?'

Tollis looked at a loss. 'Nowhere near that I know of. Beyond my grounds there's woodland. Frith Wood. My God, the common, though—Longley Common, a cursed lot of thistles there!'

'Well, well. Longley Common. Where Dale has been seen with Mrs Meryon. Who wanted him same place yesterday. Place where thistles grow. Where there might be a cartridge case of a Webley .455. I wonder. Get your wife's maid, Tollis. Want her to show us where she saw Dale and Mrs Meryon companying together.'

'Very well.' Tollis rose. 'What a ghastly business!'

'Not nice, no. The sooner it's over the sooner to sleep. We'll see Mrs Meryon on return. Have your chaps fetch her here, Underwood.'

Reggie's car, with the maid beside the chauffeur, conveyed them some two miles of a winding green tunnel of a road through beechwood before it came out on a common which spread, dim in haze beneath a sultry sky, wide spaces of coarse grass studded with thistles.

'You'd better stop now,' said the maid as they passed a rough track through the grass. 'It's along there I've seen Mr Dale.'

Reggie jumped out of the car and contemplated the track and the common. 'Lots of thistles,' he murmured plaintively.

'The devil of a lot,' said Tollis. 'Do you mean Mr Dale was here by the road, Benn?'

'Oh no, sir,' she answered. 'He took his car along the track up to those clumps of trees. But I thought this gentleman's was too big.'

'Shall we walk then, Fortune?' Tollis asked.

'Yes,' Reggie sighed. 'Do the painful right. Go ahead,' and Tollis went up the track with the maid.

'There has been a car along here,' said Underwood to Reggie's ear. 'Worn Dunlop tyres. And so are Dale's.'

'As you say,' Reggie answered. But he was not looking at the tyre marks; he surveyed the thistles on either side, the misty expanse of the common, and turned with a dreamy smile to Underwood. 'My dear chap!' he murmured.

Underwood stared about him. But Reggie's pensive attention had concentrated on picking a way along the sandy ruts. The long grass about them was wet from the haze.

The maid stopped, pointing at a tongue of open ground dividing two copses of birch and crab-apple. 'That's where Mr Dale put his car,' she said, 'and Mrs Meryon and him among the trees.'

'Thanks very much.' Reggie came up to her. 'Stand fast. Now we'll see what we can see, Underwood.'

On the dank way from the track to the copses the tussocks of grass were disturbed and some thistles had been broken down. 'Thistles enough about,' said Tollis.

'Oh yes. Yes. Plenty and fruity. Reggie stopped to collect some tufts of down.

'My God, she's right!' Tollis cried. 'There has been a car here; come and look at this.'

'What?' Reggie was putting the thistle down in a box with affectionate care and Underwood watching him. He stooped to pluck some grass. 'Go to it, Underwood.'

Underwood strode on to Tollis and was shown the traces of a car starting and turning by the trees. 'Yes, there's been a car here several times,' he pronounced, 'and once quite lately. A small car and tyres like Mr Dale's.'

Reggie strolled up to inspect and agree. 'That is so. Place where the car was. Place where thistle down is. If you find the cartridge case also, you might prove where the murder was.'

'The cartridge?' Tollis repeated. 'Oh, yes, of course; that would clinch things absolutely.' He looked about him. 'But it's almost like hunting for a needle in a haystack.'

'You think so? Should be near where his car last rested, what?'

'There is that,' Tollis said slowly. 'My God, you are keen, Fortune!'

Underwood went delicately over the crushed grass and Reggie joined the search. It was not long before Underwood plucked his arm and showed him a gleam of brass in the dank tufts. Reggie picked it up with forceps and held it to the light. 'Yes, I think so,' he murmured—'from a self-loader .455. Easy to prove it came from pistol.' He put the cartridge away and over his round face came a small benign smile. 'Now we'll go talk to Mrs Meryon . . .'

When they reached Tollis's house again a detective met them and told Underwood that the sergeant had Mrs Meryon there and Mr Meryon with her. He pointed to the study.

'You'd better come too, Tollis,' said Reggie.

'If you say so—it's a foul business,' Tollis answered. 'Anything you want.'

They went into the study, and Meryon, a swarthy, lean man, started up and limped towards them demanding which of them was Inspector Underwood and why his wife was brought to that house.

Underwood told him to sit down. 'I am investigating a case of murder, the murder of Mr Dale, the secretary of Sir Max Tollis here.'

'You're Tollis, are you?' Meryon scowled at Reggie.

'Not me, no. My name's Fortune.' Reggie contemplated the woman, while Meryon transferred his scowl to Tollis. She had not moved; she sat erect, lithe and tense, the rich, dark colours of her face set in stern calm.

'How do you do, Sir Max?' She spoke with contempt, and Tollis bowed.

'I have to ask you some questions, Mrs Meryon,' Underwood went on. 'When did you last meet Mr Dale?'

'Some days ago. I don't remember which day.'

'Was that on Longley Common?'

'Possibly. I walk there sometimes.'

'And he used to drive out there to meet you?'

'What do you mean?' Meryon roared.

'I have to put these things to Mrs Meryon, sir,' Underwood told him. 'Were you aware of her meetings with Mr Dale?'

'Yes. I knew all about them. We were both sorry for him.'

'Why?' Reggie murmured.

'He was a nice boy in a rotten job.'

'Dale never told you that,' Tollis cried.

'Didn't he?' Mrs Meryon raised her black eyebrows.

'What was rotten about his job?' Reggie asked.

'Sir Max can tell you. I never knew just what Mr Dale meant.'

Tollis laughed. 'That's the story! It won't do, ma'am. Dale was with me for years before you came here.'

'Yes, he told me that too. I don't know when he began to be afraid of you.'

'Not very clever,' Tollis sneered. 'It's no use pretending Dale wasn't happy with me. The whole place knows he was. But I had better leave the lady to you, Inspector.' He rose.

'If you please,' said Underwood. 'Now, Mrs Meryon, how often did you go alone to meet Dale on the common?'

'I never went to meet him. He sometimes met me.'

'But not with your husband there?'

'That's a scandalous question.' Meryon started up. 'I'll report you for it.'

'Been in the Army, Meryon?' Reggie asked.

'What? I'm not a regular. I was through the last war.'

'I thought so. Ever carry a pistol?'

'Why?' Meryon scowled.

'We want to know.'

'Was Dale shot?'

'We're askin' the questions.'

'I had one on service, of course.'

'What sort?'

'Webley automatic. Lots of fellows had 'em.'

'I know. Have you kept yours?'

'Good Lord, no.'

'When did you get rid of it?'

'Years ago.'

'Well, well.' Reggie turned to Underwood. 'Don't forget the message.'

'I hadn't.' Underwood was aggrieved. 'I was coming to that before.'

'My dear chap! Sorry. My error.' Reggie looked at his watch. 'Too bad.' He pushed back his chair and wandered away to the window.

'Now, Mrs Meryon,' Underwood said again, 'why did you telephone Dale yesterday to—?'

'I didn't,' she interrupted.

'A 'phone message from you to Dale was taken by the footman here after lunch yesterday saying to meet you "same place, same time".'

'It wasn't from me,' she said quietly.

'We shall be able to trace the call, Mrs Meryon.'

'Why haven't you?' she asked.

Reggie strolled across the room and went out.

'Having received that message,' Underwood continued, 'Dale left this house, and I have evidence he proceeded to Longley Common, where he had been in the habit of meeting you, and he was shot there. Do—'

'Trace the call,' said Mrs Meryon. 'I went up to town yesterday morning with Douglas. We did a matinée and—'

The door was opened and a booming voice called: 'Sir Max Tollis! This way, sir, if you please.'

Tollis bustled out. The door was shut behind him. He found himself confronting a solid man with two others at his elbows and Reggie in the background.

'I am Superintendent Bell,' the central man announced. 'Sir Max Tollis, I have to send you to the police-station, where you will be detained. You may be charged with a grave crime. I warn you that anything you say will be taken down and may be used in evidence.'

'What charge?' Tollis gasped.

'The crime I am dealing with is the murder of Robert Dale.'

'Fortune!' Tollis cried. 'You know I sent for you.'

'Oh yes,' Reggie murmured, 'to prove Dale didn't kill himself. I have. You told me you'd give your soul to get the truth clear. I've got it, Tollis.'

Tollis lurched forward, babbling incoherent panic. 'Take him away,' said Bell.

Reggie went back to the study.

'Sorry you've been troubled,' he apologised to the Meryons, who were looking dazed. 'Couldn't do without your side of it. As you see.'

'I don't,' Mrs Meryon answered sharply. 'My dear lady! You said Dale hated his job and was afraid of Tollis.'

'So he was, but he never told me why. He only moaned.'

'Look at it the other way round. Tollis was afraid he would tell you why. That's what you gave us. Motive for murder. Motive for putting it on you and Meryon. You've been very inconvenient to Tollis. Thanks very much.'

Mrs Meryon spoke loud enough for Reggie to hear what she said to her husband as she went out. 'The man's as bland as a cat.' But he was gratified. He likes cats.

Bell stood aside to let her pass and then came in. 'Well, young fellow'—he clapped Underwood on the shoulder—'you've done a good job of work this time. Tollis is an old fox. That thistle down was the smartest touch I remember. And yet it's going to hang him.'

'The thistle down?' Underwood looked stupefaction.

'Oh yes,' Reggie assured him, 'you spotted the flaw. Thistle down in the wound, thistle down in hair and car, proof Dale was not shot in the garage, but out in the open. Only the thistle down was damp. Which gave the game away. That thistle down never took the air. It never blew on to Dale. It was put. Cunning fellow, Tollis. Falls down on detail. Well, he had his engagements in town yesterday for an alibi. He knew the Meryons were not at home. So he sent a 'phone message in her name telling Dale to meet her on Longley Common and went there and collected thistle down. When Dale went to the garage and started his engine Tollis shot him, using the sort of pistol Meryon had in the war. Then planted the thistle down on the body and collected the cartridge case from the floor and went to town. Bold bad fellow. Called me in this morning to prove how fond he was of Dale and make sure the death wouldn't pass as suicide, but murder by Meryon out of jealousy. Produced the maid's evidence of meetings with Mrs Meryon and so got us to the thistles on the common. Which were still damp, as when he picked the down yesterday. Havin' led us to the place Mrs Meryon and Dale met, he left us to find the cartridge there. You noticed how well he managed that, said it was huntin' for a needle in a haystack. Devilish clever, as he said of me, confound his impudence. But he was weak on detail again. Smear of car oil round the cartridge rim. No oil on the common. But on the garage floor. Which is where it fell when ejected. I told Tollis if we found the cartridge we might prove where the murder was. He missed the point.'

'I didn't get the hang of the thistle down, sir,' said the honest Underwood. 'I just thought there was something queer about it.'

'My dear chap! You did,' Reggie chuckled. 'Your work.'

'I suppose it makes a case.' Underwood looked at Bell.

'There's more than that thistle down, my lad,' Bell answered. 'Mr Fortune 'phoned me about it being wet and asked me to have a look at the clothes Tollis wore yesterday. When we tried his flat, we found a lounge suit packed up to send to the cleaners. In the turn-up of the trousers some damp grass seed, in one of the jacket pockets bits of thistle down, and on the cuff of a sleeve a bloodstain. That's the case. And it'll hang Max Tollis.'

'Yes, I think so,' Reggie murmured.

'It's strong enough,' Underwood frowned. 'But why? I mean to say, what's the motive?'

'My Underwood! You heard Mrs Meryon. Fear. Fear she had hold of Dale, he'd tell her why his job was nasty, why he was afraid of Tollis. Tollis had to wipe him out and the Meryons with him.'

'But Tollis is a public man and all that,' Underwood objected. 'I don't see how his secretary could have anything on him to risk murder for.'

'Ah! Wait till we've gone through Tollis's papers, my boy,' Bell answered.

'My guess is blackmail,' said Reggie dreamily. 'The higher rate, big-game blackmail. Always thought Tollis knew too much.'

H. C. BAILEY

Henry Christopher Bailey (1878–1961) was born in London, the only son of Henry and Jane Dillon Bailey. He attended the City of London School, becoming School Captain and winning the Lambert Jones Scholarship, which provided him with an enormous annual grant of £80 (equivalent to around £11,000 or $15,000) and allowed him to go up to Corpus Christi, one of Oxford's oldest and most prestigious colleges. As Bailey graduated in 1901 with a first-class degree in Greats—Greek and Roman history and philosophy—one would be forgiven for assuming that he had had little time at university for writing fiction, but one would be wrong. Bailey's first novel, an historical romance called *My Lady of Orange*, had begun serialisation in December 1900 in *Longman's Magazine* and would be available in hard covers before he received his degree. It would be the first of around 30 novels dealing with particular events and personalities of European history.

On coming down, Bailey joined the staff of a national newspaper, the *Daily Telegraph*, where he worked in the editorial department for the next 45 years. In 1908, he married Lydia Guest, the daughter of a Manchester surgeon, with whom he had two daughters. Bailey's role at the *Telegraph* afforded him free rein to muse on anything that interested him—from 'British pantomime in Cologne theatre' to Shakespeare, Wilkie Collins, Lewis Carroll, the perils of smoking, Christmas traditions . . . the list of topics is almost endless. However, his journalism was necessarily more focused and purposeful during the First World War and later in the Second when his pieces damned in almost equal measure both the Nazis and Labour parliamentarians, a group that included his brother-in-law.

After the First World War, in parallel with his careers as journalist and historical novelist, Bailey began also to write crime fiction. He had written short stories since coming down from Oxford, mostly historical romances or lightly supernatural stories, including a short series about an unusual character called Quintus Harley and 'A Good Place', an eerie story that owes much to Henry James' masterpiece *The Turn of the Screw*. In 1919, he struck gold with the character of Reginald Fortune, a chatty and amiable surgeon who acts as an adviser to the Home Office, and his laconic style and affected speech would be mirrored by Willard Huntington Wright when he came to create the character of Philo Vance. But Vance only appeared in novels: Fortune appears in nine novels, 84 long short stories, one short one and a single radio play. It is a significant and impressive body of work. For his mannerisms, Philo Vance may have needed 'a kick in the pance', according to the poet Ogden Nash, and Fortune's are similarly grating after a while; even contemporary critics found them wearing. Nonetheless, Bailey's 'specialist in the surgery of crime' remains an important figure in the history of the detective story for the nature of the cases in which he becomes involved and the sometimes unorthodox means by which they are brought to a close. As Cecil Day-Lewis put it, 'Reggie Fortune is a monument of patience and a pillar of detection'. Bailey also created Joshua Clunk, a pharisaical, hymn-singing lawyer who appears in eleven novels; as with Fortune, Clunk divides critics: if you like him, you like him a lot; if you loathe him, however . . .

After the Second World War came to an end, Bailey left the *Telegraph* and settled permanently in North Wales, in the house where he and his wife had holidayed for many years. It was there, at *Bernina* in Mount Road, Llanfairfechan, that he died in 1961.

'The Thistle Down', the sole uncollected Mr Fortune story, was first published in *The Queen's Book of the Red Cross* (1939) with profits going to the Lord Mayor of the City of London's Red Cross Fund.

THE MAGNIFYING GLASS

Cyril Hare

'Come in, my dear fellow, come in!' said Mr Overton jovially. 'Have you something to show me?' Stout, rubicund, with a domed bald head burnished to copper by the sun, he swivelled round in his desk chair to greet his visitor.

The dear fellow, whose name was Harrison, was a shabby, nondescript man with a permanent frown and powerful, calloused hands.

'Walked every perishing step of the way from the station. Uphill. In this heat.' He mopped his brow.

'Ah! It's been a wonderful summer, has it not? If only our climate could be depended on! But perhaps you're one of those unfortunates who suffer in the heat? Do you find it oppressive in here, for example? '

Harrison indicated very decidedly that he did. The little room, indeed, was like an oven. Through the shut, uncurtained window the sun's rays poured in, bathing in a fierce glow the flat-topped desk drawn up right into the embrasure.

'Then you may open the window a trifle at the top, if you wish. Only in that case you must close the door of the room. I abominate draughts. Thank you. And now let us not waste time. Where are they?'

From the battered suitcase which he carried Harrison produced two small parcels, loosely wrapped in tissue paper, which he laid upon the desk. 'There's five hundred altogether,' he said. 'Three hundred in one, two hundred in the other.'

Mr Overton wheeled his chair round to face the window. His chubby fingers stripped off the wrapping and his bald head bowed low over the contents.

'Ah, yes!' he murmured. 'Just so, just so!' After a pause, he added, without looking round: 'You know, my dear Harrison, five hundred fivers are going to take a deal of disposing of.'

'You didn't give me any limit, did you? You said—'

'I know, I know, my good fellow. Don't apologise. The fault is mine—if it is a fault. And if they are all up to the standard that this one appears to be—' he held up a counterfeit note to the light, feeling the texture of the paper between thumb and forefinger—'I daresay we shall manage.'

Laying the note upon the desk, he took from his pocket a small magnifying glass, set in a square silver frame with a short thick handle. For the next five minutes there was silence in the furnace-like room.

'That,' he said at last, 'is good. Really quite good. I congratulate you, Harrison. Now for the others.'

It did not take him long, glass in hand, to count and approve the remaining notes in the bundle.

'I make that two hundred,' he observed. 'Just one thousand pounds' worth of illegal tender.' He casually dropped the packet into a drawer of the desk, and drew the second packet in front of him.

Again the glass was flourished, but this time the examination was far shorter than before. Almost at once Mr Overton's tongue was clicking in disapproval.

'Tst! Tst! What's gone wrong here?' he exclaimed. 'Your ink, my good man, your *ink*! You must have changed your formula.'

'It's the same formula for both lots,' Harrison protested. 'At least—almost. Only I ran a bit short of—'

'I'm not in the least interested in what you ran short of. All

I know is that these wouldn't deceive a blind bookie on derby day.'

He laid the glass down upon the desk. 'You can take these away—or leave them with me, just as you please. I've a very efficient boiler in the kitchen, which will dispose of them quite safely.'

Mr Overton had turned in his chair to face into the room, and he could see that the frown on Harrison's face had deepened to a scowl.

'Don't take it too hardly, my dear chap,' he went on amiably. 'Two hundred at five shillings each—just fifty pounds. If you don't mind waiting, I'll go and fetch—'

'Here, just a minute! Who's talking about fifty pounds?'

'I am, my dear fellow. That is my tariff—one shilling in the pound. With the expenses of my organization, it leaves me very little profit. It's the standard rate, I assure you.'

Very curtly and obscenely Harrison indicated what Mr Overton could do with his standard rate. 'My price for this snide is one quid per note,' he added. 'For the lot. That makes five hundred—and cheap at the price.'

Mr Overton shrugged his shoulders.

'I am sorry,' he said. 'Evidently there's been some misunderstanding. Perhaps we'd better call the whole deal off.'

He pulled open the drawer into which the first parcel of notes had been dropped a few moments before. He brought his hand out quickly, but not quickly enough. Harrison's great fist closed over it before he could raise the pistol more than a few inches.

Overton was more athletic than his figure suggested, but sitting at the desk he was at a hopeless disadvantage. The struggle was brief and murderous. Within a matter of seconds his body was sprawling backwards in his chair, a small scorched hole behind the right ear marking the bullet's point of entry.

Harrison, the man who suffered in the heat, wiped his streaming face with his handkerchief. Then he flung open the window to its full extent and opened the door. A grateful breeze rushed through the room and stirred the papers on the desk. Refreshed, he went to work with purposeful efficiency.

The desk yielded nothing of interest or value. Overton's pockets contained no money beyond a handful of small change, but a bunch of keys on the old-fashioned watch-chain looked promising. With this in his hand, Harrison moved quietly from the room, leaving the pitiless sunlight beating down on the desk and the still figure in the chair.

It did not take Harrison long to discover the wall safe behind the bed in the room above. It took him still less time to establish that none of the keys would fit it. Twenty minutes more sufficed for him to ransack in vain every corner in the tiny, sparsely furnished cottage where a key might have been concealed.

Harrison was not a man to acknowledge defeat easily. The safe was of a familiar pattern, and he had time to spare. His bag contained other and heavier objects than false banknotes. He carried it upstairs, and stripping off his coat attacked the safe with concentrated fury.

The bedroom was, if anything, hotter than the room below.

An hour went by, and Harrison's head throbbed with the implacable heat. His shirt clung to his back; the tools slipped in his clammy hands; the metal of the safe was hot to the touch, the very boards beneath his feet seemed to scorch him.

It was just as the door of the safe yielded at last to his efforts that Harrison, drugged with fatigue, realised what normally he would have noticed long before. The sun had moved from where he stood, but the room was hotter than ever.

A wisp of smoke penetrated through a chink in the floor. The air was suddenly thick with choking fumes. Barely pausing to scoop up the contents of the safe, he leaped to the door. As he reached the landing a violent gust of wind swept through the house, and the smouldering staircase burst into a roar of flame.

*

'These old cottages!' said the fire brigade chief querulously. 'Pretty to look at, but a public danger. Nothing but lath and plaster. Once set a light to them and they burn like tow.'

'And who set a light to this one, I wonder?' said the detective-sergeant.

'This is where we think it started,' the fireman explained. 'Near to where the first body was found. It looks as though something on the desk caught fire and then blew off on to the carpet. A cigarette, perhaps?'

'Or this?' The sergeant picked up Mr Overton's magnifying glass from the debris of the desk.' Leave this in the sun and it will make a perfect burning glass. Odd-shaped thing, isn't it?'

He twisted it meditatively in his hands, and as he did so, the handle slid off to reveal a small key.

'I wonder what that's meant to fit?' he asked.

But there was no one left alive who could tell him.

CYRIL HARE

Alfred Alexander Gordon Clark was born on 4 September 1900 at his parents' home, Mickleham Hall in Dorking. His wealthy father Henry was, among other squirearchical roles, High Sheriff of Surrey and a commander in the Surrey Imperial Yeomanry, and his mother Helen was the local 'Primrose Dame', in charge of rousing support for the Conservative Party, an undemanding task in that part of southern England.

An ardent boy scout and choir boy, Gordon Clark attended St Aubyn's School and later the prestigious Rugby School where, aside from his academic achievements, he was a fine cross-country runner, finishing in the top ten—just—in the annual Crick Run in 1919. On leaving Rugby, he followed in his father's footsteps and went up to Oxford University to read History. As an undergraduate in New College, he was a pupil of Dr William Spooner, an absent-minded don best known for his not always unintentional verbal gymnastics. Gordon Clark achieved first-class honours and decided to go into Law and become a barrister. He was called to the Bar in 1924 and, while living in Cyril Mansions in Battersea Park, joined the Inner Temple where he had chambers in Hare Court—the names of his home and workplace inspiring the pen name by which he is best known today.

Appearing across England, practising in civil and criminal cases variously for the prosecution and the defence, Gordon Clark was, perhaps unsurprisingly, an excellent barrister. He had also begun writing, and a handful of early short stories appeared in *The Bystander* under the name of 'T. Gordon Clark', the 'T' representing 'Taffy', his childhood nickname. He also wrote a play, *Murder in Daylesford Gardens*, which he would later adapt for his first novel. He was also active in politics locally, speaking often in support of the Conservative Party and chairing the Surrey Federation of the 'Imps', the right-wing Junior Imperial League. It was at an Imps event that Gordon Clark met Mary Barbara Lawrence, also the scion of a wealthy Surrey family. They married in 1933 and the bride—who used her middle name—entered the parish church of St Michael's, Mickleham, to a passacaglia composed specially for her by Ralph Vaughan Williams and built around the notes representing her post-nuptial initials, B, G and C.

As well as being very active socially in Surrey, Gordon Clark continued to advance his career, becoming a recorder—effectively a part-time judge—in 1938. During the Second World War he worked for the Director of Public Prosecutions and in the late 1940s he began serving as a judge. Court reports reflect the dry humour of his novels—whether delaying the issue of a caravan licence on the grounds that bad weather was coming, gently rejecting a plaintiff's offer to strip in court to demonstrate the quality of her handmade lingerie, or observing that the courts would be out of business were it not for the proliferation of television hire purchase agreements that proved unaffordable. He was also much in demand as an after-dinner speaker, on one occasion reducing members of Guildford Chamber of Commerce to laughter by observing that, while *their* customers were always right, that most certainly wasn't the case with *his*. In May 1950, he was appointed a county court judge for Surrey, which entitled him, like his father, to serve as a justice of the peace.

Gordon Clark's career as a writer took off when, at the age of 36, he submitted *Tenant for Death* (1937) to a publisher. The plots of his novels and short stories often feature constitutional or legal quirks, such as *An English Murder* (1951) and the posthumously published *He Should Have Died Hereafter* (1958). The latter is a problem of inheritance and was surely intended as a tribute to Dorothy L. Sayers, as made apparent in America where the novel was retitled *Untimely Death*. Frequently Gordon Clark drew on his own experience: *Tragedy at Law* (1942) was inspired by a tour as a judge's marshal; and a spell with the Ministry of Economic Warfare informed the opening chapters of *With a Bare Bodkin* (1946). His two main characters were the Scotland Yard detective Inspector Mallett, who first appeared in *Tenant for Death* (1937), and Francis Pettigrew, introduced in *Tragedy at Law* (1942), an eccentric and unreliable loner who owes his career—but little else—to the author.

Alfred Gordon Clark died aged 56 at his home 'Berry's Croft' in Westhumble, Surrey, on 25 August 1957. He is buried in the church where he and Mary Lawrence were married nearly 25 years earlier.

'The Magnifying Glass' was first published in the London *Evening Standard* on 10 March 1956.

THE 'WHAT'S MY LINE?' MURDER

Julian Symons

I

THE ROOM CALLED 'HOSPITALITY'

A car drew up outside a shabby building in Shepherd's Bush on which the words BBC TELEVISION THEATRE appeared in comparatively modest lighting. From it stepped, as carefully as though he was treading barefoot on pins, a portly figure.

His face was large and ornamented by a fine, thick moustache, his eyes heavy-lidded, but observant. His expression at the moment was solemn, ruminant, that of an elder statesman bothered—as elder statesmen so often are—by affairs of the Far East.

'Pick me up at ten-fifteen, George,' he said to the chauffeur. 'Ten-fifteen it is, sir.'

The car moved away. Mr Gilbert Harding moved with delicate tip-toeing walk towards the stage door.

His arrival had not passed unnoticed among the crowd queuing patiently for seats to watch the three hundred and sixty-fifth performance of *What's My Line?*, whose panel tonight would comprise Gilbert Harding, Isobel Barnett, actress Zoë Gail and character actor Godfrey Rivers. The comments were friendly, although not entirely flattering.

'There goes old Gilbert. You can see he's got his dander up.'

'Looks worried, doesn't he? Never mind, Gilbert, it'll all come out in the wash.' This was called out by a burly greengrocer from Fulham.

The girl who hung on his arm sighed. 'I'd like to marry Gilbert Harding.'

'Go on, my girl, you'd never put up with his tantrums for ten minutes.'

'I would then, and do you know why? He looks fierce, but I'm sure really he's ever so kind. I'd look after him, darn his socks. I expect that's what's worrying him; he's got nobody to darn his socks.'

'All right, you can have him. I'll take Lady Barnett or Zoë Gail.'

Mr Harding had reached the stage door. Suddenly his preoccupied expression lightened. He smiled and wrote his name in half a dozen autograph books. He had been trying to solve a crossword puzzle clue which read: 'How can the poor girl marry when, in x, he's no longer alive?' The answer, of course, was 'intended'.

Mr Harding pushed open the stage door, chuckling, greeted the doorkeeper—a new face, he noticed—and went in. The time was ten minutes to nine.

In two first-floor rooms labelled 'Challengers, Gentlemen' and 'Challengers, Ladies', the six challengers sat, three of each sex. They had arrived before seven o'clock. Since then they had talked to producer Leslie Jackson and had written their names on the stage board, taking care to stand aside while they wrote in order to reveal the names to the audience.

They had perfected the mime which indicated their occupations, and under the hot arc lamps had run through a rehearsal of their turn with Leslie Jackson. Each of them had been closeted with chairman Eamonn Andrews for further and final instructions. Then they had gone out and drunk whiskies or beers or cups of tea.

The three men were respectively an elephant trainer's assistant, the back legs of a circus donkey, and a pin-table repairer. One of the women was a tester for forged banknotes, another a teacher of deaf children, and the third a professional washer-upper. Now they sat waiting nervously in the dressing-rooms. Three of them had no need to worry. They would not go out under the arc lights again that evening.

On the stage last-minute lighting adjustments were being made.

'Come on, Professor Quatermass,' yelled a man in a leather windcheater to another in a meadow green roll-neck pullover. 'Get that spot up a bit closer. Don't stand there telling jokes to Henry. You're as funny as one of those boys on ITV. "Who was that lady you were with last night?" "That's no lady, that's my wife." Collapse of audience dying of laughing and on comes the commercial.'

'All the same, I wouldn't mind having one of those thousand-quid prizes or a new car. Just suit me, that would.'

'The ones they never win, you mean? Come one, now, Prof, get that spot closer and a bit to the right. Don't leave Gilbert in the dark.'

Meadow green roll-neck laughed. 'That's right, mustn't leave Gilbert in the dark. How is it now? All right?'

'All right.'

At exactly nine o'clock a man got out of a taxi and entered the theatre. He came in not by the stage door but by the bar door in the other side, which was opened specially for him, and locked afterwards. A scarf covered the lower part of his face, and under his arm he carried what seemed to be a large bundle wrapped in a travelling rug.

At the bar door he was met by producer Leslie Jackson, who called out: 'All clear down there?'

From the stage came back: 'All clear.'

Jackson and the man hurried down across the stage and into the producer's dressing-room. The man in the scarf was the celebrity spot of the show. The members of the panel had to wear masks while they tried to guess his identity. This week the celebrity's name was Jack Mortimer, and he was a ventriloquist.

The celebrity entered the dressing-room at five minutes past nine. There Leslie Jackson left him in the care of Eamonn Andrews. Mortimer had taken his dummy, a pretty blonde girl, out of the wrappings and was examining her closely.

'Hallo there,' Andrews came forward with hand outstretched. 'This is your new doll, is it? She's pretty. The one I remember was an old salt called Sinbad the Sailor.'

'That's right. This little lady has positively never been used before. Shall I tell you her name? It's Melanie.'

'Melanie.' Eamonn Andrews looked both surprised and upset. He hesitated, then said: 'Your wife's upstairs, you know. She'll be watching tonight.'

'Will she now?' Mortimer was a tall thin man, with prominent eye teeth which gave him a wolffish look when he smiled. 'I'm delighted to hear it.'

In a room on the second floor labelled 'Hospitality', the members of the team sat drinking and talking with friends. On a side table stood sandwiches, whisky, gin and various accompaniments. A clock on the wall said twenty minutes past nine.

A cherubic, beaming American said to a thin dark man who was splashing whisky and gin into glasses: 'You look nervous, Godfrey.'

'I feel nervous.' Godfrey Rivers fingered his collar uneasily. 'In all my years on the stage I've never been so nervous. It's the impersonality of it. You've got an audience out there, but you mustn't play to it. You must pretend it isn't there. In fact, you can hardly see it anyway, with all those arcs cluttering up the stage. Here, have a drink. Gilbert, do you know Charles and Mary Schultz?'

'The novelist? I'm one of the large company, Mr Schultz, who have read and admired your last book.'

'And Melanie Mortimer.'

An elegant, languid blonde took Harding's hand.

'We've met, ma'am. You were here last week.' Harding's eyes lost their sleepiness for a moment as he looked from Melanie Mortimer to Rivers. 'The fact is, my dear Rivers, that actors are always oppressed by the need to act. On this programme we are lucky enough to be paid merely for being ourselves.'

'And for solving puzzles, Gilbert, don't forget that,' laughed Isobel Barnett.

'We live by our wits, yes, like confidence tricksters. You must practise the art of being a confidence trickster, Rivers. Those who are fortunate, like me, are born to it.'

One of Leslie Jackson's assistants put his head in at the door. 'Ladies and gentlemen, you are on in five minutes.'

The four members of the panel went downstairs. Their guests meandered along various corridors until they arrived at a box reserved for them to watch the show.

The first challenger, the elephant trainer's assistant, waited in the wings. The five others sat on chairs gazing in a mesmerised way at a television screen which would show them the scene that was going on a few yards away.

In his dressing-room Jack Mortimer stroked the blonde hair of the elegant dummy and murmured to her, 'Melanie, Melanie, my sweet Melanie.'

As the clock hands pointed to nine-thirty millions of viewers switched on their television sets to see Eamonn Andrews's warm smile. A new session of *What's My Line?* had begun.

II

EAMONN ANDREWS STOPS THE SHOW

The panel were riding high. Zoë Gail had guessed the elephant trainer's assistant and Isobel Barnett the professional washer-upper, while Gilbert Harding himself had quickly discovered the identity of the pin table repairer.

'The thing that horrifies me,' he said, 'is that you should profess to regard this work of yours—which I've no doubt that you carry out admirably—as a public service. Surely the fact that so many people pay their pennies to shoot up little balls in an attempt to light up coloured targets is alarming evidence of the growth of imbecility in our society.'

The audience rocked with laughter. Plainly Gilbert had his dander up all right. Now the team put on their masks for the celebrity spot. Jack Mortimer came before the television screen to a burst of applause, wrote his name, held up the doll so that she appeared to write 'Melanie', and sat down beside a rather doubtful-looking Eamonn Andrews.

In the box for guests Melanie Mortimer leaned back, as if she felt suddenly faint. The features of the doll, fair and regular, resembled her own.

'Now we'll begin with Gilbert Harding.' Eamonn Andrews said.

Harding cleared his throat and asked the question that is almost inevitable on such occasions: 'Do you entertain the public?'

The answer came back, in a voice that was both languid and cloyingly sweet: 'Well, really, I'm more entertaining in private. But I suppose you *could* call me a public entertainer.'

There were some uncertain laughs from the audience. Mortimer was famous for his act with a dummy called Sinbad the Sailor, who sang sailors' songs and danced the hornpipe. This was something new.

Melanie Mortimer got up and went unsteadily out of the box into the corridor, away from the sound of the sneering voice that parodied her own so hatefully. A moment later someone touched her in the shoulder and said: 'Are you all right?'

She turned. Behind her stood little, dark Dr Mostyn, who had been with them in the Hospitality Room. 'Yes, thanks.'

'It's disgusting behaviour. I'd never believe Jack would do such a thing. Are you sure you're all right?'

'Certain. I shall just stay out here for five minutes.' Her voice was decisive. Mostyn left her and went back to the box.

Close your eyes and any voice sounds different, even one you know well. Gilbert Harding had not exchanged more than a dozen words with Melanie Mortimer but, blind behind his mask, he realized that there was something familiar about this voice. He sensed also an uneasiness in the atmosphere, he had a feeling that something was wrong.

'Have we met?' he asked.

The voice drawled: 'Oh, Gilbert, don't you remember?'

'Should I be right in thinking that your voice in fact belies your sex?'

'I have to say no to that. I'm all woman.'

The audience laughed, but uneasily again, as the puppet on Mortimer's knee pulled up its skirt and at the same time blinked its eyes in a ridiculous assumption of modesty.

Eyes closed behind his mask, Harding suddenly saw the face of Melanie Mortimer, and connected its beautiful, slightly vacuous appearance with the voice he had just heard. Yet obviously Melanie Mortimer could not be the celebrity. He had a strong feeling that somebody was trying to make a fool of him in some rather unpleasant way.

It was purely from this instinctive feeling that he said: 'I think somebody's playing a bad joke here. No more questions.'

Now the audience fairly buzzed with excitement. Eamonn Andrews said smoothly: 'No more questions. Well, we had a "no" marked up against you anyway, Gilbert, though I was very doubtful about it. Godfrey Rivers.'

When he first heard the dummy's voice, Rivers sat back in his chair as if he had been struck. Now, passing his hand quickly over his face as if he meant to pull off his mask, he said: 'We know each other, don't we?'

The dummy drawled: 'Oh, yes. Very well indeed, Godfrey. We could hardly know each other better.' Above the dummy, Jack Mortimer's face was like stone, the lips slightly parted but unmoving.

'Should I be right in thinking you dislike me?'

'Speak for yourself, Godfrey.'

At this, Eamonn Andrews leaned over and whispered something to Mortimer, who ignored him.

'Tell me this,' Rivers said. 'You're jealous of me, isn't that so?'

Mortimer put down the puppet. He said in his own voice, deep and resonant: 'If I were jealous of a thing like you, Godfrey Rivers, I should be ashamed of myself.'

As he spoke the first of these words, Eamonn Andrews hand went up. His signal was interpreted by producer Leslie Jackson, who made a signal of his own. Abruptly, and much to the indignation of viewers, *What's My Line?* went off the screen.

Within half a minute an announcer had come on to apologize for a technical hitch. And that was all viewers saw of the 365th performance of *What's My Line?*

They missed a most dramatic scene. Godfrey Rivers took off his mask, stood up and shouted: 'I know you, Mortimer, and this is the kind of dirty trick I'd have expected . . .' Then he pulled at his collar, fell forward over the little table in front of him, and slumped to the floor.

Mortimer stood staring at him across the stage, grinning wolfishly, the puppet still in his hand. The other members of the team had taken off their masks and, with Eamonn Andrews, were clustered round Rivers.

In the audience several people were on their feet. A woman screamed. Leslie Jackson made his way to the front of the stage, and spoke into a microphone.

'Ladies and gentlemen. There is no reason at all for panic. But in view of the fact that we are more than halfway through our programme anyway, and because of Mr Rivers's unfortunate indisposition, we are cancelling the rest of the show tonight. I'm sure the team would want me to say how sorry they are that you didn't see a complete show. Good night.'

Within ten minutes the theatre was empty of its audience.

Well before that, however, the little dark man who had spoken to Melanie Mortimer outside the box was on the stage. 'Make way there, please,' he said importantly. 'Let me see him.'

'And who are you, sir?' Harding asked.

The little man drew himself up. 'My name is Mostyn. I am Mr Rivers's doctor. Thank you, that's better.'

They watched while he felt heart and pulse and pulled back eyelids. Then he looked up. 'We must get him to a hospital at once. There's a strong possibility that Godfrey, Mr Rivers, has taken some kind of poison.'

III

THE MURDERER IS IN THIS ROOM

The clock hands pointed to 10.45 when Inspector Gimlet strode on to the stage of the BBC Television Theatre. 'I should like to talk to any of you who were in the Hospitality Room after Mr Rivers arrived this evening,' he said. 'Anyone else may go. Except you, Mr Mortimer. Your co-operation would be valuable, I think.' The inspector had sharp eyes and gleaming false teeth. 'Now, if you would identify yourselves, we can proceed.'

'Oh, come now, inspector,' Leslie Jackson said, 'surely you know the members of the *What's My Line?* team?'

'I am not the possessor of a television set, and I must confess my ignorance. Your face seems familiar, yet I can't quite place it. Are you Mr Andrews?'

Zoë Gail stifled a laugh, not quite successfully. Gilbert Harding said, 'If you are capable of thinking I am Eamonn Andrews, Inspector, you must be strangely unacquainted with the public prints. If, on the other hand, you are trying to make me lose my temper, you will be unsuccessful. Fortunately I am a man of placid indisposition. My name is Harding.'

'Mr Gilbert Harding? My apologies.' The Inspector flashed his teeth again and identified Eamonn Andrews, Leslie Jackson and the other members of the panel without difficulty. Then he turned to the cherubic American.

'My name is Charles Schultz,' the American said, 'and this is my wife Mary. We've known Godfrey Rivers for several years. We're on a visit to Europe, been in England a couple of weeks, and Godfrey invited us to watch the show.'

The little doctor came forward. 'My name is Mostyn. Here is my card. I am Mr Rivers's physician. I have always been interested in television and he had—ah—invited me along tonight.'

A tall, fair young man said: 'My name's Bill Bannister. I'm a freelance journalist and I've been commissioned by *Picture News* to write a piece called "A Day in the Life of Gilbert Harding". Mr Harding's been stuck with me most of the day, and I was in the Hospitality Room.'

Now the inspector turned to the elegant but no longer languid blonde. 'You are a friend of Rivers, Mrs Mortimer?'

Melanie Mortimer did not look at her husband. 'Yes.'

'Did you know that your husband was to be the—ah—celebrity guest tonight?'

'No.' She hesitated. 'My husband and I separated a month ago.'

'But not for ever, I hope.' Mortimer still had the doll on his knee. Now he stroked its hair.

'Mr Mortimer, did you know in advance that your wife would be here tonight?' The inspector's voice was sharp.

'I thought it possible.' Mortimer gave his wolfish grin. 'After all, you heard what she said. She is a good friend of Godfrey Rivers.'

Harding coughed. 'Are we to assume from this interrogation, inspector, that Dr Mostyn's original suggestion was correct? Had Rivers taken poison?'

'Yes.' The inspector allowed his hard-eyed stare to move from one to the other of them impartially. 'The hospital doctors are trying now to save his life. Poison was found in one of the glasses in the—ah—Hospitality Room. The glass had been wiped clean of prints. The poison was aconitine, the active principle of the plant aconite, or monkshood. It has a strong, numbing effect upon the tongue, and even in whisky I should have thought its taste would be discernible. Can you tell me anything about that, Dr Mostyn?'

'Hmm. Yes.' Mostyn's ruddy face was now pale. 'Godfrey burned his mouth badly a few years ago. It affected his taste buds, so that he could barely tell one taste from another.'

'He had a bottle of pills in his pocket. You prescribed those for him?'

'Yes. You'll find they are no more than a mild sedative to be taken after meals.'

The inspector nodded. 'Now, let's get down to cases. First of all, who puts out the refreshments and at what time?'

Leslie Jackson said: 'Sandwiches and drinks are put out at about 8.30 by an assistant of mine named Miss Cornelius. She's gone home, I'm afraid.'

'Does she look after them later on?'

'No. She's pretty busy with various jobs for me. Tonight she was in my company from a quarter past nine until the show was stopped.'

'All right. Now I've checked with the doorkeeper that Rivers and his friends arrived just before nine o'clock. By five past they were in the Hospitality Room and they stayed there until it was time for the show to go on.' The inspector leaned forward and said emphatically, 'I want any of you who can remember anything at all about the drinks taken by Rivers to tell me.'

'Godfrey poured them out for us,' Mrs Schultz said, speaking for the first time in an accent more markedly American than her husband's. 'And for himself, too. I had—let's see—two drinks.'

'But Godfrey only had one,' her husband said. 'Right at the end, just before the show, I remember I said he was nervous. So he was too.'

Isobel Barnett nodded. 'I was here when Rivers and his friends came in. There is no doubt about it. Rivers poured the drinks for himself and his friends. It's what we usually do.'

With his eyes closed, Gilbert Harding visualized the scene when Rivers poured the last drink. He saw Rivers at the side table, splashing whisky and gin into three glasses. Two of them he had handed to the Schultzes. Had the third been in his own hand then? No.

He said slowly, 'When Rivers got the drink for himself and his friends he brought two glasses over—Mrs Mortimer did not have one, I think . . .'

'That's right,' she interrupted, 'I didn't have a drink at all.'

'Then he turned back to fetch his own. For that time, then, he would have left his glass unattended.'

'And who was near his glass then? Near enough to drop something into it?' the inspector asked.

There was silence. Then Harding said, 'Nobody.'

'Nobody?' The inspector was politely incredulous.

'I was in a good position to see, because I stood facing that end of the room. We were all down here, well away from Rivers.'

'But when he turned, didn't he block your vision? Are you telling me that you watched Rivers's glass continuously from the time when he poured whisky in it to the moment when he turned back to drink it?'

'Obviously not. There was a time—a very few seconds—when Rivers's body obscured a view of his glass. But during those few seconds nobody passed behind Rivers or was near enough to the glass to drop anything in it.'

'I believe Gilbert's right,' Isobel Barnett said. There was a general murmur of assent.

The corners of Inspector Gimlet's thin mouth were turned down. 'We will return to that in a moment. Mr Mortimer, you arrived at nine o'clock. You were taken by Mr Jackson to his dressing room on the ground floor. Then Mr Andrews came in and talked to you. He left you at twenty minutes past. And then?'

'Why, then I just played with Melanie until it was time to go out for my celebrity spot.'

The inspector turned to the others. 'You would be prepared to agree that Mr Mortimer did not enter the Hospitality Room between nine o'clock and the time of the performance.' They agreed. A constable brought in a note which Gimlet looked at without expression, and put into his pocket. 'Then he could not possibly have put poison in Rivers's glass.'

'But none of us went near his glass,' Bill Bannister said.

'So you say. But that is impossible. In spite of what you say, somebody put poison into Godfrey Rivers's drink. Unless he did it himself, which is most unlikely, his murderer is in this room.'

'His murderer,' Bannister said. 'You mean . . .'

The inspector took out the note from his pocket. 'Godfrey Rivers died in hospital, ten minutes ago.'

IV

GILBERT HARDING TURNS DETECTIVE

The time was the day following the tragic three hundred and sixty-fifth performance of *What's My Line?* The scene was the unpretentiously comfortable sitting-room in Gilbert Harding's flat. The great man sat in a chair large enough to accommodate his considerable girth. At his feet, panting slightly, sat his black-muzzled Pekinese Cham-pu. Facing him, on a sofa, were Isobel Barnett and Zoë Gail. On the arm of a chair, near the window, sat Eamonn Andrews. And, by himself, sitting unobtrusively in a corner of the room, was fair-haired Bill Bannister.

Gilbert Harding lowered his head and looked at them like a placid bull. 'I have called you together because, after the last words spoken by that rather crass, although no doubt competent, Inspector, it is clear that those of us in the Hospitality Room must consider ourselves under a shadow until this affair is cleared up.

'It becomes plain, then, that it is in our interests to solve this mystery which the Inspector regards as insoluble, without delay. Eamonn did not enter the Hospitality Room, but I hope that he may be able to help us.

'My suggestion is this. I have had a number of occupations in my life. Now I propose that, on your behalf as well as my own, I should turn detective and solve this puzzle. Bill Bannister who, for some extraordinary reason, thinks I am what he calls good copy, will be my Watson. Do you agree?'

There was an enthusiastic murmur. 'Very well. Now I want you, Isobel and Zoë, to tell me anything at all that struck you as unusual in the Hospitality Room last night—anything at all, no matter how slight.'

Silence. Then Zoë Gail said slowly, 'Rivers was more nervous than he should have been. After all, he was a well-known actor both in stage and screen. He shouldn't have been so frightened of playing a parlour game on television.'

'I agree, my dear. And I'll tell you something else. He was much more nervous this week than last. Isobel?'

'Last week he had three or four drinks. This week he only took one, although he was so much more nervous. That seems a little odd. And another thing. It seemed to me that Dr Mostyn wasn't there just for the show. I had an impression that he was watching Rivers closely. And his diagnosis of poison was done at lightning speed.'

'Good,' said Gilbert Harding. 'I can add one small item of information. Charles Schultz, as you probably know, is a historical novelist. I am friendly with his publisher, Railton, and I happened to mention to Railton that I would like to meet Schultz, as I admired his last book. Railton said that would be impossible, as the Schultzes had their passages booked back to the United States. They should have sailed yesterday.'

'That may have a perfectly innocent explanation,' Bill Bannister said.

'Certainly. It is simply an oddity to be investigated. Now, Eamonn, we come to you.'

'I wondered when that would happen,' Eamonn Andrews said with a smile.

'You talked to this man Mortimer. What did you think of him?'

Andrews stroked his chin.

'Well now, he was pretty excited. He had this doll, and when he told me it was called Melanie I was afraid we might be in for trouble, because I'd seen his wife come in with Rivers. I told Mortimer that his wife would be there, but he obviously knew that already. I tried to get him to call the doll by a different name, but he wouldn't. So I warned Leslie that there just might be a little bother, and he'd better be prepared for it.'

'You think he staged this business of the doll deliberately to be revenged on his wife and Rivers?'

'No doubt at all about it.'

'Would he have been satisfied with this comparatively petty revenge, or would he have gone to the length of murder?'

'Your guess is as good as mine. But I don't see how he could have done it, do you, Gilbert?'

'I have the beginnings of an idea. It's based on the fact that you really can't wipe fingerprints off a glass in public without somebody seeing you. But at the moment my idea seems merely to lead into the realm of fantasy. Now for positive action. I propose to pay a call on Mrs Rivers. I have a recollection, but I must confess a vague one, of meeting her when Rivers did some shows on the panel last year. Can anybody amplify that?'

'I've met her,' Bill Bannister said unexpectedly. 'I once did a feature about Rivers in a series called "Stars of Stage and Screen". She's a rather nice quiet little woman.'

'And I shall call on Mrs Mortimer. And Mr Mortimer. And perhaps we can clear up the puzzles relating to Dr Mostyn and the Schultzes. Then I shall report back to you.'

As they rose to go, Cham-pu eagerly and joyously snapped at skirts and trouser legs.

Gwendolen Rivers received Gilbert Harding and Bill Bannister in her Kensington house. Her manner was cold. 'I've consented to see you, Mr Harding, but I really don't see that I can tell you anything I haven't told the police.'

'Now, ma'am.' Harding flung out his hands in a gesture at once forlorn, pathetic and comic. 'I am not a busybody by nature. I regard a respect for privacy as a mark of civilized behaviour. But here I can plead that I am prying in a good cause. I am trying to find out who killed your husband. Won't you help me?'

'Well.' She visibly relented. 'I will do what I can, but it is all deeply painful to me. Not only because of Godfrey's death, but—you know about Mrs Mortimer?'

'Yes.' While she spoke, Harding considered her. 'A nice quiet little woman?' Yes, she was that, but behind the quiet manner and the greying hair he sensed more determination than he had remembered or than Bill Bannister had led him to expect. A woman of taste, too, for he guessed that she rather than Rivers was responsible for the decoration of this attractive blue and white room with its faint suggestion of Regency influence. She was dressed herself in blue and white, with no concessions to conventional mourning.

'That was very bitter for me. We had been married twelve years. I met Godfrey in the war, you know, nursed him back to health when he was invalided home from the Western desert. We were very happy until he met her six months ago.' Hands clasped together, Mrs Rivers looked into the fire. Then she said abruptly, 'There is no doubt at all who killed my husband, Jack Mortimer.'

Harding stroked his moustache. 'If you will tell me, ma'am, how Mortimer could possibly have put poison into your husband's glass without entering the room . . .'

'Oh, that's what the Inspector said, but don't you see that's his cleverness? He's a clever devil.'

'Your husband seemed extremely nervous at his last performance of *What's My Line?* Tell me, to your knowledge, was he frightened of anything?'

'Of course he was,' she cried. 'And hadn't he reason to be, when Mortimer sent him a box of poisoned chocolates only last week?'

'A box of poisoned chocolates.' Harding stared at her.

V

WHO SENT THE POISONED CHOCOLATES?

'You've told the Inspector about those chocolates?' Harding asked.

'Naturally,' Mrs Rivers replied coolly. 'Perhaps you'd like to speak to Eileen. She took in the parcel.'

Eileen was the daily help, a shrewd and keen-eyed Irishwoman. Yes, she remembered the parcel coming. It had a London post-mark and was addressed to Mr Rivers. He had opened it in her presence and said with delight: 'Chocolates, Eileen. Chocolates from an unknown admirer.' He had offered her one and had eaten one himself. Within half an hour they had both been violently sick.

Eileen left them and Mrs Rivers took up the tale. 'When I came home I found Godfrey lying down. He showed me the chocolates and we looked at them. Half of those on the top layer had been crudely opened and put together again.'

Bill Bannister asked: 'Did you tell the police about this?'

'No. We simply put them in the furnace.' Mrs Rivers looked at her hands and for the first time seemed embarrassed. 'It sounds strange, I expect, but the fact is we both knew they had been sent by Mortimer.'

'How?' Harding asked.

'Why—who else could have done it? Mortimer hated Godfrey. I suppose it was natural that he should.'

'Tell me, ma'am,' Harding said with a preliminary cough. 'How was this unhappy situation to be resolved? Did you contemplate divorcing your husband?'

Slowly, but with passionate conviction, she said, 'I should never have divorced Godfrey. This was an infatuation. It was already fading, and in another month or two it would have been over.'

'I see. Now, can you tell me what happened here last night?'

'What happened? But nothing happened.' She shrugged her shoulders. 'That is, nothing out of the way. We had dinner about seven—very light, because Godfrey never liked eating much at night. Just after eight o'clock the Schultzes came in, and Dr Mostyn. They had a drink. Godfrey took only tonic water with his usual pill, a mild sedative Dr Mostyn made up for him. Just after half-past eight they left. I went to bed.'

'There was no question of you accompanying your husband?'

'No. I came along two or three times when he was on the show last year. It would have been nothing new for me. And in any case I knew that woman would be with him.

Harding rose slowly to his feet. 'You have been very patient, Mrs Rivers. And you have told me much about which I must meditate. Thank you.' At the door he paused. 'Oh, by the way, have you any idea whether your husband knew that Mortimer was to be the celebrity on last night's show?'

She had moved to the window. Her hands rested on flowers in a bowl. Now she snapped a flower stalk. 'If he did, he knew it from Melanie Mortimer,' she said sharply. 'Ask her.'

'That last question struck home,' Bannister said as Harding's car threaded a way through crowded streets. 'What made you ask it?'

'It's obvious, surely.' Harding was a little impatient. 'Leslie Jackson naturally does everything possible to keep secret the identity of the celebrity, but accidents do happen sometimes. If Rivers knew who the celebrity was to be, it would help to explain his extreme nervousness. That is the most rudimentary piece of deduction. Much more interesting is the affair of the chocolates.'

'You mean that Mortimer may not have sent them?'

'Possibly not, but that isn't the interesting thing. What interests me is the unusual nature of these so-called poisoned chocolates, which were apparently filled with essence of ipecacuanha. Now let me alone. I must think.' For the rest of the journey Gilbert Harding closed his eyes and showed every appearance of being asleep.

Jack Mortimer had a suite at Morton's Hotel. A bottle of whisky stood on a side table, and he had obviously been using it. He showed his long teeth in a smile that had no friendliness.

'What an honour to be visited by the great Mr Harding. I asked the manager to put down the red carpet, but he said that was strictly reserved for American oil magnates and White Russian princesses. So the best I can do is to offer you and your sidekick a drop of what the management calls liqueur whisky.

'No, thank you, I have three questions to ask and then I shall be happy to leave you to your career of private drinking. First, how did you happen to be the guest celebrity in this particular week?'

Now Mortimer had picked the large, pretty, vicious-looking dummy he called Melanie off the sofa, and was cradling her in one arm. When he spoke it was in the languid voice of Melanie Mortimer. 'Why, Gilbert, don't say you've turned detective. You really aren't made for it, Gilbert, not with that figure.'

Harding nodded. 'You're even more stupid that I thought you were, Mortimer. I thought you might be interested to know that those chocolates you sent have been traced to this postal district.'

Mortimer put the dummy down. He said in his own voice, 'It's a lie. The inspector's been going at me about chocolates till I'm sick of it. I never sent Rivers any chocolates, poisoned or otherwise. I'm not a murderer. I got the celebrity spot through my agent, who told Leslie Jackson I had a new dummy. So I had. I wanted to get a bit of my own back on Rivers and that wife of mine, nothing more than that.'

'So you say. Second question. Did you tell anybody—anybody at all—that you were appearing on *What's My Line?*'

Again Mortimer picked up the dummy and stroked her. 'I have no secrets from my darling Melanie.'

'So your wife came to see you within the last few days.' Harding leaned forward. 'Did she come to ask for a divorce?'

'Get out.' Mortimer's voice was high. 'I don't want to talk to you, please understand that. I won't answer your filthy questions.' He picked up the glass of whisky with one hand and with the other clasped the dummy Melanie to him in a passionately protective gesture.'

'You've answered my question already.' Harding stood with

his hand on the door. 'I leave you with this thought, Mortimer. It's a lonely man who has to drink with a dummy.'

'This is all very well,' Bill Bannister said, while they drank tea in Harding's flat. 'But I don't see that it gets us much further. How did that poison get into the glass? And where did it come from in the first place? Those are important things, it seems to me.'

'As to the last question, I understand from Inspector Gimlet that a quantity of aconitine is missing from Dr Mostyn's dispensary. Apparently he knew both the Riverses and the Mortimers quite well, and any of them might have taken it.'

'I can't see that's important. But the fact that Rivers may have known Mortimer was to be the celebrity—what of it?'

Gilbert Harding ceremonially, and with some effort, poured out a saucer of tea for Cham-Pu, who lapped it noisily. 'It helps, that's all. It helps us to see the complete picture. Now we see why Rivers was nervous. We know that Mortimer had been approached by his wife about divorce. Perhaps neither of those things is at the centre of the puzzle, but they have their place. In most murder cases the truth is simple. But it is complicated by all sorts of trivial plots and counterplots going on separately that have nothing to do with the murder.'

'Yes, I suppose so. Then there are the chocolates. To me they're almost the most puzzling feature of the whole affair.'

'The chocolates are interesting, as I have said already.'

'But I suppose they are not what you would call at the centre of the puzzle. After all, they didn't poison anybody.'

Cham-Pu jumped on to Harding's knee. 'On the contrary, my dear young man. It is precisely because the chocolates didn't poison anybody that they are so important. We are dealing with an intelligent murderer, Bannister. The chocolates, the setting, the method of murder—all these, if I am not much mistaken, are part of a plan quite deliberately designed to deceive us.'

VI

GILBERT HARDING FINDS A VITAL CLUE

If Gilbert Harding had been asked to guess Melanie Mortimer's spare-time occupation, almost the last thing he would have expected was that she might be engaged in social work.

Harding and Bannister found her that evening, however, at the Mary MacLaren Girls' Club in Deptford.

'Mr Harding,' the Chief Warden said enthusiastically. She had iron-grey hair and a handshake that gripped like a pair of pincers. 'I am delighted to meet you. I hope on another occasion that you will come and talk to our girls.'

'My dear madam, I can imagine nothing more terrifying.' Hastily changing the subject, Gilbert Harding said, 'Has Mrs Mortimer been helping you for long?'

'About five years. She's really invaluable, absolutely selfless. She's taking some girls now in the gym. I'll go along there with you.'

In the gymnasium a game of basketball was in progress. Melanie Mortimer, wearing shorts and a blouse, was acting as referee. Harding watched with interest and astonishment the authority she obviously exercised, and the way she called the girls around her at the end of the game and talked to them rather as, he imagined, the managers of American baseball teams talked to their players.

'Melanie is a good basketball player herself,' the Chief Warden said. But of course her real game is table tennis. She played for England at that, you know. We're at the top of the Deptford and District League, and she says one or two of the girls are really good. They all love her.'

It was rarely that Gilbert Harding found himself at a loss for words, but now he could do no more than feebly nod his head at this new incarnation of the languid Melanie Mortimer. She came towards them, her cheeks flushed and looking altogether more attractive and intelligent than the languid figure he remembered in the Hospitality Room.

'That's all for now, girls,' she said briskly. 'Mr Harding and Mr—Bannister, isn't it? Come along.'

She led them along a corridor to a tiny cubicle, where Harding noticed with interest cups on the mantelpiece and photographs on the wall. He walked over to look at them and saw that they showed a youthful Melanie Mortimer playing table tennis, basketball and hockey, and running.

'This is most interesting. I had no idea that you were a famous athlete.'

She laughed. 'That's putting it much too strongly. I wasn't top class at anything except table tennis. I've always loved playing games, though I love anything to do with children too. Perhaps that was part of our trouble. Jack's and mine. We never had children.'

'But your whole manner is different. You might be another person.'

She coloured. 'Jack was always rather contemptuous of the things I could do well. I just got into the way of being the kind of person he expected, I suppose.'

'And you seemed languid because you were really bored by theatres, and theatrical people, and childish entertainments like *What's My Line?*'

Now she was scarlet. She said with manifest insincerity, 'Oh, Mr Harding. I know you're all most terribly intelligent on the panel. It's just, well, not my line, I suppose. I'm awfully stupid. Jack always said so, and I think Godfrey thought so as well.'

'Nothing is so limited as a public entertainer's idea of intelligence. But it is about your husband that I came to talk. I saw him today. He told me that you knew he was to be on the programme last Monday.'

She nodded. 'I didn't tell the Inspector because—well, I felt some sort of loyalty to Jack, I suppose, and it didn't seem to make any difference. But since he told you already . . .'

'And you told Rivers that Mortimer would be the celebrity?'

'Yes. I wanted Godfrey to withdraw from the programme. I knew there would be trouble. Jack was—he was hardly sane about it. You see, I told him that I was going to start proceedings for divorce. There's plenty of evidence, you know. Jack regards himself as above the law, I think. He believes that standards which apply to other people ought not to apply to him.'

'But Mrs Rivers would never have divorced her husband.'

She looked at him in surprise. 'Oh, yes, she would. Godfrey told me so. He said they'd agreed when they were married that either of them would let the other one go if they ever fell in love with anyone else. Godfrey and I were in love. I won't try to excuse it. I can't explain it—but believe me. It was so.'

'Let's come back to Rivers and Mortimer. Rivers wouldn't withdraw from the show?'

'No. He said that he must see it through.'

'Now I want you to think carefully. When you saw your husband, did he say anything about sending a box of chocolates to Rivers?'

'A box of chocolates?' Her astonishment seemed perfectly genuine. 'No. Neither did Godfrey.'

Very slowly Harding said, 'Do you believe that your husband poisoned Godfrey Rivers? Disregard the fact that it was apparently impossible for him to do it. Was he the kind of man who would commit that sort of murder?'

Without hesitation she said: 'No. Jack is a supreme egotist. The trick he did play—that beastly trick with the puppet that looked and sounded like me—was absolutely in character for him. But murder—no. To Jack Mortimer—Jack Mortimer is the most important person in the world. He would certainly never risk his neck for me.'

Harding got up and walked over to the cups and pictures.

'First prize for the 220 yard hurdles. I wonder why modern trophies are so aesthetically revolting, whereas 200 years ago they were a delight to the eye.' His back was turned to her and there was no change in his tone as he said, 'Do you know who killed Godfrey Rivers?'

'No'

'But you could make a guess.'

Her voice was low. 'I don't want to make a guess.'

They left her sitting at the table in her little room, staring at the trophies on the wall.

'I noticed one thing in particular about what she said,' Bill Bannister said in the car. He received a grunt for reply. 'Rivers told her that his wife would divorce him. In other words, he lied to her about that.'

Harding grunted again.

'Supposing Mrs Mortimer had learned that Rivers never meant to marry her anyway—that for him it had simply been a casual love affair—wouldn't that have provided a motive for murder? She's much more intelligent than she appears.'

'She is more than that, my dear young man. She is the most interesting personality in this case.'

'But you don't think my theory is right?'

'No. It leaves too many things unexplained. What earthly reason would she have for sending a box of chocolates to Rivers that would make him sick? Does she seem the kind of woman who would poison a man she loved because he had lied to her in a way that it is easy to understand, though perhaps not easy to excuse? She knows or suspects something, undoubtedly—and I am afraid I know what it is.'

Bannister looked out of the window. 'I say. I thought we were going to see the Schultzes.'

'So we are—later. At the moment we are on our way to the BBC Television Theatre in Shepherd's Bush.'

'To reconstruct the crime?' Bannister asked hopefully.

'That may come later. We are going to talk to the doorkeeper who was on duty last Monday night. I noticed at the time that he was not the usual doorkeeper, and Leslie Jackson tells me that he is a temporary man, on duty for the first time because the regular doorkeeper is ill. An interesting point, my dear Bannister. I beg you not to lose sight of it.'

VII

GILBERT GOES TO A PARTY

Young Bill Bannister considered himself as enterprising a journalist as most, and a man as quick as any other to see through a brick wall, but he was frankly baffled by Gilbert Harding's behaviour when they got to the BBC Television Theatre, where a new panel game called *Here We Come* was being rehearsed. For the first time Harding seemed really excited by the case. He showed some impatience at seeing that the regular doorkeeper was back in duty, but the temporary man, whose name was Snell, proved to be in the theatre.

'Snell, Snell, can't call him Snell,' Harding said. 'What's his Christian name?'

And when they found Snell, a hangdog, dyspeptic man who was sitting at a corner of the stage biting his nails, Harding greeted him as Charlie.

'Why, it's Mr 'Arding.' Snell got to his feet. 'Fancy you remembering me, sir.'

'I not only remember you, Charlie, I've come here specially to ask for your help about that unhappy affair on Monday.'

Snell's natural tendency to droop reasserted itself. 'Anything I can do, Mr 'Arding, but the police sergeant asked me a lot of questions . . .'

'Not the same questions as mine, I think. You were on duty

all that evening.' Snell said that he was. Harding took off his spectacles and polished them. 'Now, I want you to think back to the period between twenty-five minutes past nine and ten o'clock. Who did you let in here during that period?'

Bannister was moved to protest. 'But you've got the times wrong, surely. We all left the Hospitality Room about twenty-- five minutes past, and Rivers had taken his drink by then.'

Harding waved him aside. 'Well, Charlie? Did the sergeant ask you that?'

'No. But I'd like to know what you're getting at, Mr 'Arding. I done nothing wrong. I never let in anybody who didn't ought to have come in.'

With elaborate patience Harding said: 'Nobody is suggesting that you did anything wrong. Just tell me everybody who came in between those times—everybody, you understand?'

Looking as miserable as a bloodhound, Snell said: 'That's a job, now. Let's see. Two of the boys what'd been out for a cuppa came in, electricians they were. Then at half-past nine, just about when the show was starting, Miss Cornelius, that's one of Mr Jackson's assistants, came in—she'd been out to get a drop of brandy for one of the challengers who was feeling a bit faint-like. And then—ah, this is what you're after, I expect—just after a quarter to ten it would be, a woman with fair hair, very smart-looking piece, came out . . .'

'Melanie Mortimer,' said Bannister.

'That's right,' Snell agreed. 'Saw her picture in the paper afterwards. Wasn't looking too well, said she wanted a breath of air. Didn't go far, just took a turn down the passage outside, then came back and went in again. That's the lot.'

Harding pondered a moment. 'You don't keep the same kind of check on people who go out?'

'No, it's only those who come in as interest me. To see that no unauthorized person gains admittance, that's my job.' He mouthed the long words with satisfaction. 'But in a general way those who come in must go out, and vicey versy,' he gave a dismal laugh.

'In a general way. The rule is not invariable.' Harding stared hard at the doorkeeper. 'You're quite certain there's nothing else you can remember about anybody coming in—or going out—between those times? No? In that case, thank you for your help, Charlie. Now, here is my private telephone number, which you will not find listed in the directory. If anything else should occur to you, anything at all you understand, ring me up.' Bannister saw the green of a pound note change hands.

When they were back in the car Harding said: 'It's a pity Charlie Snell is—well, that he's Charlie Snell. But you see where this leads us?'

'Frankly, I have no idea.'

Harding sighed. 'I should have thought one thing was obvious—a quite striking discrepancy in the evidence. But I wonder how far it helps us. We shall see what the Schultzes have to say. I don't suppose we shall be there more than ten minutes.

In this Gilbert Harding was wrong. When they entered the Schultzes' suite at the Savoy Hotel they were met by the deafening sound of two hundred people talking at once. Crew-cut Americans, men with thick and straggly beards, intelligent women trying to look beautiful and beautiful women trying to sound intelligent, were all blended together in a mass that swayed at times like a rugby scrum.

Gilbert Harding surveyed it with some dismay, took a drink from a passing waiter's hand, and moved in search of his host. He lost track of Bannister almost immediately and was soon immersed himself in the babble of sound.

He pushed his way between people who were discussing the derivative nature of Picasso's art, people talking about the Italian neo-realistic cinema, people who were saying that Kierkegaard and Kafka were both old hat, people talking about all-in wrestling as a science, people talking about deep-sea fishing. At the centre of confusion he found Charles Schultz. The American was smiling as cherubically as ever. He had on a multi-coloured jockey cap fitted back to front, and he was talking on the telephone.

'Hallo there, hallo there,' he was saying. 'I didn't get that. Speak louder. Shout if you have to. I didn't get it. Is there a party going on? No, it's as quiet as a mouse, quiet as a church. My last novel was what? Corny? Look, nobody says that to me. Put that telephone down, get your fists up and fight like a man. I don't care where you're calling from, goodbye.' He put back the receiver and beamed at Harding.

Mary Schultz came up, bright-eyed. Her husband appealed to her. 'What do you think of that, Mary? Man rings up all the way from Hollywood to say my novel is corny.'

'Hollywood?' She looked slightly alarmed. 'That wouldn't be Henry Calney, would it, the producer? You know he was interested.'

'Gee, you're right.' Schultz smacked himself on the forehead. 'Never mind, it'll keep till tomorrow. Mr Harding, I'm happy to see you. That inspector said we'd have to stay around a day or two while this mess about poor old Godfrey got itself cleared up, so we just asked a few friends in. Seems to have got a little out of hand.'

'So I see. If you'd gone back to the States on the day you planned, you wouldn't have been involved in the Rivers affair.'

Schultz giggled. 'Baby, I believe Mr Harding is suspicious of us. You tell him.'

'It was this way, you see, Mr Harding. I've got a brother named Bob Bennett, you may have heard of him, he's an anthro—anthropologist, you know, savage tribes and all that. Says civilization is terrible. "Civilization? Take it away," he says.'

Looking round him, Harding felt some sympathy for Bob.

Mary Schultz continued. 'Haven't seen Bob for five years, then last Friday we heard he was flying back, would love to see us if we could stay on a couple of days. So we stayed on. Bob's around here somewhere, says we're just as interesting as the savage tribes.'

'But that's not what we've got to tell Mr Harding,' Charles Schultz said. 'What was it we were going to tell him, baby?'

'Why, about poor Godfrey, you remember.'

'So I do.' Charles Schultz took off his jockey cap, looked at it absently, turned it inside out to reveal a different set of colours, and put it back on again. 'About poor Godfrey. We've come to a conclusion about him.'

'What's that?'

Schultz looked at Harding with his jockey cap pushed back on his head. 'There's only one possible conclusion. Godfrey committed suicide.'

VIII

WHO STOLE THE POISON?

Through one of those sudden gaps that come in the most crowded of parties Harding caught a glimpse of Bill Bannister talking earnestly to Gwendolen Rivers. He turned to Schultz and said a little absently: 'You think Godfrey Rivers committed suicide. Why? To kill yourself with aconitine is a painful way to die.'

'First of all there's the evidence of plain common sense.' A waiter came round with a tray and Harding, suddenly aware of the fact that he had had no dinner, took tiny strips of smoked salmon and salami on squares of toast. 'Mary and I have talked it over and we're certain, dead certain, mind, that nobody tampered with Godfrey's glass.'

Harding stared at him. 'I'm certain of that, too. I thought it was generally agreed.'

'Yes, but what you see—or in this case don't see—with your

own eyes is more convincing. Now, both Mary and I would be ready to swear that nobody touched Godfrey's glass before he drank from it.'

'So you suggest that Rivers put aconitine in his own glass, drank his medicine like a man, and then wiped the glass clean of prints. I suppose he did that just to complicate things?'

'How the glass got wiped I don't know,' Schultz said. He mopped his cherubic face, and in fact it was hot in the room. 'But I can tell you this too, that when we picked up Godfrey that night he was—well, queer.'

'What do you mean by that? Unhappy?'

Now it was Mary Schultz who spoke. 'Not exactly. In fact, he seemed in a way—exhilarated, I suppose you could call it. On top of the world. But at the same time he was worried about something. It was—how can I put it—as though something had happened that was too good to be true, and he just couldn't believe it.'

'That's interesting and may be helpful. But it doesn't sound to me at all like a state in which people commit suicide.'

Bill Bannister had had three drinks, and while he would have indignantly denied that they had affected his capacities in the slightest degree, there could be no doubt that they had made him unusually talkative. 'You know, I admire you for this,' he said to Gwendolen Rivers. 'For coming out like this to a party, I mean. Some people would be shocked, but—I admire it.'

Mrs Rivers shrugged her slim shoulders. In her quiet way, he thought, she was a pretty woman. 'Why shouldn't I go to a party because Godfrey is dead? What I felt for him was too deep to be touched by the conventions. Has Mr Harding found out yet how Mortimer did it?'

'I just don't know what he's up to.' Bannister took another drink. 'I have the greatest respect for old Gilbert—Mr Harding, I mean. Terrific intellect, wonderful personality, tremendously kind.' He found these long words slipping away from his tongue in the most curious way. 'But behaves in the most extraor— funny way as a detective. Asking the doorkeeper a lot of questions about times that can't mean anything.

'I mean, who cares where anybody was *after* half-past nine, when poor old Rivers had drunk the stuff anyway. And then traipsing down to Deptford to see Melanie what's-her-name. Did you know that she was a sort of champion athlete, table tennis, running and all that?'

'I know very little about Mrs Mortimer,' Gwendolen Rivers's voice was chilly.

Somehow Bannister found another drink in his hand. He was emboldened by it to leave the world of fact altogether for that of fiction.

'I tried to put him right. "Gilbert, old boy," I said to him, "quite frankly you're on the wrong tack. The important point about this crime is—"'

Bannister stopped abruptly as he felt a hand on his shoulder. Gilbert Harding's rich, sonorous voice said, 'Good evening, Mrs Rivers. What were you saying then? Just favour me with your observations about the important features of this crime.'

About Harding's expression there was an unusual seriousness, even severity, but Bannister was not to be deterred. 'The poison. Until you can explain how the poison got into Rivers's glass without anybody touching it—'

'I can explain that.'

Bannister looked at him with his mouth open. 'How was it done?'

'I know much more than that.' Harding's voice was harsh. 'I know the name of the murderer. I know the reason for the murder.'

'Then nothing remains,' said Mrs Rivers, 'but the arrest.'

Sombrely Harding said, 'That isn't so. Between knowledge and proof there is a gap. My task now is to fill it.'

*

Bannister had gone home with a headache, and Harding called alone on pursy little Dr Mostyn. 'I'm a busy man, Mr Harding,' the doctor said.

'I don't doubt it. So am I.'

Mostyn took out a watch. 'I can give you just five minutes.'

'You are very kind.' Anybody more sensitive than the doctor might have found something ominous about Harding's suavity. 'Inspector Gimlet tells me that aconitine has been stolen from your dispensary.'

'Correct.'

'And that you know both the Riverses and Mortimers quite well.'

Dr Mostyn puffed himself up until he looked absurdly like a pouter pigeon. 'I am happy to say that I have friendly relations with many figures in the theatrical profession. Godfrey and Gwendolen and—ah—the Mortimers, we're not only patients, but friends of mine.'

'Yes. Mrs Rivers said that Rivers took a pill on the Monday evening when you called on them?'

'Why, yes—if it matters.' Mostyn's eyebrows furrowed in recollection. 'Let me see, now. He took one from a bottle containing two or three only, that stood on the sideboard, and drank it with his tonic water.'

'I see. Let us return to the theft of the aconitine. Any of them might have had access to your dispensary? Doesn't that indicate negligence on your part?'

Dr Mostyn ran his hand through his thin hair. 'Damn it all, man. I've had enough preaching from the Inspector. I'm not going to take it from you. The Riverses were old friends of mine, and I'd known the Mortimers for three or four years. All of them knew where the dispensary was, and I suppose any of them could have sneaked in and stolen the stuff. My last dispensary check was made three months ago, and everything was all right then. Now, if you'll excuse me, I'm very busy.'

'One more question.' Harding's head jutted formidably forward. 'How did you know that Rivers had been poisoned when he collapsed?'

Mostyn's face was pale. 'I don't know what you mean.'

'I think you do. You gave him the most cursory inspection and said that he must be got to hospital at once because there was a strong possibility that he had been poisoned. What made you say that?'

'The poisoned chocolates . . .'

'That won't do. The chocolates did no more than make Rivers sick. Shall I tell you what I think, Dr Mostyn?' Harding's finger pointed accusingly. 'I think you had missed the aconitine already, you suspected a certain person of taking it, you were worried by the incident of the chocolates, afraid that something might happen, you didn't quite know what. That is why you were in Rivers's company that evening. That is why you came to the show. That is why you were upset when the inspector mentioned aconitine as the poison that had been used.'

Mostyn shook his head dumbly.

'The person you suspected of the theft,' Harding said, 'was . . .' And he named a name.

'Yes,' the doctor said. 'I would have spoken, but it's impossible . . .'

'It is not impossible.' Harding's face was grave. 'It is true.'

IX

GILBERT FINDS THE KILLER

In spite of the fact that his telephone number was not listed in the directory, Gilbert Harding was accustomed to receiving calls from people who thought that he could help them to do everything from winning the football pools to inducing their errant daughters to adhere to the straight and narrow path of virtue. These calls were filtered through his secretary, who eliminated the more obvious lunatics and spongers, and passed on the others. This particular call came while Harding was eating breakfast.

'It's Charlie,' his secretary said.

The whining voice of Charlie Snell, the temporary doorkeeper at the BBC Television Theatre, came on the line.

'I been thinking.' Charlie Snell paused to indicate that this was something notable. 'About what you said the other night. And I think I know what you mean. About those that come into the theatre must go out and vicey versy. You said that wasn't always so.'

'Yes.' A little regretfully, Harding eyed the scrambled egg that was solidifying upon his plate.

'I been thinking.' Charlie Snell repeated. 'And you was absolutely right, though how you knew it beats me. And what it's got to do with the case I don't see. But somebody came in that never went out.'

'And you think you could identify this somebody? Very good, Charlie. Now, can you be at the theatre at, let's see, two-thirty this afternoon?'

In the next hour Gilbert Harding made a number of telephone calls. He spoke to the other members of the *What's My Line?* team and arranged that they, with compère Eamonn Andrews and producer Leslie Jackson, should be at the theatre for what he called 'a little reconstruction'. Then he talked to the various people involved in the case, and listened with interest to their reactions.

Dr Mostyn said irritably, 'Sorry, I just can't spare the time for that kind of play-acting.'

'The case is solved,' Harding said.

'You mean you're going to name the criminal?'

'Exactly. I should like you to be present.'

There was a pause. Then the doctor said, 'All right, then, I suppose I shall have to come.'

Charles Schultz was his ebullient self. 'That was quite a little party. You know, Mary and I didn't get to bed till six this morning, and I feel fresh as a daisy. Must be something in the London air. What's that? Sure, we'll come along this afternoon, try and keep us away.'

On the telephone Gwendolen Rivers seemed her usual remote self. Faint and impersonal, her voice sounded as if she were speaking from another planet.

'So you've really cleared it all up? You've been indefatigable, Mr Harding.'

'You don't sound very interested.'

'What good will it do Godfrey, can you tell me that?'

'There is the matter of justice. There is such a thing in our society as the rule of law.'

'Is there? I suppose so. You've fitted everything in, have you, with the aid of the—what was it your friend said last night?— the doorkeeper. You've filled in all the gaps?'

'Yes.'

'Then, as I said then, really nothing remains but the arrest. And your explanation, naturally. I mustn't miss that.'

'I don't know,' Melanie Mortimer said. 'I don't think I want to come. Nothing you do can bring Godfrey back to life again, or make me feel better about what happened. It was a kind of judgement on us, I feel that now.'

'Come along if you can.' Harding's voice was gentle. 'You remember that guess you wouldn't make? You were right.'

'But I didn't say anything.'

'You didn't need to.'

*

Of them all, only Jack Mortimer treated the invitation flippantly. 'So good old detective Gilbert has solved the crime. Would you like me to confess on the telephone? I wasn't responsible. It was my doll Melanie who did it. She slipped out on her own while I was sitting downstairs, nipped up and dropped the poison in Godfrey's drink. Naughty girl. Would you like to hear her admit it?' A squeaky imitation of Melanie's voice said, 'I killed him, Mr Harding, but it was all for love. Don't be too hard on me.'

Harding said deliberately, 'Your taste is as vulgar as your manners are atrocious. You will please yourself whether you come or not. I have informed the police of this meeting, and if you are absent from it they will no doubt draw their own conclusions.'

When the time came they were all there—all except one. A note was delivered to Gilbert Harding, who read it without change of expression. Then he coughed, and began.

'Ladies and gentlemen, you are here today because you were all involved, accidental or otherwise, in what happened last Monday. Now what I propose, first of all, is that we should reconstruct the events involved in that final drink poured in this room which was so mysteriously found to contain poison. Charlie, will you play the part of Rivers? I assure you there is no reason to be afraid.

'Now, will those of you who were not in the Hospitality Room last Monday stand to one side. The rest take up the positions you sat or stood in then. A little more this way, I think, Mr Schultz. Mrs Mortimer, you were over here by me, were you not? Now, Charlie, you turn your back and pretend to pour three drinks. One each for Mr and Mrs Schultz, one for yourself. You turn round to get your own. Good. Introduce Mr Schultz to me, then Mrs Mortimer. Splendid.'

Harding looked at his watch. 'Now it is time for somebody to put a head in at the door and tell us we are on. Thank you.

Out we go, guests following closely behind us in a group. We need go no further than the door. There you are. Now, what do you say?'

'It's impossible,' Isobel Barnett said decisively. 'There was no chance at all for anybody to drop poison into Rivers's glass.'

'Precisely.' Harding nodded in pleased agreement. 'No poison could have been dropped into Rivers's glass at this time. Therefore *the poison in the glass was not the poison that killed him.*'

X

THE KILLER SENDS HARDING A LETTER

There was an uproar. Half a dozen people were talking at once. Harding quietened them with raised hand.

'Let us leave the question of *how* for a moment and turn to the questions *who* and *why*. There were four people involved who were intimately connected with Rivers in one way or another—his wife, Jack and Melanie Mortimer, and Dr Mostyn. Our American friends, the Schultzes, also knew him, but in spite of an ambiguity about the time of their leaving Britain I never seriously suspected them. The other people in the case had only the slightest connection, or no connection at all, with Rivers.

There was a whispered altercation at the door. Leslie Jackson said, 'Telephone call for you downstairs, Gilbert. Inspector Gimlet.'

While Harding was out of the room there was little conversation, and that only in hushed, slightly uneasy whispers. When he returned he spoke more briskly, but with a touch of something almost like regret in his tone.

'There were these four people then, and I talked to them all, weighing them up as possible murderers. Dr Mostyn I thought a puffy, self-important little man . . .'

'Really.' Mostyn pushed out his chest. His face was red. 'There's such a thing as a law of slander.'

'Good natured, probably. Worried, certainly. I deduced from his behaviour when Rivers collapsed that he knew something about the poisoning, had expected or feared it. I discovered that this was so. Mostyn admitted to me that he had missed the aconitine from his dispensary.

'Was this story untrue—was Mostyn in fact the murderer? If so, he had provided a clue that led straight to himself, in the poison. I couldn't believe he would be so stupid.

'So I put Mostyn on one side, and considered the situation between the Mortimers and the Riverses. Mrs Mortimer had left her husband, for which I don't at all blame her. She hides a good practical intelligence behind a slightly vacant mask. She could be ruthless, I am sure. But why should she kill Rivers? She was intending to divorce her husband. She believed that Mrs Rivers had agreed to divorce Rivers. I could see no reason at all for her to kill the man she loved.'

Quickly and furtively Melanie Mortimer wiped her eyes with her handkerchief.

'Mortimer, then? I asked his wife whether she thought him capable of murder. She said that he was a supreme egotist, and that he would certainly never risk his life for her. With that I agreed.'

Mortimer sat, pale and sullen in a corner, looking down at the floor.

'And so I came to Mrs Rivers. She was quiet, almost shy, yet in conversation with her I gathered the impression of an extremely strong character. She told me that she would never divorce her husband. She must have suffered a deep emotional injury when she learned that he had fallen in love with Melanie Mortimer. One must feel sympathy for her. Yet it is never possible to condone murder.'

'She's not here to answer you,' Mortimer said.

Schultz had a puzzled frown on his face. 'But she couldn't possibly have done it. We left her at home that evening.'

'Let me reconstruct the crime for you. I should guess that Mrs Rivers decided to kill her husband when he came and asked her to divorce him, saying that he loved another woman.

Her passion was quiet and controlled, but deep. She stole the aconitine from Mostyn's dispensary. She sent the box of chocolates to her husband. These were not meant to kill him, but merely to make him sick. They were intended to show that somebody outside his home life was trying to kill him.

In the meantime she told her husband that she agreed to a divorce. When Mrs Mortimer said this, Bill Bannister, who was with me, immediately assumed that Rivers had been lying to her. But there was the possibility that he was telling the truth—that Mrs Rivers had agreed to divorce him without, as she told us, the least intention of doing so. That seemed to fit in with Rivers's state of mind, as the Schultzes described it.

'He was on top of the world about something, they said, but at the same time couldn't quite believe it.

'Just after eight o'clock the Schultzes and Dr Mostyn came in. They had a drink. Rivers had tonic water and took a pill with it, from a bottle which stood on the sideboard. There were two or three pills in the bottle, and all of them must have contained aconitine. This aconitine must have been put, not into an ordinary gelatine capsule, but in a capsule made from one of the new plastic compounds which are more or less heat resistant but are easily melted by alcohol.

There was silence. Schultz said dazedly, 'This is only conjectural. You can't prove it.'

'I can prove what Mrs Rivers did afterwards. She knew where the Hospitality Room was from her previous visits to the theatre. At half-past nine she appeared at the stage door, said that she was Mr Jackson's assistant and had been out to get a nip of brandy for one of the challengers, and went in.

'She walked up to the Hospitality Room, put a little aconitine into the dregs of a glass, wiped the glass clean of prints, and walked out again, leaving us an apparently insoluble puzzle. At a quarter to ten Rivers collapsed and the obvious, although mistaken, assumption was that he had drunk from the glass.

'It was an ingenious attempt to provide an alibi , which broke down on two points, once we questioned the times involved. The first was that Miss Cornelius, Mr Jackson's assistant, was actually with him throughout the show from twenty past nine onwards, so that she couldn't possibly have gone out.

'The story about one of the challengers feeling faint was easily disproved. And further than that, Charlie Snell, by a magnificent feat of memory, managed to recall the fact that although somebody who called herself Miss Cornelius had come in, she had never gone out first, as she should have done.'

Melanie Mortimer said timidly, 'I thought it must be her, but I didn't feel that I could say anything.'

'Is she under arrest?' Mary Schultz asked.

'No. She put her head in a gas oven this morning. That telephone call from Inspector Gimlet told me that they had come too late to arrest her. She sent me a note, which was delivered to me here.'

Gilbert Harding took out the note that had been handed to him and read:

'Dear Mr Harding. You sounded very convincing on the telephone this morning about filling in all the gaps. And the doorkeeper, too. Very clever. I don't think I shall wait for the explanation—I do know it all already, don't I? Gwendolen Rivers.'

Harding put the note back in his pocket, took off his spectacles and wiped his eyes. 'An intelligent woman, and not without humour,' he said. 'Rare qualities, those. What a pity that she was a murderess, too.'

JULIAN SYMONS

The writer, critic, biographer and poet Gustave Julian Symons was born in 1912 in Clapham, London. His father had emigrated from Poland in the 1880s and became an auctioneer before losing all his money. Symons left school at fourteen and eventually secured a job as a clerk in an engineering firm, which gave him an income while he wrote poetry and short stories with, at that time, no hopes of becoming a full-time writer.

At the age of 25, he founded the magazine *Twentieth Century Verse* and appointed himself editor. This helped to build his profile and in 1939 the Fortune Press published *Confusions about X*, a slim volume of his largely introspective poetry that was indifferently received by reviewers.

With the advent of the Second World War, *Twentieth Century Verse* folded. At the same time, Symons' application for exemption from military service on the grounds of conscientious objection was unsuccessful, and he served with the Royal Armoured Corps until being invalided out. A second volume of poetry, *The Second Man* (1944), received a similar reception to the first and he took up a new role as an advertising copywriter, while in his spare time writing stories inspired by his experiences in the Army. His first, 'The Bull', was based on a specific officer whom Symons had loathed. He also began contributing critical articles, and sometimes light-hearted ones, to various publications and, to fulfil a boyhood ambition that had been fuelled by Conan Doyle and Chesterton, he decided to write a mystery.

The Immaterial Murder Case (1945) revolves around the absurdities of modern art and critics considered it 'a promising debut'. Symons received £200 (equivalent to around £7,000 or $10,000 today); a modest enough sum for a novel, but the experience had in every sense been more rewarding than poetry. In 1946, he replaced George Orwell as literary critic at the *Manchester Evening News*, writing its eclectic *Life, People—and Books* column intermittently until 1955. The following year, the central character of his first novel, Detective Inspector Bland, returned in *A Man Called Jones* (1947), whose mise-en-scène was informed by Symons' time in advertising. The third Bland novel was a triple murder mystery, *Bland Beginning* (1949), and was inspired by the criminal life of the bibliophile Thomas Wise and his infamous forgeries. The novel led to Symons' being admitted to the Detection Club in 1958 but, while reviewers were positive about his books, they were less taken by his detective whom they considered to be unfortunately well-named. Symons would appear to have taken note for, while he would write other detective stories, Bland would not appear in any of them.

His next novel marked a move away from the relatively conventional detective stories that make up the Bland trilogy. Although *The Thirty-First of February* (1950) initially appears to be more of the same, the novel gradually becomes a psychological thriller and the central crime is never entirely resolved. The new approach was well-received and, with a few exceptions, the detection in most of Symons' subsequent crime novels would be more psychological than physical. Among his most notable later titles are *The Players and the Game* (1972), a horrific book, and the retrospective murder mystery *Death's Darkest Face* (1990).

Over the next 30 years, in parallel with his career as a crime writer, Symons wrote criticism and biographical studies, and he made numerous radio appearances as well as writing new plays, or adapting earlier stories, for radio and television—these include the enjoyably twisty thriller *Curtains for Sheila* (1965) and *Whatever's Peter Playing At?* (1974), which pitted Ronald Fraser as a novelist against Ronald Hines as a world-weary detective.

Although Symons largely abandoned novel-length detective fiction after the Bland books, he wrote a long series of detective stories for London's *Evening Standard* and other newspapers, mostly with the sardonic private detective Francis Quarles, named for a seventeenth century English poet. As well as contributing non--series stories like 'A Mystery in Spain' and 'Don't Turn a Deaf Ear to Murder' to multi-author series of stories by members of the Crime Writers' Association, Symons also wrote puzzle stories such as 'The Cupboard Is Bare' (1955), challenging the reader to guess if it was fact or fiction, and from time to time his stories featured real people as detectives, including the television personality Gilbert Harding in *The 'What's My Line?' Murder* (1956) and the three-times Oscar nominee James Mason in the long short story *Murder in the Sun* (1957). In later years he would also write pastiche cases for the likes of Sherlock Holmes, Philip Marlowe and Hercule Poirot.

Though Symons was at times disparaging about crime and detective stories, saying once that he regarded himself as 'a craftsman working to please the groundlings', he became one of the genre's most forceful champions. In 1958 he produced a list of 'The 99 Best Crime Stories' for the *Sunday Times*, the newspaper for which he would write a book review column until 1994, his last appearing only eight weeks before his death. Building on a 30-page booklet written for the British Council, *The Detective Story in Britain* (1962), Symons wrote *Bloody Murder* (1972), a comprehensive and controversial history.

Symons also wrote about true crime in *A Reasonable Doubt* (1960), and throughout his life he produced newspaper and magazine articles about almost anything, from table tennis to spiritual movements. Poetry remained a passion to which he would return frequently and he also wrote accessible studies of notable events such as *The General Strike* (1959) and, in *Buller's Campaign* (1963), the Second Boer War. While his biographies, particularly those of Conan Doyle and Poe, are shorter than customary, they are written with passion and insight, none more so than *A. J. A. Symons: His Life & Speculations* (1950), about his older brother Alphonse.

As a writer of crime fiction, Symons spans the breadth of the genre, though there are some regular themes in his work: few marriages, and fewer families, are entirely happy—whether in modern or Victorian times—and the most devious sociopaths and cruellest psychopaths can be found in the most prosaic of surroundings. During his career he won two Edgar Awards from the Mystery Writers of America, who in 1982 made him a Grand Master. From 1976 to 1985 he served as the president of Detection Club, and twenty years earlier he had chaired the Crime Writers Association, which in 1990 awarded him the Cartier Diamond Dagger in recognition of a lifetime's achievement.

Although his views about what was good and bad about crime fiction were sometimes controversial, he was unfailingly kind to fans, always willing to stop and chat, and even sending one—unprompted—the original scripts for all of his radio and television plays. In 1994, after a long battle with cancer, he died at Groton House on the Dover Road in Walmer, Kent, where he and his wife Kathleen had lived since moving from Blackheath 53 years earlier.

'The "*What's My Line?*" Murder' was serialised daily in the London *Evening Standard* between 27 February and 8 March 1956.

ACKNOWLEDGEMENTS

'The Predestined' by Q Patrick copyright © 1953 the estate of Hugh Wheeler.

'Villa for Sale' by Ellis Peters reprinted by permission of United Agents on behalf of the Ellis Peters Estate.

'Sugar-Plum Killer' by Michael Gilbert reproduced with permission of Curtis Brown Ltd, London, on behalf of the Estate of Michael Gilbert. Copyright © 1950 Michael Gilbert.

'Vacancy with Corpse' by Anthony Boucher reprinted by permission of Curtis Brown, Ltd., New York.

'Where Do We Go From Here?' by Dorothy L. Sayers copyright © 1948 The Trustees of Anthony Fleming (deceased).

'Benefit of the Doubt' By Anthony Berkeley reprinted by permission of The Society of Authors as literary Representative of the Estate of Anthony Berkeley Cox.

'The Riddle of the Cabin Cruiser' by John Dickson Carr copyright © 1943 John Dickson Carr.

'Skeleton in the Cupboard' by Ianthe Jerrold © Ianthe Jerrold 1952.

'The Year and the Day' by Edmund Crispin published by permission of Peters Fraser & Dunlop (www.petersfraserdunlop.com). Copyright © Rights Ltd 2022.

'Murder in Montparnasse' by John Bude reprinted by permission of the estate of Ernest Elmore, copyright © 1949.

'The Thistle Down' by H. C. Bailey © the estate of H. C. Bailey 1939.

'The Magnifying Glass' by Cyril Hare reprinted by permission of United Agents on behalf of the Cyril Hare Estate.

'The *"What's My Line?"* Murder' by Julian Symons reproduced with permission of Curtis Brown Ltd, London, on behalf of the Literary Estate of Julian Symons. Copyright © 1956 Julian Symons.

Every effort has been made to trace all owners of copyright. The editor and publishers apologise for any errors or omissions and would be grateful if notified of any corrections.